STOP THE CLOCK

CASSIE SWINDON

ISBN for hardcover: 978-1-7373469-1-3
ISBN for paperback: 9798753886057

Cover Design by The Book Outfitter
Interior Formatting by DoElle Designs

OTHER NOVELS BY CASSIE SWINDON

Break the Stone
Hunt the Storm

SHORT STORIES BY CASSIE SWINDON IN THE GOLDEN CHAINS TRILOGY

Raelyn's Last Shot
Kody's Secret
Cali's Escape
William's Lies
Phoenix's Spies
Joanna's Sacrifices

SHORT STORIES BY CASSIE SWINDON IN THE LINKED SERIES

Isaac's Curse
Jadox's Spell
Kyra's Ruin

DEDICATED TO:

Mom and Dad, since I'm your favorite, of course.
This is proof, in writing & can't be erased.

Trigger Warnings

Recommended for age 18+ due to profanity, violence, sexual assault, and other sensitive topics such as PTSD that could potentially trigger the reader.

Read at your own discretion.

ACKNOWLEDGMENTS

Editor: Polished Proofreading

Trilogy Covers: The Book Outfitter

Interior Designing: DoElle Designs

Website: Jen Pavlovitz

Alpha Readers: Aubree Anderson

Critique Partner: Anna Cackler

Short Story Covers: Anna Cackler

Thank you to my husband, Matt, for being my rock during this marathon. From day one of drafting Break the Stone, through the nonsense of Hunt the Storm, all the way to the day Stop the Clock was published was an eighteen-month journey. Who knew that a worldwide pandemic would spark my passion and creativity in this unexpected way. In order to make this story possible, Matt added so much extra weight to his load of responsibilities. I was only able to write these books because of you. I super-duper appreciate all those dinners you cooked, Saturdays you spent taking care of the kids (AKA monsters), and nights you dealt with me turning into a hermit to write in solitude. Thank you for supporting my dream and having faith in my skills. Love you (most days).

PLAYLIST INSPIRATION

If you want to experience Cassie's mood throughout the book, play the following songs, which can be found on the Spotify playlist "Stop the Clock"

Chapter 1 – Raelyn
"For Those Who Wait"- Fireflight

Chapter 2 – Kody
YouTube- Suspense Music - Seeking The Truth- Greg Noblin

Chapter 3 – Raelyn
"Daddy's Little Girl" - The Shires
"Adore You" - Miley Cyrus

Chapter 4 – Kody
"Let me" – Zayn

Chapter 5 - Raelyn
"Never be the Same" - Camila Cabello
"Fall in Linc" - Christina Aguilcra

Chapter 7 - Kody
"Why" - NF

Chapter 8 - Raelyn
"Numb" - Carlos Vara
"Better Alone" - Lykee Li
"Let me Down" - Jorja Smith

Chapter 9- Raelyn
"From Where You Are" – Lifehouse
"Broken Pieces Shine" - Evanescence

Chapter 10 – Raelyn

"Don't Let Me Down"- The Chainsmokers

Chapter 11 - Kody

"Wait by the River" - Lord Huron

Chapter 14 - Kody

"Love is a Terrible Thing" - Marlon Williams

Chapter 15 - Kody

"Sign of the Times" - Harry Styles

Chapter 16 – Raelyn

"The Heart Wants What It Wants" - Selena Gomez

Chapter 17 - Raelyn

"I'll Never Love Again" - Lady Gaga

Chapter 18 - Kody

"Pieces" - Rob Thomas

"The Middle" - Zedd, Maren Morris, Grey

Chapter 19 - Raelyn

"Never Forget You" - Zara Larsson, MNEK

Chapter 21- Raelyn

"Superwoman"- Alicia Keys

Chapter 23 - Raelyn

"Salt" - Tinashe

Chapter 24 - Kody

"Pillowtalk" - Zayn

"Deep" - Marco McKinnis
"Lay Me Down" - Sam Smith, John Legend

Chapter 25 – Raelyn
"Crash and Burn" - Maggie Lindemann

Chapter 27 - Raelyn
"Fall" - Chloe x Halle

Chapter 29 - Raelyn
"Mother" by Kacey Musgraves

Chapter 31 - Raelyn
"Praying" by Kesha
"Mother's Daughter" - Miley Cyrus

Chapter 33 - Raelyn
"A Thousand Years" - Christina Perri
"She Used to Be Mine" - Sara Bareilles

Chapter 34 - Kody
"Forever Now" - Michael Bublé

Chapter 35 - Raelyn
"Dear Daughter"- Halestorm
"Fight Like A Girl" - Kalie Shorr

1

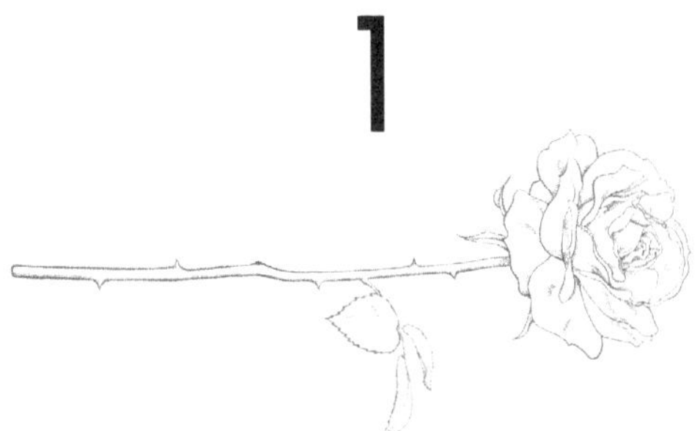

RAELYN BELL

Raelyn lit another candle. The flicker added a layer to the dancing light coming from the fireplace. Seducing Zohaib with an email of this gorgeous model might be the only way to plant a virus and access his files. Raelyn refused to let that scumbag capture or sell one more woman.

She turned too fast, sending her new Canon camera flying. The naked woman beside her reached out and grabbed the stand before the tripod toppled to the cabin floor.

"Woops, sorry." Raelyn shook her head.

"It's fine. I got it." The model followed Raelyn's gaze. "Why do you keep glancing at the clock?"

"No reason." Raelyn scribbled on a paper in red ink. "So, what's your name?"

The woman showed a sharp, brittle smile, part of a mask that hid a hint of nerves. "Why?"

"Because you look kind of familiar."

The woman squinted in the dim light. "You can call me MJ, but let's just keep this business," she said as Raelyn handed over an elaborate Venetian mask.

"I need you to wear this over your face."

MJ smiled. "We're playing dress-up?"

"The guy we're doing this for is Italian, and he likes mystery and games."

MJ clicked her tongue and fastened the mask on, covering most of her face. "Whatever you say … my cousin never told …" MJ whispered something under her breath.

"What was that?" Raelyn leaned in.

"Nothing." MJ took the sheet of paper and angled it closer to the fire. "So, this is the script?" She skimmed it silently for a beat, then read aloud sarcastically, "I'm all yours, Zohaib. Where and when can we meet?" She crunched the paper into a ball. "This is shit. I have a better idea."

"You've done this before?"

"Manipulated a man? Of course. You haven't?" MJ reached into her purse, her large breasts swinging around. "Here, rub this oil all over me."

Raelyn stepped back. "Um, I think you can reach all the necessary spots on your own."

The orange glow of flames cast gorgeous lighting on MJs golden skin. Raelyn couldn't help but pull Kody's long Cubs shirt further over her pregnant bump. MJ was remarkably fit and probably older by only a few years—she looked about twenty-two.

The baby kicked hard, snapping Raelyn's attention back to what mattered. Even at six months along, the feeling was still new and foreign. She laid her shaky hand over the bump with a smile.

MJ hopped in place. "It's freezing in here." Her nipples had completely hardened.

Raelyn tilted her head.

I won't ever know what breastfeeding feels like.

Adoption was the only choice. Each day that her stomach grew rounder, her biggest fear loomed closer— that she would turn out like Joanna. But, the mere thought that a stranger would raise her child was like someone digging a fork under her skin and peeling away chunks.

MJ squeezed the oil onto her hands and rubbed it all over her upper body, slowly moving lower. Feeling her cheeks warm at the sight of MJ's hypnotic curves, Raelyn used all her willpower not to turn away, pretending this was art, not a desperate ploy to seduce a sex trafficker. A vile taste rose in her throat. The deceptive snake who had tried to sell her and was responsible for taking Joanna all those years ago was, in fact, her biological father. Her jaw clenched tight at the memories from the desert. Raelyn looked through the camera lens in a desperate attempt at distraction.

This has to work.

"So, what position do you want me in?" MJ placed both hands on her hips confidently.

She needed the most provocative poses but said, "I'll let you decide."

"How about on all fours, hun?"

"Please don't call me, *hun*."

She nodded. "Oh, a controlling boyfriend or something? I've been there."

"No. That's what my Pa used to call me."

MJ's brow lifted. "Used to?"

Raelyn glanced out the small window framing the snow-frosted treetops toward Pa's tombstone glittered with snow. He would roll over in his grave if he knew what her life had become and the dangers haunting her.

The threat of darkness clung to the shadows as the sun's final rays inched lower through the window, sending a shiver through Raelyn's spine. As the sun dropped splashes of orange onto the horizon, chunks of snow flopped from an oak's drooping branches to the carpet of white below. She glanced at the clock ticking near the chimney.

"Okay, we need to hurry."

MJ tilted her head. "Why?"

"My fiancé–I mean, boyfriend will be here soon. And after you leave, please don't contact me again. I'm not supposed to be using *this*." She held up her phone then pocketed it.

MJ laughed. "You've got some drama. If you're hiding something, it'll never work out. If you've got conflict with your man, the only way out is through."

Kody and I will be fine.

The more Raelyn thought about it, Kody was the only person who had ever made her feel complete. Only now that they had been cooped up together for months did she understand the realness of what they shared. Kody would always be the one for her.

Raelyn cleared her throat. "Okay, when this light flashes, that means the video is recording."

MJ smiled. "Whatever you say."

"The more, um, seductive you are, the bigger the tip."

Raelyn messed with the buttons and features. The gift was probably Kody's way of making up for harboring her in a ramshackle cabin for five months. Raelyn pushed record, and MJ's creamy voice managed to be more luscious than her lips. After capturing only a minute's worth of footage, loud crunching sounds came from outside the cabin. Her heart stopped at the sound of Kody releasing an avalanche of logs, which all thunked into a barrel.

"Crap," Raelyn whispered.

"I'm back, babe." Kody's baritone soared above the winter wind's wail. "I got a deer this time."

"Your boyfriend?" MJ's eyes grew wide.

Raelyn tossed MJ's clothes over. Too late. The door flew open with a thud. A wicked gust of wind whistled its way through the cabin, whipping Raelyn's hair and blowing out the candles. Kody ducked to enter carrying Pa's old rifle and chucked it in the corner. He rubbed his hands together like he was starting a fire between them.

"Hey, babe. I've been thinking about your hot chocolate for the last hour."

Raelyn held her breath when he turned.

Kody's deep brown eyes lingered a moment too long over the curvy model before his jaw tensed. His fierce attention switched to Raelyn. "What's going on?"

Dark oil stained MJ's clothes as she wrestled with covering herself.

"Um ..." Raelyn drank in the dark gleam of his eyes and guided Kody through the small cabin, past the stove, old couch, and crooked table, toward the only other room—just as small and cold. Biting her lip, she tenderly brushed the snow off his coat. "I'll bring your cocoa in here."

"Who is that?" Kody's spine straightened like a steel beam, his voice hard. "We can't risk being tracked. She needs to leave. Just because I bought you that camera doesn't mean your art ..."

"Can you send me the money on the app?" MJ called from the other room.

Raelyn cringed, purposefully avoiding Kody's intense gaze as she responded, "Remember, I told you, we don't have phones."

"Oh, right, right." MJ's laugh carried through the threshold. "Well, can you log onto my website to pay?"

Raelyn dropped her head and looked at her toes covered in wool socks to avoid Kody's stare, a view that her belly would soon block. "We don't have computers."

Kody whispered, "You have one minute to get rid of her, or I'll toss her out of here."

"You have a heart of gold. You'd never do that."

"Tell me what a stranger is doing here. What if someone followed her?" The tight pull of his brows had returned—a look Raelyn knew too well.

"It's okay. We're still safe." Raelyn smiled at Kody, then projected her voice to the other room. "I have cash, one minute."

"Oh, that's fine. I'll finish this hot cocoa over here. You two take your time. Did I get your man all riled up?"

At that comment, Raelyn assessed Kody's stern face. His eyes were full of questions, but he shook his head 'no' and, strangely enough, followed it with a deep chuckle. Raelyn sighed. This was the most adventure they'd had since their return from the desert. The unexpected humor of the situation caught her by surprise as she joined in with him, laughing.

Kody marched over to the mattress on the floor and pulled out a wad of cash from under his pillow. "How much do you need for your ... project?"

He's not even suspicious.

"I'll count it out." As Raelyn moved bills from her left hand to her right. A collage of images overlaid themselves like a photo reel as she remembered Ma—no, Joanna—do the same thing in Zohaib's study the night of the auction, when she had placed money into the largest safe Raelyn had ever seen.

She scurried out of the bedroom to hand over six hundred dollars to MJ. "Remember what I said. This is so you don't tell anyone about our location."

MJ bundled into her coat and saluted with extreme sarcasm. "Wish me luck. If I fall off the side of the cliff, then … well, I guess there's not much to do about it."

Opening the door, Raelyn took a large gulp of the crisp air. Tiny paw prints from a squirrel trailed off toward the jagged tree line atop Ash Mountain's peak. The valley below looked like a snow globe. If Bear was still alive, he would be rolling in that powder, his fur matted with snow, radiating pure joy despite the cold. She hugged her belly again.

I couldn't even protect Bear. Just one more reason why I can't take care of a baby.

There was no way her baby would ever be safe with her when she carried the genes of the two worst parents on the planet. Her DNA showed all the proof that she could never raise a child. Returning inside, Raelyn cleared her throat, ready to finally tell Kody about her plans for adoption. He turned and looked at her, his eyes softening as he slipped off his winter coat. Maybe she could keep her plan under wraps for a little longer.

Kody's small smirk widened as he sat on the low mattress against the wall and leaned back, crossing his arms. "Can I take pictures of *you* later?"

She smacked his shoulder playfully and sat on his lap, resting her forehead on his. "Not with this enormous stomach." She moved closer, straddling him, and felt him harden under her, despite the double layer of hunting clothes.

"First off, you're gorgeous." His black eyebrows crumpled. "Secondly, why did you even contact her?" Kody tucked a loose strand of her hair behind her ear. "Am I not providing you with enough … stimulation? I mean … cooped up like this, we have sex every day. Are you bored?"

"I know you're joking." Raelyn kissed his cold hands. "But I also know you're worried."

"We agreed we wouldn't tell anyone where we are."

Agitation began bubbling in her veins. "How long can we keep going like this? I can't give birth here."

"We will be in the clear after the CIA arrests Zohaib."

"How? When? They'll never find him if we don't help. If I could research more about his past—"

"No. Prying could accidentally lead him to us. We can't waste all the effort of protecting our families." His voice turned soft. "You think it's hard for us to be living on a mountain. Imagine how Cali is surviving without her own room."

"Do you think Cali had a good Christmas yesterday?"

He rubbed her elbows softly. "Definitely not. She probably misses you too much. Plus, she probably has a dozen gifts for you full of baby clothes that she can't wait to see you open."

Tears welled for so many reasons as she whispered, "This was the first Christmas without Pa."

Kody brought her closer on his lap, pushing her into his firm abs. He ran his hand through her hair tenderly. "I know."

Raelyn kissed his cheeks back and forth, left to right. "Can my Christmas present be a laptop to research Zo—"

"Your camera was your gift, babe." His buttery soft voice melted into her skin as he kissed across her neck, but his words were jumbled and disguised through his heavy breathing.

"I can get *you* a laptop, then. And then we can research..."

Kody easily scooped her up to her feet, making her squeal with delight, then he dropped to his knees in front of her. "Let me kiss my baby."

Raelyn lifted the shirt, exposing her pale skin, allowing his request. She had grown accustomed to his daily request, yet it still baffled her since they were both aware the baby might not be his. Her heart squeezed tight from her decision about adoption, a choice that Kody wasn't aware of yet.

Kody sprinkled kisses over the arch of her belly, and his lips moved further south on her body, shaking Raelyn from her trance.

She gulped, trying to remain focused, but her body trembled. "Maybe we could go to the library after the doctor's appointment."

"Can't risk it."

She backed away and spat out a lie, "The librarians could get us access to medical insurance options."

He patted his pocket where she knew both the engagement ring and his pocket watch were tucked inside. "Insurance wouldn't be a problem if you finally agreed to marry me."

"If I agree to marry you, will you let me research Zohaib? If we know where he is, then ..."

Kody swept her close and pinned her on the bed with a deep growl. He pulled at her shirt with his teeth, lifting it over her head.

"Babe, I have a confession." Kody's lips took a break from connecting her freckles with his kisses.

"Mhm?" She trailed her lips over the scars on his bicep.

Kody wrapped his hand behind her neck. "I've got a secret."

"Oh, do you now?" Her lips found a pathway from the vein popping out in his arm.

"I know I promised to fix everything and get you out of this cabin as soon as possible, but ..." Kody's eyebrows knitted together. "Honestly, everything feels perfect here. I wish we could stay in this cabin forever, just the three of us." His mouth moved persuasively on hers, teeth gently scraped inside her lip.

I have to tell him.

THUD. THUD. THUD.

Someone pounded on the front door. Kody jumped up and grabbed the rifle as Raelyn scrambled out of bed and threw on her shirt. Her heart rate spiked as she jumped between Kody and the door.

"Go hide." He pointed to a closet.

"Not without you." She glanced at the sole window frozen shut.

We're trapped.

2

KODY WALSH

KODY'S MIND RACED THROUGH the possibilities of who could be at their front door. The floorboards creaked as he strode across the cabin, rifle in hand. He fought every neuron in his brain that desperately wanted to demand Raelyn to hide. But he had promised to be less controlling. The two of them were in this together.

THUD. THUD. THUD.

Outside the window, a blast of snow whirled around a tall thin figure bundled up in coats.

Does the woman need help down the mountain?

Trucks could only get so far, then the summit was accessible for hikers only. At least she had a heavy winter coat to keep her warm. The image of that woman completely naked in their cabin sent his body into a moment of frenzy before forcing himself to calm. It didn't matter how attracted he was to Raelyn—the sight of that woman standing there exposed would elicit a response from any straight man. Kody shook his head to focus.

THUD. THUD. THUD.

A teenager's voice cracked from high pitched to low through the howling wind. "Let me in, sis!"

"Liam?" Raelyn scrunched her sweet button nose while looking up with an arched eyebrow. The bottom of the door lodged against the wood and scraped when she yanked it open.

The gangly kid waltzed in and immediately pulled off his winter hat to reveal his wavy blond hair and his pearly white smile. "Five months!" He held up one hand. "It took me five months to find you." He stomped the snow off his boots by the front door then rushed over to hug Raelyn, almost bouncing off her round belly. Liam's blue eyes grew. "Wow, you got big!"

Raelyn's amber eyes brightened. "You got even taller!"

Liam raced to the fireplace and held his hands up to the fire. "Got anything hot to drink?"

Raelyn bustled to the tiny kitchen, soon wafting a cinnamon scent through the cabin.

"How did you know we were here?" Kody loosened the grip on his rifle.

"Raelyn logged into her social media account a few days ago." Liam pushed his glasses higher on his nose. "I hack in sometimes. I saw a message you sent to a woman about meeting here."

Raelyn palmed her forehead. "Liam, that's none of your business."

"Yes, it is. We're a team, and we have to plan together."

A shuffling sound came from outside.

Kody stepped toward the window. "Did anyone follow you here?"

Liam took the hot cocoa. "Uh—"

"Damn it!" Kody re-positioned his rifle and checked outside. The wind stung his skin. There were only two sets of tracks, one smaller set headed away, and Liam's larger boots. Kody stormed back inside. "Liam, you have to be careful! We're hiding for a reason!"

"There's no reason to hide anymore."

Raelyn bounced with anticipation. "Really?"

Has she hated our time here that much?

Kody poured himself a cup of cocoa. He purposefully let the steaming liquid singe his tongue and scorch his throat. Sometimes a little pain was necessary to snap him back into the soldier's mindset.

Liam blew on the steamy cocoa. "Officer Yohaan visited us at Aunt Aubree's. I heard Yohaan mention that Zohaib is in Oak City, so he's captured!"

Raelyn practically leaped into Kody's arms. "We can finally leave! I can go to college!"

Kody cocked his head to the side, wondering a hundred questions at once. "I'll try to contact Officer Yohaan or Dabbott tomorrow when we're at the doctor's appointment and see what I can find out."

Liam laughed. "You still sound so uptight, Kody. Relax! Everything's fine now." He gulped a swig of his cocoa, tossed off his shoes next to the fireplace, and propped his feet next to the warmth. "Can I stay here tonight?"

"Of course." Raelyn snuggled in close to her younger brother. "Did you have a good Christmas?"

The two chatted a mile a minute. Every time they paused, Kody grunted in response, but he blocked out the rest of their conversation. While deep in thought, he rubbed the black beard framing his face.

There's no way Liam's right.

Amid the snowstorm beating against their windows, Liam and Raelyn talked quietly. Their smiles were shaped the same, but nothing else. Liam inherited most of William Bell's features: tall with thick hair and a solid build. Unfortunately, it was obvious now that Raelyn and William weren't related. She had Joanna's tanned complexion, silky smooth hair, and petite frame, and Zohaib's amber eyes and thick eyebrows. How could an angel have such demonic parents?

If Zohaib was truly captured, they had a chance at a happy future. Kody swallowed hard and patted the side of his pants where he stored the engagement ring and pocket watch. When he had proposed to Raelyn for the seventh time, her face fogged over. Kody would still stand by her side if the baby was Phoenix's, so why was she so hesitant?

I know how much she loves me.

Kody walked to the back room and dug in the bottom of his emergency pack, a bag he kept full of supplies in case they needed to escape in a hurry. At the bottom, he felt the phone and pulled it out, pocketing the device before Raelyn or Liam spotted it.

"I need to go skin the deer." He charged passed them without meeting Raelyn's eye. If she caught his gaze, she'd know in an instant that he had been hiding something from her for five months.

Usually, he thrived in the woods, yet tonight, the natural sounds under the brilliant, blue-mooned night turned unsettling. Squinting and shielding his eyes from the wind, Kody snuck through the frigid darkness. An owl hooted, and strong wings flapped, making him look up for the source, but he only saw stars freckling the sky. Halfway down a hill, he tried to mask his footsteps but slipped and skidded to a spot he knew had cell reception. His body shivered, and muscles tightened together as if trying to cluster up into a ball.

The phone's screen lit up. Kody rubbed his temple, then quickly dialed Dabbott's number before changing his mind.

She picked up on the first ring. "Is that you, Walsh?"

It was so good to hear someone from his team. "Yes. Are we clear to talk?"

"Roger, that. Are you safe?"

"Yes. I need info on Zohaib."

A loud sigh came from Dabbott's end, and she paused. "He's two hours from your location."

A giant knot formed in his throat. "Is he in custody?"

"No. I bet Zohaib's looking for Raelyn."

Suddenly, visions swarmed the wintery scene like he was drowning in a drug of dreams. Agonizing memories jabbed his mind like the point of a spear. Raelyn laid in a pool of blood with a piece of metal sticking out of her stomach. The nightmare that had ripped him to pieces every single night for months returned, refusing to subside.

Kody shook his head.

It's not real. It's not real.

He clenched his jaw tightly. "That won't happen. I won't let Zohaib near Raelyn."

"Walsh, no one else knows where you two are at, right?"

His heart pounded as he stared at the footprints leading up to his cabin. "I need a team to protect Cali, and my mom, and—"

"Walsh, at some point, you're gonna need to make a choice." Dabbott's voice grew sharp. "You can't save everyone. Prioritize who matters. Otherwise, you'll have the weight of the world on your shoulders."

She was wrong. He could protect Raelyn while also keeping tabs on everyone else.

"Dabbott, I've got a lot of questions, first ..." The line went silent on the other end. "Damn it."

Kody snapped the phone shut and grabbed a fallen branch to brush away the tracks, then trudged back up as his hands turned numb. He passed by the deer still hanging from a branch and lumbered back inside. Raelyn and Liam didn't even glance up from their chatter as he jabbed at the fire, increasing the flames again. Heat filled the room as Kody started pacing.

From the couch, Raelyn quieted, cupping her beautiful belly. "What's wrong?"

Kody cleared his throat. "Liam, you shouldn't have come here."

"It's not his fault. I shouldn't have invited that model over. But, I'm so glad he came." Raelyn smiled. "Now we know we're safe! If he hadn't told us, who knows how long we'd be suffering up here."

"Suffering?"

"You know what I mean."

"No, I don't." Kody sighed. "Liam, you were wrong. Zohaib isn't in custody."

"What?" Raelyn sank back into the couch, squishing the pillows flat. "How do you know?"

"I called Dabbott."

She pointed a finger in his face. "So, I'm not the only one breaking the rules."

"I contacted someone for an emergency!" Kody barked, "Not for an art hobby."

Liam started a coughing fit, halting the conversation. He moved to the sink, hacked up a giant wad of mucus into the drain, and washed it down. "Sorry."

Raelyn massaged her temples. "Kody's right. You shouldn't have come out here. You'll get sicker. You shouldn't be up here with CF."

"I'm fine." Liam waved her off. "Plus, I'll only live once."

Kody's teeth ground together. "That doesn't excuse careless choices."

Raelyn crossed her arms. "If Zohaib is still out there, we need to go find evidence so they can arrest him. Remember, Joanna expected a thumb drive to be inside that box, but there wasn't. The drive she needed probably had proof of Zohaib selling women that we can turn into the authorities. So, we need to go find it."

"If I were crazy enough to try this …" Kody groaned and rubbed his beard. "Where do you think it would be?"

"I've been thinking about this!" Raelyn bolted upward. "It's probably in my old barn loft. I was never allowed up there, so maybe Pa put the file in Ma's trunk."

"That's a good idea. I can try the loft. Your Grandma still lives at the base of this mountain, right?"

Raelyn nodded. Fire flared in her eyes. "I'm going too."

I can't hold her back anymore.

Kody felt the smooth metal of his pocket watch under his thumb, wishing he had more time with her on the mountain before all hell broke loose again. "What if the file Joanna expected doesn't have any proof on it?"

"It will." Liam spoke quietly, "I know what's on it."

Raelyn's eyes widened. "Since when?"

"Mom told me the day we reunited with her in the safehouse."

"You're telling us this *now*?"

"You two disappeared for five months." Liam rolled his eyes. "Anyways, all the leaders signed a contract with Zohaib. If they get a woman pregnant, that child is Zohaib's property. Mom said Snyder signed one. So, Zohaib is here to collect me."

Raelyn laid one hand on her brother's shoulder. "But Snyder wasn't your father. You don't apply to that stupid rule."

"You really think that matters? The contracts don't even matter either. Zohaib gets what he wants." Liam coughed. "Apparently, Snyder didn't completely hate me. He hid me from Zohaib to train me in case I needed to fight. For years, Snyder was protecting me from joining Zohaib's army."

"That doesn't mean the things Snyder made you do were okay, don't forget that."

Liam looked away. "Zohaib must be here to collect what he believes belongs to him. Me. But I can't fight in his army. I wouldn't last a day."

Raelyn cupped his cheeks in her hands. "I'll keep you safe. He won't bother looking for you if he knows he has a chance to capture me."

Kody's heart raced, knowing she was right and what she intended to do. Raelyn would use herself as bait to save her brother.

Raelyn ruffled Liam's hair. "He won't touch you. I'll make sure of that." She stood tall. "I'll find the file in Ma's trunk, give it to Yohaan and prove what kind of tyrant Zohaib is."

"You make it sound so easy." Kody glanced between her belly and the exit, fighting every urge in his bones to step between Raelyn and the door.

I have to keep them safe. But I can't hold her back again.

3

RAELYN

RAELYN'S TOES WERE ICE cold as her boots crunched through the thick snow. As she looked up to the dawn sky, with soft strokes of purple running through it, goosebumps speckled her forearms. Pa had taught her a lot about hunting, fishing, fixing her truck, and what berries were okay to eat in the woods, but all those lessons happened in the summer, not preparing her for this harsh winter.

After tugging her wool hat further over her forehead, she crouched down and wiped the snow off Pa's isolated tombstone.

William Bell
1977-2017
Devoted Father

Shivers crept up her spine as she envisioned his mangled body below the soil. During the past five months of living in that cabin, vivid nightmares of corpses trying to crawl out of the earth, half-eaten away by cockroaches, had haunted her.

Pa had been there for her, even when she never admitted it. A smile washed over her face at the certainty that he had supported her when it really mattered. She bit on the edge of her glove, pulled it off, and then slowly traced her fingers over his name. A pleasant memory of Pa stooping before her and tying her shoelaces flickered like an old film, then was immediately replaced with Joanna unraveling the ribbon from her body at the auction—in front of all those sickening men.

A chill soaked into the marrow of her bones.

You failed me, Ma.

Rhymes hadn't come easily to her anymore, and creativity had been sucked from her spirit, but Raelyn pulled out a crumpled piece of paper from her pocket and read an old poem to Pa's grave. She wrote it long ago, but the words now rang true for a different reason.

Wandering through tunnels with shadowed walls
Chilled bones exposed like a skeleton's breath
Sliced ghosts sweep through silence as a raven calls
Asking how to defeat one's imminent death

As snow fluttered down, landing on her eyelashes, Raelyn's mind wandered. She realized Pa's grave was next to where she had buried a time capsule with her parents as a child. The earth would be too hard to dig it up, but maybe when her baby was older, she could add something special to the collection.

No. Stop thinking like that. I won't be in its life.

Liam's footsteps crunched from behind, and he wrapped his long arm around her back.

"Whatchya thinking?" asked Liam.

Raelyn glanced around, then whispered. "I can't raise this baby." She chewed the inside of her lip. "I'll mess up like Joanna. The only option—"

"You're not, Mom. You'll be fine, and I'm here to help."

A giant pit formed in her stomach at the thought of disappointing Liam too.

The sun rose higher, and cardinals flew between the oaks, flitting red feathers and floating down to the whiteness below. Raelyn pulled the collar of her coat tighter to her cheeks. Each cold breath she sucked in stung sharply in her lungs. A deep cough came from Liam, and he hunched over as she smacked his back hard. He choked out a big wad of phlegm and spat it into the snow.

"You need to get out of this cold," she said.

"Yeah, I know. I'm leaving to check in on Grandma."

"I guess she isn't really my grandparent anymore. She's Pa's mother. I'm not even related to her."

Pa's scorn possessed Liam's face. "Stop it. When I met her, the first thing she did was show me the dollhouse you played with growing up. You're the only grandchild she knew."

"But now she has you. She doesn't need a fake one."

Liam wiggled the glasses on his nose. "Oh, stop. No pity parties. You know Grandma loves you. Plus, Mom will come home soon, and everything will be fine."

The rosy love she had always felt for Ma while growing up was now slashed with black and splattered with gray. Raelyn wouldn't meet his eyes. She couldn't bear to break Liam's heart and shatter his perception of their mother. Rather she allowed him the false belief that Joanna would eventually return home.

"Liam, you probably shouldn't visit until Zohaib is locked away. Stay hidden and follow Yohaan's rules, okay?"

He smiled his wide grin and nodded. "Yes, ma'am."

"Be safe."

Liam released her and turned without another word. He waved and trudged down the steep slope. Raelyn eyed his silhouette until he faded into an ant-like spec against a giant slab of white marble. Smoke rose from their small chimney, and the scent of venison wafted through the air.

She tapped the gravestone once more and wondered if Phoenix had one somewhere and what family mourned his death. A change shifted in the wind, and snow from the roof fell onto her hat and slid down the back of her coat, making her shriek and jump as she entered the cabin for breakfast—the last meal before she headed into town

Kody chuckled. "You and winter are not friends."

"The south never gets snow like this. It's insane."

He placed a slab of venison across her plate and scooped out a mountain of steamy eggs. The plates clattered on the table as he set them down. "So, at the doctor appointment today…"

Staying silent, Raelyn concentrated on a bug crawling across the floor.

Kody rested his hand on hers. "I think we should find out the gender."

"Can we talk about this later?" Raelyn jabbed at a bite of eggs which only crumbled into smaller pieces. She stabbed at it again as Kody ate and stared at her intently.

"Babe, it's okay to be scared."

"I'm not scared." Finally successful at scooping up some eggs, she let the warmth fill up her mouth. She was tired of being cold, cooped up, hidden, and told to put her life on hold because of a psychotic man—her father— who only wanted more power.

"If you're not scared, then what are you?"

She locked onto his dark brown eyes. "Trapped. I'm trapped, Kody."

The hurt look on Kody's face, paired with the disgusting smell of the food, suddenly cut off her appetite. "I'm sorry. Can you get rid of this?"

"Are you accusing me of trapping you?"

This place is a cage.

"We're wasting time here. We have to defeat Zohaib."

"No, we have to keep each other safe."

Frustration catapulted her from her kitchen chair into the bedroom, and she lowered herself onto the mattress and stretched out like a starfish. Without caring if Kody was watching, she grabbed a pillow, put it over her face, and screamed at the top of her lungs inside the puffiness, suffocating her sounds in the fabric. Her throat burned. Again, she screamed, letting the tension drain out of her. Panting, Raelyn lifted the pillow with tears trickling as she met Kody's gaze.

He leaned against the doorframe with furrowed brows. "Sounds like you need a boxing session."

"Yes!" Raelyn tossed him a pillow to use as a punching bag, which he caught with his good arm where the snug tee wrapped his broad shoulders.

Kody widened his stance and held the pillow between two hands above her eye level. "Be careful with your twisting."

"I know." Her tone snapped as she punched the pillow over and over.

Left. Right. Crossover. Uppercut.

Raelyn's pace slowed, but she didn't stop. Panting, she threw punch after punch, trying to thrash the pillow into a million pieces. Quickly, she grabbed the whole thing from Kody's grip and chucked it on the ground, stomping on it repetitively. Feathers exploded and flew across the room. One more wild scream escaped her lungs as a line of sweat dripped down her forehead, and she gulped for air.

"Better?" he asked with a devious look in his eyes and a tiny smirk, daring her.

Immediately, Raelyn surged toward him like a beast, pressing her mouth to his, consuming his taste. Biting softly on his lip. Her heart pummeled her ribs, threatening to burst out of the cage of bones.

Escape. Every ounce of her body desperately needed to feel free. And his body always provided that feeling for her. Kody's large hands pulled off her layers in a fury and fondled her breasts. His tongue rhythmically hypnotized her, resulting in goosebumps peppering her skin.

As she peeled off his shirt, Kody's mouth moved across her shoulder blade hotter than the flames popping from the fireplace. Raelyn's lips dove into his chest, feeling his firm muscles clench and tighten in anticipation. She ferociously pushed Kody down on the mattress, and his smirk crept higher, reaching the intensity in his dark eyes. Standing in only her underwear in front of him, she backed up and slanted her body against the cabin wall.

"Damn." In a husky voice, he mumbled under his breath. Knowing all the tricks to unravel him, Raelyn tilted her head to the side and bit her lip.

His eyes narrowed into a smoldering sleepy expression. "Come here."

"No way."

Kody sat on the edge of the bed like a sprinter readied at the start. He began to move toward her like the predator that he buried deep, his eyes stripping her bare.

Raelyn shimmied off her panties. The fire cracked in the other room, reminding her how totally isolated she was from the world. There, in that cabin, no one could touch her. Maybe Kody was right; they could live there—forever, in peace. The window welcomed in the streaming sunlight. Raelyn followed a sunray to where it splashed against her belly.

Her fingertips skimmed down the edge of her hip to where she could no longer see and slowly massaged her clit, never once taking her eyes off Kody. He pulled off his jeans, and her heart sped faster, never growing tired of his toned form. His belt clunking hard on the floor. Kody's strong chest heaved up and down with desire. Raelyn took her time in scanning the shadows dipping into the valleys between his dark muscles, the bulge under his briefs, awaiting her.

"You're killin' me," he growled.

"Shh." A tingling sensation crept up her spine as she caressed small circles between her legs and walked closer to him. For a moment, the memory of Phoenix's words rang in her ear from their night in the cave when he had demanded, 'show me your power.'

Raelyn shook off his memory as her breathing became shallower as she stood only inches in front of Kody, continually massaging herself. He reached out eagerly, his eyes animalistic.

"Not yet." Raelyn gulped, feeling the pressure rise within her. Her head dropped back as she stared at the ceiling, mouth partly open. Tension built within, and all she wanted was Kody. All of him. Immediately. "Okay. Now!" she commanded.

Kody dropped to his knees in front of her, wrapped his big hands behind her thighs, and licked her in a rhythm that made her knees tremble. Savoring every sensation of his swirling tongue, she sucked in a breath.

"Oh, Kody … oh … wow … slow down."

He growled.

Raelyn tried to push him back on the mattress with all her effort, but he was a brick wall.

"Please, Kody."

His gaze devoured her. She drank in the warmth of his skin and ripped his briefs off. As her hand wrapped around his hard cock, he let out a familiar grunt. In a well-rehearsed motion, Raelyn straddled him and wrapped both hands behind his neck.

"Not until I say so." She rubbed herself over his tip.

Kody's pupils flared. "Babe, I'm so in love with you." He growled again and kissed her lips, then cheeks. "I want you now."

"Not yet." She moved her hips in a circle, feeling him caress her thighs, longing for her.

Kody's lips crushed against hers, tasting like a minty dessert. She wanted to ravish all of him at once. Raelyn positioned herself atop his cock and almost allowed him an inch inside her. He grabbed her waist, but she only smiled and wagged a finger in his face.

"Wait," she said.

A husky, animalistic grunt came from his flaring nostrils as he stared her down. Holding completely still, Raelyn savored the sight of his body throbbing for her. She leaned forward a tad, playing a game of who would succumb first, and kissed his strong neck. Her heart raced, and heat ran through her when she felt his dick twitch against her leg.

"Raelyn Bell, my love, please …" Kody moved her chin to meet his gaze. "Please, marry me."

She dropped her hands from his neck and froze. "I … why ..." She muttered as the passion faded, and she backed up. "I need to …"

If this baby is Phoenix's, Kody will never stay.

"I need to … go for a walk." She backed away.

"What?" His face became as still as the icicles hanging from the cabin window frame. "Right now?"

She turned away with heaviness in her heart and walked into their bathroom.

From the other side of the door, she heard Kody's pained voice ask, "Is it Phoenix? Is that why?"

She rested her head against the wall, feeling awful that he would even think that. "No, I just need … time."

Raelyn didn't regret her night with Phoenix in the cave. She had needed that time with him to fully understand her future with Kody and what she wanted. Phoenix had given her a gift, showing her a wildness and raw passion she hadn't experienced before. He was the first to welcome her assertive side, which had given her the confidence to tell Kody how she truly felt.

But some things were still too hard to discuss. If the baby turned out to be Phoenix's, Kody might resent her for trapping him into a life with a child that wasn't his. Everything in her gut told her this baby was Phoenix's, mostly because life would be too perfect if it ended up being Kody's. All her dreams would magically come true if they were gifted with a blessing to raise a child together, combining them into an official unit and team—forever. There was no chance her luck would turn out that way. Hot, happy tears pooled behind her eyes at the thought of Kody kissing their child on the forehead before bed. But that future seemed impossible. And even if her baby was Kody's, she would make mistakes and create a world of pain for her child, just like Joanna had done. Raelyn sat on the edge of the tub and dropped her head into her hands.

What would her life have been like if Kody had never delivered that threat or stole the marble box? Maybe life would've been better. Pa and Phoenix might still be alive. If Kody hadn't cared so much about impressing his commanding officer and used his common sense, she never would've gotten knocked up by a man who was now dead.

It's all Kody's fault.

She gritted her teeth.

Wait, do I blame him?

Kody entered, "Babe, come back to bed. Let's just cuddle."

She looked up through the crack of the door to see his erection still proudly pointing long and strong straight at her.

"Please, talk to me. I'm here for you."

Her entire future and happiness with Kody depended on the results of the doctor's test later. A life without Kody wasn't a life at all. But she needed to deny his proposals until the paternity test results.

Hiding from the love of her life, she whispered her biggest fears, hoping he couldn't see her face. "Whatever I choose, I'm going to mess everything up." Raelyn choked on her words and let the tears fall. Of course, she wasn't actually mad at Kody, and he wasn't to blame. It was Joanna. Everything was her mother's fault. Sobs exploded from her eyes as she whispered, "What if I'm the same as Joanna?"

The realization struck her, making her dizzy and the bathroom spin.

"What if I don't love my baby? What if I become just like her? I can't fail my baby the way she failed me."

Her legs shook, and she fell to the side.

"Babe!" Kody lurched across the room but wasn't fast enough.

She banged her stomach hard into the bathroom sink. Pain rippled through her body. Fear surged through her bones, and a curse escaped her lips.

4

KODY

Kody's leg bounced chaotically as he sat in the chair of the doctor's room. The scent of roasted coffee beans snuck its way under the door, but the rest of the room smelled like cleaning chemicals. Kody stood, opened, and closed the window blinds, torturing the poor things by moving them up and down repetitively. Unrelenting snow piled higher on all the cars in the lot, a record amount of precipitation in Ash Mountain for over a century.

On the patient table, Raelyn messed with the paper gown that barely covered half her body. "Kody, please relax."

He sat again, then leaned over on his knees and palmed the pocket watch, rubbing his thumb over the smooth gold surface. Flipping it open, he checked the time: 2:22.

That's not right.

He tapped the front glass and shook it in the air while checking the room for a clock. Above the ultrasound machine, there was only a calendar showing December 27th. This time last year, Kody was on a plane to visit Raelyn in Tuzlicci for her senior trip. At that point, they hadn't even kissed yet. It felt like a lifetime ago.

Kody tapped the front of the watch. Huffman's pocket watch had gotten him through so many tough times. His first army friend had never let him down when they served together, and he needed that kind of reliability in his life now.

The door swooshed open, and Cali's face peeked around the corner, her bubbly personality shining through the tension, with one eye closed like a pirate. "Arr, matey, you decent?"

Raelyn's amber eyes doubled in size as she hopped off the table and rushed half-exposed into Cali's embrace, the lemony scent radiating from her skin. "How are you here?"

With a hint of mischief on her face, Cali stared at Raelyn. "Oh, my cat whiskers, Rae! You look purrrr-fect! I can't believe I haven't seen you in five months!"

Raelyn's smile took over, pushing her high cheekbones up even further, and repeated, "How did you know I was here?"

"Your knight in shining armor called me. Kody's scared shitless, so I came to calm him down."

Raelyn fixed her gown and propped herself back on the examination table. "We're okay. She's been kicking."

Kody snapped his gaze up to meet Raelyn's, but she didn't look at him.

She. We both think it's a girl. She could be our Shanae, or Angelica or —

Cali snapped in front of his face, making her charm bracelet jingle. "Bro! Five months away from me? That calls for a reunion! Give me a hug!" Her thick black braids were twisted up in a different style than the last time he saw her, but she was the same Cali with flashy pink nail polish and a matching fanny-pack.

Kody stood in a daze and wrapped his arms around Cali, who couldn't stand still for more than a second and jumped out of his embrace faster than a rabbit.

"So, when's the wedding?"

Raelyn stared at the ground.

"Okaaaaaaaay, never mind then," Cali told Raelyn how well their mom had taken the news that she'd be a grandparent, information about Cali's band touring on the weekends, and the two people she'd been dating, Tanya and Jordan.

Kody couldn't take his attention off Raelyn, trying to read her expressions. She regularly lived in a dream world these days. The longer they had stayed in that cabin, the more distant she became. After Cali mentioned classes at State, Raelyn's eyes glossed over throughout the second half of Cali's story. A deeply rooted fear anchored itself in the middle of Kody's chest, but he didn't want to consider what it meant.

Thunk. Thunk. Thunk.

They turned their heads to the door.

"I'm ready." Raelyn smoothed the patient gown.

The doctor walked in with a bright smile. "Hey there."

Kody impatiently tapped his finger against his thigh. He joined Raelyn's side with a pounding heart, taking her small, cold hand in his. "She fell about two hours ago. Can you do an ultrasound? Now?"

The doctor nodded. "Yes. Take a deep breath."

Raelyn and Cali inhaled together and released simultaneously.

Cali laughed. "Oh man, that sigh was epic."

The tension eased a tad as the doctor asked. "Have you felt the baby move since?"

Raelyn nodded, and Kody gently rubbed the inside of her wrist with his thumb.

"Okay, lean back. The gel may feel a little cold."

Kody's phone chimed. He ignored it.

The doctor dripped the gel on her belly, spreading it around with the ultrasound probe as he pressed buttons on the scanner. Kody's phone rang, but he pushed the silencer off through the denim.

Kody leaned over Raelyn and gasped. A clearly visible baby shape floated around on the screen. "Is she okay?"

"One second, please." The doctor squinted and bit her lip. "There it is, a solid heartbeat. Everything looks good. Let me take a few more measurements."

Soft pitter-patters came from the machine.

Kody's whole body softened, and he kissed Raelyn's forehead. "Everything's okay."

A tear escaped the edge of her eye and ran down her cheek.

"You're measuring for a due date of March third. You want to know the gender?" The doctor glanced at them both.

Kody said, "Yes" at the same time that Raelyn shook her head, "No."

Cali cringed and moved to the window, her breath fogging up the glass.

"Well, I have the gender in your chart. You two decide and let me know. Anytime you call in, we can inform you over the phone." While she moved the tool over Raelyn's belly, the doctor asked, "Do you two have any other questions before the nurse comes in to go over the next trimester?"

"Can you tell which day the baby was conceived?" Raelyn spat out her words.

"No, not the exact date, but within a window. Do you have a concern?"

She took her hand away from Kody's. "Can I get a paternity test *before* the baby is born?"

Like a true professional, the doctor masked the shock on her face well, but Kody could see it in her eyes. "It's not a common procedure, but we can do that today. There are a few risks—"

Raelyn sat up slightly. "We can get the results today?"

"Oh, no. Maybe in a week."

Raelyn laid back down. "Okay. Yes, I want that, please."

"Okay. It's a long needle—"

Raelyn waved her off. "You don't have to tell me. I'll just sign the consent form."

The doctor gestured to him. "Will you be giving a DNA sample, sir, or?"

Kody stood straight and cleared his throat. "Yes, ma'am."

"Okay, follow me. It's just a cheek swab."

Kody kissed Raelyn's knuckles and whispered, "I love you."

She mouthed, "I love you too," without a sound as if fear had strangled her.

"I gotta pee." When Cali pranced by, the sound of her popping bubblegum erupted in Kody's ear.

A part of him was glad he didn't have to witness Raelyn and the needle. The thought made his shoulders shudder. Near a cart in the hallway, a nurse informed Kody of the steps and had him sign a few forms. Every fiber of his being knew that his fiancée's—no, girlfriend's baby was his. The baby would look like him, have his dark skin, Raelyn's selflessness, and determination.

Around the corner, the doctor whispered to another. "We can't save everyone. Sometimes, the only way to save one is to let the other go."

Kody shook his head, trying to push away the thought of a doctor choosing to save a mother or baby.

A nurse came out of Raelyn's room and moseyed to the counter. She hovered her hand over a few pamphlets and plucked one, then turned. At her side, the title of the brochure read: "Adoption."

The hallway spun, and his temples throbbed. There was no way he'd let someone else raise his child. Kody planted his feet on the ground and swayed back to the room in a fog. He stumbled through the door, and Raelyn yelped like she was caught in a trap. He concentrated on his breathing and grabbed the brochure from the nurse's grip. "What is this?"

Raelyn stuck out her chin and started dressing. "I want to be educated, just in case."

"Just in case what?"

"We both know the possibility that—"

"Possibility that you would let someone else raise our baby?" It felt like an earthquake created a vast gorge between them.

She pulled the pamphlet from his grasp. "It might not be *our* baby!"

Kody stepped back, his sneakers squeaking on the shiny floors.

Raelyn finished buttoning her blue plaid shirt. "How can I put you through that life if the baby isn't yours? Every day you would see Phoenix's face. You say you'll be there, but in two years, you won't be able to handle it anymore."

"Babe, William realized you weren't his, but he didn't run away from raising you. What makes you think I will? I'm not leaving you."

"Don't promise me anything, Kody. If she's not yours, you'll leave."

"You have no reason to think that. I want to be with you. Forever. Why don't you believe me?"

"I have my reasons."

"What are you trying to say?"

"You've lied to me before." She pushed the adoption brochure into his balled-up fist, ramming the wrinkled paper between his fingers. "If it weren't for *your* lies. Pa would still be alive. Everything would've been fine."

"So, you're blaming me? Well, this is new."

"Maybe my life would've been better with Phoenix." The second the words left her mouth, her eyes were full of regret, and her jaw dropped. "I … I didn't mean that."

Her admission stole his breath, but he managed to whisper, "I think you did."

Raelyn shook her head, and her lip trembled. "No, I'm sorry. I don't know why I said that. I don't know what's wrong with me."

Kody took a deep breath and moved forward, not wanting to fight with the woman he loved more than life itself. She was obviously scared, and he could be her rock. Forgiveness came easily when he adored her with his entire soul. While massaging her arms, he laid his chin on top of her head.

"Babe, I still love you when your fears are trying to swallow you whole. But please, don't try to hurt me just because you can."

She angled her head back, amber eyes glistening. "I'm sorry, Kody. I'm being awful to you."

"You can always talk to me." He wiped a single tear off her cheek. "I'm here for you. We can do this."

Raelyn kissed him so gently that it washed away all his nerves until his phone rang again.

Cali waltzed back in and caught sight of Raelyn's red face and puffy eyes. "Lord of the Oreos, what did you do now, Kody?"

He shut Cali up with one look.

Raelyn pulled away, wiped the tears, and sniffed. "Must be the hormones."

His phone kept ringing.

Cali rolled her eyes. "Jeez, I'll answer it." She almost dug in Kody's pocket, but he twisted out of the way.

He held the phone up to his ear and moved to the corner of the room. "Specialist—Uh, you've reached Kody Walsh."

"Kody! My main man!" Officer Yohaan's voice projected from the other line. He hadn't heard from Raelyn's old neighbor since they returned from the desert.

As Yohaan made small talk, Raelyn grabbed her purse and walked out of the doctor's office after Cali. He turned the corner and pulled on his coat with one arm before stepping outside into the frigid air. White instantly glittered atop Raelyn's head as she walked ahead. Kody plugged his exposed ear with his fingertip when a snow blower turned on in the distance, and a homeless man pushed a shopping cart nearby, the busted wheel scraping against the sidewalk.

"How did you get this number?" Kody projected his voice over the noise.

"Don't worry, only Liam, Aubree, and I know."

"And Cali," Kody added.

And Dabbott. This is too many people.

Yohaan clicked pens on his end of the line. "Kody, the threat is taken care of."

Just like that?

Kody stood still as a statue. "Repeat that."

"You heard me. We have figured everything out."

Kody whispered, "Zohaib has been captured? But my teammate, Dabbott, said—"

Static buzzed on the other end, interrupting the question, then the obvious sound of air freshener spraying in the background. "... and everything's fine. The police force is hosting a New Year's Eve party to celebrate. We'd love for you to be there."

Kody opened the door and glanced at Raelyn's figure down the hallway. "Uh, that's generous of you, but we still can't risk being seen by anyone until I have proof that the threat is detained."

Papers rustled. "Raelyn will go crazy cooped up in that cabin much longer. Liam told me all about how she talked nonstop about college classes."

"She did?" Car horns punctuated the rush for lunch in the distance.

"You two can move into an off-campus dorm together, and you could enroll to finish up your Bachelor's degree too. We'll talk about it at the party.

Kody cleared his throat. "A party isn't safe."

Appearing out of thin air, Raelyn grabbed the phone from his hand and put it on speaker. Her eyebrow rose to her hairline as she stared Kody down.

Yohaan continued. "The party is New Year's Eve. It starts at 21:00. Wear something fancy. It's at the same reception hall where you had prom."

"Prom? Yohaan … I don't think we should go back there."

"We'll be there," Raelyn answered for them both and hung up before Kody could grab his phone.

Kody's muscles stayed tense. Yohaan hadn't even officially confirmed that Zohaib was in custody.

His two leading ladies linked elbows ahead, Raelyn kind of waddling and Cali skipping awkwardly as if yanking Raelyn along. He had to be certain they were no longer in danger. Kody pulled out the Jeep's keys from his pocket, and the metal clanking settled his soul.

Cali shielded her face from the whipping snow and slipped into her Volkswagen. "Bye, bro." She waved.

Kody tried to memorize his sister's face, like always—just in case. Cali mirrored his broad nose, square jawline, and brown eyes. He wondered if his baby would look like Cali.

After his sister drove away, Raelyn held her knuckles at her lips, blowing hot breath on those adorable hands. "Thank you for thinking to invite Cali. I know you don't like taking risks." She started shuffling her feet to warm up.

"I thought you might've needed a woman today."

She curled her shoulders in tight. "You were right. A lot of girls expect their mothers to be at those appointments. I never thought I'd have the chance to experience an OBGYN appointment with Ma, but now that it's a possibility, the pain is almost worse. She's alive and not here. Sometimes, I'd rather Joanna be dead. I think she would've hurt me much less that way."

Kody kissed her lips. "You won't be like Joanna. And our baby girl is safe and will be happy with us."

Raelyn smiled. "You think it's a girl?"

"She'll be as amazing and creative and sweet as her momma."

Raelyn hesitated before asking once more, "And, you're sure about raising her if …"

Kody took a deep breath and pulled out the ring from his pocket. In a pile of snow, he kneeled, sinking into the coldness, but warmth enveloped him when he melted into her amber eyes.

"Raelyn, I don't care if our baby comes out white, or pink or black, boy or girl, four or five-fingered, bald or hairy, small or big … it doesn't matter. I love you. I'm here."

Her tears flowed.

Kody continued and held her hand, "I'm not going anywhere. Please, please, please, will you marry me?"

Raelyn smiled, and her eyes sparkled. "Okay."

Kody bolted upright. "Okay?"

"Yes."

"Yes!" His voice projected through the parking lot. His heart pounded a mile a minute with joy and relief as he dug in his pocket and placed the delicate gold band adorned with a ruby stone onto her finger. Kody kissed her hand and rose.

Everything will be okay.

Kody quickly kissed her lips, savoring her familiar coconut taste. He opened his Jeep door for her.

Before he closed it, Raelyn put her hand on his. "I want to find Phoenix's parents."

She's bringing this up now?

Kody narrowed his eyes. "His parents?"

"Yes."

If this baby wasn't his, he'd be wrapped up with another family for eternity. A family with grandparents who may want to spend holidays with his child, a family who may not respect his culture, rules, or parenting techniques.

Kody nodded. "Okay. January second, we can go see them."

His mind shifted back to the New Year's Eve Party. All he could wish for was a kiss at midnight to celebrate a new beginning and their new life together, yet he ignored the little voice that fired warnings in his head.

As he scanned the parking lot, a sharp wind stung his face, making him squint. Someone across the lot was watching them. A hooded figure in sunglasses leaned casually against a pickup truck, not bothering with a winter coat, a black shirt flapping in the wind. The mysterious figure glanced away as if knowing Kody had spotted him.

It's nothing. We're safe.

5

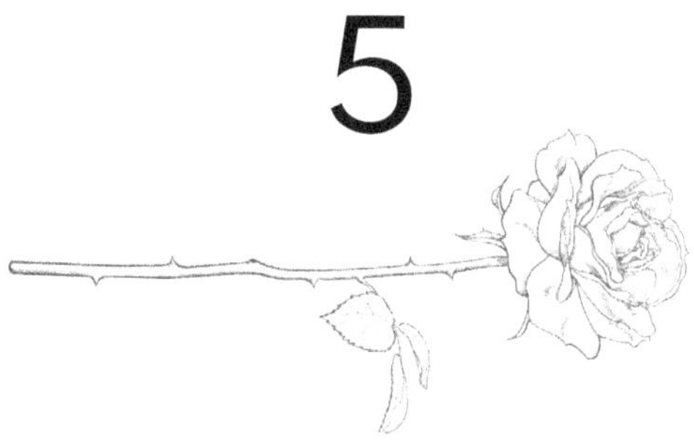

RAELYN

KODY SMOOTHED THE JACKET of his white tux, and the second his gaze fixated on her, his serious glare turned animated with a sparkle. She rose on her tiptoes, needing a kiss, which he planted right on her forehead.

"You look gorgeous, babe."

"Thank you. Not too bad yourself." Raelyn tugged at the tight black dress, making the halter neckline pull in places that shouldn't be legal. She doubted Kody would mind the view all night and smiled to herself. After wrapping her thick, red shawl closer, she cozied into his arm with both her hands wrapped around his sexy bicep. Snow sloshed over her knee-high boots as they walked toward the front entrance of the hotel. She shuddered at the memories from the same spot.

The night Pa died.

Early New Years' fireworks blasted across the sky as Raelyn slid closer to Kody. His steady hand brushed along the small of her back while purples, blues, and reds fizzed and popped above.

Raelyn jumped, lurching Kody back with her.

"You okay?"

She took a deep breath. "I'm fine."

"I've never liked fireworks," Kody mumbled.

She understood and tenderly squeezed his hand as the sounds resembling gunfire blasted into the night clouds.

Kody pulled out his pocket watch. "Someone is celebrating early. It's not even 2100 hours yet."

She gulped and stared at the side door she had snuck out through last May. A bright red emergency exit door. The memories flooded back when she squeezed her eyes shut, imagining Cali flooring the stolen cop car to the abandoned warehouse. Maybe if they hadn't rushed off to the warehouse unprepared that night, Pa would still be alive.

Fireworks exploded again, causing her to jump and grab Kody's strong arm. Her heart raced as couples in fancy attire strolled in beside them, creating a trail of slushy snow in their wake. Kody patted her hand, the warmth of his skin calming her. Raelyn took a deep breath and followed him inside the grand doors. Heat and music attacked them from all angles. The reflection from the chandelier ricocheted off the glitz of the dresses. Across a large ticking clock, a giant banner read:

To A New Beginning
2018

Atop the lobby balcony, a wide staircase led down to a central reception floor, but it looked different without the prom DJ and decorations. Televisions that hung on the walls showed live broadcasts from New York City. Police officers swarmed the area in their formal uniforms, escorting their dates to tables of refreshments, most of whom held champagne glasses in hand.

Their formal attire lessened the threatening image, but the last time Raelyn had seen the police there, they had been searching for her. She scanned the throng of revelers for Yohaan's familiar black hair but couldn't spot him below.

She had to ask his opinion on how to locate Phoenix's parents. Their grandchild may be entering the world. She had been fooling herself for the past few days of their engagement to believe that even though Kody had committed to a lifetime with her, that she could successfully raise a child. The truth was clear. She'd only bring pain upon a little one, just like Ma had done to her.

Her phone vibrated in the purse draped over her shoulder. She tilted her head at the message from an unknown number.

Leave. Now.

If the last year had taught her a few things, one thing was not to underestimate a mysterious message.

When Kody eyed her, she faked a yawn. "I'm a little tired. Can we go down that hallway and find a quiet spot?"

"Sure."

They passed two hotel employees pushing carts full of food by the back kitchen. The music faded, and owls announced the time outside the window. She glanced up to a sign showing a winery and swung open the door to an empty, dark room full of steel counters, barrels, and shelves of wine.

Kody turned toward her. Pulling the pocket watch out, he stretched the gold chain and lowered it gently over her head. His fingers caressed the skin at the back of her neck as he moved her hair aside. Shivers coursed down her spine. The metal was warm from being in his pocket.

"I need to kiss you at midnight. In case we get separated later while chatting, stop the clock, then come find me. That way, it'll still be midnight."

Raelyn glanced at the engagement ring on her finger, then rose on her tiptoes and whispered in his ear, "Why wait until then?" She pulled him further into the shadows.

Kody's excited energy trailed in her wake. She couldn't wait another minute to taste his lips again. Raelyn pushed Kody against the wall and kissed his neck, knocking a framed painting to the floor.

He laughed. "Babe, you're a sex machine these days.

Slowly, she grazed Kody's pecs over his button-up shirt. Kody chuckled. His defined chest tightened, and his biceps flexed, giving her the view she always dreamt about. Raelyn couldn't take her eyes off him, feeling the depths of her love. Hunger for him twisted through her like a tight braid, and she pulled his head toward her and kissed him deeply. His tongue darted into her mouth, swirling her into a trance. Tingles sizzled over her skin in need of more. Kody gripped her ass, covering each cheek of her dress with his giant hands. The intense need surging through her was a craving she couldn't quench.

Her lips found his ear. "What if we went to a courthouse tomorrow and got married."

Kody backed up, holding both her elbows and studied her face. "You're serious?"

She nodded. "A January wedding would be a great way to start a year."

Raelyn swiftly unbuckled Kody's belt and let his pants drop to his ankles. Passion soared through her veins. Any space between them was like torture, she needed to fill in the gap quickly, or her skin would erupt in flames. She shimmied her tight dress up over her belly and bit her lip. With a grin, Raelyn massaged his bulge and felt his warm, hard skin in her palm.

"How are you so hard already?" she said, impressed.

Raelyn pulled her underwear down and turned, leaning forward, her arms stretched on the cool stainless steel of the winery counter as she spread her legs.

Kody groaned. "God, babe."

Her body soared with heat, unable to contain her longing. She reached back and rubbed him over the soaking wet softness between her legs. His tip dipped in for a moment, making her neck arch as she moaned.

Just as she was about to push her hips back into him, a clatter of metal clanged to their right. Silencing a giggle, Raelyn swept behind a shelf of bottled wine. While quickly fumbling with their clothes, two unfamiliar voices whispered and grew louder as they moved closer.

A woman with a sinister voice whispered, "Why do you think Yohaan buried the investigation?"

A man hissed. "I'll give you one guess."

"I don't think Yohaan realized who he was dealing with when he started looking into Zohaib," she said.

"How could Yohaan ever make the insinuation that a military hero would be responsible for capturing, harboring, and selling women?"

"I bet Zohaib will make a joke about Yohaan's clumsy mistake in his speech. We should get out there so we don't miss it."

Raelyn's hands flew over her mouth to stifle a gasp. She looked up at Kody's horror-filled eyes. Heart hammering, and lightheaded, Raelyn silently dropped into a crouch, bracing herself with one hand on a shelf.

The two officers walked closer. Raelyn held her breath.

"Did you hear Zohaib's only daughter got knocked up?" one asked.

Raelyn could feel Kody's energy shift to rage next to her.

The gossiping continued in a whisper. "Teens can be stupid."

"They don't need all these. We can sneak a few away." The officers grabbed a few bottles of wine and left the way they came.

Raelyn was still cemented to the spot. "He's here? Zohaib's here right now?"

Kody lifted her chin, his eyes wild. "We'll go out the back door."

The room spun. Raelyn paused and considered her options. She'd always be running from Zohaib. If Yohaan dropped the investigation and if he wasn't pushing the FBI or CIA or whoever to keep digging for proof, then all hope was gone. She could convince all the cops out there that Zohaib belonged behind bars. She refused to stay in hiding for the rest of her life.

Kody pulled on her wrist. "Come on. There's an emergency exit in the hallway."

Raelyn shook her head. "No!"

"What?"

Terror gripped her chest tightly, but she squeezed the pocket watch hanging from her neck and gritted her teeth. "I won't be trapped."

Kody's words came out sharp as a razor. "There's no other option. We have no backup. Zohaib probably hired men to track you down. This is the man ..." Kody's voice rose. "... Zohaib's the reason why you ended up with shrapnel sticking out of your stomach."

"I know!" Raelyn's breathing came heavy. "But I will not run forever. The police out there will help us."

Kody pulled on her gently and begged. "Please. We can't risk being brave anymore. Raelyn, I can't lose either of you."

Her fingers trembled as she framed his strong jawline with her hands. "You gave me this ring and said you're with me through it all. I will *not* be caged and live in hiding. Are you with me?"

Kody leaned into her and exhaled deeply. "Always."

"Then let's go." She marched toward the door, down the hallway, into the reception hall, not glancing behind her once, knowing he would follow her through a ring of fire if she asked him to.

The music stopped, and the crowd of guests all milled in the hall around the platform. As predicted, Zohaib stood on a small stage behind a microphone stand, with his smile charming the entire room. When he moved away from the stand that had been blocking his body, Raelyn stopped and gasped.

He must have lost at least sixty pounds.

Zohaib's fifty-year-old body was covered with toned muscles, obvious under his tight suit—a drastic difference. His raven black hair was slicked up in a high bun. Each time he stressed a word, his thick eyebrows rose.

Raelyn stopped in her tracks when his amber eyes met hers. She gritted her teeth, hands curling into fists. Kody's energy was tense behind her, but she stepped forward and rose her chin.

"Hey! Zohaib!" She yelled.

Everyone turned. Zohaib met her gaze, then his eyes dropped to her stomach for only a moment with a new spark of evil plastering his face. Her hands grew clammy, but she kept walking, parting the cops like a sea. The pressure of unseen eyes of the crowd stabbed like icy pinpricks in her back.

At the top of her lungs, she screamed, "He's a liar!" making her heart rate double in speed. "Zohaib is not the military hero you think he is!"

Muttered whispers echoed around the room.

Zohaib grinned at her, his lizard eyes cold and calculating. "Happy New Year, daughter!" Each of his words was smooth and lethal.

Raelyn halted at the edge of the stage, unable to force herself closer. Yet, Zohaib's strong cologne still reached her nostrils, making her stifle a gag, bringing back memories of when he had stood so close to her at his auction. He had commanded the unraveling of her ribbon dress, making her stand naked in front of a room of local leaders—gawked at like an object. She'd never let him dehumanize another person like that again.

Kody's gentle touch on her back reminded her of her strength.

Raelyn pointed in Zohaib's face. "You …"

Suddenly, Joanna Bell walked around from behind a pillar. In a silver dress with a long train, walking with confident strides. Each time her matching high heel clacked forward, an anklet reflected a beam of light from a chandelier. Joanna approached the stage and claimed her place next to Zohaib's side, linking her arm through his.

My effin' parents.

Goosebumps formed on Raelyn's arms when Joanna's gaze flickered to her belly. If she wasn't mistaken, a look of pure dread covered her mother's face before she forced it away.

The microphone feedback squeaked under Zohaib's accent when he waved Raelyn up. "Ladies and gentlemen, we have a special guest tonight, Raelyn, who carries my grandchild."

A few people clapped around the room, but there was no steady chorus of applause this time. The cop next to her gestured for her to walk on stage, but Kody held the fabric of her dress in his hand.

Zohaib's smile crawled further up his cheeks like a slithering snake, a predator consumed with power. She ripped away from Kody's grip and climbed the few stairs to the stage. Finding herself sandwiched between the two people she hated more than words could express.

Her breathing grew heavier as hundreds of faces stared at her and meshed together like an abstract painting. Raelyn grabbed the microphone from Zohaib and tapped. *Thump. Thump. Thump.*

Below, Kody shook his head no, but Raelyn snarled into the microphone while pointing at the man beside her. "Stephano Zohaib is *not* who you think he is."

The crowd laughed as if awaiting a comedy show. Zohaib reached for the microphone, but she jumped away.

She pointed straight at Zohaib. "He captures girls and—"

Joanna's long brown hair swept over her shoulders in waves as she swiped the microphone from Raelyn and let out a laugh. "A teenager with pregnancy hormones. Poor girl."

A soft murmur mixed with nervous chuckles and whispers circulated the room.

Joanna plastered on a fake smile and pushed Raelyn out of the spotlight. "Thank you all for coming tonight and for your dedicated service. Enjoy the open bar, and Happy New Year!" She stepped off the stage, looping her hand with Raelyn's, but she jerked away.

Kody was close on their heels but still out of earshot.

Joanna pulled her into the shadows behind a pillar, her blue eyes full of despair. "You're pregnant?" Her hand hovered above Raelyn's belly.

"Don't touch me." Raelyn recoiled into the corner, blocking her view from the cops.

When Joanna sighed, the softness Raelyn had known as a child returned to her mother's face. "Why are you here? Are you trying to get yourself killed?"

"Since when do you care?"

"Hun, I've always cared. I thought you understood that by now." She swept a finger under her eyeliner, rubbing golden shimmery makeup onto her hand. "Haven't you learned anything, hun?"

"Don't call me, hun," she spat as Kody finally appeared, planting his body between them.

Joanna peeked around Kody's broad frame and whispered, "I swear, I'm trying to protect you. I faked your death so he would stop looking for you. Then you showed up in the safehouse and destroyed all my plans."

Raelyn glared. "After everything you've done, I have no reason to believe you."

"Shh!" Kody moved back, forcing Raelyn even further behind him as Zohaib came from around a pillar. The music grew louder, and no one could see them behind the pillar. They had picked a bad spot without witnesses.

Zohaib tilted his head at Joanna and pointed to his glass. "Get me more wine. Now."

"Of course, master."

As Joanna left, Kody rocketed a punch to Zohaib's stomach.

Zohaib grunted loud and bent at the waist but rose to laugh. "God, I miss the action."

His smile faded as he reached forward fast and gripped Raelyn's arm, twisting her into his control. A corkscrew of pain skidded up her forearm.

"How could you make a scene during my speech, you stupid girl?" Zohaib asked.

She could hear animalistic grunts come from Kody, but he didn't move a muscle. The gun pointed at him made sure of that. Keeping Kody calm was her first priority to prevent him from getting hurt.

Zohaib spat on Kody's black leather shoe. "I should take you back to Tahil right now, girl."

"No, you won't." Raelyn said smoothly, "If you don't let me go, then your precious mansion will go up in flames, your army will turn on you, and all those women will be free."

Like a madman, he laughed. "And how do you expect to make that happen, little one?"

"Because I know what you care about, and I can take it away."

"That doesn't answer my question." Zohaib's smile curved downward. "And, you don't know anything."

"I know what's inside the safe behind the farmhouse picture in your study."

Zohaib froze.

"I know the code, and I have spies at your place now. If they don't hear from me every hour, they'll take everything inside. You're finished."

"You're cute, not as smart as I'd hoped, but adorable." Zohaib narrowed his eyes. "This will be fun. I'll see you in the trenches." He released her, turned on his heels, and stomped away, joining a cluster of officers.

"Let's go." Kody intertwined his fingers with hers, not soft but commanding, and moved toward the exit. Raelyn wanted to stare down Zohaib in defiance, but something told her she had already pushed too far. Before they reached the double doors of the lobby, Yohaan waved at them from behind another tall pillar, helplessness reflected in his irises.

"How could you?" Raelyn hissed. "I trusted you to help me, not feed us to the wolf."

The puffiness under his eyes showed he had been crying. "I had no choice. I had to convince you to come here and hand you over."

"Why?"

Yohaan whispered, "He took my boys."

A lump caught in her throat. "How can *no* one stop him? You could go up the chain to your superiors. Zohaib shouldn't have any power over you."

"Wake up. Life doesn't always work according to the rules. There's a lot of people who he leads and believe he's a good guy. We need more proof." Yohaan gripped her hand hard. "I have to find that file."

Raelyn's heart rate spiked. "Do you have any leads on where it is hidden?"

"No, but I have to save my boys." The urgency in his voice made terror soar in her veins.

The need to find it gripped at her heart and clutched tightly like a dark promise.

I'll get it no matter what.

6

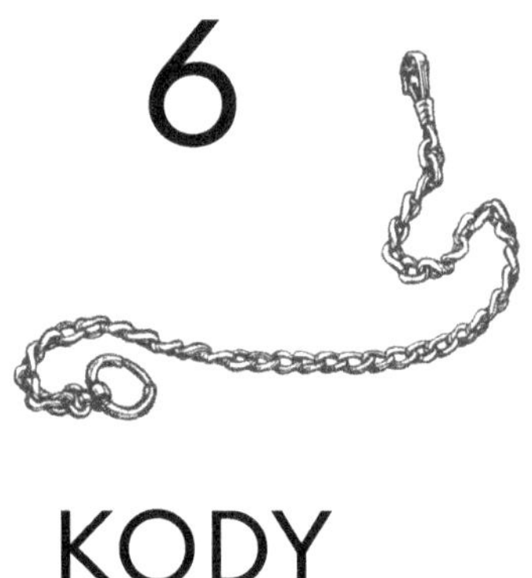

KODY

Kody tugged Raelyn toward the exit. When he opened the first set of doors to usher her out of the hotel, the techno music faded to a soft hum.

"We can't return to the cabin; it's too dangerous," he spat out, shoulders tense as they stepped through the threshold.

Two sets of doors sandwiched them. A couple of armed men dressed in black suits stepped out, blocking the exit. Fear clenched his fists into balls. The calm, snow-covered oaks on the other side of the glass mocked him for trying to escape. His veins scorched at the thought that Zohaib kept putting the woman he loved in danger.

Raelyn's energy next to him shifted, ready to fight.

"Stay behind me." Kody's gaze flickered to the guard, who was clutching a gun with white knuckles.

"Zohaib has requested your presence at the after-party, which starts at 00:00 hours in a private room," said one guard.

He isn't a cop.

Kody nodded. "Of course, we need to get her purse from my car, and then we'll be right back."

Then Kody's fist flew into the guard's gut before jabbing his fingers into both eyes. The guard swore, bent, and dropped the gun. Raelyn grabbed it and aimed it at one enemy.

"Lower your weapon!" Another guard yelled, pointing his gun at Raelyn.

"You first!" Raelyn screamed.

"Babe, drop it."

A guard swung his rifle into Kody's temple, knocking him down to the ground. Sparks of pain rippled through his head. Kody raised his foot and swiped behind the man's ankles.

"Freeze!" The guard pointed his rifle at Kody's chest as he hugged the floor.

When he looked over at his fiancée, Raelyn's trembling hands made the gun shake too.

"Raelyn, take a breath and lower the gun."

But determination claimed her eyes.

"Raelyn!"

She squeezed the trigger. The gunshot echoed in the small entryway, piercing his ears.

Her bullet penetrated the guard's black suit, and he stumbled back into the wall, dropping the gun.

"You shot me!" The guard yelled while patting his safety vest, breathing heavily but otherwise unharmed.

"And I'll do it again! In a spot not covered." She stomped forward, eyes narrowed in anger, and aimed at his thigh. "We're leaving! Don't follow."

Heavy footsteps stampeded up the grand lobby staircase on the other side of the wooden doors that separated them from the rest of the party. Loud music accompanied a dozen officers as the door sprung open. Kody's heart pounded as the officers cocked their guns and surrounded them. The sight of Raelyn's pregnant frame made some of them lower their weapons while others exchanged nervous glances.

Kody's hands shot up in the air in surrender. "Everything's fine. There's been a misunderstanding."

"Like hell! She shot me!" yelled the guard still on the ground, prompting the previously lowered weapons to revert back up, trained on Raelyn.

She held still and steady with her fingers precariously placed over the trigger.

Kody crept toward her, "It's okay. Put it down."

"Drop your weapon!" An officer shouted.

Kody couldn't breathe as he caught sight of her eyes—wild with resentment.

"Babe, it's okay. Lower it."

"It's not okay!" Her mouth set into a hard line, determination rippled through her eyes.

Taking a confident breath, Kody stepped in front of her gun. The barrel pushed against his chest.

"Move!" She cried.

Kody reached out and touched her cheek. "Babe, look at me."

Her chest rose and fell fast as her amber eyes turned unhinged.

"Raelyn," Kody whispered, "Love, it's okay, I'm here."

She locked eyes on him and gasped, stepped back, dropping the gun to her side. Guards rushed forward, intervening and disarming her. Stumbling, Raelyn leaned against the door.

"I'm sorry," her voice quivered, and her tears trailed her makeup so that her pink cheeks were streaked with black.

Before Kody could move toward her, he was slammed against the door. His cheek smacked hard against the glass, making his teeth clack together. He grunted as the cop pulled both hands behind his back and cuffed him.

Raelyn lurched forward, pleading. "No! Stop, he didn't do anything. It was me!"

No, don't say that!

Ready to sacrifice his life for hers, he yelled, "I'll kill all of you, just like I shot that moron!" Kody started to writhe against the cops in hopes that they wouldn't believe her.

Raelyn's sobs erupted to wails. A culmination of the last year of trauma and stress seemed to bear down on her as Raelyn's gaze dropped to the ground. She had been so strong for so long, and it looked as if the whole world had come onto her shoulders. The black dress blanketing her frame made her look like she was going to a funeral instead of celebrating a new beginning, a new year. And he was helpless, struggling under the officer's grip to keep the attention on himself. Every muscle clamped tight as he fought but was pulled further and further away.

"It's okay," Kody yelled from across the lobby. But before the police officer dragged him behind a pillar, he saw a cop strap cuffs onto Raelyn and eased her down to her knees in the doorway.

"Kody!" Her agonizing scream ripped open his heart.

"Let her go!"

In his desperation to break free, two officers started beating him. It felt like a forest of canes slamming straight into his back. Kody resisted the urge to cry out so he wouldn't scare her further. Despite the pain, what tore his soul more was that he couldn't comfort her, couldn't protect her, couldn't save her from pain.

In the corner of his swollen eye, the 2018 banner toppled from one corner, hanging vertically, drooping without life. As they walked down the hallway, the music faded, and the light dimmed.

Cheerful voices counted down from afar. "Ten! Nine! Eight! ..."

Every step sent a new kind of pain jabbing into Kody's heart. Fireworks crackled outside the walls, but they may have been exploding inside his body.

"Seven! Six! Five! ..."

Champagne bottles popped far off in the background while the guard kicked Kody's calf. "Hurry up!"

"Four! Three! Two! ..."

Kody thought of his broken promise in the form of a pocket watch draped around Raelyn's neck and the distant memory of a stolen kiss. A promise that he had broken. A guard threw him inside a dark conference room and slammed the door behind them.

Cheers escalated from the lobby. Kody's body ached, and his shoulder throbbed. He could feel bruises forming as the metal cuffs dug into his wrists. When the officer shoved him onto a rolling office chair, the wheels made the chair slide across the room and into a conference table with a thud.

Kody jumped up and rammed his head into the officer's skull. The man stumbled back. Kody stepped on the chair and climbed on the table, slippery underfoot.

"Sit your ass down!" The guard yelled, reaching for his gun. "Sit down, or I'll make this a lot harder on the girl!" Kody wasn't sure if this man was an Oak City officer or one of Zohaib's loyal soldiers.

Panting, Kody sat, shoulders slumped, and licked his bleeding lip.

The cop kneeled in front of him. "Don't try anything else." He tied Kody's ankles together and to the base of the chair. The officer walked out, most likely standing guard on the other side of the door.

Kody rotated his neck in a circle. Taking a deep breath, he glanced around. Chairs were the only thing he could use as a weapon—something to throw. But he couldn't pick anything up while restrained.

The clock on the wall was stopped, stuck on 11:11, showing no passage of time. Maybe the last two hours hadn't occurred. If only he could erase this party, go back to this afternoon, and stay in bed with Raelyn. His life was at the mercy of a tyrant. But his life didn't matter—Raelyn's did.

Out the sole window, snow sprinkled down. Kody jerked his body, inching the chair closer to the exit. Bit by bit, he crept closer to the cold draft coming through some invisible crack. He wriggled and twisted his wrists, but they only sliced harder against the metal cuffs. Slumping into the chair, he clenched his jaw tight. Maybe he could catapult his body and chair through the glass.

But then what?

After what felt like an eternity, a back door opened, swirling in the icy air. Kody whipped his head around as Joanna raced in and crouched in front of him.

"What are you doing?"

Joanna's gaze darted in each direction. Her long dress danced in the winter wind, and the blue sparkle in her eyes was ablaze, full of hope. Quickly she untied his ankles.

"You have to kill Zohaib. Now! He's going to take Raelyn overseas, torture her in front of his army, and enslaved women to show her as an example. If he shows them what he's willing to do to his own flesh and blood, they will fear him even more."

His words were stuck in his throat, unable to suck in a breath.

Joanna continued, whispering, "None of us are safe while he's alive."

Reality struck him like a wrecking ball straight to the gut. "I need to get to Raelyn. I'll keep her safe."

"Zohaib will annihilate everyone who stands in his way. He won't stop." Joanna's desperate plea shook in her voice as she was on her knees in front of him, tearing the last knot from his ankles.

Kody bolted to his feet fast. "Can you take my cuffs off?"

"I don't—I don't have a key."

The conference room door clicked open. Joanna faced Kody and slapped him hard across the face. Pain rippled through his skin. The hard strike hit exactly where the officer had hit him earlier.

Kody stared at her furiously until Zohaib walked in. "What's going on here?"

It didn't matter that Zohaib's wicked eyes were the same color and shape as Raelyn's—he wasn't anything like her.

Zohaib glanced between Joanna and Kody then the back door, still letting in a breeze. He lowered his chin. "I'll have fun punishing you later, darling. Wear that strappy thing I like."

"I'd rather burn in hell first," she whispered, and Kody was certain only he had heard that response.

Wrists still cuffed behind his back, Kody clenched his jaw. The man, somehow miraculously in shape enough to win a body-building contest, stood inches from Kody's face and glared at him. "Speak, boy. What do you plan to do next?" His breath smelled of whiskey.

"I want to make a trade," Kody hissed.

A slimy smirk crawled up Zohaib's high cheekbones. "A negotiator. Fabulous. Entertain me."

"I'll work as a soldier in your army for Raelyn's freedom."

Zohaib casually sat and propped his feet up on the table, crossing his ankles. "I can make you do that anyway by threatening her safety." He waved off his suggestion and picked at his teeth.

Kody rattled his brain.

What does Zohaib want more than anything?

"You want an empire, right? I'll kill all the men standing in your way."

Zohaib leaned forward. "You're willing to assassinate anyone I command? Even Lieutenant Meadows?"

"Yes."

"Good boy. Now you're coming to your senses. But we won't go to Tahil, you know that area too well. I'll send you to the jungle swampland of Niccoji."

How does he control so many areas?

"And you'll never return. You will belong to me."

Kody swallowed and nodded, sweat forming on his forehead at the thought of never seeing Raelyn again. "If you grant Raelyn's freedom."

"Nice try, it's sweet, but actually, you're in no position to negotiate. You're cuffed and at the mercy of my will." Zohaib stretched his arms in front of him calmly. "You will follow all my orders."

His heart raced. "Just let Raelyn go."

"And you'll recruit more men for my army and train them."

"Yes, anything." Kody gulped down his lies.

"You won't reach out for help to anyone."

Kody paused, digging his own grave. "Agreed. But I need proof that Raelyn is safe."

"Deal." He laughed. "Oh, and she has to stay in that cabin on Ash Mountain, so I always know where she is. You were too easy to break, soldier."

A mixture of dread and relief swirled together.

Zohaib snapped to Joanna. "Jawhara, you will take Raelyn to her cabin and supervise her twenty-four-seven. If she ever leaves Ash Mountain, you will inform me, and the deal will be off."

Kody gritted his teeth. "I want to say goodbye."

"No." Zohaib swiped a knife from his pocket and held it up to Kody's throat. "I was being nice. Listen, boy, you have no authority, no choice."

A cool trickle of blood dripped down Kody's neck as Zohaib pulled away. The gravity of the situation hit home.

Zohaib turned back. "Oh, and Jawhara, let me know when my grandbaby is born. If Walsh doesn't listen, I'll order someone to fetch it for me."

The brown table and white walls swirled together in a chaos of desperation. He gasped for air.

"The baby wasn't part of the deal!" Kody snarled and jumped up from the chair, knocking Zohaib to the floor with his powerful thrust.

Zohaib didn't even bother getting up. He folded both hands behind his head as if tanning on a beach. "Exactly, you didn't say any terms about the baby. Only about my dear daughter."

Kody's legs shook, giving out from underneath him. "Please!"

He leapt up and pointed in Kody's face. "Do what I command, and you won't have a problem."

Tears threatened to flood his vision, but Kody blinked them away. The weight of tons of stones came crashing down onto his body.

Shit. Fuck. What now?

He had no time to consider when the guard who shoved him against a door earlier walked into the room. A bag dropped over Kody's head, turning everything dark. He writhed and squirmed in restraints, but it was no use. Focusing on his breathing, Kody sucked in as much air as possible through the dense burlap. Through the tiny holes in the fabric, he spotted two figures on the other side of the back, glass window. Tires rolled and crunched snow in the back alley. A van pulled up. Doors slammed. Muffled voices called. A figure that looked to be Joanna stood outside and slid open the back door of the van. Raelyn followed, cuffed and limping.

Kody's heart beat wildly. "Raelyn! Raelyn!" He screamed until his throat was raw. "Raelyn!" Struggling against the cuffs was pointless, with the guard holding him back.

She stopped in her tracks and rushed to the window, pressing her forehead against the glass. Her breath fogged it up as she yelled something through the barrier.

"Raelyn!"

A man shoved Raelyn into the van and slammed the door shut.

"No! Please!"

A strong toxic smell wafted in the air behind him. "Shut up!" A hard hand clamped a warm, wet rag over Kody's mouth and nose.

He struggled against the sturdy grip, trying to turn his head in each direction. Kody bit the finger of the man, making him momentarily drop the rag.

"Raelyn!"

The rag returned to smother him. As the dizziness took over, Kody's lungs burned, and his eyes watered.

Zohaib stared with snake eyes that burned threats straight through his visible breath. Kody's vision twisted into a frenzied mess. Zohaib's glare was the last thing he saw before … darkness.

7

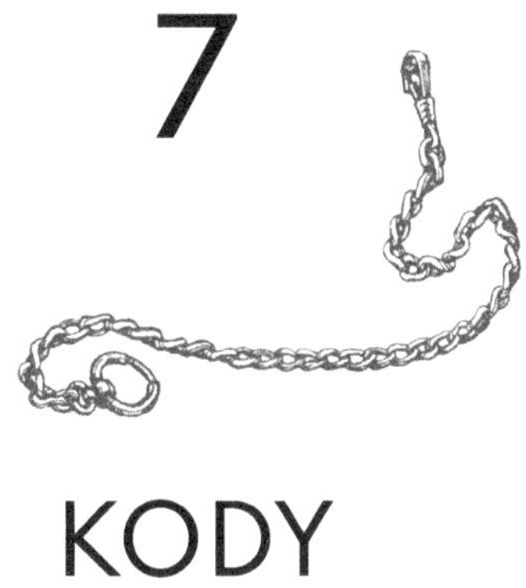

KODY

Kody opened his eyes to pitch blackness. He guessed that wheels rolled fast along a paved road underneath.

Am I in a truck?

His stomach churned as the movement jostled him along the hard floor, scraping his bare skin.

Why am I naked?

"Is anyone here?" he said to the darkness, his voice raspy. "Hello?"

Kody groaned and swept his fingertips over smooth metal to his side. At least he wasn't cuffed anymore. He brushed his fingertips over his body. He knew the sticky substance on his hands was blood but couldn't see his own hand in front of his face. Bruises throbbed, and scrapes oozed fresh warmth, shallow enough to keep him alive, deep enough that he wished he were dead.

As he tried to push himself onto all fours, a loud, strangled grunt flew from his throat. Pain swelled in every muscle. His quads were on fire, his calves felt like jello, his shoulders were as stiff as bricks, and his weaker arm shook intensely as he struggled to push up. Panting he managed to grip the metal wall of the assumed trailer, and use what little strength he had left before his legs gave out. Kody sucked in a cavernous breath, sending a piercing pain through his chest.

Need water.

The vehicle made a wide right turn, sending him flailing into the side of the metal container. His entire body tumbled and rammed hard into the side of the vehicle.

"Fuck!"

Kody crawled in the impenetrable darkness, keeping one hand out in front of him, fumbling ahead. His dry throat and cracked lips begged for water. His weight made the rough floor creak, but otherwise, only the sound of his breathing and the truck's engine could be heard. The vehicle had to be driving fast.

Out. Need to get out.

His thoughts were foggy like a dream as Kody crawled around the entire perimeter, his knees protesting with each forward movement. Standing, Kody slowly swept his limbs in each direction, hoping to stumble upon anything he could use as a weapon or food. His left foot brushed over dry leaves, his right foot mopped over gritty sand. His arms extended fully out in front, swinging in each direction so he wouldn't run into the side.

Suddenly, his foot kicked something metal, and it rolled. He followed the sound and reached for the object.

A bucket.

He chucked it hard against the side of the vehicle, making a tiny sliver of light peek through the indented metal. Kody scrambled forward and placed his hand near the light. A dot of light appeared on his finger, so he crouched and peered out the hole. The world zoomed by too fast to catch any road signs or landmarks, but the sun shone from the highest point in the sky.

Kody squatted and reached around again, feeling something rough and bristly.

A rope! Yes!

The rope went taut, tied to something. He reached forward, following it one grasp at a time.

The vehicle slowed quickly to a stop. Kody lost balance and gripped the rope to steady himself. His focus narrowed sharply in anticipation of danger. A car door slammed outside. Voices floated in the darkness, not quite clear enough to hear individual words, though the tone was enough to set him on edge. At least two people, maybe more, yelled instructions to each other. He couldn't even be sure it was English.

Kody's breathing quickened, and his hands shook fiercely as he found a knot in the rope. He felt around frantically. It was connected to a beam on the side of the truck. Fumbling, he tried to loosen or untangle it but couldn't see a damn thing. The voices grew louder. Footsteps approached. His heart rate escalated in fear.

Kody dropped the rope and stalked to the back near the trailer's large door. He held his breath, waiting for someone to open it. His grip tightened on the rope, and he bent his knees.

The footsteps faded. He waited, ready to pounce. Time passed, but he had no idea how long. Two minutes? Thirty? His legs shook so badly that he teetered over, swaying until the only choice was to sit. Crumbs stuck to his bare ass, and dizziness took over again.

His eyelids drooped, and confusing images hypnotized him into sleep.

Voices awoke Kody. He lay shivering, curled in a ball, in the same place he had fallen asleep, however long ago. No beam of light poured through that little crack from earlier.

He could hear two men laughing outside. Kody rose to his knees, trying to get ready to choke anyone who came near, but the truck's trailer door slid open before he reached his feet. Two dark-skinned men blended into the night and scanned him. One made a gesture of hanging himself from a noose and chuckled.

In a daze, Kody glanced at the rope in his hand and tried to move to his feet, but he was too sore. One man climbed up and kicked Kody straight in the face with his hard boot. He fell back, landing hard as pain rippled through his cheek.

Stop!

He couldn't tell if he had spoken the word aloud or not. Another kick to his side made it hard to inhale. The man straddled his naked body and rocketed punches to the side of his face.

Please stop!

A loud ringing in his ear escalated as he tried to shield himself. His forearms bore the brunt of the attack as the man laid new bruises over the old. Kody tried to scrunch into the fetal position, but the man wouldn't let him move. He clenched his muscles as hit after hit rammed into his body. Everything hurt. Each inhale was like needles of fire scorching his bones.

Please stop! Please!

The copper taste filled his mouth, and he choked on his own spit. Not a single inch of him was spared between the pulsing bruises, pounding skull, and multiple searing cuts. All he wanted was for it to stop, for the pain to be gone. He would have given anything to turn back time and stay hidden in that cabin with Raelyn. At least there, he didn't hurt. No matter what kind of arguments they had, nothing she could do would ever hurt as much as what these men were currently doing to his body.

Just kill me.

Gasping for air, Kody grunted, "Stop." But he couldn't even hear his own voice.

The man finally backed off. With the help of the other, the two men pulled Kody to the opposite end of the truck. Every muscle cried out in agony. The man stood on the bucket and looped the rope from a beam on the container's roof.

One smiled, pointed to it, and gestured again. Kody's eyes drooped. A heaviness weighed him down, but then water splashed onto his temple. He turned his head in time to allow a stream of water to drain straight into his throat. Before he could suck more, it stopped, and little droplets trickled down his chest and over his torso.

Shuffling sounds echoed from outside, but Kody could barely lift his head to look. Another figure appeared. Someone threw a boy into the trailer, just as beaten as he was —probably sixteen years old.

Then the door slammed shut. Darkness again.

"You okay?" Kody barely whispered, spitting out blood.

The boy coughed. "American?" Texas blood ran through that thick accent.

"Yeah. Where …" Kody gasped for air and forced out the question, "Where are we?"

"Few hours …" the boy breathed heavily between each word, "From … Rio Grande."

Pain scorched his body while he tried to crawl to the boy. "Where are we going?"

"Air … port." He let out a whimper.

"Next time … they open the door …"

The boy coughed. "Help me to the rope."

Kody allowed the kid some room but laid next to him, wondering why he'd want the rope but too tired to ask.

"I'd rather be dead."

Kody spat out blood again, understanding the feeling.

The boy whimpered. "They took my sister. Killed my parents. Please. Help me to the bucket."

Kody's heart raced, and he squeezed his eyes shut. A tear fell out anyway. "I'm a soldier. I'll keep you safe. What's your name?"

The boy reached out slowly with a shaking hand, touching the tip of his finger to Kody's. Within seconds he was snoring.

Kody's mind raced. The bucket. He could slam the bucket over someone's head to knock them out. Or catapult his body on whoever opened the door. But he couldn't even stand. His head lolled to the side, and his eyelids struggled to stay open. His limbs went limp.

Just a minute of rest.

Instead of blissful sleep, visions of Raelyn swarmed his mind in chaos. Zohaib placed a crown on her head, presented her to a large crowd, then fastened her to a wall, tying her body in a device, so she was spread-eagled before everyone. Zohaib swung a hammer by his side and pulled a nail from his pocket with a haunted look in his eye. He smiled as the crowd cheered. His snake eyes glared at Raelyn as he poked the sharp end of the nail into her palm. She writhed and whispered one name over and over, '*Kody, Kody, Kody.*' The hammer pounded the nail into her flesh, and she screamed in pain but only said one word, '*Kody, Kody.*' Tears spilled, and the entire crowd began chanted along. '*Kody! Kody! Kody!*' Only then did he realize that he was the one hammering nails into Raelyn's skin. Kody held the hammer and slammed it harder and harder into each nail until she could no longer scream. Her eyes rolled to the back of her head, and her chest heaved.

Kody bolted awake, rolled over, and vomited water on the floor. It smelled of nothing. There was no food in his stomach to hurl. The tires underneath him rolled and bounced on the road, and soft music projected from the cabin.

"Hey, kid," Kody croaked. His voice barely managed a whisper. He reached over subtly and only felt the metal floor in the darkness.

"Kid … what's your name?" Kody's body protested as he rolled over and touched the surrounding area. He crawled a little to the left, and his face bumped into something sturdy. Soft like cloth. Hanging. Kody reached up and felt pants. A leg. Dangling.

Fuck! No!

He grasped his stomach as he pushed himself up and lifted the boy up. Kody's arms trembled as the boy slipped from his grip and swung back and forth. Only the creaking of the rope made a sound.

"No! Come on!" Kody positioned himself under and pushed up again. "Come on, kid!"

The limp body bent and swerved in the air.

"Damn it!" Kody groped around in the dark for the bucket and stepped up. It caved in a little under his bare toes, so he balanced on one leg and reached up, feeling for his neck. The body twisted and swung. No pulse. He fumbled with the knot, unable to loosen it. His quick movement made the bucket underfoot crack. His foot crunched through, and the metal scraped into his skin. He hit the ground.

"Ahhhh!" Kody cowered into a ball, resting his forearms on his knees, and tried to focus on steady breathing, counting them until he reached one hundred, then started over again.

Creak.

As the truck turned, the body swung behind him. His shoulders quivered.

Breathe in. One. Two. Three. Four. Breathe out.

Exhaustion battled him into submission, and he laid flat on his back.

Creak.

The soft light in the tiny hole peeked through, disappeared, then appeared again. Kody didn't need to commit suicide, he'd die from thirst soon. He stared into the blackness, not sure if his eyes were open or closed anymore. How much time had passed? A scraping sound made Kody lift his chin, enough to see the slimy smile of the man who had beaten him last time.

"Eat." The smell of chicken wafted over. "So, the kid was smarter than you, huh?" He hopped up and strutted down the length of the trailer. "Don't worry, I'll give you one more chance.

Kody eyed the sunrise or sunset; he was unsure … and freedom outside, but his body felt like it was buried under a house.

With another bucket and rope in hand, the man threw them at Kody. He slashed the old rope, and the boy's body thumped to the floor. "You can keep him in here for company."

When Kody tried to speak, only a crackle sound came out. He tried again. "Light. Please."

"Nope. Enjoy your last meal." His boot purposefully stepped in the tray of food as he walked out.

After the door closed, Kody clung to the rope. He wormed his way to the tray, mouth drooling. Despite the strange smell, Kody devoured the cold food and gulped the warm water. He gasped between bites and ravaged every scrap possible.

He sighed. "I'm sorry, kid."

The rope near his hand taunted him, beckoning him to do the same. For only a moment, he considered what it'd be like to not have to worry about protecting others anymore. Maybe he could refuse to answer the call from deep within. A quick ending could take away a lifetime of burden. Kody squeezed the rope in his palm.

No. Fuck Zohaib. Bastard's gonna die.

8

RAELYN

HOLDING HER BREATH, RAELYN glanced at Joanna sleeping on their cabin floor. Her mother had moved the dresser to barricade the door. For the fifth time that night, Raelyn tried to crawl to freedom, but the warped wood creaked under her extra weight. Joanna rolled over and faced her, wide-eyed, almost inhuman.

"Lay down," in a tone opposite of a mother's velvety voice, "It's for your own good."

Raelyn folded her arms and leaned back against the cold wall, an icy draft seeping through. When Joanna's eyes finally closed, Raelyn stretched out on the mattress, sore from growing a tiny human. The cabin that she thought had trapped her before was now a literal prison. Joanna had boarded the windows and set a bell on top to alert her if Raelyn opened anything.

Raelyn resituated and rubbed her belly. She had enough food to survive a few months, as long as she didn't mind soup and water, enough warmth to be comfortable, and the wretched companionship of the one person she had previously longed to reconnect with but never would. There were no more chances for Joanna to redeem herself. So, the need to reunite with Kody festered stronger than ever.

He's gone, just like Pa and Phoenix. Everyone I care about leaves me.

Raelyn missed his warmth, his comfort, his steady loyalty, and even that stubbornness. She glimpsed at the sparkling ring on her finger. What will Zohaib do to him? A tear formed. She shook her head and gulped hard.

Pulling her quilt under her arms, Raelyn scooted her backpack closer to her hip and silently dug inside, keeping one eye on a sleeping Joanna. Gripping the cold phone, she turned it on. Still no signal. Her thumbs texted Liam anyway, hoping by some miracle the message would eventually transmit.

The tick-tock of the clock played percussion with the melody of Joanna's snores. Each time Joanna's snore exploded, Raelyn slowly crept across the cabin floor. In the silence between breaths, she froze, waiting. During the next snore, she stalked to the kitchen. Every other step made the wooden floor croak its age, but she timed it right. Tick tock. Snore. Creak. Tick tock. Snore. Creak. Finally reaching the stack of cans, she collected one at a time, during each of Joanna's loud breaths, and stashed them in her backpack. Raelyn turned and stared at the blocked exit. She hesitated and stared at her belly.

Raelyn tip-toed to the chimney and crouched inside. As her boots kicked up old ashes, she covered her mouth and stifled a cough. She blew out a deep, silent breath and put one shoe on the side of the bricked chimney. Good, friction. Raelyn braced her palms on the opposing side and immediately slipped.

Raelyn's heart beat faster when, mid-mumble, Joanna rolled over. She waited for the next snore, then slipped the backpack to her feet and tried a new approach. This time, Raelyn attempted to scale the chimney with her fingertips and toes latched onto the crevices. Every muscle clenched tight, and she let out a slight grunt as she reached up higher. But her belly brushed and bounced against the brick. She dropped again. Pebbles and logs tumbled and scraped down the inside of the chimney. One particularly large rock pinged into her temple, triggering an instant headache. Her lungs roared for more air, compressed by the baby.

She grabbed the can opener and moved to the window.

"What are you doing?"

"Ow!" Raelyn gasped and dropped the can opener on her boot. She hopped in place.

Joanna sat up. "I said, what are you—"

"I know what you said." Raelyn picked up the can opener, slammed it in her backpack, and marched toward the front door. "Move out of my way!" She stepped forward, dirtying Joanna's blankets with soot and ashes.

Joanna grabbed her ankles. "You're not going anywhere!"

"Let me go!" Raelyn kicked.

"Zohaib will torture you!" The frown lines etched on her face were more shadowed and deeper than before.

"He'll kill Kody if I don't save him!" Raelyn screamed. "You used to know how to love when I was little. Don't you remember what it feels like?" Their bodies pretzeled and pushed against each other's tight grip until Raelyn wiggled out.

"Of course I know, love." Joanna bolted forward, positioning herself between Raelyn and the door. "Give me some credit."

Raelyn tried to shove her aside. "I have to keep Kody safe!"

"And I have to keep you away from that monster!" Joanna swiped the gun from the floor and pushed it against Raelyn's belly. "I'll do it." Her words were so high-pitched, so desperate that they silenced Raelyn completely. "I swear, I'll kill the baby to keep you away from Zohaib."

"What?" Panting, Raelyn froze. A shiver crawled up her spine, spreading all over her body. "You're crazy! You'd kill me too." She backed up slowly, distancing herself from both the gun and the wild chaos swirling in Joanna's eyes. Raelyn crouched down in the hope that if Joanna actually shot her, she wouldn't hit her belly straight on. "You wouldn't," Raelyn whispered.

"Stop trying to leave. Death is better than what he will put you through." Her eyes watered, but she formed her mouth into a tight line. "He will hunt you down. The things he will do to you to prove his point … I can't even say them …"

"You're the same as him. You just threatened me."

Joanna dropped the gun, hand trembling. "Of course I won't hurt you. I love you."

"You're insane. You don't know anything about love. If you did, you'd help me."

"I am trying to help you!"

Raelyn backed away and collapsed in her spot by the wall again. An owl hooted outside the walls, requesting answers.

Joanna sighed. "Why can't you understand, hun?"

"I told you to stop calling me hun!" She spat and dropped her chin, hoping the shadows covered her spilling tears.

"We are lucky," Joanna spoke softly. "Zohaib, let you go. You're free, and we're together."

Raelyn sniffed and gestured around. "This isn't free!"

"One day, you'll make hard choices for your little one. You're more like me than you know."

I'll never be a mother like her.

Joanna moved toward her, leaving the gun unprotected. As she reached down for the blanket, Raelyn lunged forward across the small space and grabbed the gun.

A clank sounded from outside, then heavy footsteps crunched over snow. Raelyn glanced at Joanna, whose face was pinched with eyes watching the door. The door handle turned from the outside. Raelyn's heart hammered fast as she raised the gun.

Tap. Tap. Tap.

Raelyn winced. Her body tightened. Her finger hovered over the trigger as the door opened.

"Hello?" Liam's voice was deeper than last time.

"Oh my god!" Raelyn lowered the weapon and let her shoulders drop. "What the hell, Liam! It's six in the morning." She rushed over and hugged him tightly.

He smiled. "I know Kody told me not to come back, but—" He caught sight of Joanna. "Mom?" Liam's blue eyes grew to the size of the full moon. "What are *you* doing here?" He hugged Joanna.

Joanna took both his cheeks in her hands, kissed his nose, and sighed. "I'm so glad to see you. But you need to leave."

"What?" His gaze darted between the two. "Why? What's going on? How did you get here?"

Raelyn grabbed her backpack then marched out the door.

"Hey! Explain!" demanded Liam.

"No! Let Joanna explain that she let Zohaib steal my fiancé." She sank into the deep snow, struggling to lift her heavy boots up and over.

"Woah, slow down." He chased her into the cold. "Kody is gone?"

Raelyn kept marching down the mountain, hearing both of them speed after as she yelled over her shoulder. "We went to talk to Yohaan at the police party. Zohaib was there." White sprinkles landed on all of their coats.

"Why haven't you called me?" Liam caught up and jumped in front, blocking her.

"I tried. Ask your precious mother about her prison rules."

"She wouldn't keep us from each other."

Oak and pine trees flanked Raelyn, with Joanna quickly nipping at her heels.

"I need to get away from her! She trapped me in that cabin." She refused to let the sob escape that pushed against her chest. "Joanna held a gun to my baby!"

Liam's heavy breathing turned ragged as he coughed and spat something out. Raelyn rested a reassuring hand on his back then peered into the distance. At the bottom of that mountain was the old trunk in the loft, and inside—the other USB.

I'll find it today and take it to a different police station. Then Kody will come home.

Behind her, Liam's voice shouted up the mountain, "Is it true?"

"Liam, please." Joanna's plea was soul-crushing.

Raelyn tried to block out their conversation.

Keep walking. Don't stop.

Joanna's footsteps compacted the snow. "Liam, I have to keep you two alive!"

Keep going. Find the file.

Liam hollered. "Mom, you're acting crazy!"

Raelyn turned and stared at her brother and the woman who she was supposed to call mother.

I can't ever call her that again.

"Listen to me. I'm only going to say this once," Raelyn growled. "I have the gun. I have the food. I'm going to find the file so Zohaib will be arrested. If either of you tries to stop me …"

Liam bowed his head. "I'll help."

"No, Liam." Joanna stormed between them. The metal anklet she wore made a chirping sound, and her sparkling blue eyes turned to icicles again.

The sun started to rise in the distance, casting a golden glow over the distant forest.

Joanna swallowed hard and glared for what felt like an eternity before she finally barked, "We need to move fast, and we can't stay in one place long."

Liam grabbed Joanna's hand. "We will figure this out together. Then we're going to family counseling where they have soft, warm chairs and a giant fish tank."

Joanna ruffled his hair and zipped up his coat. "If we manage to destroy Zohaib, I won't be coming out on the other side alive."

Raelyn paused but then pushed the comment aside and trudged on. She didn't want to spend one more second near Joanna, and she also didn't want to endanger Liam. They followed the smoke rising from a chimney far below to a cozy house with lace curtains decorating each window. After another quick glance at Joanna, a pain deep in her soul crept up as they ventured further into the threatening cold.

Once they reached the bottom of the mountain, Raelyn trudged through a foot of packed snow toward the old barn loft. The morning sun reflecting off the icicles hanging from the barn roof didn't help warm her one bit. Her blood ran cold with the terror of where Kody could be.

"I'm going to fly to Tahil to find Kody," Raelyn said.

"Fantastic idea. And that's probably exactly where he is." Liam helped her stay balanced with a firm grip on her arm as they crossed the ice-slicked sidewalk. "Go back to that magical mansion full of dreams and lollipops."

"The airlines wouldn't allow you onboard in your third trimester," Joanna mumbled. The metal piece around her ankle flashed little red dots.

Raelyn pointed to her ankle. "What is that?"

"Remember your electrocution collar?"

The memory made her skin crawl.

"He's tracking me, and it'll shock me if I don't send in my location. It's why I didn't want to leave earlier."

Raelyn glanced around nervously. "Let's try to take it off."

Joanna blocked her. "No, it'd shock us."

"I've been shocked before. You'll survive."

The intensity of her blue eyes shot daggers. "I don't give a damn about myself. My fate isn't a long and happy life. I have no expectation of seeing my granddaughter's first steps one day …"

She's acting like she wants to die.

"… I just have to keep you two safe. The shock could be strong enough to cripple you." Joanna's expression turned wild. "Plus, he'll send someone after you just to make sure you're dead. If I watch you like he asked, I'm keeping you alive."

After a giant groan rattled her core, all of Raelyn's muscles clenched. "I can't do this! None of it!"

"Take a breath, sis."

"No! I have to choose between keeping my brother safe or my baby. Or I have to choose between Kody or the baby. Why can't any decision just be easy for once! I'm a bad sister if I agree for you to help me. I'm a bad fiancée if I can't find him. And I'm the worst mother if I ..." Her hands found her stomach.

Liam sighed. "You're too hard on yourself."

Raelyn laid her head on his shoulder. "What should I do?"

"What would you advise your best friend to do?"

While thinking, she walked past the oak tree with the old tire swing that Joanna and Pa used to push her on and started looking for his axe to destroy what was left of the trunk but couldn't see it anywhere.

"I know what it's like to question your choices, hun." Joanna's pale face was stone when she said, "Once I almost left you, Liam."

He turned. "What?"

Joanna sat on a bale of hay. "When you were about six, I had a chance to run and come back home—alone."

Liam patted her back. "You were a prisoner, Mom. I wouldn't blame you."

"You were six! I never should've considered it!"

Raelyn stood, mouth wide open, watching the conflicting emotions spread across Joanna's expressions.

"I'm just saying … being a mother won't get easier. You'll always question if you made the right choice for your kid. And sometimes there's no right answer."

The rickety barn provided Raelyn sanctuary from the bitter wind that bit her cheeks. She fought to control her quavering voice as she changed the subject. "Um … let's look for some tools to smash open the trunk. Last time I only managed a hole in the side."

She started climbing up the loft ladder, turning sideways so her belly didn't scrape the wooden rungs. Kody's pocket watch hanging from her neck gently jostled against the ladder, snapped apart and tumbled to the barn floor.

"I got it." Joanna picked it up.

Raelyn paused on the ladder, tempted to scramble back down and retrieve the watch herself. Joanna shouldn't be laying a finger on his things. But the lure of the mysterious trunk was too strong. At the top, thick dust coated Raelyn's tongue and set her to coughing. She spotted the place she had tucked Bear's collar away, the same place she found the list of safehouses. Crouching down with a grunt, she managed to pull out Bear's collar. Raelyn raised it to her nose and sniffed his scent. Memories of his fluffy fur sparked a fire of adrenaline. She clutched it close to her chest and squeezed it tight.A piece of home. Of normality.

Raelyn opened the small closet-like door that housed the trunk, but the tiny area only held empty crates. She swiveled. The floor was slippery from hay.

"It's not here!" She shouted down.

"What?" Liam exclaimed, then coughed hard.

"The trunk is gone!"

The sound of someone scurrying up the ladder made Raelyn turn. She met Joanna's roving blue eyes.

With a loud groan, Joanna kicked the crates into the wall, busting pieces of one apart. "How is that possible?"

Raelyn flinched. "Maybe, it's down behind the hay bales."

The trunk was the only place Raelyn could think that Pa would've hidden the file. If the file wasn't there, then they had no hope for defeating Zohaib.

She descended the ladder, careful not to slip. Behind barrels, Liam tossed items around, groping around on his hands and knees. "It's not here. There's no trunk." He sneezed, sniffed, and wiped snot on his sleeve.

Raelyn leaned against a barrel, all energy draining away. "What the hell are we gonna do now?"

Tearing, ripping, and crunching sounds echoed off the barn rafters.

Liam craned his neck and hollered. "Mom? What are you doing up there?"

Joanna emerged from the tiny closet with two huge stacks of cash in her hands. "Secret stash!" A smile rose on her pink cheeks.

Raelyn shook her head. "How much money is that?"

"If William never found it, then ten thousand dollars. I stole it from Zohaib the night …" She looked away. "… the night you were conceived. There's more somewhere." Joanna pulled out the waistband of her tight yoga pants and shoved the money in. It bulged against the elastic. "I'll go off on my own, and I'll hire someone to get more proof on Zohaib. We don't have the file, so we have to find other evidence."

Liam stepped toward her. "Mom, don't go." He held out his hands. "We can work as a team. You just said he's tracking you."

Raelyn balled her fists, still holding Bear's collar, and stomped after Joanna. At least Bear knew what it meant to stick by her side.

She whispered harshly. The sharpness could cut the winter air. "Mothers don't abandon their children!"

"Do you want to defeat Zohaib?" Joanna halted and pursed her lips together. "We already left the cabin, so now we have no choice."

Momentarily, Raelyn felt like a child, reprimanded by a parent – she'd forgotten what that felt like. She stared at the metal anklet. If Zohaib was tracking them this very moment, maybe it would be better for Joanna to leave. Raelyn stuck out her hand and stood up for herself. "Give me Kody's pocket watch."

Joanna eased the golden chain into Raelyn's palm. A cold breeze whipped her chestnut hair around as she said, "Don't follow me." Without a goodbye, Joanna slipped through the crack of the barn doors. She tried to run through the snow, having to lift her shoes knee-high.

I'll never be that kind of mother.

Raelyn looked at Liam, who looked dumbstruck.

"She actually left." His mouth hung open. "I swear, Mom wasn't always like this. It's like a switch flipped in her."

Rubbing her temples, Raelyn peeked around the door to the white yard. Grandma Viola's old truck sat idle in the driveway. The sound of a car screeched and skidded on ice under its tires as Joanna peeled away, making her cringe. Liam took his sister's elbow and guided her through the snow to the farmhouse. Flakes landed on his wavy blond hair.

"You should be wearing a hat. You'll get sick."

"I can't get much sicker than I am. Do you know the lifespan of someone with cystic fibrosis?"

Raelyn squeezed her eyes shut. "Stop it. Let's talk about something else." She stared at a spot in the yard that glistened gold atop the blanket of white. Squinting, she moved closer, then gasped. Pa's wedding ring miraculously stuck out of the snow.

"I can't believe it!" She crouched down.

"What?" Liam joined her.

"Pa threw this into an abyss of weeds, and now it's just here, plain as day." She handed it over. "Here, you keep it."

"Wow, thanks." Liam pocketed it just as the back door to the farmhouse swung open, and a loud, joyful cry came from Grandma, "My Grandbabies, come, I've got snacks!" Covered head to toe in wet paint, Grandma rubbed her hands on her art smock and opened her arms wide.

Raelyn smiled and joined her, trying to avoid the paint as she hugged her Grandma, inhaling her scent—coffee. Her gray hair was streaked with vibrant purple strands. Round glasses rested on top of her head. Her emerald eyes held Pa's glimmer, yet hers were more devious in nature.

The scent of coffee beans wafted from the kitchen to her nostrils as Raelyn tossed her winter gloves on the floor. She rubbed her fingers together and tiptoed past her snoring Grandpa to the fireplace. The heat hit her like a ton of bricks, shocking her lungs with a large inhale of warmth.

Raelyn looked around at her childhood home. It hadn't changed much. The same lacy curtains draped over the window. Most of the same old mismatched, rustic furniture decorated the living room. Thankfully, the study doors were closed. She put her back to that room and squeezed her eyes shut tight.

Raelyn gestured around. "So, you sold your other place and are living here now?"

Mr. Grumps purred loudly and stretched atop a lump of unfinished knitted blankets.

"No, we still own both houses, but we sold half our stuff at a garage sale. We haven't found tenants for this place yet." She hurried over. "But, how are you, dear?"

When Grandma spoke, the same southern accent came out that Pa had in his voice. A lump caught in her throat. "I've been better. Grandma, you two need to leave North Carolina for a few months. I thought the cops would've told you—"

"Nonsense. If someone wants to come knocking on my door hollering and demanding things, well, that's what my rolling pin is for." She nodded and turned to Liam with a giant sigh and ushered him in tight.

He flashed his pearly whites and lifted his chin. "I've got a beard coming in."

Grandma squinted, moving in closer. "Where's my glasses?"

"On your head, Grandma."

She pulled them down and inspected his jawline. "Yup, that beard is just like William's."

Raelyn left them to chat as she plugged her phone in to charge on the kitchen counter. The background of her screen was a picture of her and Kody smiling in Tuzlicci, a simple moment in her life before everything became complicated. An incoming call interrupted the photo.

Raelyn picked it up. "Hello? This is Raelyn."

A woman's husky voice on the other end responded. "Yes, this is Doctor Oberman's office. We have information about your paternity test."

Raelyn clutched the phone harder, barely able to squeak out a response. "Yes?"

"Unfortunately, in transit, the lab lost the sample of the potential father."

Her heart dropped. "You don't have the results?"

"No. It never made it to the lab. Can you ask Mr. Walsh to come in again? No appointment is necessary. He can stop by at any time."

Silence.

"Or you can have the other … candidate swing by. Any day is fine."

Raelyn's world crashed around her. "The other man is dead."

A pen scratched along a piece of paper. "I'm sorry. So, Mr. Walsh, can he—?"

"No, he's …" She clutched his pocket watch. "It's complicated."

"I see. Well, we will update you if we find the sample."

She shook her head. "That's it? I won't know until the baby is born?"

"If Mr. Walsh could come in—"

"He can't!" Raelyn screamed into the phone.

A long pause, then, "Is there anything else I can help you with today?"

Raelyn chewed the inside of her lip. "Is it a girl?"

Papers shuffled on the other end of the call. "I can definitely tell you that! Let me see …"

How had her life turned so upside down? Wasn't it yesterday she was a senior in high school, living in this house with Pa in Ash Mountain? Now she was considering giving away her baby—whom she loved more than life itself.

Adoption isn't abandoning. I'm giving her a better mother.

The baby kicked inside, showing excitement at the gender reveal, but a hollowness ran through her bones.

A scratching sound screeched in her ear. "Here it is. You are having a baby girl. Congratulations!"

Raelyn placed her hand on her belly and couldn't help but smile. She hung up without a word and turned, wanting to rush into Kody's arms and tell him the news. But he was somewhere on the other side of the world. The walls closed in around her, and a sudden sob struck her chest. Her entire body tensed and threatened to curl inward on herself, imploding from the devastation of not knowing where Kody was. Raelyn swallowed hard, bent over, and placed both hands on her knees.

Breathe. Like Kody taught me. In. Out.

A long exhale reminded her of the times Kody forced her to meditate, which slowed her heart rate for at least a moment.

How can I get him home?

Yohaan couldn't help her anymore; the man had enough on his plate. Mrs. Walsh worked nonstop at her law firm, investigating every angle to find Kody without drawing attention. Before setting her phone down, Raelyn sent messages to those who might help: Lieutenant Meadows and Private Dabbott. Kody had left her their contact information in case of an emergency.

"Grandma, do you know where the trunk is that Pa stored up in the barn loft?"

"Sold it." Grandma pawed the stack of mail. "Finally getting rid of things."

Raelyn's heart hit the floor. "Did you check inside?"

"I left that to your Grandpa, but he would've told me, so I don't think he found anything."

"Do you know who bought it?"

She huffed. "It's a good thing your Grandpa logged each transaction, down to the bucket of nails we sold." She rummaged through a drawer in the kitchen, pulling out random tape, pens, staplers, spatulas, whisks, and finally a pad of paper. "Here it is." She licked her finger and swiped open a page in an old book. "See, this page shows the item, the cost, and the person's name."

Raelyn grabbed it and scanned the list, unable to read half of it. "Where's the trunk listed?"

"Well, dear, if you were patient for once." She snatched it back and skimmed down. "Uh oh."

Grandma's eyebrows furrowed together. "This part had a bit of water and paint splashed onto it. There are three smudged names near 'trunk.' It could've gone to any of these men: Tucker, Aaron, or Jordi."

Liam pulled out his phone. "Do you know their addresses? I can find out how far they are."

"I can check in a minute, but what's this?" The wind outside roared as Grandma dug out a package from deeper into the drawer. "That's weird. This package is addressed to you, dear."

"Is it an old college recruitment letter?" asked Raelyn. "Who's it from?"

"Someone Peterson?"

Raelyn gasped and lunged forward. "What?"

She stared at the fine cursive on the front, the address from a city only thirty minutes away. Raelyn ripped open the package, and Pa's journal dropped out, flopping onto the floor. Clutching her belly, her hands shook as she sank to the floor in the middle of the hallway on the hardwood, heart racing.

"I lost this on top of the spiral tower."

Two loose papers stuck out from the top. The first read:

Dear Raelyn Bell,

I received this journal in the mail from someone named Jawhara four months ago. She included a note, which I will attach. My apologies that it took so long to send. I didn't have the energy to do much of anything since Phoenix passed.

This is all a bit strange since there was also cash in the letter. Do you know why?

Anyway, Phoenix spoke so highly of you when he called each week. I would also love to hear more stories about my son. I miss him more than words can tell.

Sincerely,

-Haydee Peterson

Raelyn held the letter to her heart, a tear sliding down her cheek. Mr. Grumps walked over and nuzzled its nose against her wrist. She folded the letter delicately, tucked it into Pa's journal, and thought about her desert journey. All she could imagine was Phoenix's smile. No amount of therapy could scrub the stain of Phoenix's death from her mind.

Does Haydee know I might be carrying his child?

Raelyn sighed. Of course, she wouldn't know. Phoenix never even had the time to find out, so he couldn't have told his parents. Taking a deep breath, Raelyn started the second letter.

From one mother to another.

Phoenix saved Raelyn's life—many times. Your son is a true hero. and I owe him much more than this small gesture. For reasons I can't explain here. I need to send this journal to you. Please mail it to my daughter at 222 Golden Street in Ash Mountain.

I know your husband is a General with combat training. If I am successful with my plan. I'm hoping Raelyn could stay with you for safety. She may have nowhere else to go.

Condolences on your loss.

Jawhara

Liam coughed behind her. "See, Mom is good. She found a safe place for you to hide."

"I don't understand. I wish I could be inside Joanna's brain for a day and figure out what she is thinking ... what she's planning." She thumbed through the pages of the journal, peering at Pa's chicken scratch of clues. "Why did Joanna give them money? Why did she send them the journal?"

"Probably not to lead anyone to this address."

Phoenix's smile flashed through her mind again, so she whispered, "What if Phoenix is the father? I can't … I don't ..."

Mr. Grumps circled at Raelyn's feet, so Grandma picked him up and placed the fluffball in her arms. "Take a deep breath. Everything will be okay."

"How do you know that? You weren't in that desert. Before anything can get better, I need Kody! I need that file!" It felt like a ton of bricks stacked on her shoulders.

Raelyn tuned out the rest of their conversation as she moved back to the fireplace. The cat followed and jumped on her lap when she sat on the hearth. Curling into a little ball, Raelyn caressed his fur. Raelyn held her hands up to the crackling fire as the scent of burning wood wafted in the air. The wind howled outside, knocking branches into the window. In the background, Liam and Grandma talked about the dander, smoke, and his cystic fibrosis while Raelyn buried herself in thought.

From the stories that Phoenix told of his mother, she knew that if she drove straight to the Peterson's house, the promise of someone who would welcome her with open arms awaited her. Maybe Phoenix's mother could give her the motherly love she had been searching for—another gift he had left her with. The closed study doors loomed before her like a fortress wall.

"Wait," she spoke to the cat like how she used to talk to Bear, "Maybe Pa never hid the file in the trunk."

She rushed to the study doors and hovered her hand over the knob. After a deep inhale, she pushed the door open to the organized office. Immediately, Raelyn ransacked the room. She flung the books off their shelves one by one, relishing in the *thunk* sound when each landed on the hardwood. Reaching under the chair, she frantically groped for anything small that might have gone unnoticed. An uncomfortable groan fled from her lips as she was unable to hold that squatting position. Raelyn rose and flipped the chair upside down.

Liam joined her, and his eyes widened. "What the heck are you doing?"

"The file must be in here."

Grandma walked in and clasped one hand over her mouth. "Young lady! You'll be picking all this up!"

"It's got to be here." She tried to tilt the desk, but it was too heavy. "Liam, look under this."

"Dear, we've completely cleared this place out before the garage sale and cleaned it. I would've found anything hidden."

Raelyn slammed her hand on the desk. "Are you sure?"

"Yes, let me get you some sugar, dear."

Liam pointed to a map on his phone. "One of these locals has the trunk, Tucker, Aaron, or Jordi. We can go to each house and ask. They're all up in Ash Mountain."

"Why not just call them?"

"Grandma's old school, she said she only has their addresses, no phone numbers."

"We can look their numbers up online."

"I tried, but we don't have service in this storm."

Raelyn glanced outside, unable to see Grandma's car through the thick gray cloud of snow. Frustrated with her luck, she let her head fall back and fixated on the ceiling.

"Grandma, do you have snow tires?" Liam asked.

"Yes, dear, but you can't use our car. Your brilliant grandpa forgot to get gas, that old fool."

"How will I get to their houses?" Raelyn asked.

"I'm going too." Liam stepped forward.

"No way, you can't go anywhere in this weather."

Grandma ushered them closer to the fireplace and pulled a blanket off the back of the couch. "Sleep here and wait out the storm. That way, I can get to know my Liam even better. I'll drive you up the mountain in the morning before we head to the airport."

"Airport? I'm confused, so you *are* going into hiding?" Raelyn asked.

"Oh no, your Grandpa and I have had a trip planned to Florida for months." Grandma handed her a cookie.

Raelyn chomped down, letting the gooiness melt over her tongue, but she couldn't savor anything. Not even chocolate. It tasted like nothing in her mouth, like ash or too nasty to swallow. "I'm getting that file tonight. I have to get Kody home."

Liam pushed his thumbs into his pocket. "How will we get to the houses in this snowstorm?"

"We hike."

"In a doomsday-end of the world-avalanche storm?"

"Yes."

A warning boiled in her blood, threatening to melt her very bones.

9

RAELYN

Exhausted and sore, Raelyn dug her walking stick into the deep snow and trudged another step up the mountain. She looked at the sky, wondering if Kody would do the same, would he see the sun or the moon. Was it day or night where he was? Actually, she could barely see the sun anyway because of the fluster of snow.

Her phone dinged.

"Hold on one second. It's Dabbott again." Raelyn leaned on her walking stick, then rubbed her sore back and read the screen.

Sorry, it's too dangerous to try and break into Z's mansion here to search for K, but I'll be on the lookout for intel. Delete all traces of our emails.

"I'm giving you one week to find it, or I'm going to that warehouse to search for more clues," Liam said.

"Absolutely not. That place is all wrong. I won't let you go there."

"One week." Liam read the message again over her shoulder. "Come on, I've never been this cold. Ever." Liam shielded his face with his gloved hands. "We're only a mile from the first house."

A glacial wind stung her cheeks as she squinted into the blur of white. Her mind whirled about Kody. Where could he be? Had anyone hurt him?

Raelyn could've sworn she saw a figure moving parallel to them behind a line of trees. "Liam? Did you see that?" She pointed through the white haze.

"What? A deer?"

"No, it looked like a person."

"Bigfoot?" He laughed. "Stop being paranoid."

Raelyn's leg muscles burned. Little chunks of snow kept edging their way further into her snow boots, but because of her offset center of gravity recently, she didn't even bother reaching down to try and pluck it out.

They reached a colossal waterfall entirely frozen to ice. The giant icicles hung like fangs bared by a cold and heartless beast.

Raelyn tilted her head. "How could something look so monstrous yet so breathtaking?"

"You're channeling Kody's big crossword puzzle vocabulary."

She tugged Liam's wool hat over his eyes. "Whatever, you said channeling."

He laughed deeply. His voice echoed around the glacier daggers pointing down like fangs. Under the frozen waterfall, Raelyn sat atop a boulder and tried to pull out Pa's journal from her pack, feeling the need to get rid of her emotions on paper, but her numb fingers wouldn't pinch together in the gloves. She bit the fabric and pulled the glove off, showing her raw and cracked pink skin.

Liam called out. "I'm gonna try to pry off one of these icicles."

"Why?"

"Why not? You only live once."

Raelyn shook her head. "Sometimes I forget your age. Just be careful."

Upon opening Pa's journal, the snowflakes saturated the page, forming little circles of blotted ink. She snapped the binding closed, unwilling to risk destroying Pa's notes. She tried to shut out the negativity, but rhymes flowed in her mind. In another time, the snow would've been comforting and beautiful, but now it reminded her of the vast coldness that would consume her future if she wasn't successful.

Tight ropes wrap around my heart, strangled in fear
The choice I made only produced a tear
I'll give you my years, my life, my everything
A promise made with a gold wedding ring

She sighed and stared at her ring finger.

"Check this out!" Liam sniffed while walking around the corner of a wall of ice, holding a four-foot icicle." Liam bent over, coughed, and spit into the blanket of white.

She banged hard on his back to help unclog the mucus. "You should go back, Liam. I don't want you hospitalized."

"Forget it, sis. If I die tomorrow, at least I know I didn't give up. Zohaib needs to stop hurting girls. Olivia died because of him."

"Olivia died because of Quincy," stated Raelyn.

"No, they were both in that position because of Zohaib. And what about Mom?"

"What about her?"

He held the icicle out like a giant sword. "I have to fix Mom. She's so broken. If Zohaib is gone, maybe she will be okay again."

"Maybe."

"But, don't worry, you'll be a much better mother to your child, him … or her."

"She's a girl."

Liam's smile reached his ears. "Kody was right."

All of a sudden, a deafening crack blasted above. Liam's eyes widened. She grabbed his wrist and pulled him away from the waterfall, but Liam twisted away.

"I need to get my backpack!"

"Liam, no!"

"It has my inhaler!"

All around them, fatal crystals plunged down fast and shattered into a thousand pieces. As she sprinted out of the cave, the ear-piercing crashes behind her made her picture the champagne glass in Zohaib's hand at his auction event when he smashed it, and glass rained down.

When everything stilled, Raelyn turned and screamed into the white abyss, "Liam?"

"I'm stuck," His voice was small and buried, muffled.

"Where? I'm coming." After looking up to check if any more seemed loose, she kicked some of the cracked icicles to form a path.

"Ssh! There's more up there," Liam whispered.

Raelyn glanced up again and stared in awe. Half the frozen structure remained.

"Liam?" Fear clamped down on her chest, and her breathing turned heavy as she tiptoed into the rummage. "Where are you?"

A soft cough came from the left. She held her breath and followed Liam's wheezes, treading slowly with soft steps through the debris. One wrong move or loud sound and the rest of the icicles would spear through them both.

Finally, Liam came into view, hunched in a ball with a sharp icicle jabbed through the tail of his coat, pinning him to the ground. Others caged him in like crystal gates. His coughing grew more intense, and Raelyn cringed, glimpsing up at the dangling weapons, sharp points directed straight at her. A vibration above made her shudder.

"We don't have time." Liam's voice had raised an octave in desperation. "Just whack it!"

Raelyn kicked it hard, splitting his ice trap in half, and freed him. The gun tucked into the side pocket flew out and skated far on the slippery ground.

"Let's go!"

As Liam rose, his boot smacked against something and clattered. An echo rattled like the call of death. Liam yanked her as they fled. Sounds imitating shattering jewels and stones clambered behind. But they kept sprinting. Running. Faster. Harder. Desperate.

Finally reaching the clearing, they both bent over and sucked in air. Raelyn checked behind. A beam of light reflected, creating tiny rainbows in the icicles for a moment before the gloom of the white-out took over again.

"Come on. That's as much adventure as we need for a lifetime." Raelyn trudged along.

"Thanks for not leaving me to rot."

Raelyn rolled her eyes. "I'll never leave you, Liam. Not like Joanna."

"Hey, that's not fair. She's probably saving our butts with that money somehow."

Doubtful.

Hiking higher and panting, Raelyn scanned the suddenly flattened surface. The river was frozen over, with a foot of snow layered on top. On the other side, bald trees towered like candlesticks on soft, smooth icing, leading to the final hill.

The pocket watch chain scratched against her chest. She never owned jewelry, but as a child, she was constantly enamored with what Joanna wore, asking to try it on. For the first time, she envisioned herself in a wedding dress, as white as this snow, smiling down an aisle at Kody. Raelyn shook her head.

He can't be dead. I'll find him. But, what if . . . ?

Raelyn stopped tromping and hollered to her brother. "Liam, I can't raise her alone."

"What do you mean?"

The wind tossed her to the side, and she struggled to remain upright. Liam moved close and latched onto her elbow.

"I'm going to find Phoenix's mother and see if she will adopt her."

He turned, and his blue eyes widened. "You got the paternity results back?"

"No." Raelyn brushed the layer of snow from the river with her walking stick, then tapped the ice.

"She's your daughter. My niece. You can't let her go." His nostrils flared.

"It's my choice." Her voice cracked as she pointed in his face. "You don't get to say that. I'm doing what's best for her."

They ventured out onto the ice, tiptoeing like ballerinas even though she wanted to storm across. Raelyn tried to picture her baby's dark brown eyes similar to Kody's gazing up at her, but only a clear blue-green shade stared back. She imagined swaddling her baby in a blanket and laying her in a warm crib, gazing up at her from a stroller, or while cradled in her arms. She'd love her little girl endlessly—no matter what. But that was the problem.

Raelyn's heart ached at the idea of Phoenix's mother rocking her baby to sleep or splashing warm water on her little head in the bath. She longed to be the first to see her daughter smile, but that life wasn't possible.

Wind whipped through the tiny holes of her knitted scarf. Her boot slipped on the ice, but she regained her footing and kept on going. Tears started freezing on her chin. She took another step onto the ice and heard the crunching of Liam's footsteps behind her. Trying to stay light on their feet, they were already halfway across the river. Only then did she realize her stupidity for not checking the thickness. Raelyn reached out for her brother. The snowstorm turned into a blizzard, and she couldn't see the other side, unable to tell if they were traveling in a straight line.

"Stop!" Liam screamed. "Don't move!" He coughed into the howling wind, his disease slowly ravaging his insides.

From the terror in his voice, Raelyn's heart jolted. She heard a split in the ice below her boot, but she didn't dare look down.

"Liam …"

Her brother backed away slowly, his hands low and steady, but the ice broke apart like an earthquake forming a divide between them.

"The ice!" Raelyn yelled.

"Crap!"

It split wider as she reached out. "Can you make the jump over here?"

"It's too far! Go without me."

"I can't leave you."

Not like Joanna left us.

Liam waved carelessly, but his face was full of worry. "I'll be okay. I need more meds anyway. Grandma has them. I'll meet you at the farmhouse, and remember, you have one week."

She memorized Liam's features—just in case—then turned and crawled as fast as she could toward the other bank. *Snap!* Another slit in the ice cracked. Her heart raced.

She crawled faster. The ice chunk ruptured in half, and her heart rate doubled. Only ten feet until the bank. A sharp crackle like thunder clapped, and her piece of ice ripped away from the larger chunk.

Raelyn's heart slammed against her ribs. She laid on her side, dipped her arm in the icy water, and started paddling. The water tortured her skin, and her drenched coat sleeve became heavy. Her heart slammed against her rib cage, terror etched in every beat. She started floating away.

Eight feet to safety!

Grappling and splashing with all her might, Raelyn cleaved her way through the water.

Six feet away!

Her teeth chattered, and her arm shook with pain like needles piercing her veins. Raelyn wrestled with the water, pulling harder using her arm as an oar.

Four feet away!

Jumping to her feet, she pushed off with all her might, lunging across to the bank. Snow crunched underfoot. She scrambled up onto the bank, heaving in shock.

I can't feel my arm!

Raelyn tore off her wet coat. Her clothes were soaked through. She stripped off her sweater and hung it on a branch, shivering. Snow stuck to her shoulders, and her whole body shook.

Wrapping her arms around her bare belly, Raelyn tried to believe her words as she said, "It's okay, Amala. I've got you." Half-naked in a blizzard, fear swirled around stronger than the snow.

So cold. Too cold.

There were no caves. She tried to remember how Phoenix had taught her to start a fire, but her mind blanked. Raelyn huddled behind a thick trunk of an oak, curling herself into a ball. Her clothes on the limb were hardened solid. In a last attempt, she dug in the depths of the backpack and pulled out one of Kody's shirts.

Keep moving. Keep walking.

Raelyn started the laborious hike through the deep snow to find help, unsure of which way to walk. She knew she needed to keep moving to maintain core temperature, but exhaustion flooded her system. Her vision blurred and her skull pounded, and an image of Pa's grave flashed in her mind.

Even if Liam got help, he wouldn't be able to cross the river anymore. Paralyzed with dread, Raelyn tried to scheme up an idea, but she was so cold her head started spinning, unable to think straight. Her teeth clattered together. Raelyn was pretty sure her eyebrows were frozen, and no matter how many times she rubbed her lips together, they had gone numb.

Trekking higher, the feeling of someone watching her racked her senses. She whirled around and felt a presence behind an oak tree, like a protective ghost or a phantom wind.

"Hello?" An unfamiliar, deep male voice called out.

A light flickered ahead.

"Hello? Help!" The back of her throat began to burn from the arctic hell. Raelyn ducked her head low into the polar cyclone that was cutting deadly chills deep within her core. While dragging the backpack behind her, completely stiff and trembling, she trudged to the light. It went out, then back on again.

"I'm here!" She wasn't even sure her voice left her throat.

She trudged forward and almost cried from joy at the sight of a house. The porch light flickered, and smoke rose from the chimney. Much slower than she wanted, Raelyn climbed the porch steps and tried to pound on the door but could barely move her arm, full of fresh cuts.

"Help!" She sank to her knees, unable to feel the landing as her bones hit the wood porch.

The door swung open.

10

RAELYN

THE CEILING FADED IN and out of focus. Raelyn awoke to the crackle of orange flames in the fireplace and heat on her cheeks. Banana bread aromas drenched the air from the oven. As Raelyn stretched and let out a soft groan, a fur blanket brushed along her shoulders, stomach, and hips. But then something tickled her toes and wiggled, making her squeal. She peeked under the fabric and spotted a huskie curled at her feet, its white and black fur matching the natural coloring of the blanket.

Blue puppy eyes looked at her, eyelashes fluttering, then the dog yawned and went back to napping. A soft smile stretched across her face until the sudden realization that she was naked made her clutch the blanket tighter. Her eyes darted around. She lay on a large bed in a one-roomed cabin, similar to the one she and Kody had hidden in for the past few months. Antlers hung above guitars.

When a kettle whistled, a bear of a man rose from the shadows in the corner, his eyes on the stove.

Raelyn gasped and groped the blankets for anything hard to hit him with.

"Feeling better?" His deep voice resonated like the perfect harmony of a church choir.

She curled into a protective ball and pulled the blanket up until her eyes. Her gaze collided with the glance of a tall, powerfully built man in plaid.

"I'm not going to hurt you."

She took in the man's features, probably late-twenties, maybe thirty, tall, with muscles like a lumberjack.

"Where's my clothes?" She tried to shake off the thought of him undressing her.

He nodded to the fireplace, where they were draped next to his plaid shirts. "It was the only way to get you warm. I'm sorry."

"Who are you?"

"Tucker."

"You're Tucker? I came up here to find you."

He stretched out both arms. "Here I am."

"Wait, did you see a blond boy?"

"No."

Raelyn moved toward the edge of the bed. "I need to go find my brother."

"You're not going anywhere. Viola will shoot me herself if you get pneumonia."

"You know my Grandma?"

He smiled, flashing a gold tooth. "Sure do."

"I need to call her and ask about Liam."

"You can try. There's not great service in here."

Raelyn groaned while digging for her phone.

"What are you doing on my mountain in these conditions?"

"I'm looking for something. Did you go to my Grandma's garage sale?"

"Sure did." He brought a mug over to her, placing it on the nightstand, and backed away without making eye contact.

"Thank you." Jitters crept over her body as she sipped the tea. "At the sale, did you happen to buy a large trunk?"

"Nope."

Her heart sank. She'd have to trudge through the storm to the other two houses and ask if they had bought the trunk. The husky rubbed his nose against her hand, then rolled over, inviting her to scratch its belly.

"That pup is Shiloh," said Tucker.

Raelyn petted the husky's fur and stroked its ears.

Tucker pointed and sat on a chair in the corner. "I did buy hunting equipment from your Grandma, though. William had a lot."

Raelyn's heart fluttered alive again. "You knew Pa?"

"Of course, everyone in town knew William. He taught me how to shoot damn good. When I was ten, your Pa took me under his wing." He rubbed his beard. "When I got grown, he invited me to his poker games."

The realization that she knew less about Pa than she assumed ripped open a new hole. How selfish had she been to not be aware of Pa's life and friends?

"Actually, I'm surprised you don't recognize me."

Raelyn gulped. "Should I?"

"Y'all's class visited my fire station. I let you slide down the pole. I guess I look different now."

"I remember now ... Fireman Tucker. Do you still work there?"

"No." He looked away and crossed his arms.

An awkward silence filled the small space until he made it worse by saying, "You're awful young to have a baby coming."

"Um—" She looked over to see if her clothes were dry so she could get the hell out of there.

"I didn't mean anything by it. I only speak from experience. I was twenty when my—" Tucker choked on his words and looked away.

Her heart dropped.

Something bad happened.

She lay a hand on her belly, trying to comfort Amala's kicking. "Do you have any food?"

"Sure, sure." He lumbered across the room, pulling out a pan of banana bread from the oven.

Her mouth watered as he cut her a slice and slathered butter on the top. It was so warm, the butter instantly melted into the fluffiness. Shiloh begged while Raelyn took a bite and let the warmth take over her mouth.

"Have you named your baby?" He pointed to her belly.

"Amala." She scrunched her nose, realizing she had only come up with that name yesterday, then ripped off another piece, allowing it to crumble under her touch. "But …"

He leaned back in his chair, making the wood creak under his weight.

"Never mind, I'll figure it out," she mumbled.

"Oh, I see, you're alone. Where's her father?"

The pocket watch still hung around her neck and was cradled between the curves of her breasts. The time on the watch hadn't ticked on since Kody stopped the clock at the New Year's Eve event—possibly the last memory she'd ever have of the man who owned her heart.

Raelyn tilted her head. "I'll tell you where he is if you tell me what happened to you when you were twenty."

"You jump right to the point."

"I don't have time to be polite these days."

"Fair enough. The whole town knows anyways." Tucker gripped the bottom of his seat and let out a huge breath. "My girlfriend died … during childbirth." The longing in his voice deepened his twang.

Raelyn dropped her bread and covered her mouth with both hands, unsure how to respond.

That won't happen to us.

Tucker cocked his head and turned to rummage through a kitchen drawer. "Actually, I have something for you."

"What do you mean?" She devoured another bite, letting crumbs spill from her lips.

He pulled out a little gold hair bow, the perfect size for a toddler. "I bought this for my little girl. I want you to have it."

Raelyn's jaw dropped. "No, I couldn't take that."

"Please. It's the only thing I ever bought for her. Since it can't make her happy, I'd like to think that it could still spread some joy."

Raelyn slowly held out her hand, watching him intently. The little metal pin used as a clasp was cold in her palm. "Thank you."

Tucker cleared his throat. "Now it's your turn. Where's her father?"

"He is … a prisoner of war. Kind of."

Tucker whistled, and his eyes widened. "Lord have mercy. What are you gonna do?"

"I need to save him." She hovered a bite of banana bread over her mouth. "Do you know someone named Aaron or Jordi? I need to ask if they bought the trunk from my Grandma."

Tucker nodded and pulled his phone out of his pocket. "Sure, I know Jordi. I'll need to go walk to where there's better service, be right back." His cheeks flushed. "How about you get changed. Those should be dry."

As he stepped outside, an overwhelming stream of thoughts and questions bombarded her mind. Did Liam make it home safely? How would she get to the next house alone? What if the file wasn't in the trunk? Would the Petersons agree to care for Amala? Where was Kody? When would she see him again? Did Joanna really take money from the loft to get evidence on Zohaib?

Naked, she moved to the clothes by the stone fireplace, absorbing the warmth. She caught her reflection in the microwave door—nothing like that gorgeous model back in her cabin. The risk of hiring MJ hadn't even been worth it since she didn't get a good shot.

Maybe I can send a video of myself to Zohaib. He doesn't have to see my face.

Thinking about sending nude images to her biological father made acid rise in her throat. Raelyn set up her phone with an automatic timer to capture a variety of angles.

"This is so messed up," she whispered to herself.

Footsteps banged on the front porch, and the door swung open. The hairs of her arm stood on end, and she backed into the wall near the hunting equipment.

When he entered, Tucker's eyes widened, then he turned away fast. "What the blazes are you doing?" He tossed a blanket to her behind his back. "Explain yourself, woman." His voice cracked as he shifted his feet, his broad back tense, then leaned his large palm on the wall. "If your man is a POW, he can't get any videos, so I'll ask once more, young lady, what in the firecrackers are you doin'?" His hand rubbed the back of his neck. "Christ, I'm too old for you."

"No, no, no, it's not for you." She cringed. "I need to send a video to a bad guy, so he will click on it. Then a virus will take over his files, and I'll have proof to get him arrested."

A slow, long exhale slid out of Tucker. "No, ma'am. We're not doing that. It's completely pointless. You could get an image off a porn site in five seconds. What are you thinking? Put your clothes on."

"But—"

"Now!"

"Fine."

It sounded like the ghost of Pa's stern voice had taken over Tucker's body. Raelyn pulled on one of Kody's shirts that she had been wearing as maternity clothes, and a groan slipped out when she bent to retrieve the stretchy yoga pants. Soon she'd have even more trouble reaching down lower.

"You can turn around now," she said quietly.

"You sure?"

"Yup, my ankles to wrists are covered."

Tucker turned slowly with one eye squinting, and his shoulders relaxed upon seeing her. "God almighty, you need to get your mind right."

She threw the blanket he had lent her straight at his chest. "You have no idea what I'm dealing with." A strangled knot in her throat obstructed her words, but she forced them out. "I'll do anything. *Anything* … to get Kody back."

A chair screeched over the floor as Tucker flopped into the seat. "You're thinking about it all wrong. That won't get ya anywhere."

"How would you know?" Desperation laced her voice.

Tucker leaned back and massaged his temples. "Listen, what you need to do is hide until it all washes over."

"No. I won't wait around helpless. I won't be like Joanna."

"Who?"

"My mother. She was forced to stay with a soldier named Snyder for like eleven years. She tolerated abuse to keep my brother safe, which of course makes her strong, but she should've fought harder to return home."

One of his bushy eyebrows rose. "So, you're more important than your brother?"

"No, she should've fought to get back to Pa. She could've tried harder. How could she have just given up?"

Tucker crossed his arms. "I don't know the details, miss, but it sounds an awful lot like you're making up a story."

"You think I'm lying?"

"No, no. I think you're stretching reality to fit what you want to believe."

"Joanna had lots of chances. She chose what was easiest for her survival. I won't be like that. I'll never put myself first."

Tucker cocked his head. "You're scared."

Her fists balled tight, and the fire behind her crackled. "Of course I'm scared. I'm terrified out of my mind."

Shiloh looked at her with alert eyes and pawed the ground. She held out her hands, and she laid her chin right in the middle, dropping the weight of her head in her palms as if trying to communicate some mysterious message. Was it a warning?

"So, does your friend Jordi have the trunk?"

"No, you'll have to try Aaron." Tucker turned away and stared up at the oaks, lined with a blanket of white.

"Can we get to Aaron's house in the snow?" Raelyn pointed to the address on her phone.

"He's not a guy you want to mess with. He doesn't like people on his property or any people for that matter."

She scrunched up her nose and walked toward the door. "How far away is it?"

"Depends on which way we go. But, with this much snow, it's not possible." Tucker rubbed his beard.

"I can't wait. Let's go."

"You have no other option. If we risk that hike now, one of us won't return."

"How long do we have to wait?"

"At least two weeks."

She clutched the pocket watch as her heart rate sped. "Two weeks?"

"Unless you can melt this snow faster."

"But I need to find it in one week or my brother—"

"It's not an option."

She slowly dropped to a chair and buried her face in her hands. "But, Liam …"

Tucker walked over and draped a blanket over her shoulders. "Also … there's something you need to know …"

11

KODY

After weeks caged in a dark box, Kody had full range of motion again in his arms, and he no longer flinched when poking the tender spots on his body. The door opened of his tiny prison opened —more than a crack this time, saving him from the crippling isolation. Kody shielded his face from the blinding sun. An orange frog hopped over his hand, probably poisonous—maybe he should let the deadly amphibian slide venom inside his veins. That way, Zohaib wouldn't have any leverage over Raelyn. No, that'd never work; he'd find some other way to control her.

When his stomach grumbled, the thought of eating that frog passed through his mind. His tongue found its way to his chapped lips, and everything felt disoriented and hazy from his hunger.

A tall man's silhouette blocked the light. This time, the guard nodded instead of simply leaving water again with a tray of feijoada, a stew of beans, and pork.

The man held a pistol loosely at his side and a machete in the other. "Come."

Kody stumbled to his feet and staggered naked out into the blazing light. A strong scent similar to a greenhouse swarmed the air, a mixture of vegetation, moisture, soil, and decaying wood.

"Where are we?" His voice croaked like a frog; he hadn't spoken for weeks.

Squinting, he scanned the environment, grateful to finally be free of that cage. When he looked around, crates were piled high along tree trunks. Huts with roofs made of woven palms were spread around in a semi-circle.

Young, armed men marched into the area carrying bins of canteens, none of them paying Kody any attention as they passed. Parrots darted between the rubber trees as he turned around to see where they were headed, and a butterfly fluttered by his ear. A palate of fresh, murky, bright, and neutral greens painted a crisp scene at every angle.

The most elaborate glass house Kody had ever seen was wedged in the trees, supported only by thick, metal beams. He took in the rest of the house through the glass walls. Every piece of elaborate furniture, from the giant circular bed to the contemporary couches and granite countertops in the kitchen were all visible from outside. On the third level, Zohaib stood at a window, staring down. He pointed down at Kody with a shotgun in hand while a sly smirk claimed the demon's face. Kody's jaw clenched tight.

A toucan flapped above, its feathers almost as exotic as the crimson flowers decorating the high branches.

The guard knocked into Kody. "Hold still. Malaria vaccine."

Kody couldn't place the man's accent but responded quickly, "Didn't think they had a vaccine for that yet."

"It's not approved." The guard pulled a needle out of his pocket.

Kody shook his head and backed away. "Is there a doctor?"

"No." He jabbed it into Kody's bad arm, which was coated in weeks of dried sweat. The man handed over a bag of water, insect repellent, clothes, and an insecticide-treated bed net. "Now go wash up." He nodded to the gnarled trees.

For the first time, Kody noticed the sound of a rushing river nearby. He walked under the canopy, trailed by the guard. The pungent smell of old leaves on the jungle floor grew with each step. A river, teal with rich blue hues, soon came into view, the only section not covered by a green canopy of foliage so far.

In an alternate reality, he imagined Raelyn photographing for hours, lying flat on her back with the camera pointed straight up, waiting patiently for a monkey to swing above or a lizard would crawl over her shoulder. His heart wrinkled up dry at the hopelessness of seeing her again one day.

"Hurry!" The guard shoved him closer to the river.

The sun shifted behind clouds, shading the river a deeper blue. Across the water, children ran into the thriving rainforest. Kody checked for crocodiles, then splashed straight into the coolness. Dread filled him at the thought of the children living so close to Zohaib. Where was their village?

Kody squeezed his eyes shut, held his breath, and dipped below the surface. Underwater, hundreds of fish swam in different directions in the clear water and tickled his ankles. His mother used to tell him stories of certain species migrating thousands of miles by instinct alone to return to their homeland. Maybe he could do the same.

At the surface, Kody swam until it was shallower, then took wide steps out. The muddy, soft earth squished between his toes. He caught the guard scanning his naked body, making him wonder how long the men had been in captivity under Zohaib's rule.

Kody forced calm into his voice when he asked, "What's your name?"

"G9."

"Is that what your friends call you?"

The guard's muscles tightened. "We don't have friends."

"How old are you?"

"Nineteen, give or take a bit." His face remained carved into a frown.

"How long have you been here?" Kody dried off and started to dress.

The man's eyes narrowed. "Twelve years."

A tightness formed in Kody's chest. "You like Zohaib?"

"Call him Commander."

Kody wiped the droplets off his arm, letting them flick onto the ground. "What?"

"Call him by his title, Commander Zohaib."

"So, there's no plan for you all to revolt?"

G9's jaw dropped, and his eyes softened briefly. "I'll … I'll pretend you didn't say that. I have no reason to revolt."

Kody pulled the flimsy, beige clothes out of the backpack. "So, you like your commander?"

"He has to make all the sacrifices and hard decisions for the security of the whole army. He protects all his soldiers."

"Have any tips for me?" Kody asked.

The man paused and locked eyes with Kody. "Follow orders."

Kody put on the rest of his clothes. A little boy across the river waved, but he didn't dare encourage the kid to move closer. Suddenly, a wailing siren screeched from the camp area.

G9 stiffened and shot a suspicious glance. "What did you do, newbie?"

Kody raised both hands, his heart thumping. "Nothing."

G9 pointed the pistol at Kody and urged him through the trees. The siren only grew louder as they approached the huts. He prodded Kody's back, making him speed into a jog.

When they arrived back to the camp, a line of fifty young men with guns stood at attention, in the same beige, long sleeves, and pants over identical ratty boots. Kody hadn't even laced up his shoes yet. No one made eye contact with him as he joined the end of the line, fighting the urge to tie his boots. He swatted at the mosquitoes buzzing by his neck.

A door opened from the glasshouse, and Zohaib stood on a balcony. Kody dared to look up, the only man in line to do so. Zohaib's slicked black hair was pulled into a bun, narrowing his eyes into slits. He raised a megaphone reciting a speech full of promises, lies layering his tongue.

When he ended with "…together we will have a better future…" Kody coughed on his own repulsion. A piercing sound in the microphone made Kody wince when Zohaib looked straight at him. "And we have a special newcomer, G55."

Like hell will I be a number!

Kody stubbornly bent over and started tying his bootlace, ready to make a difference in the camp on day one.

"Stand up, G55!"

The tension snapped tighter than a whip. G9's hand next to him trembled when he whispered, "Stand up, Shoelace." Sweat beads started forming on his forehead.

Kody rose slowly and glared at the Italian monster controlling these men.

"To celebrate our newcomer …" Zohaib prowled like a vicious lion ready to chomp. "I'll pick one of you to go home if you complete three challenges. The first task starts today."

He's bluffing.

"All of you will bring back a boy between age ten and nineteen. You have twenty-four hours. If you fail, you will be killed by a man standing next to you. G55, you have to bring two boys." Zohaib hissed his words to the line of soldiers. "The rest of you … if you find our newcomer trying to run, you can initiate him into our group however you want but keep him alive and bring him back."

Shit!

Kody whispered to the man next to him. "Where are the guns?"

"You're on your own, Shoelace," he whispered.

Zohaib smiled. "Ready?"

Kody's heart raced. He needed a weapon. None of the other men moved a muscle, but Kody whipped his head around, looking at the pile of equipment, only helmets, canteens, and rope.

Zohaib projected his voice. "It's 17:00 hours. You need to be back at the same time tomorrow with a boy, or you know what happens. It'll be worse than last time."

The sharp squawk of a bird above pierced the afternoon sky as Kody lunged toward the pile of gear. Heart pounding, he kicked a canteen, grabbed it, and dashed to the river at full sprint. Quickly, he shoved the canteen into his pocket, then dove straight into the water.

"Go, you idiots!" Zohaib screamed. "Don't just stand there."

Amid the immediate chaos, Kody swam as fast and hard as he could across the river.

I have to warn those kids.

The current swept him hard. He cupped his wide hands and paddled with each stroke. He reached forward. Kicked harder. Gasped for breath. He was drifting too far. Checking behind him, at least a dozen other guards were already on his trail.

Kody sucked in a deep breath and buried his head in the water, stroking harder, stretching his body. His lungs burned, and his heart thundered in his chest. A young boy stood on the bank, only feet away, and cocked his head.

The splashes and shouts behind him played like a disastrous symphony. Almost to the other side, Kody reached out for a branch jutting from the riverbank. Grunting, he pulled himself out. His loose boot stuck in the mud, and his foot slipped. The water carried his boot downstream. Kody crawled up on the solid ground. The boy yanked Kody up by the shirt.

"Run!" Kody tried to push him away.

The kid wouldn't move. Kody picked him up and threw him over his shoulder. His footsteps were uneven, the ground alternating hard, soft, between his mismatched feet. Thumps stomped behind him as the others gained on him. He placed the boy on a high branch and pointed up. The boy climbed effortlessly like a monkey.

Kody turned right in time as the others ran forward, panting. Drenched, they held up their fists to their chins, ready to fight. He held both his arms out wide.

"Stop!"

One man with a scar across his entire cheek swiped a knife from his own pocket.

"Zohaib is only one man. There are fifty-five of us. We are stronger than him if we stand together. I'm a soldier and can help you come up with a plan."

The rain started drizzling down, but none of the men loosened their posture except G9. His brown eyes softened in an instant. "This is the same way I was captured."

Kody brushed his hand over the pocket holding the knife. "We don't need to take any kids."

G9 spoke up, "Shoelace is right. We can all fight Zohaib together."

Four others snarled and moved forward, ready to fight. With G9 by his side, Kody tried to block their access to the boy in the tree.

G9 held up his hands. "We don't have to do this."

Two still lunged forward. Kody's bare foot slipped on the dirt as he grabbed one's shirt and restrained his hands behind his back. "Calm down! We can form a team."

G9 tripped the other soldier and sent him flailing to the ground. The others hesitantly glanced at the boy in the tree.

The soldier on the ground raised his gun and pointed it straight at Kody. "Maybe you died by accident."

Rain fell harder, sprinkling on Kody's forehead.

Kody shook his head. "After we kill Zohaib, you can all go home."

"I'm G1!" The man roared. "The first here. This is my only home!"

G9 stepped between them. "We finally have a chance to end this. Shoelace can lead us."

"It's too late." G1 squeezed the trigger.

A bullet pierced the skin between G9's eyes. Kody went rigid as his new friend fell flat back onto the ground. Lifeless. He never even knew his real name.

"Why?" Kody let go of the man struggling against his grip and dropped to his knees. "You'll kill each other? But you won't kill Zohaib? Why?"

G1 ignored him and strutted toward the tree.

Rain poured harder. The other soldiers snapped out of their stupor and dispersed, searching the trees for boys.

"No!" Kody yelled and stood.

A boy screamed.

"You're too soft, Shoelace." G1 marched out of the shadows with a boy over his shoulder, kicking and smacking his back.

"No!" Kody hollered, spinning around at the chaos of soldiers ransacking the clearing. More screams sounded in the distance. A loud smack of weapon against flesh echoed as sharp as a lightning crack. Thunder roared above, and the skies cried tears into the river. Kody's heart stampeded as G1 rushed by with the boy.

He jumped on G1's back, making him drop the child.

"Run!" Kody yelled.

G1 pulled out a knife. Kody's heart hammered as he reached for his canteen, his only current weapon. When G1 slashed forward, he blocked it with his metal canteen, and the knife dropped to the ground.

Kody retrieved the knife and grasped it tightly. He sped after G1 but tripped through the mud. Kody stabbed the blade deep in the thick tendon of G1's Achille's heel on the ground. The soldier squealed in pain and toppled over.

With the blade sticking out of his heel, G1 crawled to the river, blood trickling behind. Kody stormed after, rain splattering against his cheeks. He kicked G1 in the side, who grunted in return. Every muscle flexed. He crouched. Yanked the knife out of G1's heel before ramming it into his thigh. The man's whole body convulsed as the smell of copper filled Kody's nostrils. He straddled G1, who fought back with pure force.

Rain pounded. Another soldier climbed the tree after the boy and pulled at the kid's leg. Kody grabbed G1's gun. Aimed straight at the soldier and fired. A dark bloom of scarlet appeared on the tan uniform. He released the branch, fell thirty feet, and slammed into the muddy soil.

Underneath Kody, G1 writhed. The gun skidded out of reach. Kody tried to scramble up, but the man wrestled him. He grabbed the canteen from his pocket and slammed it over G1's head. They quickly rolled closer to the riverbank, panting and grasping at each other.

A stream of rain battered Kody's face. His hands slipped off G1's body, slick from the mix of blood and rain. The man shoved Kody's head under the surface of the river. Kody flailed. Arched back. Strained. But G1's heavyweight held him down.

Fuck!

His chest tightened.

Air!

Water claimed him, consumed him. He thrashed. Kicked wildly. No release. He tried pushing his body up. Kody resisted taking a gulp. The hand pushed his neck deeper. Straining, his chest felt like it would implode. He fought against the fatal swallow. His vision went fuzzy.

Have to breathe.

Raelyn's amber eyes blinked sweetly at him, and her beautiful smile reached her ears.

This can't be the end.

Three gunshots boomed above the surface.

Release. G1's grip slackened.

Kody pushed up, gasping for air. Panting, he collapsed in the mud. G1 lay dead face-down, three bullet holes in the back of his head. Kody clutched his burning chest and coughed.

The ally moved forward and offered a hand to Kody. "Shoelace, I'm Pedro." He was short and stocky with long curly black hair and a scar under his right eye.

"Thank you, Pedro." Kody laid flat, sprawled like a starfish.

"You're safe, for now. All the others are gone."

Kody wiped the water from his face and started to count his breaths to slow his racing heart. Once he reached number 142, he faced Pedro.

"Thanks again, man." He didn't dare look around at the slaughter that had occurred.

"No problem." They shook hands tightly and nodded.

"So, why do the men stay in Zohaib's camp. Why don't they run?"

Pedro shook his head. "Half don't want to. They agree with his ideas that he's improving the area."

"And the other half?"

"Doubt they could survive out here. Plus, Zohaib has sworn that he'll kill the rest of our families if we don't return."

Kody stood, dripping water everywhere. "That doesn't make sense. How would he even know who is who?"

"Would you risk it?"

No, I wouldn't.

Kody started walking. "So, has Zohaib snatched boys from around here before?"

"Yes."

"What does Zohaib do to soldiers who return without a prisoner?"

Pedro shrugged. "Death surrounds us, man."

Kody frowned. "We need to make a plan."

"Do you really think we can stand up against Zohaib?"

"Yes, I'll save all the soldiers." Kody rubbed the mud off the scar from his past bullet wounds and gritted his teeth. "It's my only option. I will kill Zohaib."

12

KODY

Twelve days passed in the jungle, surviving on fruit and fish. The morning sunlight couldn't fully penetrate the vibrant jungle canopy, so when Kody rubbed his eyes and stared up at the vibrant greens, browns, and yellows of the jungle all around him, he treasured the view.

Across from him, Pedro rested on the forest floor. Kody stretched his sore muscles. Each day away from Raelyn was torture, not knowing if she and his baby were safe. He didn't need the doctor to tell him the gender; he knew it was a girl. And a paternity test was pointless too. That tiny life thriving inside her momma would have his whole heart, regardless of who she looked like.

Pedro stirred, drool hanging from his lip. Kody tapped his muddy boot. Pedro jerked awake, punching the air in response.

Kody chuckled. "You get 'em, big guy."

Squinting, Pedro rubbed his crusted eyes. "What the hell, Shoelace?"

"Calm down. I'm gonna go take a leak. Thought you should know." Kody squished a beetle by accident as he rose, splattering gooey substance on his palm.

He tried to keep his footsteps as quiet as possible, but the thick mass of leaves underfoot smushed with every step. Standing next to the riverbank, he tore off his shirt. He dipped the fabric in the water to defeat the heat, then wrung it out, watching the droplets create small ripples in the water before disappearing down the current.

Rustling sound crept to his right—too big to be a monkey this time. Kody spotted one of Zohaib's soldiers and started to track him, zig-zagging through the trees. He only stepped when the man did, disguising his sounds. But the closer he got, the slower the soldier moved. Kneeling behind a bush and frozen, Kody silenced his heavy breathing. He could jump out, knock the man out, interrogate him later, or offer him fish they had caught. Before Kody could make up his mind, a strong hand grabbed his collar and yanked him backward.

Kody was slammed hard onto the dirt. In a mix of heat and dirt, they rolled atop one another, throwing punches. Adrenaline coursed through Kody's system as he pinned the soldier flat and put him in a chokehold. The man tapped out fast.

When Kody released, an accent from someone born and raised near Mississippi slid out of the man's mouth. "I'm on your side, man."

Kody stood, keeping both hands near his chin. "You're American?"

"The name's Steven." He stuck out a hand. "Zohaib's pissed that you never returned. He's taking it out on all of the men, making their lives a living hell, so I ran." His gaze darted in each direction. "Things were getting messy, and half of us are ready to fight back."

Kody couldn't hold back his smile. "Perfect. That's what we're doing out here. We've been practicing sparring daily."

Steven's eyes grew wide. "Really?"

Kody nodded. "Yeah, we just need a few more men. What else do you know?"

He paused. "They say Zohaib has a young woman trapped in his room. The men can see her through the windows."

He could barely breathe from the thought but forced out his question, "Have you seen what the woman looks like?"

"I heard she's got brown hair and is super-hot."

Kody scanned the green surrounding him just as a loud squeal came from behind them. He threw his wet shirt back on and raced back to where he and Pedro had slept. He was gone. Kody's heart rate quickened. He scanned the mud for his friend or signs of a struggle.

Multiple sets of boots.

His heart raced. "Shit!" He pulled out his knife and followed the tracks, where the long grass was folded down. His grip tightened on the blade's handle as he heard voices ahead. Kody ducked behind a tree trunk, Steven in his wake.

"What are we gonna do with him?" an unfamiliar voice said.

Who's talking?

"Kill him. There's no other option."

"How?"

"Gun?"

"Knife?" Pedro asked.

Once Kody heard Pedro's voice, he jumped out from behind the tree. Steven positioned himself into a fighting stance.

Kody caught sight of Pedro. "You okay, man?"

Pedro nodded to the others. "Amigos. This is Bernardo, and … who is *this* guy?"

"I'm Steven." The Mississippi man tipped his nonexistent hat.

Kody lowered his knife. "So, if you're fine, what was dragged?"

With a big smile on his tanned face, Pedro stepped aside to reveal a small dead pig. "I found lunch."

"Great job, we'll cook it if we have time." Kody rubbed his beard. "But we have enough men now. We need to plan an ambush and take Zohaib down as a group. Do any of you have a gun?"

They all shook their heads.

"Damn." Kody marched forward, swatting mosquitoes that nipped his ears. "Follow me and bring the pig."

The rush of the river faded behind as the four men walked in single file through the brush. Kody slashed with his knife at the thorny vines that seemed to reach for them from every direction. The rising humidity hampered his breathing. His shirt clung to his skin, clammy with river water and sweat. The animal noises around him had ceased, and the jungle quieted as if it sensed his grim mission.

They walked for hours, stopping only to roast the pig. Each man seemed to be contemplating the possibility that these could be their last moments alive. The sun soon shook hands with the moon, trading places as they finally approached Zohaib's camp perimeter. After the long journey, the fatigue made itself known in Kody's every muscle.

Kody turned. "So, Steven and I will go inside, and I'll slit Zohaib's throat. Bernardo and Pedro, you two will stand guard."

Pedro rubbed his chin. "He's got lots of guns and two guards at all times."

"I'm fast." Kody cracked his knuckles.

"Your funeral, man," said Bernardo.

"Can I have my canteen back?" He reached back for the object that kept saving his life, a bit dented in from the previous fight but still functional.

Broken can still be functional.

While sipping, Kody glanced around. "Wait, where's Steven?"

"He ran. I have a bad feeling about this," said Pedro quietly.

Kody absorbed all the sounds, hyper-aware of anything ahead. He picked up a long stick and used it to feel for any animal traps spread around under the leaves. Step after step, the tension in the air tightened, ready to snap like an improperly anchored tripwire. Kody's gaze darted in all directions. The top of the glass treehouse came into view. Other than the squawks and the distant murmur of the river, the area was quiet. Too quiet. He turned to address the others. Only Pedro stood behind him.

Kody clenched his jaw. "Where's Bernardo?"

"He's gone too, man. One second he was right behind me, then he just disappeared." Suddenly, Pedro's eyes widened as he stared up, then pointed at something high behind Kody. "Is that Steven?"

Kody winced, not wanting to check. His heart rammed inside his ribs. He held his breath, clutched his knife tightly, and swiveled on his heels to face the treehouse again.

On the rooftop, Zohaib stood with a soldier in his grasp. He dangled the soldier over the side, and the man screamed, flailing his arms.

Pedro grabbed Kody's elbow. "Don't be a hero again, man. Let it go."

Kody clenched his jaw and ran, stomping on leaves, flying past trees, barging into the camp, soaring between the huts, and storming up to Zohaib's door. He twisted the handle. Locked. Kody grabbed a helmet that was lying on the forest ground, ants crawling around the rim. He chucked it through the glass, shattering the door.

Zohaib hollered from the roof. "Bad choice, Walsh!"

Kody rushed inside. A spiral glass staircase rose in the center of the room to the next floor. Kody lunged up, skipping stairs. He hit the second floor.

Then the third floor. The stairs stopped. Panting, Kody looked around at the room. An ivory bed stood in the center with white linens. A naked woman struggled against the rope strapping her to the bedpost. Despite her body being completely exposed, a hijab wrapped around her head, allowing Kody only to see her eyes.

Why does she look familiar?

"Where's the roof's entrance?"

She shook her head desperately, her eyes wild and focused on his weapon.

"I'm not going to hurt you." He laid his knife by his feet and approached her. "It's okay."

Screams and thudding sounds came from the roof.

Running out of time!

"I can help." He kneeled by her and tried to undo the knot. "Damn it. I need my knife to help you. I'm going to get it, okay?"

Quick clomps stomped up the stairs. Kody hurried to the knife. Just as he reached for it, a scream soared. He glanced out the window in horror. The soldier's body blurred by, falling to his death. Kody cringed at the sound of him hitting the jungle floor hard.

Just like Phoenix.

Adrenaline flooded Kody's veins as he reached for the knife again, but a trap door slid open, and a rope ladder dropped, landing on the knife and knocking it down the spiral staircase.

"I'm coming, Shoelace!" Pedro yelled from below.

From above, Zohaib slid down the ladder without touching the rungs. He landed like a jungle cat and straightened. Zohaib was thirty years older than him, but that gave him thirty more years of fighting experience. Kody scanned his muscles and knew he was no match for the lethal machine standing in front of him.

The woman tied to the bed defiantly yelled at Zohaib in Spanish.

"I see you've met my most recent darling." Zohaib pulled out his gun and pointed it at the woman on the bed.

"No!" Kody jumped between her and the gun.

Pedro's head emerged from the staircase. He somehow had found a gun and pointed it at Zohaib.

"Drop your weapon, boy!" Zohaib yelled to Pedro.

"No." His voice shook. "You can't control me anymore."

Zohaib pulled out a second gun from under his shirt and aimed at Pedro. Kody held his breath.

"Go ahead." Pedro smiled confidently. "Shoelace will still kill you."

Bullets soared. Zohaib's ear slashed off and dropped to the ground. Blood spurted out of the side of his head. He screamed and squeezed the trigger. Pedro stumbled back, crashing over a coffee table, blood pouring out of his chest. He laid on the ground, panting until Zohaib shot him again. Blood splattered on the glass floor. Dead.

"Such a waste of a soldier." Zohaib smiled, blood from his ear dripping down the side of his face. "You didn't follow orders."

Kody clenched his fists.

"You must've forgotten our arrangement about Raelyn. I know where she is right now."

Kody's heart spun into a frenzy. He tried to steady his breathing, but terror and rage swirled like a hurricane inside.

Zohaib pulled out his phone. "Let me show you."

He pushed a few buttons and showed video footage of Raelyn in a barn loft, pacing around a stack of hay with Liam by her side. "Jawhara really is a loyal one." He laughed. "Actually, this little darling on the bed over here is the same way I won Jawhara over eighteen years ago. I guess the ladies can't get enough of me."

"If you hurt Raelyn—"

"I can do whatever I want. You're not running the show." Zohaib moved forward, blood dripping down his face from his missing ear, but he didn't even seem to care. "I could kill you right now. But there's more you can do for me."

Kody gulped, thinking of Raelyn's amber eyes as he stared into the barrel.

Zohaib lowered his chin. "You're going to capture three young women per week, or I'll take Raelyn."

Exhaustion hammered into his skull.

Maybe it's easier to just do what he says.

"We can keep playing this game. She has a lot of fingers and toes that could be … played with." Zohaib's slimy grin rose, but his voice rose in anger. "You agreed to follow orders. You broke the arrangement, so now we improvise. If you fail to bring me three women per week, Raelyn and the baby are mine." He scratched his black bun with his free hand. "Torturing her in front of my slaves will keep them in line. And the baby might be the ticket to keep Raelyn controlled." The whole room was filled with toxic energy, fueled by Zohaib's threats.

Kody couldn't breathe. "I'll do whatever you want. Leave Raelyn alone."

"Good boy. Now, before I have more fun with this darling … she won't tell me where her village is, I'd like you to find out for me. And I won't give you any second chances this time."

The lights flickered, and thunder crashed, giving him a moment's pause to think. Ideas and possibilities cracked through his skull like the night clouds splitting the crescent moon. Faint moonlight beamed through the glass windows, giving a gleam of inspiration.

He never has to find out my new plan.

Kody's stomach churned as he walked over to the woman on the bed. "What's your name?"

She kicked his leg.

"Where is your village?" He grabbed her throat softly. "Tell me."

Zohaib chuckled. "See, you're just like me. You'll do anything for your goal."

Since his back was turned to Zohaib, he winked at her in hopes the woman would understand that he wouldn't hurt her. Kody pretended to tighten his grip on her small throat to make a show for Zohaib. "Tell me where I can find your village." Something in her eyes told him that they shared the same plan.

She knows what I'm going to do.

13

KODY

ALONE, KODY HID BEHIND a giant tree and peeked around a tall village wall—a mixture of dried, packed clay and tightly woven branches. Zohaib hadn't given him any weapons for his journey, but at least he had his trusty canteen. During his solo voyage overnight, the jungle had not been kind through thick bushes, thorns, and endless mosquitos. At least it didn't rain every minute in January.

A frog hopped near his foot before meeting an untimely demise from the jaws of a snake.

Kody whispered to himself, "I can still convince the men of this village to help us fight."

Despite the shade from the canopy above, the thick heat stifled him. He grabbed the corner of his shirt that hung from his belt loop and dabbed the sweat from his brow. Bits of mud flaked off–he'd have to reapply his camouflage.

The wall circling the village was twice Kody's height. Four men with bows and arrows paced along the top with long hair tied back and matching brown shirts camouflaged well. Kody remained undetected–for now.

Behind the trees, Kody stalked the perimeter of the thatched wall, looking for an opening. He found a rickety door guarded by two solidly built men with long, braided hair. Large jaguar tattoos across their chests bared their sharp fangs. He wondered if they were meant to immortalize a hunting expedition in their past. They each held a sharp spear in their large hands and scanned the jungle.

Sweat dripped down between Kody's shoulder blades as he crouched. He peeked around the trunk and whistled loudly. Both the guards' snapped their focus to where he hid. One shifted his weight and tightened the grip on his spear, raising it, while Kody held his breath.

It's now or never.

He pulled the makeshift surrender flag with a white shirt tied onto a stick and waved it in the air from behind a trunk. The men hollered, and an arrow zinged through the air, piercing his shirt to the forest floor.

Shit!

One guard ran out but tripped over Kody's trap and fell flat onto the leaves. Kody seized the spear, tightening his knuckles around the shaft. The man met his gaze.

Kody raised both hands above his head. "Peace. I want to talk."

The man screamed for help. Arrows flew. Footsteps pounded closer.

Kody turned the spear around, so only the blunt end pointed out. "I don't want to fight."

The second man thrust his spear. Missed. Kody swept the dull end behind the man's legs, sending him crashing to the ground. They both clambered back up, and Kody faced him, ready for a battle.

"Peace. Who's your leader?"

It was clear that they had no idea what he was saying. Heart speeding in a frenzy, Kody's biceps tightened. His mouth was completely dry, and his ears pounded. Blood pumping, Kody knew he'd have to fight and restrain them before he could fully explain.

Kody lunged forward, wielding the dull end of the spear toward the men's heads. They were quick. Too quick. The guard lunged forward with his spear, missing Kody's arm by an inch. Kody backed up. Crunched the giant leaves underfoot. He swung, striking the rod into one guard's stomach. He grunted and bent over.

The Jaguar-man dove at Kody but accidentally thrust his spear into his allies' neck. Blood gurgled out as he clutched the wound. Kody's stomach twisted in knots.

Jaguar-man yelled and pointed at his dying buddy on the ground. Rage claimed his face. He pounced. Their spears clashed. Kody's arms burned as he pushed back with all his might. His foe held the advantage, shoving Kody's body hard.

Kody slipped. Knees collapsed. Panting, he thought all hope was lost as a gunshot thundered the still air. Jaguar-man fell to his knees with a bullet lodged in his chest. Kody held his spear tighter and ran. His breath came fast. He spotted a tree with a low branch and jumped, pulling his weight up the sturdy tree and scanned the area for a shooter.

Kody climbed higher. Twenty feet up, thick branches obscured his view, so he took a deep breath and rested on the branch for a moment. It was awkward to hold the spear in the branches, but at least he was armed. Sweating, Kody reached into his pocket, pulled out his canteen, and quenched his thirst. High above the forest floor, he allowed his ragged breathing to calm. He shook away the image of the spear slicing into that man's neck.

Crunching footsteps approached below. Between thick leaves, he caught glimpses of a man who wore the same beige, lightweight outfit as the others at Zohaib's camp. His dark skin blended into the color of the tree trunks, but the silhouette of a gun was in his hand. Kody hunched behind a branch and crouched his shoulders into a ball.

"I can see you!" A familiar voice hissed.

Kody went as still as death.

The man called up from the base of the tree. "Shoelace! Come down."

Kody didn't dare move. "Who are you?"

"I'm Bernardo. The one with the pig, remember."

Kody paused and squinted. "Are you alone?"

"Yes, and those two guards are dead."

Kody peeked from around the trunk, and sure enough, it was Bernardo. "Why are you out here?"

"I can help."

"You left us." Kody spat down. "If we had your back-up before, Pedro might not be dead."

"He's dead?"

Kody nodded. "Thanks to you."

"No … I … we can fix this."

"Nothing can bring back the dead."

"We will kill Zohaib like you said. You have a plan, right?" Something in his voice had an edge, a Judas-like quality.

Kody shook his thoughts away and climbed down. "I need to capture a woman to distract Zohaib. But, the real reason I'm here is to convince the men to join our cause and fight. They have just as much reason to get rid of Zohaib."

"You were right," Bernardo whispered. "We could have more power as a group. Everything changed after you arrived."

"If we do this … I have to trust you. You promise you won't run this time?"

"Deal." Bernardo nodded, but there was a sinister look in his eye. "We need to get into that village."

"Archers may be manning the front. I saw a back entrance from up in the tree."

They stalked like predators through the thick brush. Kody's eyes darted around for any hint of movement as the temperature cooled. He pushed away the thoughts of Pedro, the guards, and Raelyn and focused on surviving the next minute. Bernardo raised his gun as he slowed. A small door on the back side of the village creaked forward and back from a slight breeze.

Is it a trap?

"You look on that side of the village for men who can help," Kody whispered. "If I have trouble convincing any on this side, I'll whistle."

Sneaking through the door, Kody scanned the village. It looked similar to the others, built from natural materials in the jungle, but these houses were on stilts. The archers weren't atop the wall anymore.

He'd have to search inside each hut separately for strong men willing to fight. Kody scaled up a set of stairs, feeling the movements of the warped wood sag under his weight. He crept up higher, clasping the spear. The hut door swung like a ghost dancing in the wind, as if the entire village was in hiding, holding its breath.

Empty.

Why is it so quiet?

Kody searched each hut, but they were all abandoned. The shoes that laid scattered and the pots with leftover grime baked onto the sides showed that people lived here. He finally crept up the last set of stairs to the only remaining hut, desperate to find a leader to recruit.

Suddenly, Kody could feel hidden eyes on him. His heart hammered under his ribcage. He held his hand out to push the door open, revealing a small, circular, empty hut. He sighed from relief, but the haunting feeling remained.

A scratching sound made him stop in his tracks. Looking down through the slats of the floor, Kody locked onto the dark brown eyes of a child.

No! Not a little girl.

He felt sick to his stomach, knowing he still had to return with a woman to achieve his goal and convince Zohaib of his loyalty. Someone would have to make the sacrifice for his life to have any meaning again.

In an instant, he knew Zohaib wouldn't give mercy to a little one, but chain her or wait a few years or not even wait to …

I'll find someone else.

As she stared up at him, Kody put a finger to his lips. He turned toward the exit, and something hard slammed into his temple. He staggered back and raised his spear high. The floor moved, and the little girl jumped out, placing herself between Kody's spear and whoever smacked his head. Regaining his footing, Kody caught his balance and stared into the brown eyes of a woman with a water pot in hand as her eyes blazed with fear.

"Mama!" the girl cried.

Her sandals were worn through with holes, and the light-weight dress draped over her slender body past her knees. Wiry muscles bulged under the tanned skin of her arms, and determination shone through her brown eyes.

"Where's a leader?" Kody squinted through the slats of the hut, but the village seemed eerily deserted.

The woman held her stance, her eyes gleaming bright like liquid fire. Tightness overtook his gut, barely letting him breathe. If he couldn't convince anyone to help him fight, then his plan wouldn't work. Kody lowered his spear and looked around for any other options. Maybe he could take a grandmother close to death or someone ill. His chest rose and fell fast at the conclusion of the inevitable. Swallowing hard, Kody swiped the water pot from the woman and let it clatter to the floor. Maybe if he scared her enough, she'd tell him what he needed to know.

"Where are the men?"

She stared at him with brown eyes that matched her long locks.

"Husband? Brother?"

He reached out. She screamed. The girl hadn't let go of her mother's shirt. If the woman didn't quiet down, other archers would come. Dread flowed heavily in Kody's veins as he clamped his hand tightly over the woman's mouth. His heart dropped as he pried the girl's little fingers from her mother's arm and ripped the woman away. He carried her down the stairs as she wrestled against his hold. Slapping. Kicking. Struggling. The child cried and chased them outside. Desperation consumed him, feeling similar to when the guard had tried to drown him, and his lungs longed for air.

I have no choice.

He nudged the child to the ground, making the woman in his clutches fight with all her might. Tightening his hold, he stormed out of the village, into the jungle, carrying the woman along.

"Quiet down," Bernardo snarled ahead.

Once far enough away, Kody carried the woman over his back. Her thrashing and punching never weakened, as her tears ran down his neck. Her screaming continued. Mile after mile of ear-piercing, heart-shattering screams. It was enough to break open his entire soul. He had become the monster, and there was no recovery from this.

I'm as bad as Zohaib.

A zing sound whizzed by Kody's head, and a spear dug into a bush next to him.

"Run!" he yelled to Bernardo.

Bernardo shot his gun at the men chasing them. They sprinted and zig-zagged through the jungle, following the only walkable path higher and higher. Bernardo sped ahead, but Kody struggled with the woman on his back. She kicked. Clawed. But he gripped on tighter. The slope inclined, and another spear lodged itself in a tree to his right. Sweating and panting, Kody jumped off the path and catapulted through the tall brush, branches scratching up his arms along the way. She whacked his head with every limb. The ground turned to mud, and his boots sank into the thickness, slowing his progress.

"Shoelace!" Bernardo called and waved to him from behind a tree. "This way."

"I'm stuck!"

Men hollered behind them, their voices and footsteps growing louder.

Bernardo's eyes widened as he glanced at the threat, then at Kody in the mud.

"Don't you dare run!" Kody bellowed to Bernardo.

Bernardo shot at the men again, then snapped a branch off and moved forward, handing it out to Kody. He tried to grab it with one hand, but the woman was flailing around on his shoulder.

"Damn it!" Kody gripped her harder, pushing his fingers into her ribs and shaking her. "Hold still!"

She continued to thrash. Kody strained his muscles. The mud claimed him further as he sank knee-deep. "I'm gonna throw her to you!"

Bernardo braced himself, arms out.

Kody tossed her. She smacked into Bernardo's chest, and they both fell to the floor. Kody yanked his foot from his boot and made a wide step out of the mud using all his strength. Spears penetrated the ground in the exact position he had been in only seconds before. He scooped up the woman pinning Bernardo to make her stop clawing at his face.

Bernardo rolled over, rushed ahead, then yelled, "Cliff!"

Heart pounding, Kody slowed as the trees cleared, and a giant ravine stood in front of them.

"No bridge!" Bernardo started scaling down, rocks slipping away under his feet.

"I can't climb down with her on my back. We'll both fall." Kody set the woman down.

I never should've taken her.

"Let's just give her back to them."

She turned toward the attackers, then froze. A spear lodged next to her foot. He followed her gaze, then studied her face.

She's afraid of them too?

Her eyes widened, and she followed Bernardo down the side of the cliff, tumbling pebbles with each movement.

Fuck!

Kody picked up the spear and sent it flying through the air toward the pack leader. It struck him in the neck, and he fell. The men's chants and hollers quieted, but a few still followed. One lunged forward and pushed Kody into the mud. Filth splattered his face obscuring his view. A boot rammed into his stomach, knocking him breathless.

Barely able to breathe and pain surging in his core, Kody shoved the man's face into the mud and pushed down. The man thrashed around. Kody cringed but shoved down hard until the memory of G1 trying to drown him in the river flooded back. He released his grip and quickly rolled away.

Kody rushed to the edge of the cliff and followed the woman down, praying his lack of a shoe wouldn't make him fall to his death.

Left foot down, right foot lower, left hand, right hand. Muscles cramped, and his whole body shook, but he made it to the bottom.

Bernardo yelled from somewhere, "In here, a cave!"

Kody squinted, crouching into a dark hole. He couldn't get over a sudden sinking feeling that Bernardo had led them into a trap. They moved into the darkness. He fumbled around and accidentally bumped the woman. Her body trembled as she leaned on the cave wall.

Two voices mumbled whispers back and forth outside the cave entrance, then two sets of feet dropped softly to the forest floor. But the hostiles hadn't seen their cave. Kody watched, hoping they hadn't created tracks. Time lingered until the enemies eventually disappeared into the forest.

Torturous minutes dragged on, and the horror of what he had done suffocated him. While they rested, he and Bernardo hadn't exchanged a single word. Kody couldn't erase the image of the little girl, probably six years old, screaming for her mom.

I'm the villain now.

After the coast seemed clear, Kody gestured for the woman to leave the cave. She shoved him hard and rambled words he didn't understand.

"Bernardo, translate!"

"I'm not repeating any of that. Let her calm down first."

Kody held out his hand. "Give me the gun, Bernardo."

The woman's eyes widened, and she backed up into a tree trunk, but Kody laid it at her feet.

"Uh, what are you doing, man?" Bernardo backed away.

She picked up the gun and glanced between them as Kody dropped to his knees in front of her. He tried to apologize, but the words were trapped in his mouth. Folding his hands together like a prayer, his eyes watered as he saw the pain in her face.

The rage in her eyes intensified, and she aimed it straight at Kody's heart. He straightened his shoulders, offering his life as payment.

"I love you, Raelyn."

The woman's face softened, and she chucked the gun into the darkness, further into the cave. She picked up a branch and slashed it through the air, hitting the wall. She hacked the branch to pieces, sobbing. Her shoulders dropped lower with each swing. Birds screeched, matching her high-pitched scream of desolation. Kody collapsed from his knees and dropped to a seated position while the energy drained out. He stared at the woman's devastation firsthand, witnessing the consequences of his actions.

I did this to her.

A tightness hardened in his throat, making him unable to swallow the misery consuming this woman. Eventually, she stopped. The branch lay in splintered shambles at her feet. Heaving, she pointed into the jungle and rambled fast.

"What's she saying?"

"Home. She wants to go get her daughter."

Kody dropped his head. "I'll take her back."

Bernardo threw his hands in the air. "We can't now. It's too late, we'll get lost, or that group will track us."

Kody buried his head in his hands. That little girl could've been his own daughter screaming for Raelyn. What would he do to a man who did that to his family?

He patted Bernardo on the back as he walked out of the cave. "Then, don't come with us. Zohaib hasn't found you out here. You can go home too."

"I have no home." Bernardo trailed after. "Fifteen years ago, Zohaib took every woman and girl in my small village and sold them. His army took the boys to train and killed all the men." He struggled in his next words, but something about his tone didn't sit right. "I have no one."

Kody didn't have the luxury to second guess any alliance, so he gripped Bernardo's shoulders confidently and said, "Go rally the men from Zohaib's camp that you think will listen. If our side is larger than his, we can win. I will come back."

With a smile, Bernardo tilted his head. "Too late."

The woman screamed behind him. As Kody turned, a heavy bag covered his head, and someone knocked him to the ground. He rolled and fought, but someone pinned him. Kody knew that familiar musty cologne.

Zohaib.

The strong commander straddled him and latched zip ties as cuffs onto his wrists.

"Bernardo?" Kody yelled out. "You okay?"

The sound of a kick to a body and a thump, then a groan made Kody wince.

Zohaib's slithering voice hissed from his cruel mouth. "Who is Bernardo? His name is G44, and apparently, he's the only smart one here. Tighten her cuffs, soldier. I've got special plans for these two."

His heart pounded.

That betraying bastard.

The bag scratched like thick burlap, but Kody could see through its tiny holes. Zohaib raised the woman, also in cuffs. Kody wanted to reassure the woman, but anything he said would be a lie.

He tripped on a root to the ground, and Bernardo slammed the end of a gun into his stomach. Sharp twigs tore his biceps and forearms as Bernardo led him blindly until they finally slowed. He could feel small trickles of blood ooze down his arms.

The further they walked, the hotter the bag became over his head. A strong scent of a campfire grew more obvious. Soon, the crackling of burning wood grew louder, and then the creak of a rusty metal door opening made Kody's hair stand on end.

Bernardo pushed Kody into darkness and yanked the bag off his head. Another damn box. It looked like a storage container with one barred window. A plate of bread, a pitcher of water, a bucket, and blankets sat in one corner.

Zohaib tore the sack off the woman's head and clipped both of their cuffs. Every muscle clenched in Kody's body, ready to fight, but Bernardo pointed the pistol at the woman.

"It's useless to try and escape." Zohaib's smile wormed up his face. "A dozen soldiers are surrounding you."

"What are you going to do to her?"

Zohaib's sneer crept up his cheeks. "She's for sale now."

His skin crawled with disgust, and his heart plummeted, heavier than a tank.

"Your actions cost me five soldiers!" Zohaib roared. "Bernardo followed you in the jungle. Now, you'll be staying in here with her. Things are about to change."

14

KODY

Zohaib pointed to a camera in the upper corner of the cage. A grin snaked up his face, then he clicked the heavy metal door shut, locking Kody and the woman inside. Humid air circulated in from the crack in the window, suffocating his every breath. He tightened his grip on the window bars as he watched Raelyn's monstrous father walk away. His entire body twisted tight as he shook the metal bars in rage.

"Let us out!" Kody yelled until his voice was scratched raw.

He tried to fit his wrist between the bars to punch the glass window open, but the slats were too narrow. The woman started banging on the door behind him, yelling something in Portuguese.

He rushed to the steel door and repeatedly kicked his heel into it.

"Watch out!"

Backed against the wall in the tiny space, Kody didn't have much room, but he used every inch as he rammed his shoulder in the door.

He ran as fast as possible in such a cramped space and slammed his body full force against the door again. Pain shot through his arm, and he crumpled from the force.

Raising one hand to the wall, Kody's fingertips grazed the flat surface, checking for holes. Nothing. He stepped back and kicked the metal wall as hard as he could. Pain radiated up his shin. Heart racing, his fingertips skimmed each wall, feeling for any weak spots.

"Damn it!" Kody hunched over with his hands on his knees, panting. "Damn! Damn!" He clasped his head in defeat.

Silence filled their cage. Kody dropped his shaking hands to his sides while all his energy drained from his body.

This isn't happening.

Anguish chomped away at his heart until all rational thoughts disappeared. He had to get her out. Kody moved to the barred window again. Amid the greenery of the jungle, Bernardo and another guard casually leaned against a tree while picking at their teeth. Kody kneeled in front of the window, head bowed. He knew Zohaib would take his anger out on Raelyn. The reality of his situation hit him like a truck.

His whole body shook. Kody dropped to the floor and hunched in the corner burying his head between his knees. A gentle hand brushed his skin, and he met the gorgeous gaze of the woman he stole. She offered him water. Kody pushed the pitcher away gently and dropped his head. She placed a hand under his jaw and gently raised his chin. He no longer had the strength to resist, and she held the pitcher over his mouth. She trickled water into Kody's mouth, letting it drizzle over his tongue and down his throat.

"Eliza." She patted her chest. Her fine-boned face might even be considered harsh, but she couldn't be a day over twenty-five.

"Kody."

She nodded and ripped the stale bread into two, then ate her share and stared at the extra piece. He nudged it toward her, and she shoved it in her mouth, followed by a slight moan.

Night claimed them as the crickets croaked near the crack in the window. Kody spaced out, thinking of the last time he and Raelyn were in the cabin on Ash Mountain—cramped spaces but nothing compared to this hellbox. Eliza sat next to him, resting her head against the wall. Her scent was a mixture of rain and lilies.

"Do you speak English?" he asked.

"Little."

He gulped, and his shoulders dropped. "I'm sorry I took you from your daughter."

She frowned and folded her hands together. "Where you from?"

"Oak City, North Carolina."

"I know someone from there." She twiddled her thumbs. "Do you know these boxes?"

Kody shrugged, too tired to answer.

"Zohaib took friends, sister and put them here. His soldiers did …" She dropped her gaze. "All babies taken away."

A sudden lump in his throat prevented him from breathing regularly. "I won't do that to you."

"You took me! If you don't do it to me, some other soldier will."

A clicking sound came from the camera, then Zohaib's voice crackled through where the camera hung. "She's a smart girl, Walsh."

Zohaib was watching and listening in. There was no escaping him.

Eliza stood, took the tray that had held their bread, and threw it against the camera in the corner. She missed, so Kody stood and finished the job. His heart raced as he slammed the metal tray repetitively on the camera until it busted off and hung from its wires. He ripped the camera from the wall and stomped on it.

"I'm sorry. Please forgive me." He begged Eliza.

She slid down the wall and patted the ground next to her. He joined her, wondering how on earth he'd save her from this position. Eliza sighed and rested her head on his shoulder like a pillow.

His muscles tensed. "How can I fix this? What do I do?"

Eliza's eyes glistening with resistant tears. "We fight."

"How?"

"MJ, help escape. She get group and make them fight."

"MJ? Was she the woman who told me how to get to your village?"

Eliza nodded. "MJ wanted to be caught."

Why had that woman looked familiar?

"So, your friend has a plan?"

Eliza put one finger to her lips as she checked the window, then leaned in. "We get out and get group to fight."

Kody rubbed his beard, thinking of any way to escape the box.

"Promise me you make group and fight."

He sandwiched her hand between his, dwarfing her small fingers. "Yes, Eliza. I will. When we get out, I'll form a team to revolt against Zohaib. You and your daughter will be safe again."

She eyed him seriously just as the door of their cell abruptly slid open, startling Kody to his feet. Bernardo pointed his gun and grabbed Eliza by her hair. "You're coming with me."

"No!" Kody yelled.

Bernardo boomed, "Zohaib's furious after your stunt with the camera. Now you don't get a friend anymore."

As fast as he could, he reached for the bread tray and hurled it into Bernardo's stomach. Groaning, Bernardo released Eliza and fell back. Kody slammed the door shut.

Fear flamed in her eyes. "Don't let them touch me!"

Kody's hands shook as he held her close to his chest. Detest grew, fully understanding what the boxes were made for. All he could think about was Raelyn and imagining her under one of these wretched soldiers. He swallowed hard, unable to think, unable to move.

Outside, a deep scream pierced the night air. Eliza's eyes grew wide. She moved to the back corner and crouched down. Kody held the bread tray as a shield, heart racing. The door handle started to wiggle, and Kody's gaze darted around for any last resort. Quickly, he tore the broken camera from the wires and gripped it tight, ready to hurl it at Bernardo's head. Time stood still.

The door of their box re-opened, and Kody met the eyes of his best friend and past teammate.

"Dabbott?" He lowered the tray and stepped forward, worried his mind was playing tricks on him in the night. "What are you doing here?"

"Saving your ass. Let's go!" She threw him a gun.

"There's two guards," he said.

"I killed one."

Kody took Eliza's hand, and they ran into the dark jungle, past a guard with a machete in his chest, blood soaking through his shirt. "Bernardo is still out there."

Eliza stopped, stared at the guard on the ground, her expression without pity. "I never let this happen to daughter."

Kody nodded.

"Fix this. Make team." Eliza sprinted off in the direction of her village.

"Wait!" He called after her.

Dabbott pushed his shoulder. "Let's go, man!"

"But what about Eliza?"

"She probably knows this jungle. Come on."

He raced next to Dabbott until he realized he had no idea where he was, what country he was in, or how far away from transportation. His bare feet crunched over leaves, swerved around trees, jumped over logs, and zig-zagged around thorny bushes. One caught his pants, slicing a hole in the fabric and drawing a thin trail of blood that ran along his thigh.

Panting, Kody chugged the rest of the water from his canteen. Ahead, the line of trees ended as the sky opened, and a Jeep sat in a clearing. Hope soared through his veins. Dabbott positioned her gun, and Kody followed suit. In control, Dabbott slowed as they approached the Jeep and glanced in each direction. She waved him forward, and they both jumped in the Jeep. Dabbott pulled the keys out of her pocket and started the vehicle. They accelerated on the rocky road, kicking up pebbles behind the tires. He gripped the door tightly as the Jeep bounced and jerked around. She didn't turn her headlights on in the night.

Squinting, Kody looked for any sign of civilization but only saw the long road ahead and the moon. When they came to an intersection, the crossroad turned to pavement. She nodded to his gun. He held it, scanning the area for threats. The Jeep screeched as it peeled onto the pavement, and they sped faster. The first sign they came upon was in both Portuguese and English, said: Manaus Airport, 10 kilometers.

Goodbye, Brazil.

Another Jeep zoomed from the line of trees on their left and almost slammed into their side. Dabbott swerved. The man in the passenger seat pulled out a gun and shot in their direction. Dabbott floored the accelerator. Wind whipped Kody's face. He turned and shot back. Two bullets pinged off the Jeep's door.

The soldiers gained on them. More shots fired. Kody squeezed the trigger. The driver of the other car slumped to the side. The Jeep swerved and tossed around behind as the soldier in the passenger seat tried to control the steering. But Dabbott mastered her vehicle and increased the distance between them. Kody's body softened as streetlights flickered ahead. The sound of an airplane taking off into the night sky was like music to his ears.

"I promise to repay you for this, Dabbott. I owe you everything."

"Good, I've got something in mind."

15

KODY

THE AIRPORT WAS FULL of people but no signs of Zohaib's men. He sagged in the chair. Alive— smelly, muddy, and starving—but alive. At least Dabbott had bought him shoes and a shirt from a gift shop, and she had refilled his trusty canteen too. The scent of pizza from a restaurant wafted through the airport, putting Kody in a trance. He licked his parched lips as the room spun.

Stay awake. Stay awake.

At a check-in counter, Dabbott gestured back to him to stay calm as she worked hard explaining to the clerk why Kody didn't have a passport. The employee tilted her head as if not believing a word. Pulling the *'I'm in the military'* card wasn't an option anymore.

Kody clutched a new phone and called Raelyn again. Straight to voicemail. For the tenth time. Where was she? He tried Cali. Nothing.

Dabbott sat in the chair next to him, and when she held out a plate, his senses focused on the warm slice of cheesy pizza. Kody's mouth watered as he grabbed it and shoved a bite in his mouth, letting it burn his palate. She sighed and handed over bottled water. The cool liquid glided down his throat as if he was tasting water for the first time. Another bite of gooeyness smushed against his inner cheeks, but he couldn't savor the taste, not when Raelyn was across a continent, in danger from Zohaib's wrath.

Before he could ask for more food, Dabbott reached to the chair behind her and pulled out another slice. But a little boy huddled in the corner by Gate 22 caught his attention. Dirt was smeared across his forehead, and he stared at the pizza with such longing, it broke Kody's heart. He gestured to the boy, who ran over eagerly with wide eyes. Without hesitation, Kody handed over the plate, and the boy gobbled it up right in front of him, then let out a belch in thanks. He smiled and wrapped his little arms around Kody's knee.

"Here ya go, kid." Kody handed over his canteen, the object that had helped him survive the jungle. Hopefully, parting with it would symbolize leaving that wretched place behind for good.

After the kid left, Dabbott raised one brow. "You've become a softie."

Kody could barely register her words as he glanced around for any threats, keeping his back to the wall at all times.

"Walsh, you gotta calm down."

"Can't."

They sat in silence, staring through the giant windows at the planes taking off. Flashbacks of his past flights flipped on repeat—training jumps, his first deployment to Tahil, then Tuzlicci, and the flight back home after being shot. He barely remembered the last flight when Zohaib had him tied, gagged, and drugged on the trip to the Amazon. Maybe this flight home could be his last one. He and Raelyn could build a cabin somewhere where the population count was two, soon to be three.

Kody looked over at his best friend. "How am I gonna get on a flight?"

"I called Meadows. He's gonna try to call in a favor."

He glanced at the clock and checked for the security guards. "How did you find me?"

"I'll get to that in a minute." She rested her hand on his. "Walsh, when was the last time you slept?"

How could I have taken Eliza? Where's Raelyn? Is she okay? Is Zohaib on his way here?

Kody's fists balled, and his breathing sped. Civilians moseying around their area started staring at his jittery legs.

Dabbott whispered, "Walsh, take a deep breath."

"I have to kill Zohaib."

She put both her hands on his shoulders. "Hey, look at me. What happened out there?"

"I couldn't save everyone." His body released his despair all at once, dropping his head. "And we'll never be free from Zohaib's control. How will we ever be safe?"

"We'll figure it out," Dabbott spoke cautiously. "Listen, though, I've been investigating Storm Force while stationed in Tahil. I think Joanna Bell is being tracked."

Kody's eyes shot up. "Is Raelyn with her?"

"I don't know. But she's not with Liam," said Dabbott.

"How do you know?"

"Liam searched the warehouse in Oak City and found a list with more coordinates. After coming up blank with the first two, the third one on the list led me to you."

"So those coordinates lead to his fort in the jungle?"

She nodded. "I think the list has Zohaib's other army bases."

"How many?"

Dabbott flattened her hair with her hand. "Like I said, the first two were duds. But maybe ten or twelve others."

Kody jumped at a sudden pop behind him, but it was only a suitcase smashing to the ground, and he immediately felt foolish. He sighed. "Were there any bases in the States?"

"Yup. You'll never guess where."

"The warehouse?"

She nodded.

"But it was abandoned."

Dabbott brought up a picture on her phone and pointed. "I'll send this to your new phone. It's a more detailed layout of the warehouse that Liam found. There are secret entrances and tunnels all over the place."

"I'm surprised Liam found anything in the warehouse. Zohaib wouldn't leave a trail."

"Maybe it wasn't him who stored the info there. Joanna worked in that warehouse for her journalism research long ago, right?" Kody paused. "She could've stashed the coordinate list there before she even learned what they were for."

"But that must've been over twelve years ago. Who knows how many locations are still accurate."

"I'm not sure, but listen." She laid a hand on his shoulder. "I'm already gonna get in trouble for disappearing, so I need to ask you a favor. I know it's not fair that you're dealing with all this, but we need to stop contacting each other for a while. I can't be linked with any of part this, or my career is over. Let's go silent for six months and hope it all blows over by then."

"You want out?"

She sighed. "I'm always here for you, Walsh, but I've already taken too many risks. I need you to find someone else for support, for just a bit."

Kody leaned back and stared at the ceiling, pushing his palms hard into his forehead while inhaling deeply. "Right, of course, I can do that."

People shuffled by with rolling suitcases, babies cried, and the loudspeaker blared announcements in Portuguese, then Spanish, followed by English. Strollers wheeled by like they were off to the races.

Dabbott's phone rang. "Hello?" she asked and paused. "It's for you."

"Kody? Where are you?" Liam's voice was deeper than the last time they talked and fully on edge.

"Manaus Airport, Brazil. They won't let me on a plane home. Where's Raelyn?"

A long pause. "Uh, she's fine … maybe I can hack into the system," said Liam.

"I don't think that'll work." Kody snapped. "But *where* is Raelyn?"

"I bet I can get you on that plane."

Kody stood. "You're avoiding my question."

"She's probably fine. My sister is fierce."

"What do you mean, *probably*?"

Liam coughed on the other line. "Um … yeah, Mom may be losing her mind a little."

Dabbott tried to pull Kody down to the chair, but he started to pace. "Are Raelyn and Joanna still together?"

"No. Mom took off with some money right after you disappeared. Raelyn thinks the file was hidden in Joanna's trunk, which was sold." He coughed into the phone. "So, we climbed the mountain but got separated."

Kody's muscles tightened. "How long ago?"

"Two … three weeks."

His chest constricted so tight. "Are you telling me you haven't heard from her in that long?"

"Um …"

"She's alone on the mountain? She's eight months pregnant!"

"I doubt that snowstorm got her." Liam's voice didn't sound so sure on the other end.

Kody marched straight to the clerk's counter. "Get me on that plane, Liam."

16

RAELYN

THE SUN SHONE BRIGHT, making the snow sparkle like heavenly glitter. As Raelyn plodded through the endless white, she turned to meet Tucker's comforting gaze. "How many more miles to Aaron's?"

"Just one more. It'll be slow going, though."

She groaned.

"Do you want to find that trunk or not?" His voice was stern, but after growing accustomed to his mannerisms the last few weeks, she knew he was just focused.

"Yes," she said, "Your cabin is too small for the two of us."

Tucker tracks were so big they looked more like monster paws than footprints. "You mean three." He winked and patted his dog's head. "Shiloh will take care of us, just in case."

Her heart skipped. "In case what?"

"Just stay alert. Watch your footing and tell Amala to keep calm."

Raelyn held back a grin. That wasn't the first time Tucker had said her daughter's name. But the painful realization that it should've been Kody to say it first reminded her of what was at stake.

Minutes ticked by at a dreary speed. Occasionally, Shiloh kicked up snow at her while running and playing ahead.

Tucker commanded, "Shiloh, heel!"

Eventually, a narrow clearing came into view. The scenery turned into a flat thin strip on the edge of a cliffside, wrapping around the slopes. Raelyn held her breath at the beauty below. Their elevation had to be one of the highest possible points in Ash Mountain. On her left, a rocky cliff side rose straight up. To her right, the cliffside plummeted straight down. She could see the entire valley and town—a view she had never experienced before. For a moment, it felt like she was on top of the world. But they were so close to the edge. Raelyn's heart pounded, and she moved closer to Tucker.

"You want to hold my hand?" Tucker offered.

"Um …" she glanced at the treacherous path, and her eyes skimmed down the steep drop-off. "You're sure this is the only way?"

"Yup."

She grabbed his hand and nodded. "Let's go."

"Okay, but once we go out on that ledge, we can't turn back. Forward is the only way."

Her body tensed, and she used every ounce of energy not to look at Tucker for reassurance. "Do we need ropes or something?"

"I don't have any, but I've done this a hundred times ... during summer."

Raelyn gulped and held in her doubts.

Tucker guided her hips over. "Stand between me and the cliff wall."

With each step forward, she focused on her breathing. The scent of crisp winter air met her nose, and the wind stung her face.

"Keep going!" He hollered over the harassing wind.

She caught a glimpse of Tucker's boot and couldn't believe how close he was to teetering off the rim. A shotgun went off, and Shiloh scattered. Her rumbling paws knocked a giant chunk of snow from under them, making the path narrower. More snow crumbled away. Fear paralyzed her.

She sucked in a breath.

"Raelyn, jump!" Tucker screamed.

"What?" Her fingers tried to clutch the flat cliff wall with a death grip, but ice made it too slippery.

"Move!"

One.

She took a deep breath. The cliffside grew closer.

Two.

"Jump, Raelyn!"

Three!

She pushed off hard. Miraculously, she landed on a large flat clearing, surrounded by oaks. A small cabin stood in the distance with smoke rising from the chimney.

Raelyn let out a deep sigh as Tucker landed safely next to her.

"See, I told you we'd be fine." He smiled.

She caressed her belly and was about to answer when Shiloh rushed by, yapping and knocked into Raelyn's legs. She fell forward, hard, toppling on top of her belly.

Oh my God!

Raelyn panted and rolled over, her back freezing from the snow. Massaging her belly, she prayed.

Please move. Please kick.

Nothing.

Tucker turned. "Why are you on the ground?" He reached down, confusion plastered on his face.

On the other side of the clearing, a burly man in overalls ran out from his front door with a rifle in hand, cursing and waving ferociously. The moment he laid eyes on Tucker, Aaron stopped in his tracks and hustled away down the slopes, picking up momentum as he fled.

Tucker looked back at Raelyn. "I need to make sure he won't come after you. Go check out his place while I distract him."

All she could think about was Amala's lack of movement and panic latched on tight. "Tucker, I ..."

But he chased after Aaron and hollered down the hill, shouting, "You hold onto grudges too long, old man."

Raelyn glanced at the cottage.

Now or never.

She poked her belly again. Nothing. The dread of what that could mean swarmed her mind until all she could imagine was the sonogram that led to Joanna's miscarriage from so long ago.

"Come on, baby girl ... move."

She stared ahead at the freshly fallen snow that no one had stepped on yet. Two options. Forward into the unknown or down the slope toward Tucker. Aaron's house stared back at her, with a malevolent vibe hovering in the air. Doubts crept in, and it felt like the ground was dissolving underneath her feet.

Trembling, Raelyn glanced around to make sure Aaron hadn't returned from the hill. The wind went as still as death. No bird chirps. No dogs barking. When she inhaled through her nose, she couldn't even smell anything.

Absence.

The trees around her spiked into the sky like knives, creeping and stretching around her like claws ready to engulf her body and rip out everything that mattered. If Cali were here, she'd make some sarcastic comment about a horror film gone awry. The only piece still needed to complete this eerie scene was a trail of drops of blood in the snow leading her to her doom. With each step toward Aaron's wooden cabin, her heart rammed fast.

I shouldn't be here.

A deep, throaty growl came from her right. She whirled around at the menacing sound and met two gleaming yellow eyes. The elements of this new threat hit her in panic-fractured images. Thick black fur standing on end, yellowed incisors, heavy paws braced wide. With its head lowered and ears back, a German Shepherd snapped its wet fangs in a snarl. Raelyn's heart pounded in her chest as dread swarmed her soul.

She stared at those threatening canines, unable to breathe. Her hands wrapped around her belly as she slowly backed up. Her body shook, and her throat bobbed.

The dog crept forward. Raelyn grabbed granola bars from the side pouch of her backpack and threw them across the snow toward it. He didn't even sniff them but lowered its ears. His giant paws inched forward. The dog pounced, flinging its agile body forward. Raelyn screamed and streaked to the side. Its claws lashed out.

Raelyn sprinted around it and made it to the door. She slammed the barrier between her and the animal. The sounds of the dog trying to tear apart the wood sent shivers down her spine.

After sucking in a lungful of fake confidence, Raelyn stepped forward into the shadowed room. The hardwood floor creaked with each movement. Smells of rotten fish and stale beer overwhelmed her nostrils as she walked further inside. The dog continued to claw and thrash outside the door, barking fiercely. She checked to make sure all the windows were closed so the beast wouldn't jump through.

Raelyn whispered, "Hello?"

The crackle of the fireplace gave the place a sense of false life. The rest of the room looked like a carcass with guts dispersed everywhere. A skeleton of a fox laid in the back corner. The lamps were all out. As the clouds passed outside, the natural light cast shifting shadows, increasing her hesitation. Squirrel and rabbit pelts lay spread across a table with sharp tools next to them. A rack hanging from the ceiling held a variety of knives. She grabbed one—just in case. She tried not to think of Amala's lack of movements or the fear coursing through her veins. When a gust of wind blew in from the ajar door, goosebumps formed on her skin. Knives clattered together like a wind chime.

Raelyn gulped and scanned the furniture, all covered in newspapers.

No trunk.

One door led to the back, maybe a bedroom. Raelyn tiptoed, leaving tracks of snow in her wake.

Pausing in front of the door, Raelyn took a deep breath and hesitantly pushed it open. A stained mattress lay on the floor, and next to it was a large metal cage, big enough to fit six dogs. A pile of bones sat in the corner of the cage. Raelyn shuddered violently.

Need to hurry.

In the room sat one dresser—no trunk. There were two more closed doors. Wanting to flee, Raelyn wrapped her hand around Kody's pocket watch dangling from her neck for courage. She pressed the door forward. Bathroom—no trunk, five razors sitting on the counter.

Something rustled outside, and her breathing lurched into the red zone. She rushed across the room to the last door. The wooden floors groaned under her movements. Raelyn swallowed hard and tapped the door lightly with the end of the knife, but even when she tried to push it open, the door was wedged in place. Moving closer, Raelyn peeked in the crack of the door. Two brown eyes stared back at her. She jumped back, raising the knife high.

No sound. No movement. The absence was worse than something leaping out. Clutching her heart, Raelyn looked again, barely willing to keep her eyes open.

It was a stuffed raccoon.

Taxidermy?

Her chest rose and fell fast as she shoved the door open. It was a closet full of stuffed animals, all resting atop the trunk.

Wasting no time, Raelyn closed the closet door. She knocked the animals onto the floor and had to hold back a gag from a dusty smell. Fumbling with the latch was useless. Locked. With a heavy hand, she smashed the knife into Joanna's trunk. The knife sliced the wood to pieces and collapsed to the side. Nothing inside looked familiar. No wedding pictures. No journal articles. No photo albums.

She rummaged through Aaron's tools piled high in the trunk. No file. Her heart sank, and she dropped a tool that looked like a scraping device. It clunked against something hard and metal. Raelyn ransacked through the bottom, and her fingertips grazed along with a small metal container. She pulled it out. A safety deposit box with a small engraving on the side: JB+WB.

Ma and Pa.

It was locked. She shook it hard right by her ear. Just in case, she checked every last nook and cranny of the trunk for a key, then unzipped her jacket, and placed the deposit box on top of her round belly. Being the size of a tissue box, it fit perfectly. For a moment, she squeezed her eyes shut and prayed while rubbing her belly.

Please move. Please.

Absence.

Raelyn shook her head and pried open the door. A pair of dark eyes glared. This time they were a human. She screamed and fell backward, almost into the trunk.

"What the hell are you doing, lass?" A repulsive smile crawled up Aaron's face, showing several missing teeth and a wart on his chin.

Her words caught in her throat. She grabbed the knife and held it between Aaron and her, not allowing him to take a step forward.

"Calm down." He glanced behind her. "What did you do to my stuff?"

"Stay back!" Her heart hammered in her chest.

"It's okay, lass." His shoulders softened, and he reached down to offer a hand. "I'm not gonna hurt you. Come on out of there. You need to get on home." He smiled, showing black holes where teeth should be. "I bought that trunk for four dollars. So, I reckon you must be lookin for that little box inside. I've been meaning to give it back to your Grams." He pointed to the bulge in her coat. "Viola must not have known it was in there."

She backed away.

"Shucks, this place hasn't seen a female fo' twenty years. Want to stay for some cocoa?"

"Um, no, it's okay."

"Okay, well, I'm supposed to give you a message."

She stepped back again. "What do you mean?"

"Do you know someone named Marlee?"

"No, I need to go." Raelyn slipped through the room quickly.

"The name Marlee Peterson doesn't ring a bell?"

Raelyn froze. "Peterson?"

"Yes, she sent me this to give to you." He handed over a piece of paper.

"What?" Raelyn unfolded it. "How could she know I'd ever meet you?"

Raelyn,

I know about your relationship with my cousin and how much he loved you. The last time we talked on the phone, he made me promise to watch over you—in case anything ever happened. I have to admit, I blamed you for Phoenix's death for a few months, but now that I've seen you're carrying his baby, let's just say I'll stick to my word. You need to get off Ash Mountain. Immediately! Don't go back to your cabin and head to my Uncle David's. He can help. Don't wait.

The only way out is through,
Marlee Peterson

Where have I heard that before?

She shook her head, unsure what this all meant. "I need to go."

"Right, right." Aaron turned off a hissing kettle and smiled genuinely as she backed away. "You can borrow my truck on the way down. It's a long hike by foot, and you'll be much safer." Steam danced above the rim of his mug. "Make sure Tucker brings it back. That boy is always up to no good taking my tools."

"Um, okay. Thank you."

Why is he being nice?

"No problem at all, lass." Aaron pulled out a keychain. "And tell Tucker not to let his dog on my property again. It scares away all my game."

She quickly snatched the keys and ran out the door, thankfully the crazy dog was nowhere to be seen.

"You sure you don't want any cocoa?" He hollered after her, sounding confused.

Raelyn created new prints in the snow as she walked through Aaron's yard as fast as possible to Tucker. The security box slammed against her breasts as she followed tracks leading down the slope. Barren trees sagged and looked down on her in pity, and the swiftly moving clouds turned to a thick overcast gray. Tucker's shape came into view, so she slowed her pace.

He ran toward her with hardened eyes. "Did Aaron hurt you?"

"No."

"Did you find the trunk?"

She nodded.

"Then what's wrong?"

"Amala—she won't move. Ever since I fell." Tears streamed down and formed tiny holes in the snow.

Tucker dropped to his knees in front of her, rose her jacket, and hovered his hand over her belly. "May I?"

Raelyn gulped and nodded.

Down low, on the underside of her bump, his calloused hands gently pushed and prodded, giving her a cramp. She bent forward and cringed. "What are you doing?"

"Firemen are trained as EMS. We learned some tricks."

Please move. Move.

His large hand kept massaging, putting pressure on her bladder until a soft tickle moved inside her stomach, then a harder kick. A smile exploded on her cheeks as she met Tucker's eyes.

He smiled and stood upright. "She's okay. See, I told you that you'll be a great mom. This shows how much you care. The first time she scrapes her knee from falling off a bike, you have to hold it together though. Be brave for her."

Relief washed over her, followed by fatigue. Exhaustion came like a flood, followed by sore muscles.

"So, you found the trunk?"

"Yeah, I need to open this little box." Raelyn pulled it out of her coat and laid it on the hood of Aaron's truck.

"If we bust it open, anything outside could fly into the snow and get wet." Tucker picked it up and turned it over. "There's a keyhole."

"Do you have anything small that'll fit in there?"

He patted his pockets. "No. Let's head down the mountain. We can find a farmer with tools or something."

"Aaron said we can use his truck." She rubbed her sore legs.

"Really? Okay, let's go before he changes his mind, and don't worry, there's no more cliffsides."

As they drove along, she couldn't help but let her mind wander about what would be on the file. Would it prove Zohaib's cruelty and how he separated families?

I have his genes. What if I end up like Zohaib?

That fact alone should have solidified the need for adoption. Any possibility that Amala could eventually be hurt felt like poison running through her blood. This choice would make sure that Joanna and Zohaib would never learn of Amala's identity—they'd never be able to track her down and use her for their advantage. Yet, after spending time with Tucker and his devastation from missing out on parenthood started to sway her decision. He was so certain that she'd decide to keep Amala and live happily ever after.

What if I make the wrong choice?

Finally, at the base of the mountain, Raelyn glanced behind her. The mountain rose high to the gray clouds, her past. "I know where we are. My old farmhouse is that way."

The familiarity warmed her numb fingers as they passed by the neighbor's field of cows. Her farmhouse came into view with the same shutters Pa had nailed on years ago, the same mailbox he had fixed, and the same screen door he had installed. Raelyn sighed when the truck stopped, refreshingly grateful to be home where Pa's old blue truck sat in the driveway.

"This is my place," she said. With Tucker's steady hand helping her out, Raelyn walked to their door. "Thank you for all your help. You want to come in for food?"

"No, I'll head back up before Aaron hunts me down. That man is crazy." He smiled. "Raelyn, don't worry. You'll make a great mother."

No other words were needed. Tucker had saved her life—and she knew they'd meet up again. He waved with a knowing smile and turned around toward the mountain disappearing into the white wonderland.

Raelyn ran toward Pa's farmhouse and knocked. Meows escalated in volume from the other side, but no footsteps approached. She wiggled the handle. Locked. Raelyn quickly turned on her heels to see if Tucker was already gone or if he had waited until she entered. A fireman would surely know how to enter a building safely. But he was nowhere in sight. A heavy groan of exhaustion escaped her lips. She trudged around the side of the house, kicking snow along the way as shivers climbed her spine.

Back door— also locked.

Damn it!

Raelyn patted down her pockets but knew she didn't have a house key with her. One at a time, she checked every window to see if any were unlatched. No luck.

"Seriously?" She craned her neck to the sky and stared into the abyss of gray. "Give me a break!"

Glancing around, her gaze landed on a broken tree branch. She gripped it tightly and swung it at a window, smashing the glass. The way the pieces shattered reminded her of when she and Cali broke into the art museum after the school field trip. A snort came from deep within. That photograph had changed the course of her life. She missed Cali's fearless spunk and support.

Raelyn reached through the glass, careful not to scrape herself on the pointy edges, and unlocked the window. Her boots crunched over the shards as she made her way to the next room.

The air smelled of something fruity, but she couldn't pinpoint it.

"Grandma? Grandpa?"

Their cat ran forward.

"Are they still on vacation, Mr. Grumps?"

Raelyn clutched the safety deposit box. Now that the box was in her possession, she was hesitant to open it. What if the proof on the file would make Joanna go to prison too?

After a quick text exchange with Aunt Aubree, confirming Liam was safe with her, Raelyn raced to the bathroom. Amala was pushing on her bladder again. At least she didn't have to pee in the forest this time. Raelyn stared at the shower curtain, a river image that Pa had picked out. The house that used to remind her of Joanna now only reminded her of Pa.

Raelyn set the box on the counter and turned the bathwater on warm. She dropped her coat to the floor, and her phone slid out, straight into the water.

"Crap!" She pulled it out fast, shaking the water droplets off and wiping it on a towel. A large watermark appeared under her screen. She huffed, "Great."

Raelyn sighed. The mirror was the same one she had used to get ready for her first day of high school, the same one she had learned to insert earrings. That very place she stood was where Pa had taught her to floss. She stared at her reflection. Each day that passed, she looked more and more like Joanna, growing into the features of the woman who kept shattering her world. Chestnut hair, thick eyebrows, high cheekbones, tanned skin, thin, petite frame with wide hips.

But, her amber eyes were Zohaib's. She could see him looking back at her and shuddered at the thought. No one should have to destroy a parent in order to survive. Yet, here she was about to open the box with the file and turn the evidence over to the cops.

But—not yet. She had to give herself a few minutes. Now that the solution was in her grasp, it was almost too much to bear. Raelyn dipped her toe in the bath and sunk in deep, letting the heat turn her skin red.

The last time she had soaked in a bath was the morning after Phoenix died. Would Amala have his eyes, ones that shifted colors depending on what she wore? Maybe she'd have his blond hair, thin nose, and mischievous smile. Popping a bubble with her toe gave her a sense of tranquility, a false peace that everything would be okay. At least for that moment, no one was around the corner hunting her down. The apple-scented shampoo and soap absorbed into her hair and skin. As the drain sucked down the remnants of her past few weeks, it also sucked down her fears. She remembered Aaron's message from Marlee Peterson. Why would she want Raelyn to go to her uncle's?

Raelyn dried off on a towel decorated with deer images. Allowing herself the freedom, she walked naked through the empty farmhouse to the childhood bedroom she grew up in. The time spent there felt like a lifetime away. She gasped at the sight of a new wooden crib and rocking chair with chipped white paint in the corner.

Oh, Grandma.

Shaking her head, she found some of Grandma's oversized, stained painting shirts and stretchy yoga pants. The pants nearly ripped at the seams when she tugged them over her plump rear, but they worked. A laugh escaped her lips when she couldn't tug the shirt down. She left it there, rolled up, bare belly exposed.

"Oh well."

Raelyn sat on the rocking chair and stared at the mountain of pillows under her blanket. She swayed back and forth, imagining what it'd be like to rock Amala to sleep. That life could be possible. Raelyn remembered the little hairbow Tucker had gifted her and swiped it from her pocket. She stared at the box in her hand.

The file better be in here.

Time moved in slow motion, and the room whirled around her as Raelyn inserted the hair pin in the lock. She wiggled and flicked her wrist at different angles.

Click.

Raelyn inhaled deeply. Her hands shook. She lifted the top off the deposit box and examined the contents. Underneath an antique key laid a wad of hundred-dollar bills. She dumped them on the pillow and scattered them about to search for a thumb drive.

Nothing.

"No! No! No!" Raelyn's hands fumbled around, desperate to find it stuck in one of the rubber bands binding the cash together, or maybe lodged between a few bills.

"There's no file." She spoke to Mr. Grumps in anguish.

Her heart was heavy as she sorted through her options. Zohaib would find her soon, and she had no evidence to defeat him.

Just then, the lump of pillows under her comforter shifted. Raelyn screamed.

17

RAELYN

RAELYN SCREAMED AGAIN WHEN the bulge under the blankets moved. She rushed to the closet and rummaged through the piles, searching for the best weapon. Boxes toppled over. Grabbing an iron, she held it above her head, ready to strike.

A toe as dark as the midnight sky popped out from under the sheets, followed by a body and a face. "Sonic beanbags, Rae! Are you trying to kill me?"

"Cali?" Raelyn lowered her iron. "How did you get here?"

"Evil rulers aren't the only ones with a brain, Rae. I knew you'd come here, and your Grandma left me her key."

Raelyn rushed over and wrapped her arms around Cali.

"Ooh, you better name me Godmother *and* Maid of Honor, come to think of it. I'll be granting all kinds of magic wishes."

"Don't squeeze too tight, or I'll have to pee again." Raelyn backed away with a smile. "What are you doing here?"

"You need me of course."

Raelyn tilted her head, waiting. "And …"

"I was thinking about what you said about giving my niece or nephew up for adoption. You can't let someone else raise that little munchkin."

"I'm not fit to be a mother. I'm too much like Joanna."

Cali took her by both shoulders. "Stop comparing yourself with her. It's apples and zebras."

"You mean apples and oranges?"

"No. Zebras."

Raelyn threw her hands up in the air. "Joanna was married to Pa and slept with Zohaib, then had me. I was with Kody and slept with Phoenix and—"

"Were you kidnapped?" Cali stuck out her hip.

"No."

"Were you forced to have sex? Have you been tortured? Abused?"

"No."

"Were you desperate to do *anything* to survive?"

Raelyn looked at the dusty floor. "You're supposed to be hiding."

"I was *supposed* to be touring with my band."

Raelyn groaned and palmed her forehead. "Touring!? Cali, your name would be spotlighted."

"I'm not *that* famous."

"You have to stay hidden." Raelyn collapsed on the bed. "You shouldn't be here. That last night in Haavij, Zohaib asked for you specifically. You!"

Cali tapped her chin. "Actually, that's why I'm here. You know the video you tried with that model?"

"Yeeeeeeeah? Why?"

"Zohaib wanted me. I mean, who can blame him?" She winked. "It could work if it's a video of me."

Raelyn gestured a giant X in the air with her arms. "No way. I won't put you at risk."

Cali turned serious. “Rae, we don’t have the luxury of playing it safe. We have to try anything that might lead us to Kody. So, how would this genius plan work?”

“If Zohaib opens it, all the contents of his hard drive should immediately be sent back to this email. Hopefully, his files will show us where he is or have evidence to arrest him.”

Cali unzipped a backpack and pulled out body oil.

Raelyn wrapped her pinky around her best friend’s and rubbed her belly with the other. “I’m only doing this for my baby girl’s sake.”

“It’s a girl?” Cali hopped in place as she took off her shirt.

“We can talk about that later.” Raelyn glanced at a large clock hanging above the chimney. “Let’s hurry.”

Cali threw her clothes on the bed. “Oooh, it’s cold. Now, promise me you won’t blush. I’ve changed in front of you a million times.”

Remembering MJ’s request, Raelyn said, “I’m not rubbing any oil on you.”

Cali snorted. “You wish.”

Her hands shook as she changed the camera settings on the phone.

This could make everything worse.

“I’m ready, pop tart! It’s a good thing I got waxed recently.”

Cali’s dark skin glimmered so beautifully from the oil, it was captivating. Raelyn knew her body would never be the same after she gave birth, and a pang of jealousy rushed through her.

Raising the camera, she snapped a few still shots of Cali in different positions. The flames of the fireplace paired with the sun beaming in from outside created the perfect lighting. Cali twisted, turned, bent, and folded herself for the camera, making Raelyn’s cheeks turn warmer.

Still naked, Cali pushed the table away from the front door. “Let’s do some outside now.”

“What? It’s freezing.”

“Men love outside pictures. It’s the vulnerability. He wants to feel powerful.”

Raelyn’s gut clenched in knots when she remembered the man they were discussing was her biological father. That same man wanted to own her best friend, and she was willing to set Cali up for danger.

Raelyn followed Cali outside into the cold — a winter wonderland. Cali stood nude in a foot of snow and placed her hands on her hips, sticking her curves out in all the seductive directions.

"Let's do the video now."

"I hate this." She hit the record button as Cali licked her lips to give a little speech, but Raelyn cut off her best friend and said, "No, Cali, we can't do this. Let's go inside."

"Raelyn Bell, get your pregnant ass back over here and film me, or I'll do it myself."

"No, a video is too much." Raelyn ran inside. Her stomps escalated into the kitchen and the refrigerator door opened with a suctioned *pop*. Raelyn's mind wandered to Kody's smile, wanting to see it once more. If she could go back in time, she'd make so many changes to keep him safer and happier. Kody wasn't to blame for the chaos of the last year. It was all Zohaib. He deserved the worst kind of ending. A simple death was too easy for the man who demolished everything in his wake without care.

She chucked a pillow to the floor and whispered to the crib, "Kody, just come home!"

As Cali pulled her clothes on, she asked, "Did you get any good pics?"

"I don't want to analyze your body. You pick which one." She handed the phone over.

Cali scrolled through. "Okay, email this one."

Raelyn tried not to stare at the image. "I need to follow all of Liam's steps to send this right. Are you sure about this?"

Cali nodded. "We have to try, Rae."

"If Zohaib steals you away from me—"

"He won't. We will be fine."

Raelyn used an untraceable email account Liam had created and followed his directions by attaching Cali's pictures and the virus. She hovered her finger over the send button and held her breath.

Cali leaned over and pushed send, then dressed. "So, Liam texted me his half of the story. What happened to you up on that mountain?"

"I was with Fireman Tucker for a few weeks until the snow melted."

"Who?"

"Never mind, just a mountain man."

"Is he any cute?"

"Cali!"

"What, a girl can dream, can't she?"

Raelyn shook her head. "Yeah, he's attractive. But he's like thirty."

"Experience helps."

Raelyn crossed her legs like a pretzel underneath herself. "Don't think he wants a relationship."

"Why?"

"His girlfriend died in labor."

Cali gasped. "No! That still happens?"

"Apparently." She resituated, trying to get comfortable.

Cali's charm bracelet jangled as she placed her hand on her hip. "Rae, I know a lot is going on, but I can also tell when you're hiding something. What is it?"

Down the hall, the orange flames flickered and danced in the fireplace. "Phoenix's parents need to adopt her."

"You still think it's Phoenix's baby? Naw, it's definitely my niece in there."

Raelyn ignored her. "If I turn out to be anything like my parents, then I shouldn't be allowed to raise a child. I would mess her up so badly. I'm actually grateful Joanna's MIA right now so I don't have to deal with her and my father—"

"Zohaib isn't your father." Cali put both hands on her shoulders. "William was your father. What do you think he would say about your baby?"

Raelyn paused and wriggled her nose. "Pa would want me to keep the baby. His whole life revolved around me, and I wasn't even his."

"You *were* his. There doesn't need to be blood connection for love to run that deep."

Raelyn looked down and twisted her toe on the hardwood. "Do you really think Kody believes that too, or is he saying it to look like the good guy?" She imaged Kody's smile and the brilliant sparkle in his dark eyes.

Cali waved her off. "You know the answer to that. Don't even waste your breath asking, girl."

A blinding pain surged through Raelyn's lower abdomen. Shock blinded her as she doubled over the counter, gripping her belly. The agony was enough to put tears on her cheeks, but it subsided after a few deep breaths.

"You okay?" Cali asked.

I can't do this.

Raelyn grabbed the truck keys hanging by the door and raced past Cali.

"Where are you goin'?"

Hyperventilating, Raelyn rushed into the cold.

"Wait! Stop freaking out."

She hopped in the truck. There wasn't much room for her belly behind the steering wheel, and she had to back up the chair to fit. Pulling out of the drive, she checked her phone for Peterson's address. They had to raise her. Tucker was wrong. Cali was wrong. Liam was wrong.

I'm going to hurt Amala if I keep her.

After the birth, maybe she could somehow pass the news to Zohaib that the baby didn't survive, and then she'd hand Amala off safely. If she stayed far enough away, Zohaib would never find out about his granddaughter's whereabouts. The GPS shouted directions in a robotic voice, and Raelyn headed back out of the gravel driveway.

Her cell still wasn't working right, but a few spotty messages pinged. A notification came up that a picture of Cali had been sent to Zohaib. She couldn't help but check other messages while driving—fifteen from Liam. One read:

Kody is safe and on a plane home!

Raelyn slammed on the breaks, making the seatbelt dig into her belly. "Holy crap!"

When did Liam send that?

Her vision was spotted in front of her as she pulled to the side of the country road, then scrolled ferociously through her other messages. There were twenty-five from an unknown number.

The first showed:

Babe, it's me. Where are you? I'm at an airport in Brazil and flying home. Answer my calls.

She skimmed more from a second unknown number. Kody's tone increased in desperation and terror until she read the last message sent an hour ago.

Babe, I know you're probably lost in the mountains and won't see this. But, I promise I won't stop searching for you. I'll be at your farmhouse in an hour. I'll find you in Ash Mountain soon. Just hold on. I love you, always.

The heat from the truck suffocated her, so she turned down the dial and checked the road for other cars. Her chest tightened as she floored the truck back to the farmhouse. Was she dreaming? Could Kody be back? Was it possible? Her heart hammered hard in her chest.

She dialed the number and pressed the phone tight to her ear. No one answered. Trees whizzed by as the sun bore down through her windshield. She pushed the accelerator harder, but the truck sputtered a death rattle.

"No!" As the truck slowed, Raelyn rammed her fist into the steering wheel, making the horn beep. Pulling to the side of the road again, Raelyn shifted gears. No luck. She turned the keys and tried to restart the truck. Nothing.

Only half-a-mile. I can make it!

Raelyn shoved the deposit box and her keys in the coat, then jumped out of the truck, landing with a thump. She waddled toward the farmhouse, but the heavy snow boots crunched through the snow, slowing her down. Her breath came heavy, and her gait was awkward from the extra weight, and she could feel the stretch marks queuing up to pull her thigh skin to pieces. Underfoot, the road turned slick from black ice. Raelyn concentrated on each spot to place her foot as her speed increased, trying to race in the direction of where she hoped Kody would be.

A cramp seized her body, and she gasped and pushed against it with three fingers digging into her side. A car rolled by, splashing a pool of melted snow on her boots. Panting, she dared to glance up long enough to squint ahead. His green Jeep sat parked in the farmhouse driveway.

He's here!

Raelyn's heart slammed fast as she tried to jog. Her boots clomped like a horse stomping on a knot of snakes. A tall figure moved inside the study window in the dim room.

"Kody!" Raelyn screamed into the crisp air.

A door banged from the side of the house, and a broad shape with dark clothes and a backpack walked off toward the mountain trail.

Breathless, Raelyn ran faster. Her throat prickled as she shouted at the top of her lungs, "Kody! Wait!"

He's too far away!

He walked further, camouflaging into the line of oaks. A tight pinch racked her stomach, and Amala kicked hard. Raelyn stopped in her tracks, bent over, pressing her hands into her knees to keep herself upright.

Hunched over, Raelyn took a deep breath and screamed as loud as she could as if practicing for labor. "Kody!"

Her throat burned and she sniffed in the little trail of snot dripping over her lip. Staring down, she wiped her nose on her sleeve.

"Raelyn?" Kody's deep voice boomed from the forest line far off.

Panting, she looked up.

"Kody!" She wanted to run into his arms, but her legs shook.

He ran toward her, kicking his legs up high to better navigate the snow. His arms frantically pumped the air. That one moment stretched into an unbearable eternity. She needed to be in his arms faster. The closer he moved, the more surprised his brown eyes seemed.

Her heart cartwheeled as she held out her hands to him.

Closing in, Kody rushed into her arms. "I'm here."

Raelyn buried her face in his chest, whimpering his name over and over.

He scanned her up and down. "Are you hurt?"

"I'm fine. You?" Just one look from him healed the hole inside of her. She pulled his neck down and laid a kiss on his warm lips. Their two beings fused into one as Kody cloaked her in his strong arms. Her body defrosted at his touch and eased into his embrace.

Unable to hold back, Raelyn snuggled her head into his chest. "You're here." His touch awoke her consciousness that she had been struggling to survive the last month. "You're here."

Kody held her steady. "Shh, it's okay."

She swallowed hard and licked the salty tears. "How are you here?"

He covered her in kisses as his answer, then whispered into her cheek. "Babe, you're shaking."

Raelyn wanted to merge her whole body with his and never allow separation again. She almost climbed up his side, latching on like an animal. As he guided her through the melting snow to the farmhouse, his hands moved under her coat to her stomach, exploring how round she had become. Raelyn looked up at him, and he smiled, but it was strained and layered with anguish.

What happened to him?

"Kody?"

"Let's go inside," he said.

"Okay, Cali's in there."

His eyes should've shown joy at the mention of his sister, but only exhaustion showed on his face when he whispered, "That's good."

His footsteps were heavy up the back steps, and when he pushed the door open, it appeared the effort of a broken man. The sound his coat made when it slumped to the floor was like the last huff of a dying animal. And when he collapsed into the couch, his weight sank into the cushion as if he would be glued to the spot for eternity.

Raelyn curled into a ball next to him, his warmth seeping into her. He was all she'd ever need. She took his hand and kissed his knuckles. Kody stared ahead, seemingly hypnotized by the abandoned hummingbird feeder swaying in the cold. She unzipped her coat and sat on his lap.

"I thought I lost you." His voice cracked.

"Kody, look at me." She lifted his chin with one finger. "Hey, look at me."

He did. Strain was written all over his handsome face.

Raelyn nuzzled into him as close as Amala would allow and lay her chest on his chest. Amala kicked as if to let them know she was happy her family was reunited. His heavy breathing made his chest rise and fall, and her head followed suit.

Up. Down. Up. Down.
"Always stay by my side," she whispered.
"Okay." He slowly twisted her engagement ring around and around
"I mean it." She kissed him softly.
"Forever." Kody tugged her in closer. "Everything will be okay now."
"You're sure?" Uncertainty shadowed his eyes.
"I promise. Nothing can hurt us now."

18

KODY

HEAVINESS STACKED ON KODY'S every muscle despite Raelyn's kisses all over his shoulder. Sitting on the couch together, Kody couldn't believe he was looking into Raelyn's eyes. Even though her face was pale, drawn, and worn, relief still washed over him like a tsunami. New Year's Eve was the last time he had seen her. A month of hell had put them worlds apart. He had expected to find her body blue and in the snow atop Ash Mountain the entire flight home. But everything about her was alive.

Maybe everything will be okay.

Kody set her on his lap and raised her tee. He looked down as the skin over her belly jutted out, maybe the baby's knee or elbow. "Babe, does that hurt?"

She didn't stop kissing every inch of his neck while quietly mumbling, "I'm fine. Amala's an active one."

Kody leaned back so he could take in every detail of her face. Unable to contain his grin, he asked. "What did you say?"

Her eyes widened to the size of saucers. "Oh, um, Amala..."

"I love it."

"Her name means hope."

"Hope," he whispered, "You picked a good one."

Her skin tasted like an apple with each kiss, and when he ran his hands through her silky hair, she leaned into his palm like a kitten being petted. The flavor of her lips was the same as always — cherry Chapstick, which gave him comfort in the familiarity. He wanted to ask what the paternity results had concluded, but it didn't really matter.

That baby girl is mine.

Footsteps creaked down the hall, and his sister's sarcastic voice rang clear. "I can't believe you just left me here, Rae. Not cool. Did you at least bring back some cake?" She stepped around the corner. "Holy spaghetti! Kody?" Cali dropped the backpack she was clutching and raced over. "You're here! How are you here?"

He forced a smile and sighed. "Dabbott."

"Remind me to buy her a cake. Are you hurt?"

Kody yawned and shook his head. "I don't even know."

Cali lifted his arm. "Can you see okay? Count to ten. Touch your nose. Does the air taste weird? Any pain here?"

He swatted her hands away. "I'm fine. I just need some rest. How are you?"

"Other than needing some sugar? I'm fine."

Kody nodded. "Can we have a minute alone, Cali?"

"Not excited to see me, bro?"

"I love you, Cali, but gimme a minute. Everything is ... it's a lot."

"Uh, okay, right. I'll go shower."

The couch groaned when he shifted to the side. Raelyn latched onto his body so tightly.

He kissed the engagement ring on her delicate finger. Her soft lips ravaged his cheeks and forehead like a famished tigress.

"Babe ... I need some time before we ..."

She tilted her head to the side.

He turned away, not willing to risk her read the shame covering his face. This was the house he had broken into to steal the marble box and leave the threat. He stared at the wooden doors that led to the study. That was the room that had started it all. William. Joanna. Liam. Zohaib. Her family.

My family.

Flowery wallpaper peeled off the walls, wooden beams stretched across the ceiling, and natural light pouring in through the lace curtains. On the kitchen wall, the daily calendar showed February 2, 2018. Her due date was less than a month away. Each thumb circled slowly on her temples. Raelyn purred under his caress, and he stiffened, then shook his head and moved out from under Raelyn's embrace.

"Kody?"

I'm a monster.

"Kody?" Raelyn cleared her throat. "Do you want to talk about anything?"

"No." He stood.

"Okay." She had tried to disguise her voice to sound strong, but it wavered. "Let me cook for you. That'll help."

"Thank you." Kody sighed and slid into a barstool as if standing for only a minute was too difficult. He could feel her assessing gaze as he studied the granite pattern in the countertop. Speckles of gold and greens swirled in a dizzying haze. In his mind's eye, he saw the boy's body who had hung himself in the trailer, which snapped into images of the guards' oozing blood, Pedro's face in death, the woman tied to Zohaib's bed. All the trauma blended until Kody pushed his palms hard into his forehead and inhaled deeply.

She turned the stove on. That metal click of the knob reminded him of the click of the trigger. He bolted upright, and the stool slammed to the ground with a loud crash.

"Kody?"

"I'm fine." He shook his head.

Raelyn's amber eyes widened, and she opened her mouth to speak. "Ko—"

"I'm fine!" The screaming volume wasn't intentional but slipped out anyway.

Raelyn's bottom lip quivered.

He backed away as anguish sandwiched his body from all sides. After looking at her stricken face again, his heart plummeted. "I'm sorry I yelled."

She rolled her lips in and nodded but focused all her attention on the kitchen pot.

"I need … I need to be alone for a minute." Kody trudged down the hall, his own voice ringing in his ears. He didn't want to scare Raelyn with his confusion, so he went inside a bedroom, silently closing the door behind him.

It was the master bedroom, full of her Grandma's knick-knacks and pictures of Raelyn as a child. Kody's shoulders sagged at the thought of having to admit to Raelyn what he had done to Eliza, capturing an innocent woman from a village, separating a mother and daughter.

Clanking sounds echoed from the kitchen, and the scent of scrambled eggs and toast wafted down the hall. Starving, Kody licked his lips, but he didn't deserve food or an easy life.

Eliza should never forgive me. Raelyn should never forgive me.

Kody fell onto the wrinkle-free bed and squeezed his eyes shut. He had to find a way to let go of Zohaib's manipulative hold on him and focus on the next task, what he planned with Eliza. But, it'd have to stay a secret. Raelyn shouldn't have to hear the vile level her fiancé had stooped to.

"Your food is ready." Raelyn's angelic voice rang down the hall.

Everything immediately snapped back into focus.

"Where are you, babe?"

"In here."

Kody followed her voice and pushed open the door to a room. Raelyn sat on the carpet with two plates and forks in hand. A crib was angled against the wall, stealing his breath away. Kody pointed, unable to get a word out.

"Grandma must've bought it." Raelyn exhaled deeply. "Um … are you okay?"

Kody gulped and approached. "I need time before I can process the last month." He could tell she wanted more. "Zohaib held me captive in a jungle and commanded me to do unthinkable things." A bird chirped outside the window, a reminder that life could maybe be good, safe, and solid.

Raelyn studied him intently.

Kody stared at the birds fluttering, then he said, "Zohaib has many more camps spread around the world."

"How many?"

"I don't know." He bit into the eggs.

Cali interrupted by walking in wearing a fresh set of clothes. "So, why do you think someone is following you, Rae?"

"What?"

"In the mountains, I kept seeing shadows and eyes peering back." Raelyn paused. "It was probably an animal."

"You don't believe that, or you wouldn't have mentioned it."

"Only Joanna knew I was out there. But she abandoned Liam and me for a pile of cash."

"What's Joanna gonna do with the money?" Cali asked.

"Her excuse was that she was gonna pay some investigator to find more evidence on Zohaib, but I don't believe anything she says anymore."

Kody sighed. "Zohaib believes that you're still in that cabin. We need to find somewhere safe for you and figure out a long-term plan."

"You mean, *we*, right? We can't split up again."

Eliza's face pushed its way to the front of his mind and the promise he had made her to assemble a team and fight Zohaib.

"I think I might know a place we could be safe." Raelyn bit her lip. "Phoenix's parents."

Kody's chest tightened. "The Peterson family? Why?"

"Phoenix's dad served. Maybe he has some ideas. And Ma, I mean Joanna, sent them money. She must have had a reason."

"But you said you don't trust Joanna," said Cali.

"I don't, but …" Raelyn hid her face behind the letter. "Don't make me say the other reason."

The pain of her words sliced through his soul. "So, the baby is Phoenix's?"

"I never got the results." She wouldn't look at him.

Kody stood and looked down at her on the floor. "Babe, I told you, it doesn't matter if she's black or white or has four toes or hiccups every other second. She's mine. Why can't you understand that?"

With effort, she stood and backed up against the window. "Everyone leaves me … eventually. There's no guarantees you will stay with me."

Kody crossed his arms. "I could say the same to you. No one can predict the future, but that doesn't mean we live in fear."

Her voice rose in frustration. "I can't risk it. If you left, there's no way I could raise a baby alone. I'd fail like Joanna failed me."

"What are you trying to say?"

She gulped and turned away, looking out at the melting snow. "I want to talk to Mrs. Peterson about adopting Amala."

It felt like a truck had hit him head-on. His breath was sucked out of his lungs. "You can't be serious? After everything I've done to keep you two safe? After all the sacrifices I've made … you'd give her up?"

Raelyn whirled around, and tears rushed down her red cheeks. "You think *I'm* not making sacrifices?"

"That's not what I said. We need to keep her safe and do what's best for Amala."

"I agree." Her voice shook with each word. "And what's best is giving her to someone who knows how to raise a child."

Kody outreached his hands. "We can figure out how to raise her together."

"I don't know what I'm doing." Raelyn let her arms drop to her side as if they each weighed a ton. She shrunk before him. "I'll disappoint her and make horrible choices." It sounded like a sob ripped out her throat. "I love you both too much to risk hurting either of you. So, I choose you. If it's just you and me, we can last, and you won't have any reason to want to leave."

He wiped the wet streaks plastered onto her face and held her close, cradling Raelyn into his chest. "We will raise her together, as a family."

With all her heart, she wanted him to be right. "What if I mess up?"

"Every parent makes mistakes." Kody gazed at Raelyn. "It's okay to be scared, babe, but I'm in this forever."

Raelyn nodded and eased her head onto his chest, letting out an epic sigh. "I already love her so much." Her voice steadied. "But, I need to stop being so scared. You're back now. Maybe I can do this if you're completely sure.

"I'm sure."

"Okay." She sniffed. "I still want to visit Mrs. Peterson, though. Maybe she and Mr. Peterson can hide us."

Kody paused.

Kody was sure that if he could find a list of Zohaib's soldiers loyal to him here in the States, he could convince them to revolt. But they weren't living in the warehouse, or Liam would've been caught when he had investigated alone. So where were they?

Raelyn crossed her arms and dabbed the corner of her eye. "You'll come with me, right?"

He didn't remember what she was talking about. "What?"

"You'll come to the Peterson's with me, right?"

It'll delay my promise.

"Of course, babe."

He glanced out the window so she wouldn't see his expression. In the distance, a car was parked on the side of the country road with a hooded figure sitting in the front seat. Watching. Kody gulped and reached behind Raelyn to close the blinds.

19

RAELYN

In the Jeep, Cali stretched, knocking her knees against the back of Raelyn's seat. "Oh, sorry, Pumpkin. Are we there yet?"

"Guess I'll need to get used to annoying, child-like questions, huh?" Kody snapped.

Cali kicked the driver's seat purposefully. "Shut up, ass-face."

Raelyn studied him, but his aviator sunglasses blocked her out. She was unable to determine why he was so short with his sister. She repositioned the seat, fighting the urge to trail her fingertip over his strong jawline and meld their lips together.

Can't believe he's back. Everything will be fine now.

The snow seemed to be melting the further they drove until only slush was left in the Peterson's neighborhood. They parked in front of a two-story brick house near a large puddle. Kody's jeep almost skimmed the side of a brick mailbox with a large 'P' engraved in the side. A large bulldozer sat idle between the house and the remains of a shed, where lumber rose in a tidy stack. Mounds of dirt drew Raelyn's eye. They dotted the otherwise immaculate yard randomly, each with a deep trench nearby at least seven feet across.

"They must be renovating," said Cali.

Raelyn covered the deposit box with her winter coat, then hopped out. The right moment hadn't come up yet to tell Kody about the money she had found. It had to be over twenty-thousand dollars. She gripped the pocket watch around her neck, still stuck at the same time as when he stopped the clock on New Year's Eve.

"Let me fix that for you." On the hood of his Jeep, Kody laid the pocket watch down and fiddled with the back clasp.

"Actually, my fingers are too big. Can you pinch this piece?"

Raelyn mocked his deep voice. "Okay, Mr. Macho, let me fix that for you."

Kody smiled as the pocket watch came undone. "What's this part for?" He pulled out a small metallic-looking chip.

"I don't know."

"That's suspicious. I'll look into it later." He tucked it in his pocket. After restarting the clock, he draped the golden chain over her neck, then smiled. "Is there anything of mine that you *aren't* wearing?"

She glanced down at his oversized Cubs hoodie. "Be nice. It smells like you."

Cali came beside her, entwining their fingers together. "You sure you want to do this?"

"Yeah, Joanna must have sent the Petersons Pa's journal for a reason."

Her gaze darted around the yard, past the white picket fence to the tree line in the backyard. Kody pointed silently to tiny black cameras tucked into over a dozen locations around the perimeter of the house.

"It could be a trap," he said.

"I trusted Phoenix."

"You don't know his parents, though."

"Let's go." Raelyn marched forward to the easy access up the long driveway, but Cali playfully jumped over one trench, then lowered herself into another and climbed back out with a big smile on her face.

"A minefield of obstacles!" Cali hooted as she brushed off her dirty clothes.

Dozens of bird feeders decorated the lawn. It was only February, but spring would bring the pollen and new life before she knew it. Amala kicked wildly inside.

Is she nervous too?

"We got this, baby girl."

Raelyn knocked her knuckles on the bright red door. *Thunk. Thunk. Thunk.*

A middle-aged woman with long blond hair answered, she had Phoenix's thin nose and piercing eyes.

Raelyn smiled. "Mrs. Peterson?"

"Yes?" She opened the door fully without fear or care.

"I'm Raelyn Bell. I think my mother sent you a letter," she cleared her throat. "And … some money."

Mrs. Peterson's eyes widened. "Oh! It's you. Yes, come in."

"This is my fiancé, Kody, and his sister, Cali."

Kody stuck out his hand. "Specialist Walsh, ma'am."

"Walsh? I've heard that name before."

"Your son and I were on the same team for a while."

She smiled with a flicker of sadness in her eyes as she shook his hand.

As the sun peeked out from the clouds, natural light flooded the open living room that led to the kitchen. The scent of ham in the oven made Raelyn's mouth water and her stomach rumble. As Mrs. Peterson led them to the kitchen, photographs of every type of bird she had ever imagined were framed on the walls, woodpeckers, finches, cardinals, wrens, bluebirds, robins, sparrows displayed in all their beauty. Raelyn couldn't help but stare at the professional Canon cameras on Mrs. Peterson's lace tablecloth that hung low, meeting the fresh vacuumed lines running parallel to each other with tiny paw prints heading to the couch.

Mrs. Peterson patted a chair. "Let's get y'all warm." She hustled to the thermostat and pushed the red button up four times. Her straight hair swooshed over her shoulders as she turned around.

"Oh, it's okay. I'm actually always hot these days." Raelyn peeled off the hoodie and held it at her side.

Mrs. Peterson stopped short when she saw Raelyn's belly. "Oh, goodness, dear! Well, look at you." Her cheeks flushed as her gaze flickered to Kody's, and she watched Mrs. Peterson and Kody nod to each other in a silent exchange.

Raelyn gulped.

Do I tell her now?

Her whole body felt jittery as she took a small step forward.

"Mrs. Peterson—" Raelyn started.

"Call me Haydee." Faint lines fanned her face when she smiled, and perfect teeth showed the evidence of professional dentistry work at its finest. "Would you like some water?"

I'll have to pee every two minutes.

"No, thank you."

Haydee Peterson turned off the oven and pulled out the ham before clasping her hands together behind her back. "Well, your mother's letter was definitely interesting. I wasn't quite sure what to make of it."

"Yeah, as long as we have the great and powerful Joanna on our side, nothing can go wrong." Cali rolled her eyes.

"Cali, be polite!" Raelyn patted the purse where the journal lay inside. "Thank you for mailing my Pa's journal."

The ceiling creaked, and footsteps thumped softly.

Kody looked up. "Is someone else here?"

"Yes, my husband, David. He's usually at work by now."

Raelyn cleared her throat. "Kody, Cali, can I talk with her alone for a minute?"

Kody nodded and led Cali around the corner. The grandfather clock ticked in slow motion next to a picture of Phoenix with his arm looped around some friends. Her fingertip covered Phoenix's striking face and landed on a brunette next to him, with a smile that matched his. She tilted her head, not quite able to place the familiarity. It must've been taken a couple years ago.

"That woman … I think I've met her."

"That's Phoenix's cousin, Marlee Jane. She's a Navy SEAL."

Raelyn leaned closer to investigate. "I thought there were no female SEALs."

"None that you're told about, dear."

"I wonder why she told me to come here," Raelyn whispered to herself, then was about to ask Haydee the dozens of questions in her mind when a rattling sound started her. Haydee was digging through a drawer in the kitchen and pulled out a large knife. She sliced thin strips of the ham, letting the meat fall into piles, and nodded to a chair.

"I need to carve the ham while it's hot."

Plates banged together as Haydee brought over a plate full of ham. Raelyn ripped off small pieces, slipped a piece onto her tongue, and savored the meat.

Haydee sipped from a mug on the counter, waiting. "So, how can I help you?"

"Um, so to be completely honest, a man who sells women is trying to find me."

"What?" Haydee clutched her heart. "That is not what I expected, but I guess I've heard crazier stories."

"It's not a story. I think Joanna wants your husband to keep me safe given his military background. I bet the money is to convince y'all to agree or something."

Haydee glanced at the stairway. "I'd rather not get my husband involved. He has a stressful job." She tapped her fingernails on the table. "I could help you find someone more qualified than me. I don't think I'm right for what you need."

How do I tell her?

A cat uncurled from the heating vent on the floor and stretched two black paws out. It circled around Raelyn's feet, purring until she picked it up.

Kody emerged from the corner with wide eyes, his heavy boots clunking onto the kitchen tile. "We need to leave. Now."

The cat dug its claws into her forearms and darted away.

Cali ran in and pointed to a picture. "Is that picture of your husband?"

Haydee craned her neck. "Yeah, that's David. Why?"

Cali gasped.

Kody held out his hand to Raelyn, his lips in a tight line. "Babe, please. We need to leave."

"Hold on, Kody. Wait a second."

It's now or never.

Raelyn locked eyes with Haydee. "I wasn't a stranger to your son." Her voice broke a little as she rushed out the words.

"I know. He told me about his feelings for you and ..."

Raelyn naturally looked down to her belly. Haydee studied Raelyn, then a spark of realization ignited. She dropped her mug to the counter, shattering it to pieces, and backed up, knocking a stool over to the floor.

Haydee pointed to Raelyn's stomach. "Is that baby—?" Something had shifted in her face, but it was too difficult to read her expression without knowing the woman well enough. Shock? Hope?

She stared at Haydee. "There's a possibility that I'm carrying your grandchild."

Haydee's thin fingers trembled as she covered her mouth.

"This may be Phoenix's child."

Kody stood solid as a sculpture next to her.

Haydee backed away until she hit the counter.

Tears pooled, but Raelyn held them back. "I … I'm sorry. We shouldn't have disrupted you. We'll go."

Kody tensed and tried to lead her toward the door.

"No!" Haydee held out one hand. "Please stay!" The desperation in her voice shattered Raelyn's heart to pieces, mirroring the cracked mug at her feet. Haydee dashed across the kitchen.

Raelyn took a deep breath and ran her thumb over Kody's clenched fist. When he finally glanced over, his jaw was set hard, and his eyes blazed with the fire of protectiveness she was used to, but there was also a glint of something else in his look.

Haydee inched forward. "So, you're telling me … that there's a chance my *only* child's baby is about to enter into this world. And a man is threatening to hurt you?"

"That man is actually my biological father, Amala's grandfather."

"What?" Haydee held out her hands. "Oh, hun. Come here."

Raelyn rushed into her arms, allowing this motherly presence to completely consume her.

I need a mom like this.

"Everything will be okay. I'll help you," Haydee said.

"Thank you." She wiped away her tears. "I can't promise that she's Phoenix's though."

"A girl?" Haydee hugged her even tighter until Raelyn wiggled free.

"Yes, Amala."

Haydee untangled a small knot in Raelyn's hair as if she'd been doing it for eighteen years. A reel of memories sparked comforting ease when she recalled Ma teaching her how to measure flour for baking cookies, how to tie her shoes and twist a braid through her hair.

We had good times once.

"We'll figure it out. When's your next doctor's appointment?" Haydee asked.

"I haven't had the best prenatal care. I've been in hiding and—"

Kody slowly brushed his fingertips against her shoulder. "Raelyn, we need to leave now." She knew how patient he was trying to be by the tone of his voice. He reached down for Raelyn's hand and tugged her toward the door.

"One more second."

"No way, I'm out of here!" Cali ran out to the front yard, carelessly leaving the door wide open on the way.

What's going on with them?

Haydee shook her head. "Wait, can you tell me something about your relationship with my Phoenix? Anything at all?"

Raelyn's heart raced as she remembered the sensual night with him in the desert cave. Her hands turned clammy, and she was grateful Kody wasn't at an angle to see her flushed face. "Phoenix saved my life a few times. Once, we were hanging from a bridge over a ravine, and he pulled me up."

Out of the corner of her eye, Raelyn watched Kody shift his weight on his feet. "I'm gonna check on Cali," he said as he marched out the front door.

"I'm sorry. This hasn't been the easiest time for us."

"Did Kody know about you and Phoenix?"

Raelyn nodded. It felt like needles were pricking her temple, forming a headache. "Kody believes Amala is his."

"You don't?"

"I want to, but …" Raelyn could feel her lip tremble. "I don't know, and either way, I'll mess everything all up."

Haydee looked so much like Phoenix when she smiled knowingly. “My boy would only love someone strong. Don’t let fear control you.”

“Phoenix didn’t love me.”

Haydee placed her hand on Raelyn’s. “Of course he did. That’s how my boy was.” After they sat in silence for a bit, Haydee started picking up the mug’s broken pieces.

Heavy footsteps clonked down the stairs. “Haydee? Why is there a Black superhero-looking man standing at attention on our front porch?” A husky voice filled with humor followed the creaks of his steps.

“Come in here, David.” Her voice teased. “We have guests.”

A bald man appeared around the corner, dressed in army fatigues. David’s eyes widened, and his razor-sharp glare immediately scanned the backyard through the windows. “Hide her in the bunker with you! Don’t come out until you see my face!”

“What?” Haydee tilted her head. “What are you talking about?”

David glanced around. “Is *he* here?”

Raelyn’s heart pounded, but words wouldn’t come out.

“Answer me! Is *he* here?” David’s husky voice projected.

Haydee grabbed David’s elbow. “No, David, listen. She *knew* our Phoenix.”

David studied his wife’s eyes for only a moment before glancing at Raelyn’s belly. He pushed against the back of a chair abruptly. The sudden screech of the wooden legs was like nails on a chalkboard. His chest rose and fell fast, but otherwise, he was frozen in place.

Raelyn glanced at the picture of Phoenix on the wall again and didn’t risk speaking.

David exhaled slowly, and to Raelyn’s surprise, a glitter of a tear rolled from the corner of the giant’s eye. “You’re telling me … that you’re carrying my boy’s …” He choked on his words. “My son’s little one?”

Despite her wobbly knees, Raelyn stood taller. “Or she may be Kody’s.”

Before Raelyn could shake her head, the front door flung open. “You!” When Kody met David’s eyes, his nostrils flared wide. “Raelyn! Let’s go!” he roared.

“Why are you here?” David’s voice weakened.

Haydee glanced between Raelyn and her husband, a man even taller than Kody. "What's going on?"

With the speed of a cheetah, Kody lunged across the room and quickly shielded her with his fighting stance. Her back pressed against the cold glass door.

"What are you doing?" Raelyn managed to squeak out.

A metal shimmer caught her eye and guided her to a short blade in Kody's hand.

"Why are *you* in my home?" David backed up. "How do you know Jawhara's daughter?"

"You know my mother?" Raelyn's heart skipped a beat as she moved around Kody.

"She saved my life," David admitted and ran his hand over his shiny head.

"And Kody saved mine. He's my fiancé."

"Okay, okay." David's shoulders loosened. "Put your knife away, soldier."

Raelyn rubbed tiny circles on Kody's forearm until he folded his blade and straightened tall. The two men stared each other down like it was a poker game. Their intense reactions didn't make any sense. Did they know each other from the army? David leaned back against the kitchen counter and folded his arms, blowing out a long sigh.

"Kody, how do you know Phoenix's dad?"

"He's responsible for almost killing Cali a few years ago."

She tucked her belly behind Kody's dominating stance.

Haydee finally spoke up. "David, what is he talking about?"

"Remember the car crash a few years ago?" David asked. "Walsh is the name of the girl who pressed charges."

Haydee clapped her hand over her mouth together.

"I'm so confused," Raelyn whispered.

The veins in Kody's neck seemed to almost pop as he pointed straight at David, "… this man kidnapped Cali in the middle of the night from a bus station, threatened her, and told her to deliver a suitcase to some stranger."

"That's not what you told me!" Haydee's jaw dropped.

David buried his forehead in one hand. "Listen, it all was a mistake. I owed Jawhara my life. She sent me a random message asking for a favor to deliver a suitcase to someone for her. But that day, my best friend had died. I was in a bad place and wasn't thinking straight. I went about it all wrong. I was drunk and high."

Haydee gasped. "David! That's not like you."

He hung his head. "I swear, I never meant to hurt your sister, Walsh."

"You harassed her." The words were barely audible from Kody's lips.

How have I never heard about this?

David glanced at Haydee's stricken face. "I don't remember doing that. I'm sorry. I know it's not an excuse. It was the worst day of my life. My best friend ..."

Kody stepped forward. "I know what it's like to lose someone!" He boomed. "But I don't take advantage of teenage girls!"

Raelyn waited, her mouth frozen open. The visit was going south quick, so she needed the answers to her questions before Kody dragged her away. "How did Joanna save your life? How did you even recognize me?" All the air was sucked out of her lungs. "When was this?"

"Two, maybe three years ago," Kody mumbled.

"Let's all sit down." Haydee took control of the room, but Kody didn't move an inch.

"Please, start from the beginning." Raelyn slid into a chair across from Haydee and gently kicked out a chair with her boot for Kody, who stayed by Raelyn's side. She continued. "Why do you owe Joanna?"

David sighed. "A few years ago, I was stationed in Tahil. There was a cunning woman with long brown hair discretely distributing books to girls in the marketplace. She thought I didn't notice. After approaching her, I decided she was harmless, but her attempts at trying to be so secretive had me suspicious."

"That was my mother?"

"I believe so." He swallowed hard. "I didn't think I'd see her again, but a few weeks later, she was out in the market passing out books again. After a few months, she finally told me her name was Jawhara but wouldn't tell me anything else. Her eyes always darted around as if being hunted. I should've known that something wasn't right."

"The next time I saw her, she slipped something in my pocket without a word. When I got back to my barracks, I studied the picture she had given me—a teen girl with similar long brown hair down to her waist and honey eyes."

"Me." Raelyn gasped. "She gave you a picture of me."

David nodded. "Yeah, it had your name on it too, but I didn't know what she wanted. On the back, she had written a warning of an ambush at our fort at 2300 hours. I didn't know if I could trust her, but I played it safe and prepared my team. She was right. A force attacked that night, and a soldier died, but I saved the others because of her."

Haydee took his hand.

"I memorized that girl's … your features … vowing to pay back Jawhara for her warning. After that day, I never saw her again." He dropped his chin. "I should've known she needed help."

Kody cleared his throat and shifted the weight of his feet. "Then how does the briefcase play into it?"

"Much later, I received an email from her that said, 'Z is coming. Be on guard. He can't know about Raelyn,' then it showed an address in Ash Mountain to deliver the briefcase to."

"What was inside?" Raelyn rushed out her question.

"I don't know."

Raelyn inched forward. "Did you deliver it?"

"Yeah, it was a challenging night, but … yes, eventually."

Haydee bit her lip. "David, this doesn't sound like you. Anything could've been in there. A bomb, drugs …"

"I was hammered and devastated. A man can make mistakes."

She tried to return home. Ma didn't give up.

"So, that's my story. Like I said, I'm sorry."

Kody stepped forward. "Raelyn needs protection. She came here for your help. But I see we wasted our time." He gripped Raelyn's hand and leaned into her ear. "We need to find somewhere else."

"Haydee, maybe you can hide Raelyn while Walsh helps me hunt for a man my team is trying to locate."

"That man wouldn't be Zohaib, would it?" Raelyn asked.

"Yes." David cocked his head. "How could you possibly know that?"

Before she could answer, Kody shook his head. "I'm not going anywhere with you."

"Listen, it'll work." David continued, "This Zohaib commander is creating all kinds of shitstorms for our troops, and I found some intel on him with a list of his possible locations. If he's not there, we can take out his remaining affiliates. Haydee could help you raise the baby while Walsh goes undercover."

The world stopped turning for a moment. David was offering exactly what she had come here to ask for—Haydee could give Amala a better and safer life—someone who knew what they were doing. But, hearing the words from someone else turned the option into a reality. His proposition sliced like a dagger to the heart.

There was no way in hell she could give Amala up for adoption. Not to them or anyone. Just the sound of it sounded insane. It didn't matter how many mistakes she'd make, Amala was her child, and she'd never let her go.

"No. Kody and I are raising her. He's no longer in the army to do that work, and he is this baby's father."

David rubbed his beard. "But, you said that, Phoenix ..."

"Amala may look like Phoenix, and your son will always be important to me, but Kody is this baby's father, and nothing will change that." She laced her fingers between his and felt a tiny squeeze of comfort in return.

Then there was a hard knock at the front door.

"Crap! Cali, where is Cali?"

20

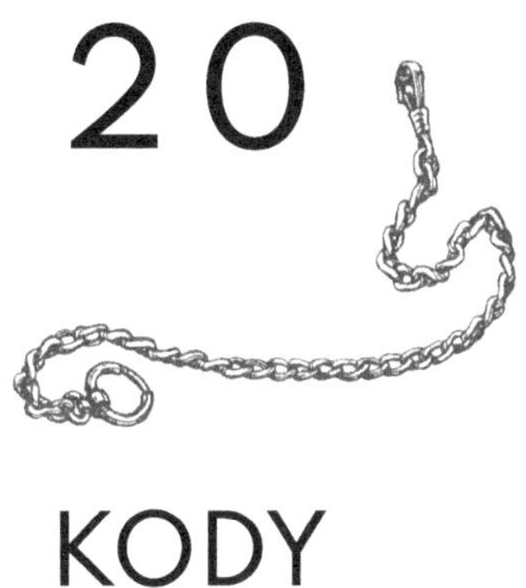

KODY

CALI RUSHED INSIDE. "A car just flew up your driveway!"

Kody scooped his arm around Raelyn's back and pulled on Cali's shirt simultaneously, wrapping them both into his chest. "Where can we hide?"

"We have a spare room upstairs," said Haydee.

"What about that bunker?" The last place he wanted to be was a dark, claustrophobic area that reminded him of the box Zohaib had caged him in for so many weeks, but he'd do anything to keep them safe.

"The bunker is only for emergencies."

They scaled the stairs as David closed the shades against the morning sun.

His gut tightened. "Listen, everything with Raelyn's safety is serious. Understand?"

"It's probably our neighbors." She led them through a hallway to a closed door at the end of the hall. "Lock the door on the other side, just in case."

Kody put one finger to his lips and glanced around inside a bedroom— a door led to a bathroom. Only one exit, the second story window. No trees or branches to help them down. Raelyn instinctively moved toward the closet and wedged herself inside, hidden from view.

Cali crouched behind the side of the bed, next to a nightstand. Kody's heart hammered. Opening the dresser drawers, he dug around for any weapons. Instead, he found a jewelry box. He popped it open and stared at a small engagement ring.

Who was this for?

For a moment, he could hear Phoenix's witty voice in his head, teasing, *I loved her red lingerie, big guy.*

Shaking his head, Kody kept rummaging around. He found a medal with David Peterson's name on it with a bomb dismantling certificate underneath. No weapons.

Kody pressed his ear against the locked door. A male voice laughed downstairs, pitched higher than David's. Haydee's cheerful hum floated from the hall.

They're not worried.

He sank to the floor, resting his back against the door. The room held a dresser, queen-sized bed, and small desk. This was Phoenix's room. Images of Raelyn under Phoenix in the cave were replaced by visions of Phoenix rolling over Raelyn on the bed to his right. A mixture of regret, jealousy, and grief struck him from all angles. He could've been the one who fell off 'The Spiral' instead of his teammate.

Kody shook his head. But it didn't help to erase the reel of images burned inside of his eyelids.

Raelyn's amber eyes peeked through the crack of the door. "Can I come out?"

"For now." He sighed, letting the strain from the previous conversation drain out from his body.

Raelyn crawled to him and sat in his lap. A strong wind whipped the window, and she jumped a bit. She curled into his chest, instantly slowing his heart rate, like his personal prescription to keep him sane and level-headed.

Cali groaned like a wounded animal. “This can’t be happening. How did Phoenix’s dad end up being that asshole?”

Raelyn held her hand. “What do you need?”

“To erase that night, sophomore year.”

“I’m sorry, Cali. We should’ve left earlier.”

“Yeah, but we’re stuck here now, or I could drop out the window and try my luck.”

Raelyn looked up through her long lashes. When they locked eyes, the love for her consumed every ounce of his body.

“We’re not separating again. None of us. All three will live together for eternity and never leave my sight.”

He couldn’t help but chuckle. “Yes, ma’am.”

“It’s not funny.”

“I know. You’re just so …”

Loveable. Stubborn. Perfect. Adorable. Sweet.

“Right.” Raelyn scrunched her nose. “That’s what you were gonna say. I’m so right.”

Cali rolled her eyes. “You guys are so gross. Get a room.” She threw one of Phoenix’s old shoes at Kody’s head, which he blocked effortlessly.

Kody wrapped Raelyn in his arms tighter as he asked, “Did you mean what you said downstairs?” A sudden constriction gripped his throat as he waited.

She bit her nail, and he noticed the raw skin around the edges gnawed away. “Yes, you’re Amala’s Daddy. We can do this.”

Kody lifted her chin. “I need you to promise me something.”

“Only if you keep this scruff.”

His lips twitched. “I’m serious.” A breath trapped itself in his lungs. “If something happens to me…”

“Kody, don’t say …”

“Listen, if something happens to me, I want you to promise you’ll still raise her. Don’t give Amala up to anyone.” His chest tightened and twisted so intensely he was afraid it’d combust. “Please, babe. Please. She needs you.”

“I need you.” She laid her head back on his chest.

Footsteps approached from the hallway, and Raelyn waddled to the other side of the bed, ducking low. Kody reached for the blade in his pocket again, the cold metal familiar on his skin. A soft knock.

"You three okay?" Haydee—someone who could be a mother figure to Raelyn.

"Yes. Everything okay out there?" Kody whispered.

"Yes. Can I come in?"

He opened the door.

In hand, Haydee carried toothbrushes, snacks, towels, extra clothes, and a gun. "It was only a neighbor asking about our yard renovation."

"Did David go to work?"

"Yes, he doesn't want to attract any unwanted attention. We'll figure out a plan when he's back from work this evening. We agreed that you can stay as long as you need."

Cali crossed her arms. "I don't want to stay."

Haydee made the same face Phoenix did when contemplating a situation then outstretched her arms. "I'm so sorry for what my husband did. It's not like him, but I shouldn't excuse his behavior."

Cali tilted her head. "I'll stay if he sleeps at his office while we're here."

"Yes, of course." Haydee rubbed her temples. "It's just so out of character that he did something to make you that uncomfortable."

Kody glanced at Cali. "Anything else you need?"

Cali wrung her hands. "Do you have a guest room?"

"Yes."

"Does it have a lock?"

"Yes, dear. You'll be safe."

"Okay, I'll be good." She pushed her tongue into her cheek, signifying her fear.

I shouldn't make her stay here.

"How close is the nearest hotel?" Kody asked.

"Please, stay here, at least for tonight." Haydee pleaded.

Cali nodded. "I'll be fine." She took a toothbrush and disappeared into the hall.

Haydee folded her arms and scanned Raelyn's form again, making every protective bone in his body stand to attention. "Kody, if you were on the same team as Phoenix … do you have any stories about him?"

Kody raised his chin. "Your son was a hero, ma'am. He risked everything to keep Raelyn …" A pressure slammed on his chest. "He was extremely brave and made the ultimate sacrifice. I wish I could thank him."

Haydee wiped a tear. "And a smart-ass. He always said what was on his mind."

Raelyn glanced at her tattoo. Kody could tell she was asking him for permission, but it wasn't his to give.

"Phoenix convinced me to get this." She showed Haydee her rose tattoo. "He got a bigger one, wanting to match."

Haydee ran her fingertips over Raelyn's wrist, then took Raelyn's hand. They stared at each other for far too long, communicating something Kody didn't necessarily want to understand.

He shuffled his feet and cleared his throat. "Can I keep one of those tonight?"

She handed a gun over. In his hand, the gun felt all wrong—thirty pounds of lead. Everything felt different since he had returned from the jungle.

Don't want a gun around my baby.

"It may be best for y'all to stay up here all day until we figure out the risk. David is going to try and gain some intel on where Zohaib is. I'll bring up a meal in a few hours. Keep the curtains closed."

"Thank you." When he turned around, Raelyn was directly behind him, rising on her tiptoes. The warmth of her body immediately centered his racing mind.

She pulled his neck down. "Kiss me."

"Here?" He glanced at Phoenix's trophies. "Now?"

"You always make me feel better." She brushed his lips over hers. Soft. Eager.

But he pulled away, saying, "I'm really tired. Let's rest."

Her lips trailed down his neck, sending shivers up his spine. "You're … different."

Backing up, he caught the confusion in her face.

"Are you okay, Kody?"

"I need some time," he admitted.

"For what? You can tell me, I'm here for you."

The moment slipped through his grasp. He tried to keep his voice calm as he changed the subject. "So, I thought we agreed not to tell Phoenix's mom until we knew who the father is."

"That's the first time you called him Phoenix."

"Well, if you're so sure it's his, I better get used to talking about him more."

"Amala isn't an 'it.'" A harshness in her voice sliced the air.

She didn't even give me a chance to help decide on a name.

"We need to make decisions together." He moved further away.

She shook her head. "We're both on edge. I'm gonna go shower … and pee … she's always pushing on my bladder."

Glad to avoid the tense conversation, Kody grunted and dropped to the floor for pushups. Like always, exercise helped. The soft carpet tickled his fingertips as he pushed up and down. His chest brushed against the material over and over, and his shoulders burned after he hit fifty repetitions. Jumping jacks shook Phoenix's trophies. Lunges across the room. Punches soared in the air as Kody faced the mirror.

Finally, he laid flat on his back and spread his arms out wide, stretching his sore muscles. Tiny chips in the paint hung from the popcorn ceiling, and little holes speckled the corner. Kody closed one eye and aimed a pretend dart between two fingers, pinging it in the direction of the corner.

Yup. Darts.

Phoenix had sacrificed himself for Raelyn. If Peterson blood ran through Amala's veins, the least Kody could do was be cordial with her relatives. And as much as he wanted to stay in hiding with Raelyn, he had to accept David's offer. That way, he could assemble a team like he promised Eliza and eliminate the threats. Otherwise, Raelyn would always live in fear. If Phoenix could pay the ultimate price to keep Raelyn alive, maybe that was his destiny too. He closed his eyes and absorbed the sound of Raelyn in the shower. But the scent of blood and the image of broken bodies haunted him.

I'll keep my promise to Eliza.

21

RAELYN

RAELYN TRIED TO SHAKE Kody awake again, feeling an ounce of comfort in just touching him. Moonlight glinted in the window, shining on a stack of books on the desk.

"Eliza," Kody whispered while thrashing under the sheets.

Who's Eliza?

"Kody! It's a dream." She had to punch his shoulder to wake him.

He bolted upright, sweat drenched the linen under his back. Tears spilled, making small drops in the blankets. Panting, he scanned the dark room, full of Phoenix's trophies, then buried his head in his hands.

Raelyn curled into him, wrapping both arms around one bicep. "Ssh, it's okay."

His deep brown eyes met hers, completely defeated. "Did I hurt you?"

Hurt me? What's wrong with him?

"I'm fine." She caressed his chest, circling his skin with her fingertips. "It's okay. I'm here."

He flopped backward, flat against the pillows.

Raelyn nuzzled into the crook of his arm, using his muscles as a headrest. "Do you want to talk about it?"

Kody covered his face with one hand. "Zohaib is … he's a monster." His whole body shuddered, so she curled in even tighter, protecting his heart in the only way she knew how. His throaty voice was full of pain and regret. "Men have died under his hand. So many. And families torn apart. Villages ripped to shreds."

Goosebumps formed on her arms. "We can defeat him."

"What if he has already won? Some things we can't undo. The dead won't return. People won't reunite. And the women that he …"

The feeling of a spider crawling over her spine didn't cease when she pulled the covers closer, shielding them from whatever he was about to admit.

"I know he's terrible, but I don't need you to save the world. I need you by my side."

The bedroom door flew open and slammed against the wall. Kody's eyes looked wild as he sat up and swiped open the dresser drawer within reach. A red cloak flapped in Raelyn's peripheral as she rolled herself off the bed.

"Don't come any closer!" Kody's voice boomed.

Raelyn dipped her head. The shoes on the other side of the bed moved closer.

"Get out!" Kody yelled.

"No. I'm here to help," Claimed the voice that had caused both Raelyn's dreams and nightmares. "Zohaib's men are on the way to take you both!"

Raelyn popped her head up. "Joanna?"

"Haydee, let me in." Joanna raced to Raelyn's side and grabbed her hands. "Raelyn, you have to believe me. Hurry, you don't have time."

Raelyn dropped her hands from Joanna's. "How could he know where I am?"

"He made me put a tracker in your pocket watch. The signal on it activated a few hours ago and sent an updated location to him."

Kody dug in his pocket where a small rectangle piece sat, and he squeezed it tight in his palm. "Damn it, Joanna!"

A sharp pain squeezed tight in Raelyn's stomach. She hunched over and gripped the side of the bed. Focusing on her breathing, Raelyn gritted her teeth until the cramp passed. She tried to focus on the loud debate in front of her. Neither had noticed the contraction.

Raelyn was still partially bent over as her voice rose. "How could you have put a tracker on me? Do you *want* me dead?"

"It was the only way to protect you. If Zohaib knew where you were at all times, he didn't feel threatened."

Raelyn shook her head. "That doesn't make sense, and we have no reason to trust you."

"We don't have time for this!"

"You could be setting Kody up for another trap!" Raelyn yelled.

"I'm not. Please! You have to leave!"

Raelyn's entire body boiled with rage. "Since when do you even care?"

Joanna dropped to her knees and grabbed the bottom of Raelyn's shirt, begging. "You're my baby girl. I always care. I'm sorry. I've messed up so many times. Forgive me!"

"No."

"Okay, then just hide. Please."

Raelyn's heart jackhammered.

She met Kody's eyes, and he pleaded the same.

"Okay, we'll hide," Raelyn said quietly.

Kody took Joanna by both shoulders. "How much time do we have?"

"A few minutes."

Kody's eyes grew twice their size. "Raelyn, grab our packs."

Her bladder wouldn't hold out during whatever escape plan he was planning, so she ran to the bathroom. Raelyn's heart pounded as she stared into the mirror from the toilet. Zohaib's amber eyes stared back at her and Joanna's eyebrows, facial shapes, and lips, all a sign that she would corrupt her daughter the same way they had demolished her.

"I've got Cali, come on." Kody's voice snapped her back to focus.

Raelyn joined them, and Kody led them down the stairs. She gripped the railing tightly as her weight tipped her forward.

“This way.” Moving items under the bottom shelf of the pantry, Haydee lifted a lever, and a hole led to under the house. “Hurry! Go!” Right as she said it, three mice sped out from the hole and skidded through her kitchen.

Raelyn descended the ladder into darkness, and Cali followed silently.

“There are supplies down there.” Haydee pointed. “I will let you know when it’s safe.”

Haydee leaned down and placed a little baggie in her hand. She whispered in Raelyn’s ear. “This is a fast-acting serum that temporarily paralyzes the victim, so you’ll have time to run. They can still see, hear, and feel things, but they won’t be able to move. Stab the syringe in someone’s arm if anyone tries to hurt you.”

Raelyn hid the baggie behind her back, feeling the shape with her hands—two syringes.

I couldn’t paralyze someone.

Kody looked at Haydee. “Is David here?”

She shook her head. “He’s at work.”

He glanced down at Raelyn. “I can’t leave Mrs. Peterson unprotected. I’m sorry.” His face held so much agony as he commanded, “Don’t come out.”

She latched onto Kody’s eyes before Haydee closed the door. Complete darkness enveloped them.

22

KODY

STANDING ABOVE THE BUNKER'S secret door, Kody's heart rammed against his chest. He knew he should join them, but fear took control for the first time in his life. There was no chance he'd go back into a small, enclosed cage. Not after the box Zohaib had trapped him in for weeks. He'd rather face hostiles than that agonizing darkness.

"Is there an access to the bunker somewhere in the yard?" he asked Mrs. Peterson.

"Yes. If they need a way out, they'll find it."

"Which means someone else could get in." His heart raced, hoping he made the right choice.

Haydee patted his shoulder. "They won't find it."

"Do you have more weapons?"

Mrs. Peterson was already dragging a stool into the pantry. Climbing, she reached up and pulled a handle. A trapdoor on the ceiling dropped down, hanging on hinges while she lowered a shelf full of guns and knives. Before it completely steadied, Joanna jumped up and grabbed the largest weapon, checking for ammo. She sprinted out the door and yelled behind her. "I'll be on lookout out front."

So much for a plan.

Kody picked up a Glock and held it by his side. Adrenaline coursed through his veins, disguising the fear threatening to explode inside his chest.

He turned to Mrs. Peterson. "Do you know how to shoot?"

But before he could finish asking, Mrs. Peterson racked a round.

"Okay, then." Kody gritted his teeth. "They're going to come in with force."

"Did Raelyn's mother lead them here?" she asked.

"Maybe … I'm not sure." Kody peeked around the corner.

Haydee blocked him from leaving. "The henchmen may not know you're here, so stay in the back dining room and listen in."

"These guys might take you. Selling women is their thing."

"Don't underestimate me."

He gritted his teeth. "Killing someone isn't that easy."

Mrs. Peterson nodded. "Self-defense. I've done it before."

Kody hustled past a glass door leading to the backyard and entered the dining room. Exits: two windows. Crystal-lined shelves and glass frames could be broken into sharp pieces. Four chairs that he could slam over the enemy's head.

Kody flipped over the dining room table, sending the white lace tablecloth to the hardwood. He hunkered low behind it, putting his weight on the balls of his feet, ready to lunge forward. Mrs. Peterson paced near the door, her heels clicking against the floor. The clock ticked, and a slight breeze rustled branches against the back window. *Tick. Tock. Tick. Tock.*

He quieted his breathing, trying to inhale through his nose. The light from the sunrise streamed through the window, creating a rectangle of white on the floor by his boots. The damn cat crept over and meowed, basking in the first rays' sunlight. It nudged against Kody's leg. He pushed the creature away, but it purred and jumped on his bent knees. Kody dropped the cat to the ground.

"Go away."

Rustling sounds came from the backyard, strengthening his grip on the gun. He had no vest, no helmet, no team. Four women and his baby girl were all under his care.

I'll sacrifice myself if I have to.

Mrs. Peterson's voice whispered from the front hallway. "I can't see Joanna in the yard."

Kody whispered, "Stay away from the windows."

A shadow loomed across the light that the cat laid in. Kody held his breath. Someone large stood outside the window next to him. His heart slammed under his ribcage.

If Kody jumped out, he'd have the element of surprise. But it'd be stupid to give away his position too early. He needed Dabbott and a team. He needed comms. A dark silhouette moved in front of the window. The man was big. Tall. Muscular. And armed.

Damn it.

Kody rolled his troubled shoulder.

Mrs. Peterson whispered, "There's a big guy out front."

Kody cringed. The one in his sightline turned the handle of the back door. Locked. He shoved the barrel of a gun through the window. Glass shattered. Mrs. Peterson screamed.

The intruder raised his gun toward the hallway and yelled, "Where's the girl?"

A gunshot exploded.

The man staggered back and fell to the hardwood. Kody bolted upright and ran across the room. He scanned the area then pointed his gun down at the man, still very much alive. Kody squeezed the trigger, but the man rolled out of the way.

Another shot pierced the air. Mrs. Peterson had lodged two bullets straight into the man's chest. Keeping his eyes on the intruder, Kody swiped the tablecloth from the floor. Kneeling over the man, he tied the tablecloth tight around the man's wrists.

"Is he dead?" Mrs. Peterson's voice quivered.

"Not yet. But he won't get out of that knot."

Where's the other man?

Moving outside, Kody kept his back to the brick house and moved around the perimeter. He held the gun high, aiming at the yard. Someone might be behind a tree or the shed. Heart thumping fast, Kody sidestepped toward the trucks. Kody dropped to his stomach to check for shoes underneath. Nothing. A scream stabbed the air again. He dashed over the uneven yard and through the front door to be met with a chaotic triangle standoff combusting with fury and desperation.

A man pointed his gun at Mrs. Peterson.

Mrs. Peterson held her gun directly at Joanna.

Joanna pointed her gun at the man.

They were all screaming nonsense. He didn't have a good shot at the man without risking one of the women.

"Give me Zohaib's daughter!" The man yelled.

"Leave now, or I'll shoot!" Joanna screamed.

Mrs. Peterson's hand shook. "You liar! You led them here."

Kody couldn't move. If he distracted any of them, then Mrs. Peterson might die.

Joanna's posture stiffened. "You're right." She lowered her weapon and stood next to the man. A smile crept up her face.

Shit!

The man tilted his head at Joanna, then focused back on Mrs. Peterson. "You have until the count of five to lower your weapon, lady. I'm not here for you. I don't want to shoot you."

Kody charged. Before he could get to them, another shot fired. The man shouted in pain and fell over. Joanna stood over him and shot again, bullet after bullet ripping through his body. Chest. Shoulder. Neck. Stomach. Over and over. Until the gun clicked. Empty.

Joanna's eyes rose to meet his, completely animalistic.

Sirens wailed in the distance. Joanna's eyes turned even more panicked as she stood over the bloody body.

"Whose side are you on?" Kody growled.

"Raelyn's. Always." Joanna wiped the sweat from her brow. "I'm not the bad guy that you think I am. I've saved her over and over, and no one trusts me." Her arm shook as she dropped the gun to her side, then let it clatter to the floor.

Sirens grew louder.

Kody picked up her gun from the floor. "Let's go. I'll keep you all safe."

Joanna shook her head. "It's too late." She collapsed into the kitchen chair and stared at the pictures on the wall. The sirens grew louder outside the house as she whispered, "I can't be saved."

"I told you, I'll keep you safe."

"What about the hundreds of women Zohaib has captured, tortured, hurt? You can't rescue all of us. We're all broken beyond repair."

"You're almost done, I promise. Stay strong for a little bit longer. I have a plan."

Thud. Thud. Thud.

A knocking on the door silenced them.

He could let Joanna get taken into custody. She might be safer with cops anyways. Thud. Thud. Thud.

Wait, that's not the door.

23

RAELYN

The gunshots finally stopped. Still trapped in the bunker, Raelyn's heart rammed so hard she could've sworn she was about to have a heart attack.

"Kody has to be okay," Raelyn whispered.

Only Cali's terrified breathing could be heard next to her. In the darkness, she groped at the dirt for a weapon. Nothing. Her eyes had adjusted enough to pull a container to place it directly under the ladder leading up to the pantry. Raelyn climbed atop and started rapping her knuckles hard on the wood.

"What if … Zohaib's men are the … only ones left?" Cali's voice shook.

Raelyn glanced into the dark tunnel. "No, Kody has to be fine." Wood creaked above, and light poured into the bunker. Raelyn shielded her eyes then met Kody's gaze.

"Thank God!" She searched his face. "Are you okay?"

He nodded. Behind him stood Joanna and Haydee. Kody pointed to the bunker. "You two, jump down."

Joanna did, landing like a panther, blood splattered on her legs.

"No, I need to work with the authorities," Haydee said, "I'll see my granddaughter soon enough."

Kody's eyes widened. It felt like his presence had turned wolf-like. But she didn't have time to address his feelings now. Raelyn climbed the ladder rungs. Behind Kody's feet was a man sprawled on the ground in a bloody mess. Her stomach rolled, and acid burned up her throat. She leaned over and emptied her stomach, feeling it splatter and splash back up to on her ankles.

"You okay?" Joanna patted her back.

"Since when do you care?" Raelyn wiped her mouth.

Joanna's blue eyes turned to ice. "Let's go."

"Why do we have to go through the tunnel?"

"There may be more men outside."

"Kody, come on." Raelyn tugged on his shoe. "Please."

He glanced between her and the man on the floor.

"The cops are here," Haydee announced.

Raelyn reached up. "Please, Kody."

Kody nodded and dropped down with a heavy thump, then closed the bunker door.

They were surrounded in darkness again. At least Kody was with her this time. His sweaty scent calmed her as she grabbed his forearm. For a moment, Raelyn could only hear all their faint breaths until Kody rummaged through his pocket. A light flickered on from a phone.

"Me and Cali will jog up ahead to scout."

"Oh, sure." Cali raised her arms. "This is the perfect horror film scene."

Kody nudged her quiet. "You two take it slow." He handed over one phone. "Keep this flashlight on so Raelyn doesn't trip."

Their silhouettes disappeared ahead, and they walked in silence. Raelyn stared at Joanna but couldn't see her face with only the flashlight beam guiding them. She scuffed her boots carefully on the ground so she wouldn't trip on anything.

Finally, she asked her mother, "Why did you send money to the Peterson's?"

"To give them enough reason to protect you. And, you need to give that baby to someone who can't ever be found by Zohaib. The Peterson's have amazing military connections to keep her safe." Joanna took the lead in the tunnel. "Listen to me, sometimes a mother has to leave their children to protect them."

Raelyn grabbed Joanna's wrist and twisted her around. "No! I won't be you. You had plenty of chances to make the right choice. And what's worse is you hurt Liam too. Why did you leave him in the farmhouse?"

"Liam is safer without me around."

"Do you even know where your son is right now?"

Joanna raised one finger as she twisted out of Raelyn's grasp. "Don't test me. I had someone check up on you both in the mountain."

I knew someone was following me.

"Who?"

"It doesn't matter. I left to keep you safe, just like you'll do for your baby."

"No! I won't be like you."

Joanna pinned Raelyn to the wall.

"Ouch!"

"You want the whole story? And force me to relive those days? Fine!"

"Stop shouting."

Joanna sighed and released her grasp. "In 1998, after sleeping with Zohaib, I fled home to William, unaware that I was pregnant with you." She cringed as if the very thought of carrying a child was torture. "When I started showing, William was so happy, and everything was great."

"Did you really love Pa?"

"With all my heart." Her eyes glistened. "When you were born, I knew right away that you weren't William's. I swear that there was a fraction of a second in the delivery room where I could tell William knew too. But it was never brought up again. And not once did he act differently or say anything about it."

Raelyn's heart grew heavy at Pa's commitment.

Just like Kody.

"The article I wrote about the sand tunnels won an award a year later, and our family's portrait was all over the newspapers. That week someone climbed into your nursery window. If you hadn't cried out, you would've been gone."

Raelyn's stomach churned. "You think it was Zohaib's men?"

"I know it was."

"How did Zohaib even know I was his?"

"That detail didn't matter to him, then. He was mad at me for leaving and wanted control over all his possessions. Anyways, I convinced William to move to the middle of nowhere in Ash Mountain."

"I thought I always lived in that farmhouse."

"No, we started out in an apartment near State's campus." Joanna shook her head. "You don't remember."

"Wait, but Pa always said that he was the one to hold you back. He blamed himself that he trapped you in the country so you couldn't fulfill your dreams of traveling."

Joanna faced her, despair lining her wrinkles. "He said that?"

"Yeah." Raelyn's heart turned heavy, coiling into tight knots.

"God, I wish I could've seen him once more." Her head hung, and she continued down the dark tunnel.

Raelyn hurried to keep up. "So, no one found us after you moved to Ash Mountain?"

"I was really careful. I quit my job, but I did undercover research about Storm Force based out of the warehouse. When you were four or five, one of Zohaib's men found me there. He demanded that I return to Zohaib with you. I had to …"

Raelyn leaned forward.

"I set the man on fire." She paused. "That's why half the warehouse burnt down. I didn't even go home before heading to the airport. I couldn't risk anyone following me to you." Joanna's voice quieted. "I never got to say goodbye to William in person."

Raelyn realized she was holding her breath and released the air.

"I called William from the airport, letting him know about a last-minute work assignment to Iraq."

Raelyn reached out desperately to try and get Joanna to face her again as she was putting the pieces together. "But you weren't working at that job anymore."

"William never knew I quit."

"But, you must've received a paycheck for all those years?"

"I had stolen cash from Zohaib on the night we were together. Enough to last a long time. That's probably another reason why he never gave up looking for me."

Raelyn waited, unsure if she was telling the whole truth. A rat scurried by on the tunnel ground, its tail whipping against her ankle. She hopped in place until Joanna tenderly lifted Raelyn's chin.

"Not in a million years would I have thought I'd miss your entire childhood."

Raelyn gulped down the pain. "So, you landed in Tahil and met with Zohaib?"

"Yes. His mansion was being built, so he was easy to find, such a well-established man in the area. Everyone knew the Battalion Commander. I told him you were his baby so he would trust me, but that you died in a fire in hopes that he would stop chasing after me."

Goosebumps formed, sending a shiver down her back. "He didn't let you leave."

"We were in a public place, so he let me walk away free …" She cringed. "… into the marketplace."

"Then the car bomb exploded?"

"Exactly. Zohaib commanded Snyder to create a diversion. The car bomb went off, Snyder snatched me, and the rest is history."

"But if Zohaib wanted you so badly, why did he let Snyder keep you as his fake-wife?"

"Raelyn, I was passed around at Zohaib's command. Zohaib did whatever he wanted with me."

"So, how did you know Liam was Pa's son?"

Joanna was just like me when she was pregnant. Terrified.

"I was already showing symptoms before I had been with Snyder. If I was smart, I never would've left William for the airport that day." Joanna cleared her throat. "As awful and as jealous as Snyder was near the end, he did save Liam's life by protecting him from Zohaib for so many years."

"You were trying to protect us both."

"Yes, this whole time. I even sent a briefcase of money to David Peterson once. He was supposed to deliver it to William to take care of you."

"Money doesn't make up for anything."

"No one can be fully prepared to be a mother. It's not like I had a magical formula with all the right answers. I did my best. When Snyder threatened that he'd send a soldier to your farmhouse, I even convinced him to choose Kody. I'd been watching him during his patrols and knew he wouldn't hurt you."

I met Kody because of Joanna?

A stabbing pain struck deep in her stomach. She leaned forward and grabbed the tunnel wall, dirt coating her hand.

She let out a deep breath.

"How far apart are they?" Joanna asked.

"I'm fine." Raelyn straightened. "Listen, I'm glad I learned more about your past, but it doesn't erase everything you did to me in the desert over the summer. I can't forget."

I want to. I want to forgive.

"What can I do to make it better?" Joanna asked softly.

"No, I'm done talking, Ma. We need to get to a computer because my phone got wet and barely works. I have to get onto my email."

"You called me Ma again." There was a smile in her voice.

"No, I didn't."

Kody returned from scouting ahead and broke the tension. "It's clear up ahead, but I overheard that last bit. Why do we need to get to a computer?"

"Um ..." Avoiding his eyes, Raelyn explained. "I sent Zohaib an *alluring* email. If he clicks on it and the virus works the right way, then I'll have access to his current files. We can send them to the CIA or FBI or whoever."

"What do you mean, an alluring email?" Kody blocked her path, then understanding lit his face. "Is that why that model was at our cabin?"

Raelyn nodded.

"So Zohaib is going to see that innocent woman? How could you put her in danger like that?"

"I didn't. We never got good footage after you interrupted. I used someone else."

"Who did you use?"

"It doesn't matter." Raelyn squinted ahead at a tiny light shooting through the dirt ceiling. "I need a computer."

They walked further through the tunnel. Slivers of light filtered through the end of the tunnel, where tree limbs blocked their exit. Hypnotized by the flashing blue police lights, she released a sigh.

Kody looped a strand of her hair behind her ear. "You *did* call her Ma again."

"I did?"

He massaged her back in slow circles and whispered, "Maybe you and Joanna will be able to mend things—with time."

"It would be nice, but I doubt it. I need to see if that email worked."

"So, if you didn't use that model, who did you use? Don't tell me that you did it yourself."

She cringed.

"Raelyn!" The anger in Kody's voice was evident.

"I didn't. Tucker stopped me." She sat in the dirt, then rested her forehead between her knees.

"Who's Tucker?"

"A man from Ash Mountain who saved my life."

"I'd like to thank him, then."

"I'll introduce you to him later. I've got his cell in my phone."

"Back to the topic," Kody said sternly.

Cali stepped forward. "I volunteered. We sent pics of me."

Kody leaned away abruptly. "What?"

"The images to Zohaib are of me."

"How could you do that to your best friend?" Kody glared and mumbled under his breath. "You're afraid of turning into Joanna, yet you end up just like Zohaib."

Did he seriously just say that?

Raelyn's heart pounded fast, and she felt her own jaw drop. "If you think that, then I definitely can't be a parent. Amala will be safest without me. I was right before and need to give her up." Her chest tightened, threatening to explode. She pulled the gold chain off her neck and threw it at his chest. It bounced off and landed with a thunk in the dirt. Kody scooped it up, face full of dread.

"Babe, I …"

"I was desperate, and I didn't force Cali to volunteer," she screamed, "Cali's strong and brave and made her choice. It'll work. Zohaib likes her. But, if you think for one second that I'm like him, then why are we even together? How could you even look at me if you seriously think that?" Raelyn's body went rigid.

She stared at the darkening clouds. Despair beat her down. All her fears had come true. Kody was going to leave her again. She'd be alone to figure out who to give Amala to. Sinking to the level of photographing her best friend naked for Zohaib was an all-time low. She was putting Cali in danger for her own gains. Just like Zohaib would do. Kody had been right about her. She may as well have dumped Cali's dead body into a ditch. There wasn't any escaping the doomed future that choked her with uncertainties.

Kody knelt in front of her. "I'm sorry. I shouldn't have said that. I'm just so tired. I'll fix everything and ... and I'll keep you and Cali safe. And Amala."

"You can't keep everyone safe, Kody!" Raelyn spit out her words. "You're not some superhero."

"I can." His eyes narrowed. "I can protect you."

"You think you're protecting, but you keep abandoning me. You left me on New Year's Eve!"

"You can't be serious!" Kody threw up his hands. "They tied me up! Threatened me!"

"Did you volunteer yourself to save me?"

"Yes, of course."

Raelyn's voice rose, "And you left me in that bunker. You left! Just like Ma left when I was a kid! Just like Pa left me! Just like Phoenix left! One way or the other, you won't stick around. Maybe you'll leave me if this baby isn't yours, or maybe you'll get yourself killed! I can't do this alone."

Kody's clamped jaw loosened, and his breathing slowed. His mouth opened and shut again, then he peered up into the sunlight shining through a hole. "I'm not going anywhere."

She marched up to his face, inches away from his nose. "I know you. Don't pretend that when David offered for you to help him that you didn't consider it."

His glance to the ground was the only confirmation she needed. He sidestepped her and started climbing out of the hole. "It looks like all the cops are gone. Come on." Kody lifted them to the surface.

Raelyn sniffed in the earthy grass scent. The ground was wet under her boots without snow or flowers, like the earth lingered in-between seasons. Three squirrels scurried by and ran up a hill in the Peterson's backyard toward the forest behind.

They marched toward the driveway as Raelyn trailed, arms crossed, knowing that Kody had plans to leave her—again.

Everything's falling apart.

Sliding inside his Jeep, Raelyn sat in the passenger seat, reached under her boot for the safety deposit box, and handed it over.

"What is this?" Kody popped it open with his knife. "This has to be forty-thousand dollars. Where did you get this?" He took a deep breath and studied her.

"Ma's trunk."

He snapped the deposit box back and shoved it across the console. "We need to turn this into the police."

"But what about our daughter? We could start a fund for Amala. Whoever adopts her will be taken care of for a bit."

Kody slammed his palms on the steering wheel. "Exactly. What about her! You're giving up on her before she's even here. It almost seems like you *want* us to fail."

Joanna snorted in the back seat. "There will be a day in your future where you'll look back and regret a choice … there are so many times I wish I had … never mind."

A lump formed in her throat, and she turned so Kody couldn't see her face when she said, "Can you please start driving."

"Where?" He put the Jeep in gear and drove away from Phoenix's parents.

"The closest hotel with computers in the lobby."

Raelyn pulled Pa's journal out from the depths of her purse and wrote a poem as the Jeep jostled over potholes.

STOP THE CLOCK

Each step is dangerous when you dig your own grave
Tragic if eaten alive, it's the destruction you crave
Claw, scratch, and burn to suck in one last breath
Dragged down deep underneath until death

An eerie feeling crept up her spine that they were being followed. She glanced in the side mirror and met eyes with a woman in the car behind them.

Why does she look familiar?

24

KODY

GRAVEL CRUNCHED UNDER THE tires as Kody's Jeep rolled into an empty hotel parking lot. The pavement quickly turned into weed-infested dirt. He glanced in the rain splattered rear-view mirror to confirm no one had followed. Raelyn's tense energy in the seat next to him was like a balloon about to burst. Cali jittered her leg against his seat in the back, and Joanna kept tapping her fingers on the window. Each woman seemed to shield themselves with invisible walls, all three in their own mental world of fears.

Kody reached for the deposit box, swiped a few bills into his pocket, hid the gun under his shirt, and nodded. "Come on." He hopped into the rain.

"Dun, dun dun," Cali whispered. "This place is freaky." She pointed to yellow 'caution' tape wrapped around the front pillars of the hotel's entrance. "Was someone murdered here?"

Kody shook his head. "I researched it quick before we came. Everything should be okay, that's for painting, but stay close to me, just in case."

They quietly walked around the tape, bending around the yellow ribbon as if it would poison their skin if touched. The run-down lobby smelled of wet carpet, and a bucket collected droplets that fell from a hole in the ceiling. Raelyn and Cali linked arms while Joanna stared at a spider dangling from the ceiling.

"How much for two rooms?" Kody asked.

The clerk didn't even glance up from the tv. "Fifty a night. First, fill out this form with your name, and I'll need your ID with a twenty-dollar security deposit."

Kody slid four hundreds over the countertop. "We aren't here."

The man's eyes widened as he pocketed the cash. "Sounds good to me."

Before Kody moved down the hallway, he caught the eyes of a woman employee behind the desk.

Something else about her seemed oddly familiar as if he knew her. Kody craned his neck around the corner of the clerk counter and started to get her attention, but she quickly turned her back and disappeared from view.

"I'm losing my mind," he whispered while handing Cali and Joanna their key.

"You already lost it a while back." Cali smacked his shoulder.

Kody shook his head. "We're in the room adjoined with yours. Please don't leave unless we communicate."

Cali frowned. "Rat cakes, I probably won't even leave the bed. Do you think those devil zombies will find us here?"

"No." Kody patted her back.

Joanna's blue eyes seemed desperate when she looked Raelyn's way.

Kody bent down to Joanna. "I'll talk to Raelyn for you. She'll come around in time."

The hope sparkled in her irises for only a moment until she disappeared into a room with Cali. He would need to thank Joanna for warning them about these men and killing the threat back at the Peterson house.

Inside, stains sprinkled the room carpet. Kody double-locked the door then slid the hotel's dresser in front of it. He hung the comforter from the curtain rod, darkening the room.

Kody faced Raelyn. "You need to forgive Joanna."

"I don't know how."

"What if I had secrets to tell you … about things I did in the jungle … that you couldn't imagine. Would you forgive *me*?"

"I would blame Zohaib, not you."

"Then why can't you blame Zohaib for Joanna's choices? She's been manipulated and abused."

She rolled in her lips. After a thread of silence, Raelyn asked, "Can we take a shower?"

"Now?"

Her face softened as she slowly stepped forward and wrapped her arms around him. "Let's just be us again … and forget all these problems and drama. You've been acting different since you returned … distant." A tear rolled down her cheek. "Everything is strangling me, and I just need you right now. I need to be us again."

"Oh, Raelyn." He lifted her in one swoop and carried her.

"Hey!" Her sweet smile claimed her face again. "I'm too heavy for you!"

"Oh, hush." He shook his head and set her down gently in the bathroom. The mirror reflected his complete exhaustion, but glancing at his features, he wondered if their baby would have his dark eyes, a wide nose, and thick lips. He turned on the hot water of the shower. At least the hotel had sufficient water pressure.

Raelyn lifted the sweater over her head and flopped it over the edge of the sink. She rose on her tiptoes and kissed his neck repeatedly, not missing an inch. She shimmied out of her yoga pants, shirt, bra, and panties in front of him. Kody stared at her naked body in awe, unable to glance away. Raelyn's breasts were now twice their usual size, with pointed nipples begging him closer. But it was the passion and understanding in her eyes that he had been needing.

Raelyn unzipped his jeans, and raw desire consumed him. Longing. He needed her lips. Skin. All of her. Her amber eyes turned to fire as she pulled out his full erection. Technically, she would need three fistfuls to cover his length —but that hadn't ever stopped her from pleasing him.

I need her. Now. Everyday.

Kody helped her into the shower, watching her footing on the slippery floor. Steam surrounded them as Raelyn covered them both in soapy bubbles, rubbing their slippery bodies together, slowly healing him. He breathed in her new, strong coconut scent— so different from that of the jungle, invading his senses and providing relief.

She started stroking his shaft firmly. He stared at the ceiling, feeling her move on him with the slick water between his skin and her palm. Bracing himself on the shower wall with both hands, he let out a groan that echoed in the small room. "Mmm, babe, that's good."

Fuck, I love her so much.

"Babe, it's been so long since …"

She slowed down, the tension building as he grew thicker and harder in her hands.

"Aaaah … fuck … this is perfect …"

Her intoxicating eyes fixated on him as he gently pinned her against the shower wall. Water rained down and splashed on his feet. She didn't need to say a word. One bite of her lower lip told him everything he needed to know. He cupped her breasts and rubbed his thumbs over her hard nipples.

Kody's mouth crushed hers as his blood turned to lava. Their kisses moved deeper—harder— as water poured down. He threaded his hands through her wet hair and kissed a path from her neck to her breasts, making her back arch. Kody massaged a finger between her thighs, feeling her reposition. He moved a finger inside, craving the soft heat she offered.

Raelyn moaned at his touch, and he could feel her muscles tighten. "The bed."

"But, we're both soaked." He grinned.

"Bed. Now."

"Not yet," Kody added another finger, swirling deep inside her, reveling in how hot she looked. Endless love for her encompassed his entire soul.

Dropping to his knees, Kody held her hips as water splattered down on his back. He kissed the droplets trailing down her round stomach, then angled over to lick her upper thigh. He could cum just from watching her and listening to her moaning.

"Kody, you're too tall." Raelyn laughed.

He gripped her ass with both hands and spread her legs, moving his tongue over her clit. Her hands found the top of his head as she moaned, demanding more.

He sat in the shower. "Stand over me." Water beaded over her plump breasts.

Her eyes hooded in desire at his new position as she smiled, chest heaving. "What?"

Kody didn't wait and moved her exactly where he wanted her and used his tongue and fingers—caressing, massaging, licking in circles until her legs shook around him. She tasted so sweet. He wanted more.

More.

"Kody!"

He sucked faster, harder. Her skin on his lips felt like heaven. Above him, her body jerked, and she caught herself with two hands on the shower wall as a louder moan confirmed what he already knew.

"Damn, babe. Okay, the bed." He picked her up, water cascading over both of them, and carried her out of the steam into the room.

She licked her lips when he laid her soaking body on the blanket.

"Can we do this when you're—"

Raelyn laughed. "When I'm giant?"

"I mean, will I hurt you?"

"No. I should be fine."

Kody moved over her, but she shook her head.

"No way. We take turns. Lay down."

He groaned, and his thoughts faded away as she scooted lower, her belly rubbing against his skin on the way. Somehow, she was even sexier now, carrying his child.

Her eagerness sent shivers up his arms. She skimmed her fingertips up his inner thigh. Kody knew her patterns, and he ached for what came next.

"I can't believe you're gonna be my wife."

"Mhm." She smiled just before her perfect lips wrapped around his tip. Kody throbbed inside her wet, warm mouth. The way her tongue swirled around his cock sent a shudder shooting through his core and spread over his entire body. His heart slammed against his ribs, and his fists tightened in ecstasy.

I can't live without her.

He groaned, using all effort to not stare at the ceiling in disbelief. The love in her eyes amplified each time he let out a grunt, urging him on. His heart spasmed in his chest. The sounds she made sent his brain whirling as she sucked harder, faster, and wetter. Nothing had ever felt so good. His body jolted and twitched. He couldn't think straight. Raw need. Her lips. Her tongue. Her eyes.

Kody grabbed a pillow, covered his face, and grunted into the fabric in spurts. Shallow. Deep. Shallow. Deep. She knew where to touch and lick to send him over the edge. His entire body tensed in ecstasy. When he cast the pillow aside and locked onto her amber eyes again, her slight smirk set him ablaze. Raelyn ignited something within him that another woman could never replace.

"Babe, you gotta stop, or I'll ..." Kody bit his lip as she continued. "Oh. My. God."

Raelyn slowed and pulled away, licking small circles at his tip as if in a hypnotic trance. Her fiery smile rose. "More?" The alluring gaze cast a spell on him.

Unable to contain himself, Kody stood and pulled her up. The room spun, but he wrapped his hands around Raelyn's waist. Her doe eyes worked their magic.

Quickly, Kody turned her around onto all fours on the bed as pillows flopped to the floor. Her curves felt different now but still as ample and soft. Raelyn faced the wall and spread her knees apart, giving him the most gorgeous view.

"Jesus, babe ... don't move."

Raelyn arched her back like a wave, positioning her ass in the air. Kody softly caressed her round ass then spread her cheeks. Heart hammering, he pressed his rock-hard cock between her thighs, tantalizing her inviting folds. Raelyn reached back, trying to guide him in, but he placed her hand on the mattress.

"I said don't move," his voice deepened.

She whimpered in need and spread her legs further apart. A frenzy shot through his body. Kody bit his lips and reached between her cheeks, massaging her clit gently from behind. Her warmth radiated onto his wrist.

"I can't wait," she said, her voice thick, dripping with passion.

His heavy breathing turned into a pant. He stared at her electrifying form. The bed frame squealed in protest as Raelyn writhed against his hand, demanding more.

The tip of his cock pushed against her entrance. He held himself there, frozen.

She tried to buck her hips. "Kody! Please!"

He held her steady, unmoving. She was soaking wet, and he let out a groan in anticipation, slowly rotating his hips to feel all of her entrance.

"Please!" The urgency in her voice heightened his senses.

Kody slid inside of her, penetrating. Slowly. So slowly. She moaned and clenched her muscles around him. He thrust his hips up higher, groaning at each movement. Her moan matched. A sound came out of her like he'd never heard, and she backed into him, embracing all of his length. Slow. Steady. In. Out. He watched himself slide and disappear, holding back curses on the tip of his tongue.

"Like that?" The bed creaked under their weight as he slowly moved deeper.

"Let me do it." Her voice was raspy.

Kody watched her curves move around him. Her body absorbed him entirely. He couldn't tell where he ended, and she began.

In all his life, Kody had never expected to feel a love so powerful, to find a woman who obliterated his chance of surviving without her. Consumed by the feeling of being inside her, Kody held off as long as he could, focusing on pleasing her. Panting, she tried to speak, though only moans came out.

His eyes rolled in the back of his head, and he gripped her waist harder. Rocking his hips forward and back, forward and back, he could feel her trembling under his touch.

She's close.

Kody widened his stance and sped up, thrusting harder. Sliding all the way in and out each time, watching his cock move inside of her. Raelyn moaned and leaned forward, burying her face in a pillow. Her muscles clenched around his cock. So tight.

Fuck!

"Kody!" She screamed into the pillow, shaking from head to toe again.

"Yes, babe, that's it." Kody choked on the words, trying so hard to hold off as long as she needed him to.

"Turn me," she commanded, her voice smooth as silk.

Kody rotated her and stared into Raelyn's deep eyes.

This raw, primal need for one another united them to a level that was more than sex. For the first time, it felt like a true lifetime commitment. This time symbolized his promise to do the dishes with her, pick out a stroller with her, drive Amala to preschool, and retire with her. Raelyn was his everything, and nothing could change that.

Repositioning, he sat against the headboard. Still full of his hardness, she started moving up and down, riding him. Kody watched her rise and fall and helped her momentum by lifting her body with each movement.

"Babe!"

Raelyn slammed herself down on him like a hammer onto a nail. Dumbfounded, Kody's body tightened, and muscles flexed while watching the woman he loved using his body. Unrelentless, she kept at it.

"I'm yours," he said.

Raelyn gasped and licked her lips. Her face was red from the exertion as she rose and fell onto him. She leaned in and kissed him deeply, hard. Faster. The mattress shifted, skidding across the bed frame. She screamed. He knew she was close. If he kept up that same rhythm, she'd bust in a few more thrusts. Her body tensed. He was ready for the magic.

"I can feel you, babe. Come for me." Kody demanded her to let go.

He gripped her waist tight, driving into her deeper. The build-up was about to explode, and after Kody dove into her once more, Raelyn released everything at once. An intense orgasm took over him deep within, spreading like an intricate web in every direction.

His cock pulsed inside her as a shattering shockwave burst through his body. He rode out his climax and filled her up as her body quivered and loosened below him, releasing a scent of sex he never wanted to forget. They both moaned out in unison, and her body slacked, but he held her, still moving her hips higher and lower over him until finally slowing, then stopping.

She took a deep breath and leaned into his chest, resting her chin on his shoulder. Beautiful belly in between. The golden afterglow of sex on her skin glistened like dew.

Kody kissed her shoulders. "I love you so much."

"I love you too." Leaning against him, the smile in her voice was evident.

With his hand on her belly, he felt his baby girl kick hard. "I love you too."

I won't let anything happen to them.

Still in bed, savoring the rare peace, Raelyn eased into the crook of Kody's arm. He wanted to keep her there, forever, as close as possible.

"Did you leave that little tracker piece at Haydee's?" she asked.

"Yes, she's going to destroy it, just in case we didn't deactivate it correctly." Kody looked around the room, choosing to ignore the dark stains on the walls. Not a luxurious resort—but better than a box.

Her voice held so many layers when she asked, "What are we going to do?"

I need to form a team.

Kody sat up. The bed creaked under his weight. "Take one day at a time."

"But, we have no plan. I searched for the file all over Ash Mountain and never found it, so if Zohaib doesn't open that email, then we've run out of options." Raelyn's voice cracked a little. "Will we always be on the run? Can Zohaib's men find us here?"

Kody laid his hand on hers and kissed her forehead. "I don't know what I should tell you."

"Tell me the truth."

"Yes, they might find us here."

She rested her head on his shoulder and curled closer. "Kody?"

"Yeah, babe."

"I'm scared." Her words punched him hard in the gut.

"Me too." He swallowed hard, but it felt like a rock was lodged in his throat.

When Raelyn lifted her chin, those long lashes batted away a glistening tear. "Really? You?"

"Of course, you said things about giving away Amala … that terrified me." He rubbed his beard. "Please believe that I'm here for you."

"You're not scared of the bad guys?" Raelyn smiled slightly. "But my words make you nervous?"

Wrong. I'm scared shitless.

She smiled a little wider but still held back.

He tickled her side. "I almost got your real smile. Keep it coming."

She squirmed, giggling. "Stop it! I can't smile right now. Things are too serious." Her cheeks rose as her grin spread.

"Serious? Nah, we're on vacation." Kody teased. "Where should we go next? I'm thinking no deserts, no rainforests, so I guess we're running out of options." His hands roamed her most ticklish spots as she pretended to slap him away, ending up lying flat on her back.

"How about Tuzzlici?"

He lay next to her, letting her hair fan over his ear. "That was a pretty good trip. Only if we stay in that grotto. No fires."

"Deal schmeal." She rolled closer, allowing her belly to nudge against his side. "So, will you ever tell me what happened in the rainforest?"

Kody's whole body felt heavy like bricks burying him in guilt. Eliza flashed in his mind. Something in his gut convinced him that she was still alive and safe. He latched onto the reassuring feeling and didn't let go. How many others had suffered the same—just like Joanna. Raelyn's mother had every right to be inconsistent, paranoid, and desperate if she had experienced years of inconceivable trauma. Trauma he had put Eliza through.

His jaw clenched, but he nodded and looked straight into her amber eyes. "Babe, I don't know if I should tell you."

She guided his chin toward her. "Nothing can make me change how much I love you. I can have negative feelings and still want to be with you forever. We're engaged, right? That means for life. I don't want secrets between us."

Kody squeezed his eyes shut.

She doesn't know about my promise.

Thoughts of the lives Zohaib wasted, Eliza, the boys in the village, and a yellow snake-like smile all swarmed in his mind.

"I did everything I could to get back to you." He could tell she wanted more. "I don't have anything else to say right now."

"You're holding back."

"Raelyn, please understand."

She studied his face but softly ran a hand over his cheek. "Do you blame me for being trapped in Brazil?"

"No, not at all."

"Then why won't you open up about it?"

He cleared his throat and glanced out the window. "Did you know Liam thinks he found the coordinates of all Zohaib's other camps in the warehouse?"

"You're changing the subject."

"Babe, please!"

"I wish you'd talk to me."

Kody pulled his clothes on and moved toward the door. "I need some fresh air." And he left.

In the hallway, he caught sight of that familiar woman again, and the same eerie sensation sent prickles up his arm. "Excuse me, miss."

She darted behind a corner.

"Wait, miss, excuse me ..." He rounded the bend and found himself staring into the barrel of a gun.

"Don't come closer."

Kody's jaw locked tight.

"You recognize me?" She asked. The way her hair was tied up in a tight ponytail made her eyes spark with intensity.

He nodded.

"But you don't know who I am." She spoke confidently.

He quickly scanned her hotel uniform to check for a badge or ID, then shook his head.

"Don't move." The woman pressed the gun against his temple, and he could tell from her eyes that she wasn't messing around.

Kody gasped. "You're the woman tied to the bed in the jungle."

She nodded. "What did you do with Bernardo?" Her fake accent dropped, and the American accent was as clear as day.

His jaw dropped. "Bernardo? You mean, the man with the pig?"

"What pig?" She pressed harder. "Where's Bernardo?"

He flinched. "I don't know. Who are you? How did you escape Zohaib's house?"

"Are you working with Bernardo?"

"Not anymore. He betrayed me and helped Zohaib."

A flicker of shock was quickly disguised by determination. "I was afraid of that unless you're lying." The gun scratched against his skin.

"I wasn't ever going to hurt you that day. I swear." Sweat dripped down his temple.

She studied him. "Tell me, where did you move the people of that village?"

"What?" Kody raised both hands. "I didn't. The village was already empty."

Now she looked confused and alarmed simultaneously. "You didn't clear it out?"

He shook his head. "There was only a woman, Eliza, and her daughter."

She paused, her lips parted slightly.

He took her moment of hesitation, twisted her wrist, and grabbed her gun. Kody pointed it at her. "How do you know Bernardo? He's a traitor."

The woman's eyes narrowed, but she didn't seem at all concerned that the tides had turned. "We're engaged. Or we *were* engaged, and he volunteered to infiltrate and spy on Zohaib's base to learn his plan and report back. But, he didn't show up to the last three meetings. You swear Bernardo helped Zohaib?"

"Yeah. Now explain yourself because I don't have time for games."

She chuckled and leaned against the wall casually. "All this time, I've been keeping my eye on you, Walsh, and you truly did turn out to be a good guy."

He dropped the gun to his side. "Explain."

"We need to form a team. Eliza has made progress, but it's not enough."

The woman widened her stance, her firm build taking up more space than possible with that confidence. "Zohaib has a bigger objective."

"Which is what?"

A door clicked open and shut down the hallway. They both froze and clamped their lips shut. Kody peeked around the corner to see a cleaning lady with a cart of towels.

He rubbed his beard. "Go on."

"Sex trafficking gives Zohaib power and money, but why? What does he really want?" she smirked while watching his wheels turn.

The way Zohaib stood on the balcony of his glass house with his soldiers lined up below flashed across Kody's mind.

"That's right, soldier. He wants an international dictatorship," she said.

"That's not possible."

She nodded. "If he gets enough influential rulers involved and gets his hands on enough militaries, he can blackmail each one when needed. So he has control over their decisions, and they'll follow his orders instead of their superior."

"It'll never work."

"It already has. A war will start."

His lungs crushed to nothing, sucking his air dry. "We can still defeat him."

Her blond hair swooped in front of her face when she laughed. "You don't stand a chance without me."

"Who are you?"

The way her smirk covered her face seemed familiar, and Kody realized he hadn't seen her mouth under the hijab that day in Zohaib's glasshouse.

He cocked his head to the side. "Wait a second, you look like—"

"Don't you dare say his name." She took out a hidden gun and smirked, "When the time is right, we'll need a signal to communicate."

25

RAELYN

RAELYN WOKE AFTER A nap to the scent of McDonald's fries wafting through the hotel room. Her stomach rumbled and saliva formed under her tongue. Kody strutted over with a smile and a Big Mac in hand. She tilted her head, wondering what caused his mood shift. If only she could wrap his smile with a bow and tuck it in her pocket for safekeeping.

"My hero! How did you get this? I can guarantee you didn't leave the hotel."

"I made a friend in the lobby." Kody winked. "I wasn't sure what you've been craving." His voice laced with a hint of gruff sexiness as if he had a bottomless appetite for her. "Me though, I'm craving round two."

"No way. First, milkshakes and fries."

He laughed.

When she bit into the junk food, flavors blasted her palate, making her moan. "Mmm, the recipe for a perfect relationship."

"Jeez! You're enjoying that more than sex."

Raelyn rolled her eyes. "Maybe I'll lick food off your chest next time."

Kody's hearty laugh came from such a deep place it made her stop eating.

I haven't heard that sound in a long time.

"What?" He eyed her.

"It's just nice to see you happy again."

Raelyn sighed. Their time in the shower earlier was what they had both needed to reconnect. But Kody's avoidance of his experiences in the rainforest worried her to pieces.

One day at a time. We'll get through this.

Kody devoured his share of the takeout burger and slurped a thick chocolate shake through his straw as she pulled out her journal and wrote a poem.

What if the challenges were more than you care to bear?
Would you rely on me and be willing to share?
What if the time you had was too rough?
Would the support I give be strong enough?

"So, you asked what we should do next. I don't want you to worry. I'm not going anywhere with David now," he reassured her.

"What made you change your mind?"

"In the hallway, I met —"

A knock came from the door adjoining their rooms, followed by Joanna's voice. "You two decent?"

Raelyn's cheeks flushed warmly. "Let her in."

Kody unlatched the lock, then asked, "Where's Cali?"

"In bed. I swear that girl could sleep through a sandstorm." Joanna's voice sounded impatient. "I need to talk to both of you."

Raelyn swallowed her last bite and crumpled the wrapper into a ball, throwing it across the room into the trash. She raised both hands. "Score!"

Joanna raised one brow. "I'm guessing you two made up?"

Kody cleared his throat. "Do you need something?"

"Yeah, we weren't having any luck logging in. The connection at this hotel is awful. But, I've been looking through William's journal. He drew a symbol here." She pointed to a page. "It looks like an old graffiti painting in the warehouse."

"Really?" Raelyn inspected a page and pointed to an hourglass symbol, half full of sand. "I never saw that."

"Well, it may be painted over by now. I haven't been to the warehouse in twelve years. Have you ever been to the computer room there?" Joanna asked.

"No. We should go!" Raelyn stood. "What if it means something? I'll text Liam to meet us there."

"Okay, we need to ask for backup," Kody pulled out his phone.

Didn't expect him to agree so quickly.

"Liam knows all about computers," Raelyn spoke confidently.

"That's not really the backup I meant." Kody walked to the far side of the room. She heard the name Dabbott roll off his tongue as he paced.

Unable to wait, Raelyn rushed around the room and threw their few belongings into the backpack, but her walk felt more like a waddling penguin. Her stomach squeezed tight, and she stopped in her tracks, digging her nails into her palm until the tightening ceased.

Joanna whispered behind her, "Maybe we should get you to a hospital instead."

"I'm not due for weeks. She's not coming yet."

Kody ended his call. "Dabbott will meet us at the warehouse, but she's not thrilled about it. I promised her I wouldn't ask for help for a while."

"You did the right thing, thanks. We'll be in and out." Raelyn grabbed her purse, glancing at the syringes in her bag that Kody wasn't aware of.

It's a good thing I won't have to use those.

Joanna cleared her throat. "Kody, can I speak to you in the hallway for a moment?"

Raelyn tilted her head.

"No." Kody widened his stance. "Joanna, whatever you have to say, you can tell Raelyn too."

"It's not that. I'd just like to apologize and have a heart-to-heart with the man who will marry my daughter. Just in case something … happens to me."

"Nothing will happen to you when I'm around." Kody walked to the door. "But fine, Raelyn, can you give us five minutes?"

"Sure." She stared at the syringes again, then wrapped the straps of the bag around her shoulder.

Once the door clicked shut, their whispers murmured from the hallway. Raelyn started thinking. Where did Haydee get the paralysis formula from? Did David have access to chemicals in the army? How potent was it? Could someone really hear and see and feel everything but not move?

I'm glad I'll never find out.

A scratching sound clawed at the other side of the adjoining door that harbored Cali. Maybe time with her best friend was what she needed to calm her nerves. If she could carry some of Kody's pain, maybe Cali could help loosen some of her burden. Plus, she had to inform Cali of their new plan to go to the warehouse. Raelyn moved closer to the door and heard a thump from the other side.

Footsteps shuffled along the carpet in the room. Raelyn jiggled the handle. She knocked on the door. "Cali?"

The footsteps stopped.

Raelyn pushed her ear against the door. "Cali?"

Two deep male voices whispered something. Raelyn's heart hammered fast. Just as she turned to warn Kody, the door adjoining her room with Cali's flew open, and she stumbled through to the other side. A masked man caught her in his arms before she hit the floor. He clamped a hand over her mouth. Sharp stings pierced her bicep. Raelyn glanced at her arm in alarm. A long needle stuck into her skin as the man's thumb injected the clear liquid into her body.

Raelyn tried to roll, hit, anything, but she had no control over her body. Her body went limp, and she melted into a useless blob in the man's arms. Warnings screamed in her mind to kick and thrash, but her muscles felt like jello sloshing around. As her head lolled, she saw Cali laying on the bed like a rock, eyes full of fear. An icy breeze rushed in through the window as the two men whispered in another language.

Amala! What if this hurts her?

One masked man threw Cali's dead weight over his back and climbed out the window with a heavy grunt. He ran across the parking lot to a van, slid open the door, and threw her inside. Raelyn wanted to yell, but words wouldn't form. Her breathing felt like a robot on autopilot instead of the desperate panting she expected. Her heart rate stayed steady, but fear consumed her.

Help!

The other masked man set two digital watches into the middle of the bed and smirked at her.

Don't touch me!

Somehow, he managed to lift Raelyn through the window, hitting her head on the frame as they moved through. She couldn't yelp in pain or grab her temple but felt the throbbing pain without the ability to respond.

Let me go!

All she could do was watch the sky as the man hurried across the lot. Any moment now, Kody would come back to the room and find them missing. His footsteps would thunder behind her. Terror gripped at her bones and latched on tightly.

At least I'll be with Cali. We'll survive this together.

But the first van holding Cali pulled away.

No! Come back!

She tried to read the license plate on the back, but there wasn't one. The man put Raelyn in a van and slammed the door shut. The cold, metal floor sent shivers up her spine, but that didn't compete with a new contraction pulsing through her stomach.

This can't be happening!

The engine roared to life, and the van zoomed down the street. Every turn the man made sent her body skidding from side to side in the back, but she had no way of stopping her movements or protecting her belly. Each fiber of her being screamed in protest, wanting to cover her stomach, but her arms flopped around wildly. A tear rolled down her cheek as it trickled down her neck and lingered.

Where are they taking me?

26

KODY

STANDING IN THE HOTEL lobby, Kody nodded to Joanna. "Thank you for your kind words, but I have one more thing I need to ask."

"Sure." Joanna smiled, relief on her face that their conversation had gone well—so far.

"Why did you send money to the Peterson's? Did you really think I wouldn't protect her?"

"Let me explain." Joanna sighed. "In the spiral tower in Haavij, I had cameras to monitor the girls. I heard a few conversations between Raelyn and Olivia."

"Let me guess." He rubbed his beard. "She was frustrated about me being controlling?"

"I see you two are stronger now. Raelyn doesn't seem worried about that anymore. Maybe you've grown."

"I'm trying."

Joanna started walking back toward their rooms. "Anyways, I'm glad you have forgiven me. Maybe Raelyn eventually will too."

"We have time."

"I'm not so sure."

He matched her stride down the hall. "What do you mean?"

Joanna dropped her head and lowered her voice. "I won't be able to … never mind, it's nothing."

Before unlocking the hotel room, Kody looked at Joanna. "We're family now. Whatever you're worried about, I can help."

Those blue eyes glistened, almost playing a video for him of her years under Zohaib's control. "Kody, you're a good guy. But, you can't protect everyone, especially people like me."

He waited, allowing the concept to sink in. But he didn't want to focus on anything worrisome. At the moment, he was hopeful and confident after forming his new plan. It was conveniently helpful that Raelyn wanted to go to the warehouse, too—the very place where he could form a team and help Eliza. Everything was lining up perfectly to work out to his advantage.

Just need to remember that signal.

"I'll wake Cali for some food." Joanna clicked open her hotel room door.

When he walked into the room, he stopped in his tracks. The nightstand was overturned, and pillows were scattered along the floor.

"Cali?" His fists balled tightly as he ran into the bathroom. "Cali?"

"The window's open," Joanna shouted as she sprinted to her bag and pulled out her gun.

His attention snapped to the adjoined door, which was swung wide open.

Kody ran through the adjoined door to his room. "Raelyn?"

Their room looked untouched. Her phone sat charging on the nightstand. He stormed to their bathroom, and his voice rose. "Raelyn?"

"Do you think they got food together?" Joanna's voice turned fierce.

The rest of the McDonald's food sat untouched on the table.

"Shit!" Kody's gaze darted around. "Her purse is gone." Rushing back into the other room, Kody took inventory of all of Cali's belongings—still there.

"What's this?" Joanna picked up three watches from the bed. "There's a blinking light on this button."

"Don't touch it!" Kody jumped forward to stop her, but she had already pushed the button.

A video on the face of the watch started playing. Despite it being small, the image came in crystal clear, and Zohaib's sly smirk taunted him.

"Walsh! I'm glad we're able to continue to play our game." He ran his hand over his slicked-back hair into the bun on top of his head.

Kody held his breath.

"In a moment, you'll gain access to live feeds." Zohaib snickered. "I split them up, making this so much more fun."

An agonizing scream erupted from Kody's throat as every muscle tightened, which cut off Zohaib's directions for a moment.

Joanna gripped Kody's shoulder and shook him. "Quiet!"

Kody gulped down his rage and listened as Zohaib continued. "… punishment for leaving my rainforest, one woman will die today. You need to understand the consequences of your actions." He paused and took a swig of whatever alcohol was in the glass he grasped. "We made an agreement together, and you broke the contract."

Kody's hands shook with rage and fear.

"The live stream will show Cali at the warehouse, Raelyn in your cabin at Ash Mountain, and Joanna is at Slate High."

Joanna growled, "He meant to take me too."

"You can only save one." Zohaib's thick eyebrows arched. "And Walsh, the clock is ticking. You have one hour. Enjoy!" The video faded to black.

For a moment, the world stilled, and only the ticking of the clock on the wall centered him to reality.

Kody swallowed hard, fighting the urge to snap something in half. "I can't choose!"

Who do I save?

59:99

At the bottom of one watch was an address, the same location that had given him nightmares. "That's the address to the warehouse."

"Where Cali is." Joanna peered over his arm at the screen. "The warehouse is fifty minutes from here. How far is the cabin?"

"Sixty." Kody's heart hammered as he thought through options. "Ash Mountain is close to David. He can save Raelyn. I'll go to the warehouse since it's closest." He rushed around, grabbed his pack and weapon, and called David, but it went to voicemail, so he texted instead.

Emergency. They've taken Raelyn. I need you to rescue and evac in Ash Mountain.
Sending address. Confirm.

Kody quickly sent a mass text to every military contact he still had, asking for help, but most of the soldiers he knew were overseas. Joann was on the phone with the emergency line, but it didn't sound like they believed her claim. Kody's gut squeezed at the thought of either Cali or Raelyn in pain or injured. He wrapped the watches around each wrist. A video showed a gray, fuzzy background and the sound of an engine. Then a horn. A metallic clank sounded on the live video stream, but no voices or images of a person appeared.

"They're still in transit."

Joanna's eyes were wide. "What if David doesn't answer? We can split up. I'll go after Raelyn. You get Cali." Joanna jumped toward the open window. "Maybe we can catch them en-route."

Kody froze. "Wait. Why did Zohaib's men take Raelyn and Cali at the very moment I left the room with you?" Kody pulled out his gun, pressing it to Joanna's temple. "Did you do this?"

She turned her head, so the barrel pushed between her eyes. "I wouldn't hurt Raelyn, and you're wasting time."

Kody slowly reached for the sheet and tied Joanna's wrists together in a tight knot.

"Stop! I'm on your side."

"Raelyn was right. We can't trust you. You did this."

"I didn't. I swear. Let me help her."

Pulling her toward his Jeep, his keys jangled together in his hand as he shoved her in the passenger seat. After the door slammed shut, he jumped inside with a death grip on the steering wheel and zoomed away.

On the highway, he scanned every car in the area for signs of suspicious activity. The sound of a man coughing came from the video feed on his left wrist. Swerving past cars, Kody glanced at the watch. The address continually flashed at the bottom, and something new popped up in the corner.

52:09

Fuck you, Zohaib.

Metal screeched, and light crept into the live stream, beaming onto a body lying sideways on the floor, motionless.

No! Please be alive.

The video jostled, and a man spoke in a foreign language, maybe German. The camera moved, showing the bare feet he had massaged so many times, the belly holding his child appeared, the slow rising and falling of her chest, and the shocked, paralyzed expression of Raelyn's wide-open eyes.

"What did they do to her?" Joanna shrieked.

Kody gulped hard. "She's alive. Look, her chest is moving."

"But she's not moving!" Joanna rocked back and forth, trying to unknot her wrists.

The man coughed again, and the video blurred out for a moment. Kody tapped on the watch and shook his wrist. When it came back into focus, a vest was strapped around Raelyn's body. His heart sank.

"Oh my god!" Joanna's voice was full of panic. "That's a bomb! They put a bomb on my daughter! Why isn't she fighting?"

Realization struck, sending panic through his veins. "They've paralyzed her."

"What? No!"

Kody accelerated to 100 miles per hour. He tried not to think about how David hadn't responded. Or that Raelyn was even farther away from him at this moment, headed toward the mountain cabin. Dread took over.

I can't save them both.

He untied Joanna's wrists with one hand. "I need your help. Can I trust you?"

27

RAELYN

I'm not going to die.

The heavy vest chaffed against her skin as Raelyn rolled against the floor of the van uncontrollably. Her arms were pinned to her sides, and she couldn't move an inch. A tiny hum came from inside the vest. She couldn't panic, hoping the ticking sound wasn't a bomb like she assumed.

Kody will come. He will.

Wind howled as the man opened the van and carried Raelyn to the warehouse, looming atop the hill like a dark castle.

"You're so small for being pregnant." The stranger's accent was thick. "Too bad your baby won't see the light of day."

A tear rolled down her cheek that she couldn't wipe away.

The skeleton of the building was half damaged by fire, scorched, and tattered on one side—and now she knew the whole story.

Ma burned it down to protect me.

There was more graffiti painted on the bricks outside, and a few more windows had been shattered, shards of glass scattered along the ground. So many questions ran through her mind, but she couldn't voice any of them. She had overheard the drivers saying Cali would be brought to the cabin in Ash Mountain, but that was an hour away. Did they put a bomb on her, too?

The sunset cast a red glow between the trees, and the air smelled woody with a tinge of pollen. A snapping came from the darkness as if someone had stepped on a twig.

Is it Kody?

But it was only a squirrel climbing higher. Her heart sank. The man's boots clomped on the earth until they reached the top of the hill. He pushed the door open with his shoulder. Metal creaked loudly in protest. His breath smelled of cigarettes when he exhaled onto her, but she couldn't even turn her head away. Inside, he laid her on the dirty floor, and the bomb dug into her side.

Stay calm. Maybe it's a decoy.

The man pulled over a chair. He set up something on a stand in front of the chair— his body blocking the view. If only she could roll, crawl, run away. But it was useless.

He muttered to himself and lugged Raelyn up and tied her to a chair. Slouching over and unable to hold up her head, Raelyn stared at the shadowy concrete. A dagger symbol was etched into the floor at her feet. She had met Kody at that very spot, where she had brushed her fingertips along the shape of that dagger. She wiggled her fingers, and hope surged through her veins that she could move them.

"Look at the camera. It'll make a better show," the man laughed gruffly.

Fear flooded her body. Amala wouldn't survive the stress if this man was about to induce pain.

He bent over and pulled something out of his backpack. "Want to see the last friend you'll ever make?" He crouched into her sightline near the floor and held out a large digital clock with red numbers flashing:

47:07
47:06

No!

She tried to strain against the rope, but her muscles weren't working. Sweat dripped down her temple. He set the clock at her feet, the only place she could see.

"Goodbye, sweetheart." Footsteps faded, and the metal door creaked in the distance until she was alone.

Kody will come.

She wanted to suck in a giant breath and fill her lungs with strength and relief that he had left, but voluntary movement was out of the question. Only the steady in and out of shallow breaths kept her heart ticking. The intense smell of gasoline hit her nostrils.

Oh God!

The minutes passed, but no flames came, just the heavy smell of raw fuel.

42:48
42:47

She squeezed her eyes shut and forced her mind to replace the odor with the smell of coffee, cinnamon, or freshly cut grass. She imagined birds singing. Fishing in a boat with Pa as the river water gently rocked the boat back and forth near the comforting roar of a waterfall. The warm sun beating onto her cheeks. Climbing a tree. Bark scratching her skin. Bear barking. Kody smiling. Cali singing. Cali struggling against a bomb strapped to her chest. Raelyn's mind reeled at the thought.

No. Stop. She'll be okay. We'll both be okay.

Raelyn wiggled her fingers again, able to move her wrist in a small circle. The need to keep Amala safe singed all fear as she tried to move her forearm— nothing.

I have to get this vest off.

She opened her eyes.

39:37

39:36

Stop! Stop ticking!

The sun had sunk, and shadows crept closer from moonlight in the high windows. A contraction seared through her insides and pulled at her stomach like a rubber band. Realizing that Amala was on her way sooner than expected gave Raelyn a strange sensation. Ma had been right. She was in the early stages of labor. For a moment, it felt like she had floated outside of her body and was watching from above. Flashbacks rushed back in a thunderous wave. Books from the library with the theme of motherhood. Going to Ma's funeral as a child. Staring up at Ma's article hung in their study for so many years. Wishing Ma had been at the photography contests.

Ma had let me down. But I still love her. And she still loves me.

Raelyn knew she had made a mistake in not forgiving Ma earlier, but resentment gnawed at her. All she wanted was to be free of the torment, free of the bomb strapped to her, free of Zohaib's control. Free.

Maybe if I'm dead, I'll feel that freedom. No more worry or pain.

37:27

There's no point. I can't escape. This is it.

A clatter echoed down a hallway, and someone ran toward her. She managed to raise her neck as the paralysis faded by the minute.

"Raelyn?" Liam's voice rattled through the warehouse.

No! Run!

She tried to yell but couldn't speak. She tried to raise her arm to point to the exit door, only lifting it halfway before it flopped down.

Liam came into view and raced over frantically but tripped on a dumbbell that sat on the floor by the workout equipment. His glasses fell off his face onto the floor, and he fumbled on the floor and placed them on his nose. Only one lens was intact. Crawling closer, he met her gaze. "Is this … is this a bomb?" His nose scrunched. "There's a lot of gas somewhere close. Oh my god, okay." He hovered his hands over the buttons on her chest. "Okay, I'll get you out."

How?

"Tell me what you know. Did they give you any information? Clues? Tools? Maybe I can cut the right wire." He stared at her, waiting.

She couldn't form a word.

"Okay, you can't talk. I got this." His eyes darted around the room. "Okay, hold on." Liam closed his eyes for a beat and inhaled deeply. "I can do this."

35:05

"It looks like I need a code. Six digits," Liam said.

Zohaib's voice calmly came through the camera. "Having fun yet? I should broadcast this. People would love it. Edge of your seat kind of stuff."

"You asshole! What's the code?" Liam screamed and hovered his finger over the buttons, about to punch in a number into her vest.

"I wouldn't do that if I were you. If you enter the wrong one, it'll blow you both."

Liam paused and turned toward the camera. "Tell me the code!"

"No."

Liam's veins pulsed in his neck. "She's your daughter! How could you do this?"

"That Walsh boy deserves to watch you both blow up after what he did to me."

Oh my god, Kody can see us.

Liam's eyes widened. "What?"

"That's right. This video is live streaming to them. They can see your every move. It probably hurts to know that Kody decided to save his sister instead."

A moan escaped her lips. Raelyn could swallow now, and she pried open her mouth. Only a puff came out.

"What was that? Speak up, daughter."

Liam's fists clenched, and he went rigid and screamed. "Tell me how to get her out!"

Zohaib smiled. "Nah, maybe I'll cut a few minutes off to make this more exciting."

Raelyn's heart strangled her. "She used every ounce of energy to push the words out between breaths. "My … baby…" Fatigue drowned her senses, but she started to regain control of more muscles. She moved her knee, then straightened her shoulders.

"What would you do for me to keep your baby safe?"

"Please." She forced the word out.

"Would you sacrifice Kody for her?"

She stared at the camera.

"I didn't think so. What about Liam?"

Liam stiffened and glanced between her and the camera.

"Now we know your favorites." Zohaib paused and chuckled. "It's good to know where your priorities lie. I can definitely use that to my advantage if you survive, but the odds aren't looking good, huh?"

27:05

More tears ran down her cheek.

"Oh, I know, how about Jawhara. Would you kill her to save the others?"

Using all energy, she nodded.

"Great. So, if Joanna arrives, kill your mother, then I'll give you the code."

She cringed at his words.

"We won't have time for that, you ass. Give us the code!" Liam yelled.

Raelyn's mind whirled as she used every effort to tap Liam. "Turn … it … off."

Liam turned off the camera and disabled the battery.

"Run!" The word sounded weak, so she pleaded with her eyes, wishing she could say more of a goodbye. But she had to keep Liam safe.

"I'm not leaving you." Liam started texting on his phone, then repocketed it and exhaled deeply. His green eyes latched onto hers. "I love you, sis." His crooked smile melted her heart—he looked so much like Pa.

"Liam."

"Don't give up now!" He turned a knob at the top of the vest. "I can do this!"

"Liam … go." She struggled to push out each word.

She knew it was the end. There was no escaping this. Zohaib had won. At least Kody would still have Cali, the only person who'd be able to keep him afloat in the aftermath.

23:54

He backed up and rubbed his sleeve over his sweaty forehead. "Raelyn, I … I don't know how to take it off."

"Leave." Tears formed behind her lids, but she held them back.

Liam's phone rang. "It's Kody." He held it out with trembling hands.

She swallowed hard, and her chest twisted into knots. Instead of just her hand, her whole arm shook as she reached out. "Ko … Kody?"

"Babe! Oh God! You're okay."

I'm not okay.

"Wait, you're at the warehouse? I thought … Shit! Shit! Shit! Okay, it's okay." He panted on the other end. "I'm running there, now. I'm only three miles away."

He can't get here in time. This is goodbye.

"Cali …?" Raelyn forced out a plea.

He was breathing hard, and she could hear his feet thumping as he said, "David Peterson and a man named Tucker disarmed her bomb. She's safe. Cali is okay. They're on the way to the police station."

A sob escaped her throat, and she used every bit of energy to force out the next words. "Ko … dy … love …you."

"Ssh, don't say that, Love. I'm close. I'll save you both."

Tears flowed down.

17:14

Any words weren't enough to show him how she truly felt, the enormity of how much he meant to her. She'd be ripping apart his life by not surviving but not being strong enough. "I love …" Her head dropped from exhaustion.

"No!" His heavy breathing exploded between crazed words. "Raelyn, hang on."

I know what I have to do.

28

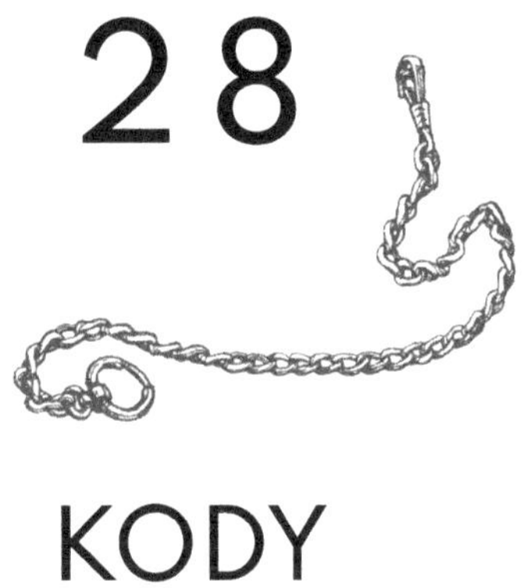

KODY

In the cloak of darkness, Kody sprinted faster than he'd ever run before, his muscular legs beating the pavement. The call dropped with Raelyn, or she had hung up.

She'll be safe. Almost there.

He checked the live stream—of course, Zohaib had switched their locations. On his watch, it was now clear that Cali was strapped to a chair in their old cabin, crying. David Peterson hadn't arrived yet. Kody had lied to Raelyn about her best friend's safety. On the screen, a man named Tucker paced in measured steps around the cabin with a rifle, no longer even trying to disengage the bomb. Kody's heart thumped harder than he thought imaginable. His watch flashed the countdown time.

8:24

His lungs burned, and his legs spasmed as he pushed harder. The navy sky embraced the incoming inky black. Headlights blinded him, and lampposts dotted his vision, but Kody's eyes remained straight ahead. A long road. Pebbles underfoot pressed into his boots and wind-whipped his face as he pumped his arms.

I'll get there in time. She'll be okay.

The traffic started moving again, and the cars on his left picked up speed, rushing past. Gusts of wind threatened to blow him over when the vehicles accelerated to their usual highway pace. A loud horn honked behind, and the gravel rumbled. Kody turned. Joanna waved from the driver's seat of his Jeep. He hustled to her and jumped in, sweat drenched his shirt.

He glanced at the clock.

5:06

Panting, he called David. "Are you with Cali yet?"

"I'm pulling up! Can't be distracted. Hanging up." But David didn't end the call, and Kody could hear everything. A car door slammed in the background, then heavy breathing. Another door.

"Hurry!" A deep voice barked, must have been Tucker, from Raelyn's contacts.

"Back away! Go down the mountain half a click."

"No! I'm not leaving the girl." Tucker bellowed.

Kody's stared at the live visual feed on his watch. His heart slammed under his ribcage as he pressed the phone hard against his ear.

Cali stifled sobs in the background and said, "There's only three more minutes."

What! No, we have five!

On the highway, Joanna peeled to the right. Their exit finally appeared, and Kody pointed to a road. "Turn!"

Rattling and clicking sounds came from the other side of the phone.

Cali moaned. "It's not gonna work!" For a moment, the camera faded to black then the image showed again.

"Quiet down." David sounded calm, focused.

Kody's leg bounced under the glove box, and his temples throbbed as Joanna swerved full speed through the intersection.

Cali squeaked on the other line. "Tell Kody I love him."

"No!" He yelled, and all his muscles tightened.

More rustling sounds came, then Cali's voice came in clear. "Kody? You're there?"

"Cali, everything's gonna be okay. David's got you. Just sing something. It'll just be a few more seconds."

Amid their conversation, the warehouse came into view behind a line of bare oak trees. The car jolted to a stop, and Kody rushed up the hill, legs shaking.

1:57

Have to save one of them.

Kody was sprinting to Raelyn. Leaping. Panting. Running.

"Take care of Raelyn. You've got her safe, right?" Desperation laced Cali's voice on the other end of the call.

He gulped down the dread ripping apart his insides. "Yeah, I've got her. We're leaving the warehouse now and headed to the hospital. Yohaan is here and keeping us all safe."

Cali's sobbing slowed, and her breathing turned regular. "Okay, good, good. Can Amala's middle name be Calipescia?"

Atop the hill, Kody froze for just a moment and bent over, agony tearing him apart. "Yes, Amala Calipescia Walsh. And you'll teach her how to sing," he choked on his words.

She sighed, seeming to understand her moments were up. "No, she'll be a boxer, like you."

Kody couldn't wait any longer. "I love you, Cali."

Cali laughed, music to his ears as she said, "Finally. It only took you eighteen years to say it."

A sob and painful laughter mixed together, burning a hole through his entire body.

In the video stream, Cali smiled, but it didn't reach her eyes. "I love you, too, Kody, and …"

The call dropped. Static on the live feed. With shaking fingers, he called her cell. Nothing. David's cell. Nothing.

Kody stared at the stars. Choked on tears, suffocated on the pain erupting inside. A painful scream scorched his throat and projected out into the night sky. Cali was gone.

She's gone.

He dropped to his knees and screamed and screamed and screamed again, his body raw. Unable to breathe and paralyzed with grief, Kody's head dropped heavy. He stared through the warehouse window. A large clock was flashing red.

00:50

Next to it, Liam knelt in front of Raelyn, fumbling with the bomb vest. Red numbers flashing on her chest too.

Kody shook his head, stumbled upright, and jolted forward, but just as he was about to swing the door open, Liam burst through with the bomb vest in his hand, running toward the tree line.

"Liam!" Kody shouted, "Liam!"

00:30

Liam darted away into the woods. Kody ran into the building where Raelyn was struggling against the rope taut around her chest and legs.

Her amber eyes widened. "Liam?"

As soon as Kody looked toward the doorway, flames engulfed the trees at the base of the hill, igniting the area orange and red.

"Liam!" Raelyn screamed and wrestled the ropes, but her movements looked like she was drunk. She didn't have any coordination or strength.

He dug a Swiss Army knife from his pocket and cut her free, then held her sagged weight in his arms.

"My brother," her voice sounded broken, forced, and hysterical.

Kody let his tears fall on her silky brown hair as he held her, clutching her close to his chest. "You're here, alive. Breathe. Ssshh, stay with me. You're okay."

Cali's not. She's gone.

He stared up at the cobwebs lining the old windows high in the warehouse.

The room I met Raelyn.

In a mental fog, a flashback whirled before him of the first time he laid eyes on Raelyn in this very space. The same gym equipment that he exercised with and lighter weights were missing since the last time he was there, and dozens of cigarettes littered the floor. He inhaled deeply, and the smell of boxing gloves was obscured by gas, assaulting his nostrils. He could barely think straight, unable to focus on the present moment and not allowing his mind to think of Cali yet.

Raelyn felt so warm to the touch while she weakly stood and fought against his grip. "Liam!" She leaned on Kody, using him as a crutch.

He supported her and led the way, terrified of what they might find outside.

As they stepped through the door, Raelyn leaned on him.

"Liam?" Her voice turned frantic, but her strength seemed to be returning. "Did you see him?"

Kody gulped.

"Liam?" Her voice rang loud between the trees where black smoke rose.

He tugged her hand and pulled her into his chest. That beautiful belly stayed protected between them both. His future. Their future.

"Babe, I don't think he—"

"Raelyn?" Liam's voice cracked from behind a tree.

She gasped and hobbled off, slanted sideways, gripping the trunks for support.

Liam poked his head out from behind a tree where he was sitting on the ground. "My glasses broke. I can't see which way to go."

Raelyn fell into Liam's arms, sobbing. "You're okay!"

But Cali's not.

Shock overtook his system, and he just stood there, staring at the two hugging. Everything felt numb.

Liam nodded. "I threw that vest as far as I could, and there was enough time to run in the other direction."

They walked silently back to Kody's Jeep, and he wrapped one arm around her waist, unable to get out a word.

She curled into Kody's body, and her faint whisper of gratitude about cracked his heart in half when her voice trembled, "Thanks for always keeping us safe. I love you."

He dropped his head.

But … Cali.

Raelyn winced and hunched over.

"Babe, are you—?" The way she was squeezing his hand so tightly sent his pulse racing. "We're going to the hospital."

She stood straight. "How did your Jeep get here? I thought you were running."

He barely heard her question. "Joanna ..."

"Mom's here?" Liam looked around. "Hey, mom. You used to carry a spare set of my glasses. Do you have one now?"

Raelyn tapped Liam's arm. "She's not here at this exact moment."

"Well, where has she gone?" Liam asked.

Gone. Cali's gone.

Kody felt like a zombie, walking through nothingness. The forest didn't make sense around him. The night sky seemed to laugh at him. It seemed like he was the one drugged and paralyzed, and the world was pushing him down, burying him alive. His mind felt blank. No feelings rushed through his heart. Emptiness. Absence, like time itself, had truly stopped. Maybe he was dreaming.

Like a ghost, Kody pushed the metal gate open, making it creak under his touch. Ants crawled over each other up the gate, creeping over his hand. The bugs moved in and out of focus like he was drunk.

Cali's gone. Cali's gone. Cali's …

"What now?" Liam asked.

"Follow me."

Kody just stared, unsure if they had even said anything or if it was his imagination. Did it really matter anyway?

"Kody? Come on."

STOP THE CLOCK

With Raelyn in the lead, Kody trudged up the steep hill aimlessly, wondering when he could just sit down. Maybe he wouldn't have to get back up again. Ever.

Four geckos scampered up the side of the warehouse wall. How strange. If Cali were here, she'd make some joke. But that would never happen again. Kody held in a laugh at the absurdity of that fact. It was real. How would he even move tomorrow? Or the next day? What was the point?

He thought he heard Raelyn speak up and focused on a few words "... hourglass symbol ... Pa's journal ... computer lab."

I should've gone after Cali. I didn't even save Raelyn. Liam did.

Raelyn stepped through the threshold. "Let's go look for Ma. I don't want to be here any longer."

Unable to think, Kody allowed her to tug him along like an old, tired dog on a leash.

Cali is dead. She's dead. She's gone. She'll never sing again.

Bile rose in his throat, and he swallowed it down, then palmed his forehead and squeezed his eyes shut tight.

"... my email ... proof ... Zohaib guilty." Did Raelyn say that, or did he imagine a conversation?

Cali! Need to sit down. I can't breathe.

"... lab has power." That must've been Liam talking. Maybe.

Numb to everything, Kody peered down the hall, watching for movements. An eerie feeling gnawed in his gut that something else was about to explode and ruin their last chances of making it out of there alive.

Raelyn moved forward and pushed the old door the rest of the way open with her foot, making a loud groan. "If we can't find anything, then we'll go to someplace that has a signal. That way, we can call Cali too."

I can't breathe.

Kody's heartbeat accelerated as he laid one hand over his chest. They stood in front of a door with three bullet holes, a warning to turn back. The rusty hinges ground as Raelyn pushed her shoulder into it. Kody followed, in a trance, stuck in a whirl of cloudy fog. This was all just a nightmare, and he'd wake up soon.

On the other side of the threshold was a long, dark hallway lined with more closed doors. Kody's heart ticked faster at the possibility of anyone in one of those rooms who might be armed.

"Are you okay, Kody?" Raelyn's voice sounded a world away, fuzzy, and thick.

He stopped abruptly, and Raelyn's large belly bumped into his back.

"Oh!" Liam ricocheted off of her, and they almost fell like dominoes until Kody caught Raelyn in one arm and Liam in the other.

"… bunch of beetles crawling up … ceiling." Someone was talking, or maybe he was hallucinating.

Kody smacked his cheeks hard and tried to focus on what they were saying, but all he could think about was Cali's scared face the moment before her bomb detonated.

Liam turned to the mass of insects that covered much of the wall. He grunted. "Freaky."

"Where's … hourglass drawing?"

Kody stopped trying to concentrate on their conversation and leaned against the wall in defeat, attempting to block out all sounds, sights, and feelings. It didn't work, but everything seemed to move in slow motion.

Liam pointed to the wall. A large, drawn hourglass. Sand poured out in graffiti gold.

Before Raelyn turned the handle of the door, she faced him. "Okay, y'all. It all ends tonight. Here and now. Zohaib won't win. We got this."

He's already won.

Inside the lab, the smell of decay wafted through the air. Liam sneezed, then again and again. Wrought iron detailing rusted through the ceiling pipes. He shoved over tables of old dusty computers that filled the space, then flipped on the light switch, but none of the lights had bulbs. A hint of moonlight beamed through three windows on the southern wall.

Raelyn pulled Kody's hand, her skin soft and warm, snapping him out of the abyss for a moment, then reality sucked him back down, tainting all sensations into a cloudy flurry of confusion.

"Any zombies?" *Liam's voice.*

"No zombies. And no Ma." *Raelyn's.*

"I'll see if I can figure out a way to turn these on."

"Can you see?"

"When I squint, it's better."

They droned on and on about whatever. The conversation didn't matter because it wasn't about Cali. Boulders stacked on his heart. Jagged glass shredded his heart. Poison flooded his veins. A noose gagged him lifeless.

"Kody? You don't look good." A fingertip brushed against his, but whose?

"Hm? What?"

A flicker of movement was reflected in the computer screen.

"Is someone outside?" Raelyn said that one, he was sure of it. But it was hard to see her lips move when images of pieces of his sister's body spread dead on the floor behind her, bleeding out.

I can't breathe.

A shifting shadow swayed somewhere. Slowly, he moved closer to the window. Bracing himself against the brick wall, he peeked his head around the window frame but didn't check all angles. His shoulders slumped. Liam was fiddling with cords, and Raelyn crawled, groping under the tables, her belly almost sweeping the floor.

Why are we even here?

Kody stared at them, dumbfounded.

"Can you look for the file up there, Kody?" *Raelyn.*

Right, the file.

He blindly fumbled on the shelves above his head. Dusty books toppled as he slid his hand across the grain.

A soft floorboard creak came from the hall.

"Mom?" *Liam's voice.*

Joanna stood leisurely against the door frame.

"How did you get here?" *Raelyn.*

"I had to sweep the perimeter and make sure no one was coming." *Joanna.*

Does she know we were too late? Does she know Cali was blown up?

Raelyn ran to her. They wrapped their arms tightly around each other as if squeezing away all the trauma from the last year.

I'll be the one who has to tell her about Cali.

Joanna took Raelyn's cheeks in her hands. "Everything will be okay."

No, it won't.

Kody used the wall as a crutch, supporting all his weight, unsure how long he could stay standing. A world without Cali wasn't a place he wanted to live in.

Liam coughed. "This computer works. You followed the exact instructions I gave you when sending that email to Zohaib, right?"

"Yeah, why?" *Raelyn.*

"I added a feature. If Zohaib opens the email and if the virus works, we won't be the only ones to gain access to his files, and it'll go straight to Yohaan's email too." *Liam.*

"Isn't that the cop who stopped investigating Zohaib after their precinct was bought out? Why would he help us?"

God, everyone just shut up.

Shadows covered the wall, but a beam of light hit the corner, in a spot he hadn't paid much attention to before.

Liam pointed. "Look, there's another faded hourglass symbol there." He dragged a chair closer to the wall, making the legs shriek, and stood atop to reach up on a shelf. He coughed from the smell of mold and pushed aside books. Dust flew, making him sneeze.

"I can't reach."

Kody knew he had some sort of duty, but what exactly that was, didn't feel clear anymore. He felt his jaw hanging loose and snapped it shut at the sound of his name.

"Kody? Did you hear me? Can you reach that?"

Mindlessly, Kody took Liam's place and reached. His hand lingered over the last book. There was a keyhole in the wall. Surrounding it was a faint square—maybe a safe.

He inserted his knife and twisted it. Inside the safe sat a little white box, similar to the one he had stolen so long ago. His heart jolted. "Something is here."

Raelyn lifted her head, and her amber eyes grew wide. Her jaw dropped as she opened the little box. She inhaled deeply. Inside lay a small USB. "Could this be it?"

A door slammed down the hall. Joanna jerked into a fighting stance and aimed her gun.

Something's not right.

"Let's go." He had no more energy to fight off Zohaib's other threats.

Footsteps approached too fast.

"What do we do?" *Liam.*

Kody froze.

"Kody?" *Raelyn.*

He stared. "What?"

"Jesus Christ! Wake up, soldier!" Joanna flipped the nearest table onto its side and moved Raelyn behind it.

"Liam! Get behind here!" *Joanna.*

Liam rushed over and covered Raelyn's body with his. Footsteps echoed down the hall closer. In a daze, Kody pulled out his gun with shaky hands and stumbled toward the door. But Joanna jumped in front of him into the hallway and squeezed her trigger. Two shots were fired. A loud grunt.

A thump. Loud groan. Female pitch.

"Crap!" Joanna said, her electric eyes spiked fear inside him. Silence. A citrusy orange scent wafted through the air, followed by a copper tinge of blood.

The next sound bombed his core. "Walsh?" From the darkness, Dabbott's voice cracked with weakness.

No!

That voice smacked him back into reality. Kody rushed into the hall, squinting. Heart thundering. His foot thudded into Dabbott, sprawled on the floor. He dropped to his knees. "No!"

He glanced down the hall. Dabbott had come alone—as his backup—just like he had asked.

Raelyn raced out, phone in hand, shining a light. It reflected off the red soaking Dabbott's neck. Blood rippled out, draining into a pool on the floor. Raelyn gasped, frozen to the spot.

Kody pushed his hand against the wound. Warm stickiness flowed over his fingers. He cradled her head in his lap. Dabbott choked on her own blood. Her brown eyes locked onto Kody's, showing her pain. They glistened and lost their focus, giving up.

"No! Dabbott, hold on." Kody pressed hard, but his hand was drowning in her blood.

Joanna's voice was flat behind him. "I thought it was Zohaib."

Panting, Kody's chest tightened. Her gurgling sounds scorched against his heart. "It's okay."

Dabbott pointed to Joanna's ankle with all her remaining effort, where a silver metal piece flashed little red dots. Her hand went limp, and Dabbott's last breath shuddered out from her body.

Kody's head drooped. He pulled his blood-soaked hand away and stared down at his best friend. An image of Cali dying flashed spotty in his vision. Then the boy who had hung himself in that truck. More bloodied bodies of soldiers and innocent people haunted and threatened to take control.

I couldn't save any of them.

Sniffing, Raelyn put a shaking hand on his shoulder. Kody wanted to hold Raelyn, hug her, melt into her comfort, but he was soaked in Dabbott's blood. Liam stood at the doorframe, wide-eyed. Next to him, Joanna slowly backed into the computer room, out of sight.

"It's not your fault." Raelyn squeezed him.

Agony consumed him as he screamed."

His throat went dry at the crimson pool spread beneath Dabbott and the hallway floor. He gently placed Dabbott's head on the cold floor and wiped his hands on his pants. Kody stood in a trance and gripped his gun hard.

I couldn't save William … because of Joanna.

Kody marched down the hall, ignoring Raelyn, who clung desperately to his elbow.

I couldn't save the soldiers!

Kody rammed his shoulder against the door on the way into the computer room and pushed Liam into the hall.

I couldn't save Dabbott because of Joanna.

Joanna picked up a chair and smashed it through a window. Glass rained down. She was only halfway through when Kody raised his gun took aim.

I couldn't save Cali! Someone has to pay.

29

RAELYN

Raelyn's heart battered hard. "Kody!" The stagnant air smelled thick of fresh blood, causing her to suppress the urge to vomit. She used all her strength to pull Kody away from the smashed window. "Kody, focus on me."

With flames in his eyes, he turned away from Ma fast and punched the wall, screaming in agony. A hole gaped in the middle, and cracks crept up to the ceiling.

"Here, say goodbye to her." Raelyn guided him back to Dabbott, knowing he'd want a minute alone with her body. She brushed a reassuring hand over his back. He had been acting strange but couldn't spend time talking with him about it yet

She stepped away toward the window, calling loudly, "Ma, wait, I need your help!"

Ma moved out from around the corner of the building. "I didn't know she was a friend."

"We'll talk about that later."

"I may not have a later."

"What?"

"Nothing." Ma shook her head.

"Tell me about your anklet. You're still being tracked, aren't you?"

Ma nodded. "As long as the tracker was on, he wasn't supposed to come for you."

She gritted her teeth and lifted her chin. "Okay, listen to me. I have a plan. Please keep watch behind the trees just in case. Can I count on you?"

"Yes, I'll be in the shadows, as always."

Raelyn stepped back in through the broken window, carefully avoiding the sharp edges.

"Come on, Kody. We can't stay here." She dragged him up.

"My best friend …" he mumbled and staggered.

Kody didn't seem to process her words, but she tugged him down the hall. His weight bore down on her as if he had lost the will to move. She gripped the box tightly in her palm until they reached fresh air. Kody's best friend was dead. Raelyn supported Kody, trying to hold the distraught pieces of him together. Each heavy step he trudged along looked like he was allowing himself to seep into a crack in the earth, dooming himself to a life in a fiery hell. Kody staggered away and trudged down the slope with a phone to his ear again. Watching him in agony made her whole-body ache.

Standing atop the hill, Raelyn looked down at a cemetery—still as death. The marble tombstones were chipped and had eroded into rows of crumbling mounds. Raelyn stared at a cracked angel statue half-covered with moss, guarding the sea of the dead. How could one place feel so full and yet so empty at the same time?

Every name on the stones had their own adventures, worries, fears, successes, hardships, and triumphs. They each knew love, loss, mistakes, and regrets. And they each found themselves resting for eternity here in front of her eyes. The dead souls around her sent prickles up her spine and made the hoots of the owls in the thicket's shadows more noticeable.

She trailed down the path, taking small steps to avoid falling. Raelyn followed Kody over a stone bridge while her fingers traced carved letters on a nearby tombstone.

Did this woman have a daughter?

The skeleton under her feet had probably made hundreds of mistakes in her lifetime.

Just like Ma. Just like me.

Raelyn sighed. There was no chance of being a perfect mother or giving her child everything in this big world. Something Pa had said once came to mind, his voice crystal clear. *Family always forgives. There's no need to hold onto anger. It only poisons the water.*

Raelyn slid her fingertips over her belly. "Will you forgive me when I make mistakes, baby girl?"

Amala kicked.

"We can do this, and maybe I can forgive Ma too."

The night was unusually quiet, with barely a breeze as if the world was holding its breath, expecting something big to happen. Raelyn breathed in the moment; despite it being full of Dabbott's loss, she was finally certain of her future—motherhood. She gazed down at the murky waters below as he looked over to her.

"I need to tell you something," said Kody quietly.

She nodded and took his hands.

After a big breath, his eyes dropped. "In the jungle, Zohaib commanded I capture women. I was locked in a box for weeks." He couldn't meet her eyes. "I think that's how Zohaib commanded his soldiers to get the victims pregnant."

So many moments passed by as she struggled to digest this information. Her fingertips trailed along his bearded jaw, and those dark brown eyes searched hers.

Kody's whole body went rigid. "I took a woman … away from her child and village ... I'm sorry."

She let out a breath she had been holding while searching his face for answers. "And did you … um … do the other thing?"

"No, but everything in my gut points to the fact that a box he trapped us in was meant for that." He shook his head. "If Dabbott hadn't rescued me,

I'd still be there now, caged and forced to ..." His eyes began to glaze over, and tears ran down his cheeks. Sobs erupted from deep within his chest, his entire body racked, releasing all the pent-up emotion. "I failed Eliza. Then I failed Dabbott. And now C—"

Raelyn wrapped her arms around him, squeezing him so tight that he could scarcely breathe. "You didn't fail, Kody. Some things are out of our control."

His head dropped into his hands, so she rubbed his back softly and said, "We've got each other."

Finally, Kody looked up with red-rimmed eyes, then nodded. "Do you need more details … about ... what I did?"

"I'm here to listen if you want to share, but I'm not going to push you."

Kody stared at the bugs crawling over the hard ground. "I made Eliza a promise. I'm going to keep it. I need to form a team to revolt against Zohaib. I couldn't save my best friend, but I can still save you."

Her heart ached for him.

"She didn't even know she was my best friend." He sounded so broken as his voice cracked.

"Dabbott would have known."

He dropped his head in his hands. "No, not Dabbott." But his words faded.

Confused, she kneaded his muscles deeply with her thumbs. "How can I help?"

He turned toward her and moved to his knees. "Please, please go into hiding without me. I can keep you two safe if I form a team. I won't let anyone else die. I promise."

Her stomach contracted. "Kody." She had never seen him so distraught.

"And please don't give our baby up for adoption. If I survive, I'll come back and feed her and get up with her each night." Kody leaned into her body. "Don't worry. I'll change all the diapers and—"

She sighed and stroked his head. "We're keeping her. I won't be a perfect mother, but I'll do my best. We're strong together, and we can fight through the challenges."

Still on his knees, Kody exhaled and wrapped his arms around her. "Thank God." His shoulders softened as his glistening eyes met hers. "It's what Cali would've wanted."

"What?" She stared at his face, knowing she heard him wrong.

His face looked like a lost schoolboy. "You'll go into hiding with Amala? And when this is all over, I'll join you?"

"No, Kody. I won't live in fear. We are keeping her, but I refuse to be trapped."

He shook his head. "How can I guarantee your safety?"

"You can't."

Kody's eyes grew wide, and his mouth dropped. "I have to. You're all I have left."

What does that mean?

Raelyn pulled him up. "Kody, just love me. If we have one day, one year, or one eternity, just love me in the time we have." She covered his thick lips with her fingertips.

"No matter what happens, someone gets hurt."

"You won't be able to save everyone. But if we keep fighting, if we keep pushing forward, we can save at least someone. You've already saved me. One person matters."

Kody leaned against her.

His intense deterioration scared her a little, but she knew she had to hold it together for his sake and asked, "What do you need?"

"I need a minute." Kody's face was full of dread as he walked away behind an oak tree.

Liam silently appeared next to Raelyn, rubbing his eyes. "So … Dabbott just died. That was messed up. We're all gonna need counseling."

Unable to think too far in the future, Raelyn confessed the only thing she was currently sure of anymore. "I told Kody we're keeping Amala."

"I knew you would."

"I refuse to be like Ma."

"Maybe Mom isn't as bad as you think."

"Okay, if Ma ends up being this perfect specimen, then what if I'm like Zohaib? I used Cali's body as a means to an end, selfishly, without caring for her safety."

Liam coughed. "I thought you said Cali volunteered to send the video?"

"She did."

"Then you can't dismiss that. After that douchebag captured her in the desert, she should be able to get revenge too." Liam nudged her shoulder gently.

Raelyn twisted a blade of grass between her fingers. "I'm so glad David got to her in time. Phoenix always talked about how his dad was his hero, and he even messed up a few years ago."

Liam faced her. "Every parent makes mistakes, Rae. You won't be perfect."

She sighed deeply. "How do I know everything will turn out okay?"

"You don't, but you can't avoid being a parent because you're scared. I bet our dad was scared out of his mind when he had to raise you alone, but he didn't run."

Memories flashed in her mind of when Pa first taught her how to use a wrench, how to track animals in the woods, and how to swing an axe.

"You're right." Raelyn looked at Liam. "If Pa could do it, I can too. He taught me what I needed to know. But, I'll have Kody to help anyways."

"That's right." Liam coughed. "Guess what, I memorized one of your poems."

"You did?"

Liam cleared his throat dramatically. "Inky pens drip, ooze and smear. Rhyming words of hesitation and fear. Liquid drops of unknown on a page. Keep me trapped in this iron cage."

"I wrote that about fear." Raelyn lifted her chin. "I can't hold onto my fear anymore. I'll raise Amala with Kody, and everything will be fine."

Small buds covered the branches where flowers would soon sprout. Spring was around the corner, harboring new life. As the moonlight reflected off the pocket watch around her neck, an idea popped into her head. The ticking of the watch couldn't compete with her racing heart.

I know how to make things right.

Liam nudged her side. "You have me and Cali to help too."

"Let's call her to check in. I think I'm still in shock." She looked at her trembling hand. "I hope she's not too worried."

As she dialed, the gloom of the cemetery lifted when the moon popped out from behind a cloud, showing textures of mother nature's browns she hadn't noticed before. Afar, Kody was still sitting in the cemetery, staring into the darkness of the forest.

The phone stopped ringing, and shallow breathing came from the other side.

"Cali?"

A soft sigh came then Cali squealed. "Oh my God! You're alive! I've been trying to call you. Is Kody okay?"

"He's … grieving." She tilted her head at the sight of Kody in the distance, hunched over a tombstone and utterly defeated. "Dabbott died."

"Oh, shit. How?"

"Um, Ma shot her by accident."

"Damn. I can't even think straight, Rae. We were both just attached to bombs."

Raelyn's body tightened. "I'm trying to forget about that for a minute."

"I have bad news." Cali's voice lowered. "When David got the bomb off of me, Tucker ran off with it into the forest. He died, Rae."

She gasped and clamped her eyes shut. "Tucker? Are you sure?"

"Positive. I'll have nightmares for years." Cali spoke softly. "He was a good guy."

"I don't know what to say."

"I'm taking Shiloh with me down the mountain. Can I talk to Kody?"

"Yeah, hold on." Raelyn walked over to Kody and held out the phone. "Cali wants to talk to you."

His head snapped in her direction, and he bolted upright. "What?"

"It's Cali, and she wants to make sure you're okay."

His hands shook. "She's alive?"

"Um … yeah, David saved her, you told me that, remember?"

Kody's dark brown eyes widened when he grabbed the phone. "Cali?"

After a moment, Raelyn watched Kody drop to his knees and lean his head on the dirt. He pounded one fist into the ground repetitively.

Raelyn covered her arms over his broad back, feeling his trembling body under hers.

"I thought you were dead," his words were so soft, so vulnerable.

Her jaw dropped, finally understanding.

What? Oh my god. Oh, Kody…

Tears threatened to spill. Raelyn rubbed her hand up his back in small circles over his skin. Cali was rambling fast on the other line, but she couldn't make out the words.

"Don't you EVER scare me like that again," he said as if that was all he could muster up. His shoulders shook as he kept listening to his sister.

He thought he had lost her.

Eventually, Kody said goodbye, hung up, then stretched his arms to Raelyn, pulled her onto his lap, and kissed her forehead.

"Cali's okay," he said. "She's okay." His glistening eyes turned focused again as he rose and straightened. "We won't leave Dabbott's body here."

"I'll call Yohaan, and he'll know what to do." The phone only rang once, then Yohaan picked up.

"Raelyn? Is that you?" Air freshener sprayed in the background. "Zohaib clicked on the link you sent him. We have access to enough of his files to put him away for life."

"Really? It worked?"

"Wait! Aah! No! Crap!" Yohaan's voice boomed.

"What?" Pens clicked in the background as Yohaan said, "That virus just brought down all our computers. We lost it all!"

Raelyn paused. "I have a plan."

An abrupt sound of a chair leg screeching against the floor on the other line was followed by Yohaan's desperate pleas. "Raelyn, don't put yourself in any danger."

"Listen. I have to make sure my baby girl won't ever fall into his hands. Zohaib could make Amala's life a living hell. I have to be one of the good guys. Amala won't have to be afraid because I'll take care of her. I can finish this."

Heavy breathing on the other side was followed by, "What do you need?"

"Drive here to the warehouse. I'll bait Zohaib."

Crickets played Marco-Polo during the rest of their conversation. After she finished her call, one owl hooted. Raelyn walked to the man she loved.

"You okay, Kody?" she asked.

"Cali's alive. She's safe."

Wrapping her arms around him tight, she buried her head in his chest. "I can't believe you went through that alone. Always lean on me. That's what I'm here for."

A sudden tightness clamped hard in her abdomen. She hissed sharply but did her best to not move.

"I'm taking you to the hospital."

"In a few minutes. I have to do something first."

His eyes narrowed.

She gestured toward the cars. "Let me send Liam ahead of us to alert the doctors and get us a room."

Her gaze moved across the scene. Atop the hill, the warehouse towered into the night clouds. As they walked hand in hand, a strange light floated in the air near the black gate. It looked like a ribbon of blue haze, a steady glow hovering.

Raelyn pointed. "Do you see that?" The faint light didn't move or reflect. It was just there.

She stared at the light, feeling an overwhelming calm soothe her racing mind until another contraction bit down on her muscles, twisting them together like Pa used to ring out a towel. She groaned.

Kody pulled his keys out fast. "You need to get to a hospital. There's one ten minutes away."

"Okay, but first, I need to lure Zohaib here. That way, Yohaan can take him into custody." Raelyn raised a hand. "Don't worry, none of us will still be here by the time Zohaib arrives. I need Liam to help me send a message, and we will all drive away unharmed." She winced at her words, somehow forgetting Dabbott for a moment. "I mean, us three will leave unharmed. Um, Liam, can you see the screen if you squint?"

"I found spare contacts in the Jeep." Liam sneezed all over her phone. "Uh, sorry." He wiped it with his sleeve. "So, what do you want me to type?"

She peeked over his shoulder. "You're using that fake email that's connected to Yohaan, right?"

"Yes."

"Um … tell him Jawhara and I are tied up and waiting for him."

While Liam typed, Raelyn tilted her head at the sight of so many beady eyes watching her from high tree branches. She couldn't remember seeing so many forest animals.

That's spooky.

"It's all ready. All you have to do is press send." Liam handed the phone back.

Before Liam hopped in the driver's seat, Raelyn kissed her brother's forehead. "Please go to the hospital on State Street and let them know I'm on the way."

"You're in labor, aren't you?"

She nodded softly so Kody wouldn't see.

He smiled and slid the seat belt on. "I'm gonna be an uncle!"

Watching Liam drive away sent a strange buzz through her system. Her nerves planted an irrational fear that she would never see Liam again. The bluish light nearby grew and then disappeared in an instant, like the blue flash from an electrical short-circuit. Raelyn shook her head in disbelief.

Her finger hovered over the screen. "Let's finish this." She glanced at Kody quickly.

After he nodded, she pushed the 'send' button.

There's no turning back now.

30

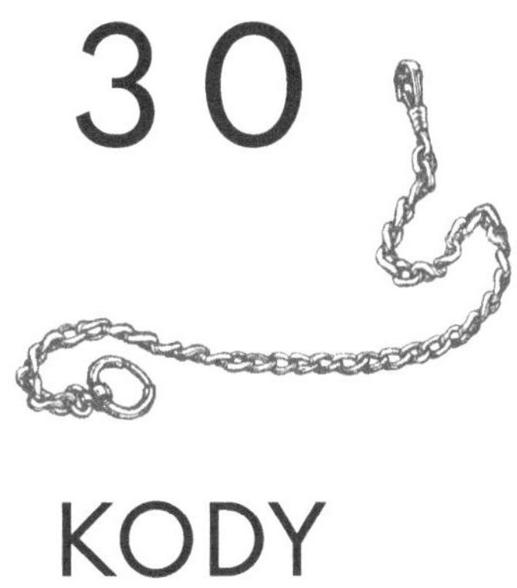

KODY

"Ready to go?" Kody asked. "Seems like Amala is eager to meet you."

"Yeah, let me text Cali to meet us at the hospital."

I'm gonna be a dad!

Nearby, a rustling sound crept from the cemetery. A hooded figure ran from behind oak trees, kicking pebbles onto his boots. Kody's eyes darted up and locked onto Joanna's wild blue eyes. As he was about to apologize for his earlier outburst, a heavy hand grabbed Kody's other wrist and yanked him backward. His troubled shoulder popped out of place. Raw pain. Kody roared as he slammed into the dirt.

"Raelyn, run!"

Two figures silently moved in the shadows. Someone jumped closer and kicked Kody behind the knees, but the other rocketed a punch to the attacker's face. The two strangers scrambled in front of Kody until a fist slammed his cheek. Kody's head snapped back, and he fell to the side, a metallic taste covering his tongue. Everything went black for a moment when he heard a man whisper in his ear, "Eliza got us together. Wait for Marlee's signal."

The signal.

A foot clobbered his stomach, and he went rolling over weeds, cuts scraped open his forearms. After catching his breath, Zohaib's eyes stared down at Kody, infected with power.

"Get up. You've caused me so much hell. Your death won't be clean or pretty."

Zohaib stalked between gravestones like the predator that he was, holding an AK47, wearing a bullet-proof vest, and pockets, no doubt stuffed with other weapons. He kicked Kody straight in the jaw. Bone ground on bone and his teeth chattered hard. His body struck the earth again. Ashes billowed up from the ground. Pressure throbbed in Kody's entire face and one eye was already swelling shut.

Fuck!

In front of the metal gate, Zohaib paced. "I'm gonna cause you so much pain for leaving the jungle." He swiped his knife out and pushed the sharp point against Kody's temple. "Do you want to guess what happened after you disappeared?"

Kody was breathless as he tasted copper but stayed as still as a statue as Zohaib broke open his skin. A drip of warm blood slid down his cheek to his neck.

"Your pretty jungle girlfriend convinced half my soldiers to revolt against the others. Now you've lost me those men. I needed them. And you completely fucked up my bomb game. How did you even do it? No, don't tell me. I'll have fun getting the answers out of you."

"I'm not afraid of you."

Zohaib laughed. "Let's change that." He pulled Kody up with a fistful of his shirt.

He lifted his rifle high in the air and struck it hard across Kody's cheek. Then again. Again. It slammed. Over and over. Kody spat out blood, splattering onto the ground. He tried to yell, but an intense throbbing spread all over his body. Zohaib kicked him to his side, rolled him over, and pinned him. He pulled out ties from his pocket and cuffed him tightly. The unforgiving plastic dug into Kody's wrists. Zohaib kicked dirt in Kody's eye. His heavy boot stood on Kody's temple, pushing his face hard into an exercise mat. The scent of the sweat overtook the smell of blood.

"Afraid yet?"

Raelyn's scream pierced the air.

What happened?

"Oh, that makes her easy to find," snickered Zohaib.

His heart rammed hard and heavy. "Leave her alone, and I'll do whatever you want."

"You said that last time." Zohaib crouched and wrapped a rope around Kody's chest. Then he whistled a high-pitched, screeching call that made birds in the ceiling rafters fly away. Immediately, dozens of figures marched from the shadows of the oak trees, blending into the night. Kody could barely see. They walked closer. Armed soldiers.

We're surrounded.

Kody begged the soldiers, mirroring his pleas in the jungle. "There's more of you than him. We can take Zohaib down and be done with him."

He could still see through one of his eyes, but the other was sealed shut. One soldier gave him a slight, intentional nod.

What does that mean?

Hazy figures approached from the corner. Bernardo emerged behind a tree and pulled Raelyn to a trunk stub.

"Where's my Jawhara? Her tracker should be on." Zohaib boomed to Bernardo. "You, go search the forest. She's not far."

Some soldiers swayed nervously, glancing between each other.

Zohaib pointed the gun at Raelyn and hollered, "Where is your mother?"

She glared flames of fire at the abusive monster. Her face was flushed and sweat glistened her forehead.

"Fine." Zohaib snarled. "Punish her."

The soldier pulled her in front of Kody. "Babe, I'll figure this out."

Her frantic eyes met his. "Amala's coming. Now. I can't do this."

"What? Now?" He wanted to hold her hand, to rub the hair away from her face.

She took a long, labored breath in and squeezed her eyes shut, then dropped her head back to the stars. "It hurts. I can't." Her knuckles turned white from clutching her purse.

Kody swallowed hard, his heart shattering. He needed to take away her pain and fix it all. He kissed her sweaty forehead. "You can do this. You're so strong. We'll be okay."

The rope ranked against him, sliced into his chest like a razor, and pulled Kody backward. His head crashed into the ground. The forest spun above him.

"Tie him to the gate."

The rough ground scraped into his arms as they dragged him. Exhaustion and pain took over. The rope dug into his chest. He tried to roll to his side and kneel, but the soldiers kept kicking him down.

Raelyn's whimpers grew more desperate. Kody's head felt heavier than a bowling ball as someone tied him up and metal poked into his back. The restraint cut into his wrists. He spat out blood.

Zohaib pointed at Raelyn. "When she's done pushing that nuisance out, I'll have more leverage up my sleeve. But I've seen enough births to know she's still got some time. I wanted to let you know that when she's put back together, in a month or so, my boys will sure have some fun with her back in Tahil."

Rage boiled in his veins, scalding hot, but he couldn't move. Across the clearing, Bernardo fiercely lifted Raelyn to her feet. She let out a howl and hunched over, grabbing her stomach. Bernardo slid off his belt.

"Leave her alone!" Kody screamed at Bernardo, making his throat raw.

Zohaib sneered. "Ever been whipped, Walsh?"

"Stop!" Kody shouted. He wanted to fall on his knees and beg, but the rope restrained him too tightly.

"I wonder if she'll even be able to feel the whip with all those contractions." Zohaib tilted his head. "Let's run a test."

Raelyn gripped a tree trunk as they lifted her shirt up a bit, exposing her bareback.

"Tell me, soldier. Are you afraid now?"

"Yes." He choked out the word, unable to breathe in a full breath. "Let her go."

A loud crack smacked something hard, and she screamed.

Oh my god!

Zohaib leaned in and whispered. "You can still save her."

"Let her go."

Another crack. She cried out again.

"Let her go!" The restraints dug further into Kody's skin, and his voice cracked just like his broken spirit.

Another crack across the clearing. Raelyn's scream pierced his soul.

Zohaib dug a little hole in front of Kody and buried the hilt of his dagger in the ground, blade pointed straight up to the moon.

"What do you want?"

Zohaib stared him down. "Kill yourself, and I'll spare Raelyn."

It's the only way.

Kody leaned forward, yet was still strapped to the gate, so he paused. "And our baby. You'll leave them both unharmed and never bother them again."

Zohaib nodded with a sick smile. "Always a negotiator ... just like me."

"Swear it."

His smile crept up higher. "I swear."

There's no other option.

"I'll do it. Untie me from the gate." Kody stared at the silver reflecting off the sharp point.

Zohaib grinned and loosened the rope around his chest. With his wrists still tied behind his back, Kody kneeled in front of the dagger.

Zohaib blocked him from the blade. "Wait, I want her to see what she is making you do. This is her fault. The women are always to blame."

Raelyn can't see this. I have to do it now.

Ready to launch his body onto the blade. Kody stared at the tip of the dagger. He projected his voice as calm as possible. "Raelyn, I love you."

At that moment, he caught sight of a familiar female face among the soldiers, giving him the signal.

This is it. Our one chance.

"Now!" Kody screamed into the night air.

31

RAELYN

Across the clearing, Kody was kneeling, staring down at a dagger that pointed straight to the sky.

The whip cracked against Raelyn's back for the fifth time, blazing her skin on fire. Tears streamed down like a waterfall.

Kody yelled something. His voice sounded frantic, as wild as ever.

Immediately, the soldiers split into two opposing lines, yelling at each other and turning their weapons on each other–and Zohaib. A bullet pierced Zohaib's arm. He stumbled back.

Bullets zinged around, lodging into tree trunks. In another reality, she'd use all her effort to help those brave enough revolting against Zohaib, but Amala was coming.

A sharp, piercing pain whipped Raelyn's back, and she screamed in agony. Cornered.

Her legs shook, and all muscles throbbed.

"Bernardo!" A woman's voice yelled, "Stop!"

That woman reminded Raelyn of Phoenix in her coolly confident expression. Then the realization hit her hard like a train.

Oh my god, it's the model, MJ!

The one she'd hired all those months ago to seduce Zohaib.

MJ is Marlee Peterson!

"Bernardo, what are you doing? Christ, stop!" Marlee yelled.

Using the distraction, Raelyn desperately searched her purse, looking for anything to use as a weapon. The syringes Haydee gave her met her fingertips, begging to be used. Quickly, she turned and sank it into Bernardo's arm, injecting drugs into his system. Only half inserted before he ripped it out and the rest of the fluid sputtered onto the ground. He staggered and drooped to the side in a partially paralyzed trance, but his pained eyes focused on her, alert.

Raelyn swung the second syringe like a sword toward the soldiers closing in. "Back off!"

Mid-contraction, the pain twisted Raelyn's insides, and blood dripped down her back when she rolled her shirt down over the stinging lashes, the fabric sticking to her skin. Another contraction came, clamping down so hard. A scream scratched her throat.

Suddenly, the ground shook under her knees. She froze on all fours. A trembling climbed up her legs through her core. A thundering sound followed. The ground shook and lurched and the air filled with a low, gut-deep crack that came from the earth beneath.

"Earthquake!" Someone shouted.

The ground split, creating trenches that spread further and deeper. One man close by fell, swallowed by the earth.

She glanced toward Kody. He wasn't there. The entire area where he had stood was now a crater.

"No!" Her lungs emptied as she screamed in anguish. "Kody!"

There was only silence in her head, suffocating her, trapping her. She screamed and screamed.

Heart slamming. Body shaking. Sweat dripping down her neck.

"Kody!"

But she couldn't see or hear him.

Come back.

"Kody!" Her throat tightened, the word clawing down to her empty heart. Empty.

Come back.

Atop the hill, in the distance, the entire warehouse vibrated. Brick crumbled. Guns fired. Men rolled, ducked, and hid behind gravestones, facing off, shooting at the opposing group. Bullets soared. Soldiers collapsed.

Raelyn leaned against the tree trunk, pain overwhelming her. A shiny object caught her attention. She squinted and gasped. Pa's axe rested a few trees away, covered in cobwebs, and his engraved initials were half-covered by dirt on the handle. She crawled over, groaning, and gripped it hard.

A hand clamped over Raelyn's mouth, and she instantly knew it was Zohaib from his alcohol smell. He pulled her away, far from the group, through rough gravel. Pain streaked her back as scrapes burst open from the sharp pebbles. Raelyn kicked and writhed under the steady grip. She could barely breathe, barely think straight. Raelyn bit down on a hand.

"Wretched bitch!" He screamed. "God, I'll have fun torturing you."

"I have the file! The one you've been looking for." She staggered to a standing position and weakly pointed the axe up at him. "It's buried in a hole in the cemetery."

"You will obey me now, child." His eyes shot venom at her as he swiped a thin metal piece from his pocket and dangled one of the electronic shock collars from his fingertips.

"No!" She scrambled back, then slashed Pa's axe at the air.

He laughed ruthlessly and knocked it out of her hand.

Zohaib took a fistful of her hair and snapped her head. Raelyn fell flat on her back. Rocks poked into the bleeding welts on her back. Tightness cascaded inside her stomach, moving lower. He hauled her toward the cemetery. The gunshot sounds faded into muffled pops. Zohaib dragged her through the rough dirt by her hair.

She had no voice left to shout for help but reached into her purse and fumbled for the syringe.

"Let's see if your little one is strong enough to survive this."

Determination struck deep within.

"Show me where the file is," he growled. "Where is it, girl?" He yanked her hair in all directions. "Here?"

Sharp pain radiated down her back, but she finally gripped the syringe.

Heart pounding and sweat dripping, Raelyn twisted off the cap. She reached toward Zohaib and stabbed the needle into his bicep. He howled and released his grasp of her hair.

"Bitch! Though this will be more fun than I thought if you keep putting up a fight." His words were already beginning to slur. "Don't worry … I'll eventually break you. Just like all the others."

She scrambled away on all fours. It felt like her ribs were sawing each lung in half.

Zohaib stumbled in front of her, weakening by the second. He dropped to his knees on the ground, then fell to his side, sprawled in front of her, twitching. His eyes darted around in a paralyzed panic. She crawled as far from him as possible toward the line of trees. Her entire body was a landmine of goosebumps.

Shouts escalated in volume from the warehouse atop the hill. The smell of smoke hit her nostrils, and she whipped her head around. Flames consumed the building, and black tendrils rose to the stars. Men ran out, tripping into divots in the ground.

Focus. Amala is coming.

The dates on the tombstone in front of her split down the middle as another tremor absorbed the stone. There was nothing to grab onto as the earth opened, inviting her into its depths. She shrieked as the ground tumbled around her. Raelyn slowly sank lower into a sinkhole. Smoke floated above, kissing the sky with blackened haze.

Raelyn's middle tightened and pressure built in her abdomen, spreading to her groin. A shadow moved above.

Impossible.

She prayed Zohaib hadn't defeated the paralysis already.

A gasp left her lips when Marlee Peterson stood above her wearing a Navy SEAL. uniform. Raelyn knew for sure it was the same woman she had photographed to seduce Zohaib months ago.

Marlee kicked Zohaib's side hard above. Mud and blood smeared his face. The woman cuffed Zohaib's wrists.

"That's for my cousin," Marlee said, "Raelyn, stay here. The police are on the way. I need to go help the injured."

"MJ? Where's Raelyn?" Ma's voice pleaded. "Have you seen her?"

"Down there. I kept her alive, just like you asked. Now, my job is done."

Ma's blue eyes poked over the edge of the hole. "Oh my god, hun! You're okay."

Raelyn grasped at the air. "Ma! Help! She's coming"

Ma dropped into the hole and kneeled next to her. "It's okay. Breathe." She smelled of gasoline.

"Did you …" Raelyn gulped in air. It smelled like burning leaves above. "Did you set the fire?"

Ma nodded.

An unbearable pain made her dig her nails into Ma's skin. Ma worked Raelyn's pants to her ankles and shimmied her underwear off.

As sweat dripped down her face, Raelyn panted and screamed in a shrill voice, "I can't do this. It hurts too much."

"Yes, you can." She rubbed Raelyn's sweaty cheek.

"Where's Kody?"

Silence. Exhaustion stripped her down to the moment. Bare from the waist down, Raelyn pawed at the air, seeking relief. A terrible battle raged inside her belly, and her muscles seized.

Ma locked on her eyes, determination settled deep down. "I'm going to touch you, okay?"

Raelyn nodded. A warm hand brushed along her skin.

"You're close to pushing, hun. But not yet."

Hun. Pa called me hun.

The ground shifted again, splitting a new rip in the earth above, creating a clear view of the bodies of dead men laid in the bloodied grass. The warehouse collapsed above from horrific red flames. She could feel the heat from there, but no, it was closer. Around her, the forest was alight, fire spreading.

Ma kissed Raelyn's forehead. "I'm sorry, hun. For everything." A tear rolled down her cheek.

A hunched silhouette approached above them in the smokey darkness.

Raelyn gasped and pointed behind Ma. She pivoted fast as Zohaib kneeled above them, looking drunk, half of his body drooping in weakness.

Ma gripped Raelyn's hands. "I love you so much. You can do this without me. "

Raelyn was unable to respond as another contraction crunched down fiercely.

Ma scrambled out of the raw earth and pushed Zohaib. "You bastard!"

He fell to his side, slamming the ground. Zohaib grunted, fighting the paralysis.

"You devil!" Ma screamed as she kicked his side. "By the way, I gave all your money to the families of the women you murdered and stole." She slammed her heel into Zohaib, and his body convulsed.

Raelyn dug her fingernails into the dirt at her sides. From the angle in the trench, she could see the entire scene unfold as the baby tore apart her insides.

Ma picked up Pa's axe. Raelyn knew what Ma was about to do when the flames of the forest fire matched her destructive eyes.

Zohaib might have known too, but he smiled and said, "See, we're two of the same, willing to do anything to get what we want. If I'm a monster, so are you."

"Ma!" Raelyn shouted.

Ma held the axe above her head and chucked it down hard into Zohaib's leg.

Blood spurted out. Zohaib laid flat on the ground, crying out.

"You deserve this!" She rammed Pa's axe into Zohaib's chest. His body shook at the same time as Raelyn's body—one life ending, one beginning.

Ma pulled the blood-soaked axe out and hacked it into Zohaib's stomach repeatedly, shouting with each hack she made in him.

"YOU'LL. NEVER. HURT. ANOTHER. GIRL. AGAIN!"

Ma carved holes in Zohaib with all her fury.

Over and over. Ma slashed apart Zohaib's face. The thick smell of blood coated the air.

Another burst of pain pressed against Raelyn's torso from the inside, the worst one yet. She couldn't move – terror and agony fought within. There was barely a separation between where she laid and the massacre above.

An intense pressure pushed. Ribs split. Bones cracked. Muscles tore. A scream built and grew in Raelyn's soul, expanding fully until it harmonized with Ma's screams— together, their pain swallowing up the universe.

No matter how much she tried, Raelyn couldn't keep her eyes closed to block out the madness. She tried to focus on the dancing smoke, with any last hope that Kody's form would come walking confidently toward her.

With the last swing, Joanna sliced the axe into Zohaib's throat.

Finally, the blade, dripping with blood, clattered to the ground next to Zohaib's mangled head. Ma spat on his face. "You took everything from me." She kicked his corpse and turned toward Raelyn, covered in deep scarlet. Her blue eyes had turned into ghosts in a world far away. "I killed your father for you. You're safe now."

Somehow, unable to process what she had witnessed, between severe pants, Raelyn muttered, "No, Pa is my father."

Ma's voice belonged to a ghost, and her eyes were unnaturally wide. "That's right. And William's grandbaby is coming. You need to push." Her voice turned abnormally soft.

Raelyn's back muscles twisted in agony and a fresh surge of pain jolted through her pelvis. It felt like knives were rupturing her insides apart, shredding her body. A force was bursting her skin and splitting it into two, like the earth surrounding her.

Ma stared down at her. "I'm leaving now, hun. I can't be here anymore." Her voice sounded on the brink of snapping into insanity. "I can't stay. Please understand."

As if in slow motion, Raelyn watched Ma pull out a lighter from her pocket. Her blue eyes held so much trauma, the spark had disappeared. She flicked the button, and a flame flickered from the top.

In an instant, Raelyn realized Ma's plan.

Raelyn clenched her teeth hard from the wreckage her body was going through. "Ma ... I need you." Waves of heat lapped against her bones.

Her entire life flashed in a series of moments. Hikes in Ash Mountain with Pa. Picnics by the river with Pa. Building a treehouse with Pa. Learning how to drive her truck with Pa. First kiss with Kody. Karaoke with Cali. Jokes with Liam. None included Ma, and now Raelyn knew with sinking clarity that none ever would. That was never meant to be her life, but Ma had sacrificed everything so Raelyn could live in safety and freedom.

"I forgive you," Raelyn pushed out the words.

"I did everything I could, but now my job is done. I can't stay after what he did." Her eyes turned hollow. "I can't. I love you, but now I need to go." The sound of the lighter igniting was possibly the worse sound Raelyn had heard. Ma lit her shirt on fire, and her entire body, doused in gasoline, erupted into a bright flash, then a red blaze.

Screams pierced Raelyn's ears. Ma yelled and fell out of sight. The smell of burnt flesh singed the air. Fire crackled. The weight of a hundred bricks stacked on top of Raelyn's heart, but they still couldn't compare to the pain gushing through her stomach. A burning sensation ignited her groin.

"Kody!"

The fire crackled above.

Tears spilled down her cheeks. "Ma!"

Hollers and gunshots continued to blast above.

Panting, Raelyn bore down with all her might and let out a savage scream, shocking her system. Pressure. Pain.

"KODY!"

32

KODY

In a sinkhole, Kody punched a soldier straight in the jaw. The man rocketed a punch to Kody's gut, making him trip over Bernardo, who squirmed on the ground, half his body sluggish like he had suffered a stroke. Kody sidestepped him with ease and thrust out a foot to send the soldier stumbling. While trying to regain his balance, the man jabbed an elbow into his spine. Biting back a yelp of pain, Kody slammed the soldier to the ground.

Kody clawed at the steep wall again, but Bernardo kicked with his strong leg and knocked him down. Dirt caked his hands on landing. The other man jumped on Kody's back and held the blade to Kody's throat. He bent, flipping him over his back.

The man dragged his shirt, pulling Kody down with him. They rolled in the dirt, punches landing on his cheek. His eye. His ear. His body thudded hard. A flicker of gold splashed his vision. His pocket watch laid in the dirt, calling out to him. He tried to reach forward, but the guy pinned Kody to the side and snapped his shoulder.

"FUUUUUCK!"

Laying on his side, Kody kicked the man's side hard, then rolled and dug his knee into the soldier's throat, pressing down. Harder. Sweat dripped. Rage boiled. The man's face turned red, and he dropped the blade to the earth. He tapped Kody's knee, surrendering.

A screaming came from the surface. One he knew too well.

I'm coming, Raelyn.

Panting. Desperate. Kody grabbed the blade and rammed it hard through the soldier's temple, straight through and out the other side. Holding the man's sweaty forehead in place, he jerked it back out, blood dripping.

"For Eliza," Kody growled, then turned to Bernardo. "Marlee's deal was she wants to be the one to take care of *you*."

Bernardo blubbered gibberish, half his face still paralyzed as Kody tied the traitor's wrists together with shoelaces.

Kody grappled with the wall and finally managed to climb out into the chaos. Scrapes lined his forearms. At the top, flames surrounded him, and bodies were strewn on the ground, soon to be rotting flesh. A group of soldiers hid behind charred trees as the remaining marched forward, shooting mercilessly in a brutal attack. Which side was still working with Zohaib?

Sweat dripped. Kody ducked his head, held his breath, and limped through the flames, pain shooting through his leg. Heat scorched his skin, and his lungs filled with smoke. Gray fumes blocked his vision, blinding him. His chest ripped open with a coughing fit. Blood-stained smoke choked the sky.

"Raelyn!"

Trenches from the earthquake had split the hill. Below, a fiery red ball rolled across the ground chaotically at the end of the cemetery.

What is that?

Limping, he barely jumped over holes. A stream of others' blood trailed like a river at his feet, and he didn't want to think of how many casualties there were. Another scream gutted his soul. His breath hitched. He raced faster and saw the red ball of fire was a person.

As he grew closer, he instantly recognized it as the charred remains of Joanna.

I can't save her.

Dread consumed him at the thought of where Raelyn could be. But then the distracting sight of Zohaib's mangled body and decapitated head struck him with surprise. Blood, a rich shade of lipstick, streaked the grass surrounding his severed limbs and hacked face. Panic consumed him.

"Raelyn!"

"Kody!"

His head snapped to her distraught voice, hidden low in the fractured ground. He jumped, landing in the loose dirt by his fiancée, who was covered in filth and naked from the waist down. "I'm here, babe."

Her eyes rolled to the back of her head, and she struggled to suck in air but reached out to him. "She's coming."

"You can do this. Amala needs you." Kody knelt next to her and grabbed her hand. "Push!"

Raelyn screamed. "Ma!"

"We can't save her." Kody rubbed her cheek, then resituated her legs. "Amala needs you. Push!"

A whimper escaped her lips. "I can't …"

"Yes, you can. Now, Raelyn. Push!"

She screamed and bore down, grabbing a fistful of dirt. After the third painful screech from Raelyn's mouth, Kody caught his warm daughter in his hands. Amala wailed into the night air. Kody locked onto his baby's gaze as he wiped mucus from her nose, and his heart fluttered. He knew without a doubt who her father was.

Kody kissed Raelyn's forehead. "You did it, babe."

"Amala," Raelyn said, then rested her head against the dirt wall. But her whole body went slack and slumped over as her eyes closed.

"No … no … no, babe." Kody glanced between the two, unsure how to get out of the landslide with both.

He patted Raelyn's cheek over and over.

"I need you."

No response. Kody's heart hammered in his chest. He checked her pulse. Steady. But so much blood lay between her legs.

Approaching sirens wailed. Blue lights flashed and reflected in the haze.

"Help! We're down here! Help!" His voice drowned out the loud crackling as the warehouse crumbled further in the background.

The sirens continued past, toward the warehouse despite his yells. The heat escalated as a few trees caught on fire, quickly spreading into the forest. Red embers sprinkled from branches above, and trees creaked as they split and fell.

"Help!"

Amala cried in his arms. Kody used what he learned from basic training, severed the umbilical cord with his knife, and then clipped it fast. He could save at least one of them. He knew what Raelyn would've wanted.

With Amala in his arms, slippery and bloody, he struggled to climb out of the earth. The dirt crumbled under his weight. He tightly grasped a root with one hand and heaved himself up, sliding, but he kept fighting. He climbed out of the hole and hobbled around Zohaib's mangled body. He held his breath as he passed the blackened, scorched remains of Joanna. He desperately waved to a police car. It stopped with a screech, tires digging into the ground.

Yohaan jumped out. "Kody?"

"Raelyn's down there! She fainted."

Yohaan commanded assertively. "Give me the baby. You look like death."

When Kody handed Amala over, Yohaan wrapped her up and radioed for help. "I've got her, Walsh."

Kody limped as fast as he could back to Raelyn. He lowered himself into the crack, gasping from putting pressure on a now obviously broken arm, unsure how many other bones were broken. His heart plummeted at the sight of Raelyn lying unconscious, sweaty and pale. Scooping her up in his arms hurt, and his injured shoulder snapped again, making him wince. But when he cradled her, a soft moan escaped her lips.

"Stay with me, babe."

Struggling, Kody raised her up and had to lay her on the grass. When he reached the surface, Raelyn looked asleep, next to both of her parents. A shudder shot through him at the sight of her body almost as still as theirs, helpless and broken. The finality of what happened to her parents overwhelmed him, but he wouldn't allow Raelyn to have the same fate.

He cradled her sweat and blood-soaked body in his arms, stumbling back to Yohaan. An ambulance and EMS team had arrived and were checking on Amala. She continued to cry in their arms like a healthy, strong girl.

Thank God.

Two paramedics hustled to Kody and laid Raelyn on a gurney. They huddled over her, sticking and prodding her veins to insert an IV. After what felt like a lifetime, one medic turned to Kody with a concerned look on her face.

"Are they okay?"

Just as the medic opened her mouth about to speak, Kody's legs crumpled beneath him, and he collapsed to the ground. Everything went black.

33

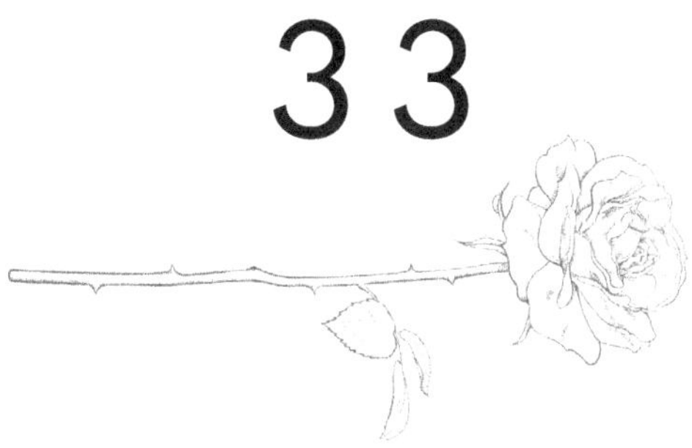

RAELYN

BEEPS AND CHIRPS ORCHESTRATED the most irritating melody. Raelyn readjusted her uncomfortable bed and kicked the hospital sheets from around her ankles. Her eyelids drooped as she stared at the clock ticking in front of her.

Kody should be out of surgery already.

She wondered how much Kody would remember. The doctors had kept him in a coma for forty-eight hours, and any minute now, she would receive news about his most recent surgery.

Amala softly cried out from her arms, so Raelyn re-positioned her on her nipple. The pinching from suckling was manageable compared to yesterday. She ran her hands through Amala's thick dark hair, features that resembled her father's. As Amala looked up and paused, Raelyn took a deep breath looking into those striking eyes.

She's perfect.

Rain showers sprinkled the outer hospital walls and trickled down the open window screen, foreshadowing an early spring—a new beginning. That refreshing scent of rainfall from a thunderstorm relaxed her, plus all the pain meds were helping. A breeze blew in and toppled the congratulation cards on the hospital dresser, splattered with little watermarks.

Raelyn looked down as the pressure in her breast eased while Amala drained her of milk. Her baby girl was a curious and quiet one. She only cried when hungry and was already taking in the world with her inquisitive gaze. When there was a knock at the door, Amala paused her meal for a moment, then continued drinking.

Cali strolled in with Liam by her side, both holding a tray of ham and bread. As she sat, Cali's long black braids swished against her back. She picked at the food with her fork, but no charm bracelet jangled on her wrist anymore. The girl without sound wasn't like the best friend she'd once met in Slate High's parking lot—a lifetime ago. Cali eased into a chair next to the bed and laid her forehead on the sheets as Raelyn covered herself up with her hospital gown.

Liam placed his tray in front of Raelyn, but she couldn't eat while holding Amala. He stood next to her and rested one hand on Cali's shoulder. Each day he looked more and more like Pa. Now they were both parentless. His voice cracked. "How do you feel, sis?"

Relief.

Her thoughts surprised her since Ma was gone. But, Zohaib. Well, he could rot in hell.

Raelyn gulped. "I'm on pain meds, so I feel fine."

"That's not what I meant." His blue eyes stared her down. The only one of his features that resembled Ma's.

Raelyn stared at the clock again. "I'm holding my breath until we hear from Kody's doctor. Do you have any updates?"

Liam shook his head. "What are you gonna do with Amala, if …" He looked out at the rain. "If Kody doesn't make it?"

Cali whimpered into the sheets.

"He has to be fine. He will, but …" Raelyn lifted her chin. "I'm keeping her. No matter what."

A knock tapped on the door. Haydee, David, and Marlee Peterson's faces peeked around the corner. Balloons bobbed in, followed by their tip-toed movements.

Raelyn's heart spasmed for a moment, wondering how Phoenix's parents would truly feel about who Amala's father was.

Haydee smiled and whispered, "How are you feeling?"

Raelyn gulped and hugged Amala closer to her chest. "Tired."

Haydee stepped forward while David's eyes glowed with hope. "Can we see her?"

"Yeah." Raelyn scrunched her nose and rolled in her lips for a moment, then confessed. "She's Kody's."

Marlee sighed as Haydee patted her husband's back and approached the hospital bed slowly. "Amala doesn't have Peterson blood, but Phoenix loved Raelyn, so this precious angel still connects us to him."

Raelyn released the breath she had been holding. "Maybe you can visit regularly?"

"I'd like that," Haydee wiped away a tear.

"I think Cali is planning a baby shower in a few weeks," said Raelyn, "I'd love you to come."

"We'll be there. We won't stay long today. I just wanted to check on you."

Raelyn rested her hand on Haydee's wrist. "Thank you for everything." She nodded to David across the room. "And for saving Cali."

David cleared his throat and nodded. "I'm sorry about your friend, Tucker. He seemed like a good guy. He didn't think twice but just took the bomb and ran."

"He saved both my life and Cali's."

Marlee snorted. "I don't get any credit?" She leaned against the wall.

"We'll let you two catch up." Haydee patted her shoulder and disappeared into the hallway with David.

Raelyn stared at Marlee. "So, you're a spy or something?"

She clicked her tongue. "Naw, just doing my cousin a favor. Phoenix asked me to watch over you, in case, ya know ..." She rolled in her lips. "I guess I won the bet, though. He always thought he'd die from a jet skiing catastrophe gone wrong. I told him, nope, it'd be from saving someone." The pause held the whole room. "He was my best friend."

Raelyn nodded. "We've all lost someone we love."

I'll never see Ma again.

Marlee looked up. "Did you love Phoenix?"

Raelyn gulped. "I think there are different kinds of love. I'll never forget him."

Marlee sighed, then turned to leave.

"Wait, there's one thing I don't understand. How did you know I was at Aaron's house? He gave me a message that you wanted me to go to your uncle's?"

She sat on the edge of the bed. "Joanna was strong, cunning, and powerful. She asked Phoenix to help protect you, and he formed a whole team to look after you— Tucker, Aaron, probably even your local mailman. I sent a message to everyone I knew she had previously contacted to help. That mountain has the worst reception."

Raelyn chewed the inside of her lip, thinking.

Marlee softly rubbed Amala's thick brown hair. "Look at that scowl, as serious as a boxer."

"Boxer … Kody." Raelyn gripped the hospital blanket. "Can you check on Kody?"

"Sure. I'll be back."

If Marlee stuck around in their lives, maybe she could keep a part of Phoenix with her. She envisioned the future–summertime in a backyard playing basketball with Kody, Cali baking in the sun on reclining chairs, Haydee setting up a picnic and photographing birds, Liam teaching Amala how to code, and Marlee sipping a soda. The future looked hopeful as long as Kody survived his surgery.

Liam spoke from the chair in the corner, "So …"

Raelyn jumped, forgetting he was there.

He continued, "I have your money from the safety deposit box. It's actually sixty-thousand dollars."

"Wow." She blew out a slow breath. "Ma would want you to have half."

Liam's brow creased. "Did she say anything about me before she—?"

Raelyn's heart shattered at the sight of Liam's face. She could lie and tell him that all of Ma's last words were about him. No one else was there to know what really happened. No one else had seen the crazed look on Ma's face. When she hacked into Zohaib, Ma truly wasn't Joanna anymore. Her identity had been stripped away by the years as a captive in the desert. She murdered him as the fierce prisoner, Jawhara.

A shiver crawled up Raelyn's spine at the image that had haunted her sleep the last few nights. Ma's job was complete. She had gotten revenge, but now the ashes from Joanna's body were as black as Zohaib's heart.

Raelyn nodded to her little brother. "Ma said she loved you, and she's sorry."

"I didn't get to say goodbye. The last time I met Mom's eyes was after she shot Dabbott." He angrily kicked the base of the furniture.

Raelyn reached out her hand. "Liam, I don't think she was fully there anymore."

"When I was little, we had a decent life for many years. I'm gonna remember her like that. I wish—"

"I know." She realized he might blame himself for Ma's death, just like she had blamed herself for Pa's. "But we found each other. We'll be okay."

He coughed into his sleeve. "Until this CF kills me off."

Raelyn cut the air with her hand. "Stop it. We will talk to specialists and get you treatment."

He nodded and fixated on the pouring rain splattering the window.

A nurse walked in, her voice much too cheery. "Hello, there!" She peeked at Amala's face. "She fell asleep while nursing?"

"Yes."

The nurse nodded and typed on her tablet.

"How long did she nurse for?"

"Twenty minutes." Raelyn could hear how flat her voice was as Cali's snore vibrated the bed.

The nurse glanced at Cali, then lowered her voice. "How often is baby Bell eating?"

"Walsh. Her name is Amala Walsh." Raelyn looked at the clock. "Do the doctors have any updates on my fiancé's surgery?"

The nurse's smile rose. "Of course, dear. I thought you'd been informed. Mr. Walsh is out of surgery and awake already."

"What?" Raelyn's heart leaped with relief. She jolted upright in her bed, waking Amala. Despite her pain meds, the sudden movement made her flinch. "Can I see him?"

She kicked up her leg, jostling her best friend.

Cali jolted upright from her sleep. "I didn't steal the cheetah, I swear!"

"Cali! Kody's awake. Go find him!"

Her eyes grew wide. "Huh? Okay. Right." She swayed out the door but turned the wrong way down the hall.

The nurse typed again. "You're both doing great, and it looks like the doctor has discharged you. We can stock you up on supplies, and you have an appointment scheduled with our psychologist next week. There's no rush, but in a few hours, we can arrange for your ride home."

Home. Where is home?

When the nurse left, Liam moved close. The fluorescent lights made the blond streaks of his wavy hair stand out.

"Where will we go?" Liam asked.

Raelyn considered her options. It was February, not a popular month for rental agreements to begin. She wanted to start classes at State in September, but that was too far away, and the on-campus housing might not allow infants. Cali's house had spare bedrooms, but Mrs. Walsh had already been so accommodating in the past. In a split second, the perfect place came to mind.

She tapped Liam's hand. "Let's talk about that after we see Kody."

Bags shadowed his eyes.

"Can we have a moment to remember Ma, right now?" She sighed. "Just you and I?"

"Like a funeral?"

"Yes."

"Okay." They held hands tightly.

Raelyn cleared her throat and focused on the pitter-patter of rain on the window. "Ma, I used to think only you could love me. And that no one else would come close to our bond. I was wrong. I had Pa … and now Liam." A tightness wedged itself in her chest, then crawled up to her throat. She could barely get out her words. "But, then Pa left us. So, I searched and searched. I did everything I could to find you, Ma. I promise I didn't give up."

Liam squeezed her hand.

She continued. "And then, there you were. Standing right in front of me in that safehouse, after all that time. I wanted you to love me so badly, Ma. I felt so lost when you didn't welcome me with open arms. Something shifted, and I was afraid to be like you, to be closed off to love. But I was wrong. I hope I can love as fiercely as you did."

Raelyn paused, and they both had tears running down their faces. "I guess what I want to say is … I'm sorry, Ma. I shouldn't have thrown out blame. You were broken, but I didn't understand. When I was scared of turning out like you, I was wrong because you fought for us and protected us until your dying day." She swallowed hard and stared at the rain. "We're all a little broken, and that's okay."

Liam nodded and buried his face in Raelyn's shoulder. His sobs erupted. "I'm a little broken now too, Mom."

Raelyn patted his back and swallowed hard, but it felt like a rock had formed in her throat. "Ma, we're not mad that you chose to leave us. You did the best you could. And we love you."

Her hands shook as she swiped a piece of paper from her hospital tray with a recent poem and read aloud.

Juggling pain and strength at the same time
We will rise up and continue the climb
Create a new path toward the mountain peak
Along the hike, we can find what we seek

They held each other quietly.

It's okay if I'm like Ma. She loved us in her own way.

Raelyn's childhood had been full—even without the motherly presence she had always longed for. And now, adulthood was already upon her, and Raelyn knew she would eventually be okay. Pa taught her everything she needed to know, and Ma had given everything so that Raelyn could do the same for Amala.

Footsteps shuffled in the hallway, and doors squealed open and shut.

Suddenly, Cali ran into the room, followed by her lemony scent. Her eyes were full of hope. "Kody's alive! He's fine! And he's furious they won't let him see you yet."

Raelyn allowed a smile to overwhelm her face. She brushed Amala's hand and let her baby girl's fingers grip onto her pinky. "Your Daddy is okay."

34

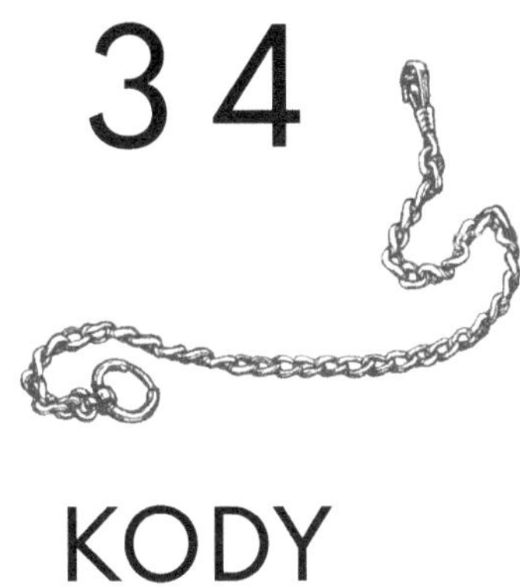

KODY

RAINDROPS SPLATTERED THE SKYLIGHT, and a shock of lightning cracked the sky as a nurse's footsteps entered Kody's room. "Pain level?" she asked.

"I'll be fine."

The nurse frowned. "I've heard that before." She checked his bandages. "Maybe you should think about taking some time off."

Retirement from action sounded like a good plan—even for a twenty-year-old. He was too beat up for anything more demanding than a chess game.

"Where's my fiancée?"

"She's resting."

Kody's arm was stiff and sore, and the nurse injected more pain medication into his system, which created a jolt in his thinking. Images cleaved their way through his mind— Dabbott dying in his arms. Joanna lighting herself on fire as he had sprinted down the hill toward the cemetery. He should've realized long ago that Joanna had been too far gone to save.

He shook his head and pictured Raelyn smiling at prom last year. Then his daughter's dark brown eyes—Amala's trusting look in that ditch after she was born. Unconditional love for her ran through his veins.

He looked at the nurse and opened his mouth to speak.

"They're on the way."

Squeaky wheels grew louder from the hall. Cali's dramatic voice sang like a song when she projected her question before Kody could see her face. "What room number is he in? This is freakin on the other side of the moon."

He sighed. "Everything will be okay."

The nurse leaned in to check his machines. "Take a deep breath, sir."

Kody's heart beat faster when his door swayed open, and Raelyn's toes emerged into view.

The nurse shook her head and stepped away. "I'll be back to take your vitals later."

Raelyn came into view, holding Amala in white blankets. She smiled and whispered, "Kody."

He started to get off his hospital bed, but Cali pushed him back down. "Don't even think about it."

Raelyn looked worn, but her eyes lit up when he smiled.

"You okay?" He scanned her body.

She nodded and caught one tear rolling down her cheek.

Cali rolled their beds next to each other. "Awe, y'all could get married like this. Two hospital beds kissing one another."

Kody waved his sister over. "Thank you."

"For what, butthead?" She stuck out her hip.

"Never mind, I take it back."

Her voice softened. "Whatever, I heard you're rich now. So, if you love me at all, just buy Amala's godmother a new guitar."

"You got it."

Cali leaned in and rested her forehead on his. "Make me a promise, bro."

"What?"

"If we're ever in another epic battle again, then don't you ever try to save the day without me."

"Deal." He nudged Cali's shoulder playfully, then asked, "Can I hold Amala?"

Raelyn scrunched her nose. "Will you drop her?"

"No." His stomach hurt when he laughed.

Cali helped Raelyn pass her over. Kody had cradled his baby in his arms once, but this time was different—real. She was so light and tiny.

"Hi, Amala." It flowed off his tongue like honey. Her dark brown eyes were his. Her wide nose was his. Her full lips were his. A tear rolled down his cheek as he was entranced with Amala's tiny fingers.

She's mine.

Raelyn sighed. "Now we know."

Kody glanced over. "I still would've stayed with you if she looked like Phoenix."

"I know."

He gently brushed his fingertip over Amala's perfect cheek and asked Raelyn, "Are you happy, babe?"

"Somehow, yeah, I really am." She nodded. "You?"

Kody choked on his words and snuggled Amala closer in the crook of his elbow. She slept silently, smelling of soap and something fresh, new. "You three are all I need. We're all gonna be okay." He leaned over and kissed her cheek.

Cali moved to the doorway. "At least you included me in that three." Her sneakers squeaked when she turned, then puckered her face like she'd eaten something sour. "Oooh, smacking chipmunks, your baby stinks like Kody after he's eaten tacos."

Kody laughed as he watched his sister disappear out the door, thankful she hadn't lost her spunk.

Raelyn brushed a finger over Amala's thick hair. "The nurse said I can leave today."

"Where are we bringing Amala home to?"

"I was thinking we could buy Pa's old farmhouse from Grandma. Where I grew up."

"I had the same idea." Kody rubbed her wrist and leaned over for a kiss.

Don't worry, William. We kept each other safe, just like I promised.

35

RAELYN

One month later

Raelyn rocked Amala in her arms as she moseyed toward her barn loft. The soft purple shades of the sunset swept the sky through the slats of the barn wall. She thought back to early in her pregnancy when she and Kody spent months isolated in the wintery cabin atop Ash Mountain. At the time, it had been difficult, but looking back, it might have been some of the happiest, calmest days of her life. Then she looked down at Amala's piercing brown eyes.

No. Our best days are still to come.

She now accepted that her journey of motherhood would be drastically different than Joanna's. However, she couldn't help but wonder how Amala would view her over time. Would five-year-old Amala see her momma as a superhero? Would ten-year-old Amala wish they could spend more time together? Would seventeen-year-old Amala need a mother to talk to about her crush?

We'll be okay.

Raelyn lugged in Amala's car seat and set her next to Pa's old tool bench, now covered in boxing gloves. Kody had plans to redesign the barn into a training center business. The oak trees swayed in the breeze out the open door, along with the tire swing still hanging. Little white buds popped and sprinkled all along the branches, spreading the scent of pollen. One day Kody would teach Amala how to climb those trees.

Just like Pa taught me.

Raelyn hovered her hand over the rung of the ladder to the loft. With a bag full of her journals, she scaled up slowly. She could smell the spring pollen in the air the higher she climbed. In the back area, where Ma's trunk used to rest, she filled an empty crate with her journals. She stared at a poem she wrote last night.

Started this journey climbing a ladder
A choice sits before me on a platter
I could let deep grief suck hope from my blood
Or start over with a soon blooming bud
Fear can no longer crack apart my bones
I don't need to hide away from unknowns

She snapped the journal shut, closing the chapters of her past. The sound of a heavy axe slammed down outside the wall.

Thud. Thud. Thud.

A soft rustling approached, and his deep voice asked, "Babe, where are you?"

"Up here."

"What are you doing?" Most of the scrapes on Kody's handsome face had cleared up except for a small scar on his chin.

"Secrets I'll never tell."

Kody rubbed his ever-growing black beard. "Get down here."

"What for, soldier?"

"I need a kiss. Pronto." His white tee flapped in the breeze.

Raelyn descended the ladder and landed with a thud. Her boots scattered the fallen flower petals. She rose on her tiptoes and pecked Kody's lips—minty fresh. His beard tickled her skin, making her giggle.

"That's all I get?"

"Maybe." She rubbed her palm over his angular jawline, then locked lips once again, never wanting to pull away. Her muscles flooded with water as her body melted into his.

Kody's deep laugh filled the barn as he pulled away. "We can't start for baby number two quite yet, babe."

"You want more kids?"

"Of course. You?"

"Two more."

"Deal, but there's no rush." He took her hands softly. "Listen, Yohaan called."

"What did he say?"

"The virus email worked, and they have evidence of hundreds of email conversations between different leaders, meeting locations, times. They have a list of his followers who worked with him, and they already got two in custody."

"But?"

"It was handed over to the CIA. They need to work with a bunch of different countries and their government agencies to find and arrest them all."

Raelyn rubbed Kody's forearm. "You're not leaving, right?"

"No, I'm staying right here, but Yohaan says it may take months or even years to find all these criminals. We might not be fully safe until they're all accounted for."

Raelyn nodded. "What are our options?"

"He says the safest would be to split up under the witness protection program. Two of us in one location, and the other—"

"Not an option," Raelyn said coolly. "We're not splitting up."

"I agree." Kody shrugged. "We can stay remote here on the farm, but eventually, they'll ask us to testify."

Raelyn and Kody glanced at each other, then at Amala.

"I'll testify, but I won't separate from you."

Kody wrapped his arm around her waist. "There's no guarantee that every one of Zohaib's colleagues is listed on that file."

Raelyn straightened. "I won't live in fear, and I won't hide."

Kody kissed her forehead. "Okay, it's settled."

Raelyn brushed the dust off her jeans. "Good. Maybe I need to send Yohaan and his boys some cookies."

"That'd convince me to do anything." Kody crushed his lips to hers.

"Hey …" She snuck in words between his perfect kisses. "When is Amala's next pediatrician appointment?"

"It's on the calendar, on the fridge."

"Right." She tucked a piece of her thick hair behind her ear.

Careful not to press on his bandage or touch his shoulder, Raelyn wrapped her arms behind his neck. She hovered her mouth with only a sliver of space between them. "Do you have anything we should stash up in the loft?"

One of Kody's eyebrows rose, and a slow smirk rose as his gaze settled on the loft. "I wish I didn't lose that pocket watch."

"That's how I felt when I lost Ma's necklace and Pa's compass." Raelyn leaned back against Pa's workbench, and a piece snapped off, sending her falling to the hard ground. Tiny pebbles dug into her palms. "Ouch!"

"You okay?"

"Pa's workbench broke." She leaned over, inspecting it.

"I can fix it."

Raelyn grazed her fingertips underneath where a broken wooden chunk poked out. "Wait, there's something under here."

Wrinkling her nose, Raelyn angled her arm sideways and down. "What the?" She crouched and stared at a mound of cash. "Kody! There's *more* money."

He accepted a wad of bills. "Jeez, how much did Joanna steal?"

"Wait, this is Pa's bench, so he would've put it here. I don't understand." Raelyn moved bills from her left to her right hand. "Did Pa know that Ma sent him this?"

Kody shrugged. "Maybe it wasn't from Joanna. Maybe he kept a secret stash here."

Her heart sped. "No way, there's so much."

"Maybe William had a side hustle." Kody smiled.

She nudged his arm gently. "Don't tease."

A piece of paper fluttered down between the pile in her hand and landed on her boot. For a moment, time stood still, like when Kody stopped the clock on his pocket watch. Raelyn picked it up and immediately recognized Ma's handwriting. "It's unopened and dated from the summer before my sophomore year of high school." A lump formed in her throat.

"Open it."

She ripped the seal and read it out loud.

My William and my Raelyn,

I know you may never see this ... it could be intercepted in so many ways.

But I'm alive. And I'm desperately trying to return home. I can't tell you where I am because he might find you and hurt you both, and it's the only way to protect you. Keep this money. That way, I'll know I did some good for you two.

This may be the only chance I have to reach out, so know this ... I imagine your faces every day. I'll always be looking for a way out of here, and I won't give up until I can see you again.

William, I know you'll take care of our girl. For now, a mother has to do what a mother has to do. Now, brace yourself. We have a son, too. He is here with me, little Liam. But it seems like things are about to change. I promise I'll die before I let anything happen to him. William, I know you'd make the same sacrifice.

Trust me. I'll get him home to you one way or another. I love you both so much.

Joanna (Your Ma, always and forever)

Raelyn pressed the letter to her heart. "She did. She got Liam to me."

Kody brought her head into his chest. The wind blew, and she watched it knock off a few rose petals in the yard, which scattered along the grass.

"She really tried to be a good mother. And I'll do my best to keep Amala safe too."

His lips brushed her forehead. "We both will."

"Maybe it's okay to be a little like Joanna. Strong. Determined. Fierce."

In the distance, near the farmhouse, Cali set up the microphone on the makeshift stage for the baby shower. Purple balloons blew in the breeze while a few streamers wrapped around the strings of Cali's guitar leaning next to the back porch. She smiled and waved to them as a polka-dot tablecloth flapped in the wind, knocking over the plastic cups, spreading them around the yard. Cali howled giddily like a schoolgirl as she hopped around retrieving them all.

Raelyn snorted mid-laughter while listening to Cali's random song she made up during the décor catastrophe.

"Auntie of the day, hanging streamers in the hay. Maybe you should pay, the Auntie of the day," Cali sang.

Above, thousands of new spring leaves fluttered, carrying the hope that the wind would gift them with flight.

A spluttering sound clanked from the road, and Pa's old blue truck groaned as Liam drove it into the long drive. He waved from afar and opened up the side door. A tiny fluffy paw flopped out, followed by another.

Raelyn felt her eyes widen. "Kody? What did you do?"

He raised both hands. "I didn't do anything." He craned his neck to the rafters like he was laughing a silent prayer.

A puppy jumped out of the truck, sniffed the grass, and sprinted across the long grass straight to the barn, ears flapping in the breeze. Raelyn smiled as she glanced between the puppy and Amala sleeping.

New beginnings.

Raelyn crouched down, straw tickling her ankles, and opened her arms wide, accepting the new life colliding face-first into her chest—knocking her breathless.

EPILOGUE

10 years later

"Liam S. Bell," she repeated my name, snapping me out of my trance.

The Department Head of the Computer Science Graduate Program at Duke University projected her voice in the microphone as I walked across the stage. A ray of light temporarily blinded me when Raelyn lifted her camera from the front row, reflecting the bright sun. Wind swooshed under my graduation gown with each proud strut. Flower petals crunched underfoot while more floated down, sprinkling the ceremony. I glanced at my untied shoelace and smiled.

Don't trip. Amala will never let me hear the end of it.

As I lifted my gaze, three sets of dark brown, adorable eyes took turns threatening me with an attack of hugs if I didn't scoot across the stage faster. Amala held each of her little sisters on her lap, trying to contain their squirming and high-pitched giggles that whispered through the breeze.

Kody swept one toddler onto his knee and bounced her ever so gently as a grin spread across her sweet face. It was a good thing they chose an aisle seat since Kody's legs spread wide, requiring twice the normal space. He nodded to me briefly then handed his youngest a stuffed animal from his camo backpack. That man was always prepared—always a soldier.

"Dara M, Chan," the Dean announced the student behind me.

And just like that, one name sucked me back into the moment.

Dara.

I could feel her energy behind me—the same as always, full of poise and brilliance. An electric pulse surged between the space between us. If I slowed down just a tad, there was a possibility she'd bump right into my back. My heartrate sped at the thought of her skin brushing against mine, but I stepped forward, off the stage and into the lawn, following the line.

During undergrad, I had managed a few successful relationships, but there were too many hurdles, and women simply weren't my focus. Until the first day of grad school, when Dara braved sitting next to me in the front row. When the letter "s" on my keyboard fell off and skidded under the teacher's desk, Dara kept peeking over at my notes, giggling at all the misspelled words. No person or situation had ever paralyzed me in the way her smile did. It had taken me a week to work up the courage and ask for her notes from that lecture.

On stage, the dean listed off more names as we moved across the quad, behind the audience, and finally dispersed around the table of refreshments. Despite it being only nine in the morning, sweat dripped between my shoulder blades. At least the speeches were over with. But if the temperature today rose to the same as yesterday, we were about to have record-breaking May weather in North Carolina. I fanned myself with my new diploma and ran a hand through my annoyingly thick hair, then ripped off the long robe to drape it over a branch of an oak branch. Leaning against the trunk, I chugged a cup of lemonade. The little beads of condensation on the exterior brought back a sudden flashback of my time in the desert when Mom had handed me a bottle of water.

I wish Mom were here to see me graduate. Or William.

A robe swept against my ankles. I swiveled to my right and caught sight of Dara staring at me. My breath hitched. It didn't matter that we'd spent countless hours coding during our thesis project. I'd always be swept away by her eyes. Plus, that round face, confident smile, and long black hair distracted me so intensely it was a surprise that I even passed my classes. Sitting across from her in the library for so many hours all last semester gave me a new definition of longing. Thoughts of her consumed me, from the time I woke in that measly one-bedroom apartment to the minute we'd walk out of the library together. If only once I had enough courage to grab her hand into mine. But I had waited too long. She had clearly designated me into the friend zone.

"Congratulations." Dara leaned in for a hug, and my heart thundered, threatening to burst free.

I had to hunch down quite a bit to her five-foot-two height. When she released, I thrust my arms through the sleeves of my graduation robe again in an attempt to hide the bulge throbbing against my pants' zipper.

Pushing my glasses higher on my nose, I smiled. "You too. Nice speech, smartie-pants."

A rose color flushed to her cheeks. "Stop it. You earned it fair and square. I still don't know why you asked me to give your speech."

"You mean, *your* speech." I folded my arms and leaned against the tree again, trying to look casual while a swirl of panic and desire and need and excitement all cycloned inside my veins.

Dara playfully shoved my shoulders. "Did you hear me stumble over my joke about analogs?" She palmed her face. "And then I'm pretty sure no one got the one about encryption either. It was like crickets out there."

I bit my lip, holding back every impulse to kiss her right then. "Naw, they were probably just hypnotized by your genius."

She shook her head, chuckling. "I still think you should've given the speech. You never told me why you let me."

Take her hand. Hold her hand. Now. Do it.

I inhaled a deep breath and moved forward, just as Cali popped out from behind a nearby tree. "Liam!"

Cali's long braids were thinner than when I saw her, and purple streaked through the twists. Huge sunglasses covered half her face and almost slipped off when she catapulted herself into my side, almost knocking me over in the process. "You've got to be the youngest kid to finish grad school with a doctorate. Only twenty- three! I was lucky enough to finish my one music class by that age."

Dara's jaw dropped next to Cali. "You're only twenty-three?"

"Yup. Just skipped a few grades when I was younger, that's all." I shrugged, trying to hide my discomfort. Of course, it would only take Cali a few seconds in front of the woman I was madly in love with to blab one of my secrets, and at least it was the most innocent one.

Cali stuck her hip out as she grabbed a cup of lemonade from the table. After a slurp, she asked. "So, where are all my nieces?"

I pointed across the lawn toward the chairs set up in the shade.

"Oh, those poor tortured souls. Don't worry, I'll save them."

The Dean was still rattling off names, but Cali yelled in the distance, waving her arms. "Rae!"

"Ssh!" I lowered Cali's arms but couldn't hold back my laughter. "You're making a scene."

"Of course I am, my chipmunk. There's no other way to live." She jumped up and down. "Yoo-hoo, Rae!"

Kody turned in his chair with a stern look claiming his brows. It didn't matter how intimidating he looked, completely ripped in his tight tee with his fitness training business logo plastered on the front. After knowing the man for ten years, I knew he was ecstatic to see his sister back home again.

Dara pointed to Cali. "Wait, you're …" She tilted her head, and her eyes grew wider. "You're THE Cali Walsh!"

Cali shimmied her hips and batted her eyelashes. "In the flesh."

"I've seen you on a billboard on the way here! Weren't you just up for a Grammy?" Dara pulled out her phone from her pocket and showed the screen to me.

I nodded with a smile. "Don't get her started, or she'll go get her guitar from her tour bus."

Cali dramatically placed the back of her hand on her forehead. "Oh, Liam, I'm so sorry for embarrassing you. As my punishment, I shall leave and never return again."

When she turned, I gripped her elbow and swung her around, teasing, "Oh, hush, go get me some cookies."

"Scrumptious. I'll grab a plate for the girls, none for you. That way, I'll forever be their favorite aunt."

I shook my head. "You're their only aunt."

After Cali marched off, Dara snuck closer, but I pretended not to notice. "Well, she's … something," she said.

A deep laugh escaped from my belly. "You could say that again."

"How do you know her?" The touch of the sun couldn't melt me as quickly as Dara's curious voice.

"It's complicated." It dropped my gaze to the grass, hoping she wouldn't press too much. "Well, it's a long story. Her brother is married to my big sister."

"That sounds simple enough. The way you're looking had me worried about some top-secret organization or something."

I froze. "Uhh—"

"I'm just joking." Dara nudged me again but scanned my face. I could see her wheels turning, likely calculating how many classes I was absent for during the last year and making assumptions.

Change the subject.

But she beat me to it.

"My parents are headed this way. Let's get a picture together." Dara handed me her phone. "You take it because you know your arms are twice as long as mine."

"Sure." I reached my arm out for a selfie.

Every muscle stiffened as she wrapped her arms around my waist, rose on her tiptoes, and kissed my chin. Miraculously, I snapped the shot, proof that her lips were once mine but fumbled her phone, and it fell to the grass.

"Oh, sorry." I crouched, ready to scoop it up, when two tiny bodies slammed into my chest, crushing me to the ground.

"Ucle Li! Ucle Li!" Little Willow squeaked out, age two and unable to pronounce my name, yet capable of destroying a tiger with her strength.

"That graditatun was soooooo boring!" Six-year-old Joelle rolled her eyes while still atop my prone body. "But you got a prize, right? That paper is your prize? Mommy told us to tell you good job and give you the biggest hug, so ta-da, it's done." She rolled off of me, grass stains already overtaking her white shirt. "Now, how high do you think I can climb that tree?"

Dara laughed and held her hand out to Willow. "Can I get a high five?"

That fierce little one stepped back five feet and used a running leap to slam the biggest high-five a toddler could possibly achieve. Dara laughed with a twinkle in her eye then tilted her head. "Well, Liam, my parents are waiting. I'll see you at Evan's party tonight?"

My words caught in my throat. All I could do was nod as she turned and walked away. The sight of her leaving my side sent a turmoil of intense need through my body. My gaze left her slender form and rose to catch the frowning face of her father. One brow lifted as he studied me with a knowing look.

Crap.

And then Amala jumped on my back, knocking my attention back to the three hopping, Energizer bunnies. At ten years old, she had already mastered all her events in track and field with trophies lining her pink shelves back at the farmhouse in Ash Mountain.

Amala climbed on my shoulders with a little boost from me, leaned over, and whispered in my ear. "You like that Asian girl, don't you?"

I whispered back, "Amala, what would you say if someone called you a mixed-girl?"

Her body tensed over my neck as she took a moment and tried again. "You like that woman you were talking to, don't you?"

"I don't know what you're talking about."

"Liam and pretty girl sitting in a tree … k … i … s … s …"

"That's enough."

Kody and Raelyn, hands interlaced, walked across the short-trimmed grass. Raelyn's light blue summer dress swayed in the breeze by her knees and her chocolatey hair whipped by her waist. I could tell they didn't sense my eyes on them as Raelyn tugged on Kody's hand a little and pulled him behind a thick oak tree. Before their frames disappeared from view, I caught a glimpse of Kody's hands wrapping around my sister. To replicate their relationship was my Everest—the ultimate goal, yet something that seemed impossible.

Amala easily managed Joelle and Willow, sitting them cross-legged on the ground with lemonade in their hands. They followed her instructions obediently like their big sister was their guiding princess in arms.

Cali magically appeared with her fairy godmother plate of cookies. "Who loves me best?" She waved cookies in the air.

"Me! Me!" Willow's eyes lit up.

"No, me!" Joelle raised her hand and was about to jump up, but with one quick look from Amala, she stayed right where she was.

After Cali passed them each an abundance of sugar, she turned to me. "So, what does the 'S' stand for in your middle name?"

I swiped a cookie from her plate and let the chocolate melt over my tongue before answering. "My middle name is Samuel."

She cringed. "Why?"

"That was Snyder's first name."

"Really? You're named after that awful guy?"

I sighed. "At least he wasn't my real father."

Cali clicked her tongue. "Today's about celebrations. Let's not talk about all that. What are you planning on doing now that you have a Ph.D.? Become a father of your own?"

I choked on the last bite of my cookies. "Right, like that's possible." Yet my eyes searched for Dara's silhouette among the newly crowded area.

Cali flopped her sunglasses back on. "Why not? It's not like you're gonna die when you're thirty anymore."

Joelle looked up from the ground. "What? Who's gonna die?"

Cali brushed the girl's bushy hair behind her ear. "Nothing, monkey." She pulled Liam away. "Seriously, now that they found a cure for CF, you're still gonna hold yourself back from dating?"

I swallowed hard. "I … it's … there's ..."

"There's no reason not to date. I have the perfect girl in mind."

My stomach clenched tight. "Oh, really? You do?"

"Of course, this girl Maya is on my music video production team. She's totally perfect for you because she's your opposite in every way."

I crossed my arms. "I guess you've got it all figured out then."

"You've got what figured out?" Raelyn approached from behind another family, all smiles, with Kody in her wake. Even an ex-military man couldn't hide the satisfaction on his face.

What the hell did they do behind that tree?

I shook my head from the thoughts about my sister. "Oh, Cali has picked out my wife."

Raelyn's amber eyes popped as her smiled grew even larger. "Oh, well, I'll only charge you half of my photography fees."

"How generous of you."

She put a finger to her chin. "Though, I happen to have a perfect woman for you. I know what'll make you happy more than Cali."

Completely entertained, I widened my stance and gestured for her to continue.

"Tanea is just like you and works for the … well, I can't say … but y'all could do all those computer games, and she also speaks five languages. I can see you traveling the world together." Raelyn's gaze focused on the sky dreamily.

Cali pointed in Raelyn's face. "No way, they'll get bored. To live happily ever after, you need someone to balance you out, someone to push you out of your comfort zone."

Kody winked at Raelyn, who wrinkled her nose in return. Their silent exchange spoke volumes.

I tuned Raelyn and Cali's friendly banter out and watched Dara walk toward the parking lot. Even though ten years had successfully buried the trauma from my childhood … even though the doctors' new medicine had eliminated my Cystic Fibrosis symptoms, giving me a new chance at a full life … even though top-secret government agencies were recruiting me for my hacking skills … the thought of finally kissing my dream girl stole my breath away.

I'll ask her out at Evan's party tonight. What's the worst that could happen?

Sign up for my newsletter here at
www.cassieswindon.com
for updates and bonus material.

Cassie Swindon

Isaac's Curse

Cover Design by Anna Cackler

ISAAC

The fierce wind flapped the sheet in my hand, so I tightened my grip, shaking out the crumbs from last night's dessert. At least Zephyra had licked most of the cake off my abs, so it didn't end up staining the blankets. The morning clouds camouflaged into the fabric, taking the form of a full sail, and I couldn't tell where the sky ended, and the sheet began.

Another gust blew through my loose shirt, the cotton shifting against my skin and exposing the gray and white Mobius loop tattoo claiming my hip. It'd be another sweltering day. I stripped off my shirt and pinned it on the clothesline next to the dancing sheet. Craning my neck to stare at the washed-out, dusty blue sky, I took in the swirls of white and crisp blue stretching through Vayu.

"Isaac?" Zephyra's voice gave me goosebumps every time.

"In the flesh." I cleared my throat to get rid of the groggy morning sound and turned to face her.

At age thirty, Zephyra didn't look a day over twenty when she batted those long lashes that knocked my breath away. I longed to kiss those high cheekbones and wrap my arms around her slender form again.

"Wes is in trouble."

"What?" Alarm coursed through my muscles to my quickly clenching fists. "What's wrong with Wes?"

“I heard him screaming.” Long ringlets whipped her face. “He’s outside the dome wall.”

My heart stopped. “How?”

“I don’t know.”

My skin stung as though pricked by needles as I snapped my attention in each direction from the skyscrapers atop the peak to the green treetops that stretched below for miles but couldn’t see my son—even with my enhanced vision.

“Follow me.” Zephyra sprinted down the trail of the steep slope.

I ran after, questions soaring through my mind. The only way my son would have exited the safety of Vayu’s barrier was if someone had taken him. How did they find us?

Terror hummed in my bones, and I could feel I was losing control of my calm. My tattoo scorched, summoning my power, and surged a pulse through my body to my fingertips. But I shouldn’t manipulate the air this close to the dome—too dangerous. We could be exposed.

Panting, I found my pace next to Zephyra, hitting shade at the tree line. Sweat dripped down my neck. My sneakers skidded over loose pebbles, and dirt kicked onto my shins as we descended. Only half a mile left. My calves burned, and my feet thumped on the gravel so quickly, like flying instead of running. When the adrenaline hit this strongly, the sensation of wings always overcame my body, putting me in a focused trance—heightening my sight even more. Immediately, I spotted every angled curve of leaves and the indents on a beetle crawling up trunks as I sped by.

Zephyra pointed straight ahead where I knew the invisible perimeter of Vayu met the rest of the world. Wes had once termed our dome “The Bubble.” Outside the barrier, a pair of his blue sneakers laid next to a tree trunk. My heart rate quickened.

“Isaac, what if—”

“Don’t say it,” I shouted over my shoulder as I passed her and pumped my arms faster.

Knowing I was about to transfer through the wall, I squeezed my eyes shut for only a moment and braced for the electric-like pulse. A sharp shock pinged in my tattoo and zapped my whole body from head to toe. Gasping, I landed on the other side of the dome seal, sprawled flat on the earth— Zephyra already out of view, protected inside the shield. At least the dome was still functional, and whoever had taken Wes hadn't destroyed the future of our entire city.

Outside of Vayu's seal, I always felt different—vulnerable. The thrum of my powers sliced through me. My sight telescoped in. Exactly one mile to the east, I could see a group of deer grazing. One point two miles to the south, a car curved around treacherous, steep roads. I couldn't see who was inside, but they were moving too fast for a lazy Sunday morning drive.

Some son of a bitch stole my kid. Out of practice, I begged that my abilities were still strong enough.

Widening my stance, I inhaled a deep breath and raised my arms straight to the sky, desperate for help. My heart rate quickened as I summoned every ounce of energy, making an intense pulse surge through my blood. Suddenly, a gust of wind rose and chased the car in the distance. *Form a blockade.* The wind followed my command, soaring forward at my will.

About a mile off, the gust snapped an evergreen trunk in half. A loud crack echoed up the mountain hillside, and the giant tree landed with a thud over the country lane. The zooming car slammed on its breaks and slid to the right on the shoulder, jerking to an abrupt stop. A woman jumped out of her vehicle and raised both arms in exasperation, but now that the car was at an angle, I squinted from afar and searched the backseat. Wes wasn't in there. *Damn it.*

"Oh my god, seriously? What did you do?" Zephyra's blue eyes studied me.

I jumped and swiveled on my heels, unaware she had merged through the Bubble too.

"I couldn't think of anything else." I pushed both palms to my temples with such force I swore I could've snapped my skull in half.

"No, literally, what did you do? I can feel your energy, but you know I can't see that far like you."

"Uh, nothing."

She cocked her head, bent down, and reached into Wes' shoe. "Look, there's a note inside."

"A ransom note? Is it someone from Draven? I'll give them anything." I grabbed the flapping piece of paper from her hand and read Wes's sloppy ten-year-old handwriting.

Went to see Mom. Don't be too mad. I'll do extra laundry tomorrow to make up for it.
P.S. You didn't tell me the tattoo would burn me. You LIAR!

I stared, re-reading the last line a dozen times, then finally dropped the paper to my side. Looking over at Zephyra's stunned face confirmed my assumption.

"He already tattooed," she whispered in awe with such certainty, paired with knit brows.

"It's not possible. He's too young."

"You know better than anyone that this has happened before. Not everyone is seventeen. Maybe he's as strong as you."

"I was twelve, and *that* was unheard of when we were kids. He's only ten."

Zephyra massaged my shoulders like she did last night before she snuck out of my room. "Then maybe Wes is stronger than you."

I could only hope she was right because I couldn't consider the alternative but muttered it anyway, "Or a Draven monster wrote this."

"No, it's his handwriting," she said calmly.

I started walking down the trail, needing to find a car … and a shirt. "Anyone from Draven could've threatened Wes to write it."

After she scurried after me, Zephyra laced my hand into hers. "If someone took him, they wouldn't leave a note, and no one from Draven has any use for Wes."

She's right.

"But Wes wouldn't leave. We're a team."

"Maybe it was one of his pranks," she said.

"No, he knows better than to leave the dome."

Zephyra sighed. "When his tattoo formed, he was in pain. Do you really think he'd want to show you that weakness?"

"Pain isn't weakness."

"Well, then maybe he's mad at you."

I didn't know how to deal with my son already maturing—I wasn't ready, and neither was he.

"So, you never told Wes about the tattoo scorch?" she asked.

"I didn't want to scare him," I mumbled and moved faster through the woods. An eerie sensation crept over me that we were being watched. I checked over my shoulder. No one. Shaking my head, I continued, "Zeph, a ten-year-old shouldn't have to know all the responsibilities that come with our powers."

"I know you want to protect him, but the last day for that was yesterday."

"No, I will always protect him."

She laid a strong hand on my bare chest, yet with less assertion than she did in my bed last night. "In our world, Wes is now an adult. You need to respect him as one."

A laugh escaped my gut. "You're kidding, right? He doesn't even clean his toys. Toys, Zeph. He is a child. And he decided to run down the mountain alone, without shoes. Why on earth would he go barefoot?" As I side-stepped around her, I nudged into her shoulder a little harder than I should've.

"Ouch. Isaac, come on, I'm on your side." She hustled after my long strides. "I care about Wes too, and you know I'm better about making decisions when it comes to his well-being. You two can still play pranks all day, but he also needs a firm hand with structure."

"First, we need to find him to lay down any rules." I pinched my beard, trying to contain the wind howling in my heart, not wanting to be held back. "I'm sorry, Zeph, but *I'm* his parent. Maybe you should go back to Vayu."

Time stood still. She tilted her head, holding the long pause between us like a cage of tornadoes threatening to escape. "You don't want me to meet Wes's mom, do you?"

"What? Don't start that again. This isn't about Reese." I stared ahead with each continual step, catching a blurry charging station for cars in my peripheral. Maybe the Ordull owner would have a tourist tee-shirt of Mount Evans. I couldn't show up at Reese's half-dressed, or I'd get myself into another mess that Zeph would never forgive me for. Sleeping with Reese had been too risky. I couldn't let her find out who I really was or about my Magik. The information would only put her in danger. Ordulls couldn't find out about us, Mystiers, which is why I never should've fallen for her in the first place.

Zephyra stared at me suspiciously, eyes narrowed.

I cleared my throat before saying. "Plus, you and I are just friends, right? That's what we agreed to."

Her jaw dropped. "Fine. But when you find Wes and have trouble choosing what to do, don't complain to me about it." Zephyra turned quickly and jogged back to Vayu.

Alone again, I raced towards the charging station, hoping I wouldn't have to interact with too many Ordulls. Past the trees, over the bridge, and across the street, a squirrel fumbled cracked nuts between its teeth and climbed up the side of the brick building. Despite the distance, my gaze darted through the dirty windows of the shop. No touristy shirts were inside. Damn.

I tapped my solar-powered watch, realizing it was the first day of a new month, so the charging station would be closed anyways. The screen flashed the date, "Red Moon 01-81T," with a bright image of Wes on the front. His gray eyes were replicas of mine, just like his long blond hair pulled back in a high bun mirrored mine. That devious smile matched the one I wore, but his skin tone was darker, more like Reese's.

The clouds shifted overhead, turning darker by the second. Local weather forecasters would be frantic about the drastic change. But, I didn't care until Wes was by my side again.

Rain splattered my bare shoulders and trickled down my arms as I headed closer to the road and quickly spoke into my watch, faking a casual tone to my voice, "Hey there, sunshine. You awake?"

Reese's sweet voice was peppered with sarcasm when I heard her comm float from my watch, "I thought you only sent that at one in the morning?"

I kept jogging. At least I knew if Reese was calm, then she didn't know Wes was missing yet, and I wouldn't be the one to tell her.

I stopped at a crossroads. One headed straight down the mountain, and the other path led to winding paths, eventually ending at Reeses's. *Which way?*

Rain soaked my hair and drenched my workout shorts. *Focus*. In an instant, the storm mellowed, and the pitter-patter of droplets plunked into the puddle by my shoe. Through thousands of tiny gas molecules, I stared ahead, primarily nitrogen and oxygen with a small amount of argon. *Where are you, Wes?*

Wind howled, and the storm started rapidly again. That wasn't me. He might be close. I could feel Wes's unsteady energy. Afraid. Determined.

Proud. Hesitant. Angry. His emotions flickering faster than a lightning bug. Protectiveness whirled, and my tattoo throbbed, urging me to stop restraining my potential to find him. But I hadn't been training. Magik was too risky to use.

A littered bag plastered to my face, directing me to go down the mountain. I stepped toward Reese's house, and more trash catapulted into my body. A fast-food cup smacked my ear. After it dropped to the ground, my shoe crunched the cup underfoot, splitting it in half. A projection of straws hurled and stabbed into my cheek like arrows into a target.

"Wesley Isaac Nilson, I know you can see me. Stop throwing trash at me."

But why couldn't I see *him*? Was he truly stronger? No one at Vayu showed my intense. abilities, which is why they relied on me to run the teen training program.

The wind whispered, tickling my ear: *You didn't tell me about the pain.*

A chill ran through me from the secrets compacted inside that bluster of wind. What kind of powers did my son possess?

"Wes, come here." I scanned every tree branch, unable to spot my son. "Wesley, now!"

Then silence. Autumn leaves swirled down into my hair. I pulled one out of my high bun and tossed it to the ground. The energy encompassing me didn't allow the leaf to hit the trail but kept it dancing by my side, weaving in and out of my knees like a game.

I searched for seconds, minutes, what seemed like an hour, growing more desperate by the moment. Then I felt it again. A presence. Someone nearby. But not Wes's energy. I turned on my heels. Nothing was there. Just space. Goosebumps prickled my arm. Maybe someone from Draven really did capture him, and this was just a trick. If so, I was running out of time.

My watch vibrated. A still shot of Reese's smile and dimples covered the screen, but right when I clicked accept, her voice screeched, "I can't ever rely on you. What did you do? Wes just busted through the door, all scratched up, and looks like he's been in a wreck. What the Abyss is going on?"

Relief blanketed my soul for just a moment. My chest rose and fell fast as I picked up my pace. "He's okay, Reese. We just had an argument."

In my mind, I could see her eyebrows crinkle in that adorable way as she was looking out her window.

My breathing turned heavier with each fast step. The road turned narrower around the cliff's curves, and I had to watch my footing— so close to the edge. "We went for a run, that's all."

"In this weather?"

"Yup. He likes the … uh … wind … But we started talking about his karate class, and he got pissed and raced off."

She snorted. "He's faster than you?"

"Apparently." Panting, I swallowed down saliva. "Reese, I'll be there in five."

I picked up my pace, grateful that Wes was safe. Luckily, I wouldn't have to deal with a threat anytime soon. My feet pounded the wet pavement, splashing through a puddle

Reese's horses came into view first, all umbrellaed and miserable under a tree. As I rounded the bend, a trail of flapping flags led to a view of my sanctuary. Reese's cozy, wooden cottage was sandwiched between two windmills. She'd never believe me that the view from her front door wasn't just trees and mountains, but skyscrapers atop a peak, protected by an invisible shield.

I finally reached the path of stones in her yard, starting from her quaint mailbox, painted all shades of blue, leading to her front door, also painted blue. And I would know because we worked on it together. Wes was a toddler at the time and had knocked over a bucket of paint, and I chuckled at the memory. His baby feet tracked little footprints all over the front patio, and we didn't have the heart to cover them.

As I stared at the prints of baby toes, faded by the sun, my hand hovered over her door. A calming, weightless sensation floated around me like a scarf dancing in the breeze. A tumbling crash exploded inside, followed by a short shriek. I burst in. Wes was chasing after the cat, who darted away, toppling the chess pieces off the coffee table, knocking over the telescope, and scaling up the toybox.

"Dad, Mrs. Puff is scared of me now." Tears streaked down his face as he hopped up and down in place in front of the astronomy charts, desperately trying to hug the cat so dear to him. I remembered too well how animals first responded to my power when it was uncontrolled. Nature always knew.

Reese exploded into the room, holding Wes's meds. "Here, hun, your pill will calm you down."

"I'm fine." Wes swatted it to the floor, making the canister roll across the hardwood and land by my shoe.

Reese shot him a look, then one just as deadly to me. "Isaac? Can you please …?"

"He doesn't need these anymore." I threw the bottle across the room, and it sank into the trash.

Her jaw dropped. "You're not a doctor." Her thick auburn hair fell in waves over the white silk robe with a slit open just high enough to show the black lace hugging her curves.

I bit my lip. "Trust me, babe."

"Don't …"

Her eyes lasered into mine as she sped forward, tugging me into the kitchen. I'd consider that an open invitation any other day, but now wasn't the time for playing games. Once on the other side of the door, she pushed me against the bay window, her hand pressing against my rain-coated chest. Her fingertips grazed my beard, and the cyclone of passion lining her eyes veered me off-topic. A smile crept up while imagining her body trembling underneath me— always leaving me thirsty for more. But no matter how submissive she was in bed, the hammock, and the shower … she was a fierce momma bear when it came to our Wes.

"What is going on? Tell me right now, or I'll …" When she paused, her nose scrunched up in that perfect shape. "Don't you DARE smirk at me like that." She slapped my hip near my tattoo, sending a jolt of fierce power through my veins, and for a brief moment, all I wanted was to fuck her—hard.

I gulped and rubbed my beard, then let out a deep breath. "Let me talk to him. It's been a rough day."

"No shit. He's acting like a lunatic, and our cat seems to think he's some alien. Now, tell me what happened."

"Nothing. Wes is fine. You know, angsty mood swings."

"I know you have good intentions, but if something like this EVER happens again, I want to go back to court. No more equal custody." She stepped closer, pointing a finger in my face.

Wind whipped against her windowpanes, making her shudder. "And is it Armageddon or something out there? What is with this bipolar tornado freak out? One second I'm hiding in the bathroom with Mrs. Puff, and the next, the air is as still as a statue, and our son busts through the front door."

I crossed my arms and leaned against her counter. "Is that a hypothetical question, or would you like me to educate you about weather patterns?"

She threw a dishtowel at my chest. "Don't be a smart ass." A smile poked at the corner of her lip, giving me the invitation, I was waiting for.

Stalking forward, I hovered so close that her intoxicating honey scent momentarily distracted me from all the other thoughts spiraling out of control. *Just one kiss.* Her pouty lips hovered under mine, sucking all the air from my lungs. Reese rubbed my earlobe, then ran a long fingernail slowly down the side of my neck like the edge of a dagger.

Her hands found my chest. "You haven't come over in weeks." It was a dare.

"Dad!" Wes hollered from the living room.

Reese pushed me away. "Go put on a shirt. I have an extra for you in my bottom drawer."

I winked. "Waiting for me to move in, huh?"

"Shut up. Don't even get me started on that. I have still never seen your place." She left to console a weeping Wes.

A kettle whistled, sending steam rising. I passed my hand through the heat, collecting the power and harboring it for later. Would Wes also be able to manipulate steam the same way? I had researched for years to find answers as to why I matured at age twelve and eventually gave up since there hadn't been enough information recorded in our Vayu database to reach a conclusion. *I need more answers.* I grabbed a pen from Reese's counter and scribbled a list:

Where can I find other ~~mixed kids~~ hybrids?
Do all hybrids have powers?
Are any hybrids stronger than their Mystier parent?
Are they all hidden in their dome or do some live with their Ordull parent?

I cringed from the static distraction humming in my mind. Peeking up, I saw the television was on, just muted. No wonder. It flashed a news story that read about an increase in earthquakes. An interviewer held a microphone up to a brunette girl with streaks of red in her hair that matched her red crop top. She stood in front of a car, and the ribbon on the bottom of the screen read:

Kyra Kozelski fell into a crack caused by an earthquake after performing at local pub.

"Dad!"

"Okay, bud, I'm coming." I turned off the death machine. That tv had the same toxic energy as all the other electronics in the house. Once it was off, I my mind cleared, and my powers strengthen. Taking a quick moment to make the day easier, I also unplugged the toaster, microwave, and coffee machine, breathing an immediate sigh of relief. As I swung the door open into the living room, Wes's little body smacked into mine in a full embrace.

"Why does my cat hate me now?" He buried his head into my stomach as I rubbed his back.

"Can we have a minute to chat alone?" I asked Reese.

"Wes, hun, what do you want?" She glanced at our boy.

"It's okay, mom, this is man stuff." He sniffed and rubbed his eyes.

She eyed me carefully again before we retreated down the hallway. Watching her form had me wishing it was already past Wes's bedtime. I'd have to come back tonight.

"Dad? Why didn't you tell me the tattoo would hurt?" He sat on the edge of the couch, but it was so old the cushions absorbed half his body.

I kneeled in front of him and pushed the blond, rain-soaked hair from his eyes. "I'm sorry, bud. We can talk about everything, but not in front of your mom."

"It hurt so bad." He lifted his shirt a little and showed me his Mobius loop tattoo, gray and white like mine and in a similar spot, diagonally below his belly button, close to his hip bone.

I peeked behind me to make sure Reese hadn't seen and rolled his shirt back down, then whispered, "I know, bud. I should've told you. But it won't happen again."

His shoulders softened as he slouched further into the couch. "Are you sure? There's no way I'll get another one, right? Don't lie to me again."

"Well, there's one way, but we don't need to talk about that yet. You're too young."

He sat straight; his eyebrows knit tight. "You told me I wouldn't get Magik until around when I'd be driving."

I smiled. "I guess I need to teach you to drive. Think you can reach the pedal?"

He huffed. "This isn't funny, Dad. I even disappeared."

My heart stopped, and my body froze in place, unsure what to say next when a thousand questions ran through my mind. "What?"

Wes nodded. "You told me all about wind control and weather and stuff and the great eyesight. I mean … when I was running around, I could see super far away, like a superhero. But you never told me I could disappear."

I brought him in close and hugged him to my chest, terrified of what it could mean but so glad he'd have an advantage.

"Ew, Dad, you're all wet." He pushed away.

"Tell me exactly what happened when you said you disappeared," I whispered while Mrs. Puff sniffed the air and tentatively snuck closer.

Wes held out his hand and flipped it over slowly, inspecting his tanned skin while speaking. "In the forest, when I looked down, my body wasn't there."

"Okay … Um, did it hurt?"

"The tattoo or the disappearing?"

I held his hand. "I know the tattoo hurt, and that was probably scary. But, when you disappeared, what did it feel like?"

He smiled. "Like everything made sense in the world, and I was free-floating."

I knew that feeling. I leaned back and studied him, whispering to myself, "Where can I find answers?"

"What did you say, Dad?"

"Nothing, bud. I'll figure it out …" I rubbed his messy hair. "Now, remember, you can't tell Mom, and from now on, she can't see your stomach. It looks like your swimsuit will cover it, so you should be okay at the pool."

He saluted me. "Yes, sir." His boyish grin turned devilish before he skipped away.

At least he had his energetic spirit back, but I needed to learn the answers to why he matured so early and if this had happened to anyone else. The old wooden clock chirped at nine am, warning me that I didn't have much time.

The breeze shifted, making the windchimes outside strike a faster chord. After a quick glimpse out the window, a small silhouette stood far off in the distance, leaning against an Evergreen. Reese didn't have any neighbors. Who was out there? My heart rate quickened, and a jittery sensation crept up my legs. What did they want?

Without taking my eyes off the person, I prowled back to the yard and crossed my arms—claiming what was mine. That should send a clear signal. The guy didn't move an inch but whistled a high pitch call. A brown Labrador dashed out from behind a tree and ran straight toward me, ears flopping and tongue hanging out the side. What on earth? Its paws thundered over the dirt road, casting up a cloud of dust. Once it was a few paces away, the dog stopped and lay down. It carried a little backpack vest wrapped around its brown torso. A piece of paper flapped out the top pocket. I glanced at the silhouette, and he waved.

The pup whined, so I grabbed the paper and unrolled it to read:

I heard you're the Library Keeper of Vayu.
I need access and am willing to make a trade.
It's about The Link.

Jadox Griffin, from Draven

My shoulders tensed, and a tornado of leaves swirled at my feet. Fear coursed through my gut, and I glanced through Reese's window to the sight of Wes jumping on the couch with a smile on his face. Everything could be taken away if two Mystiers linked. I couldn't let this happen again. History couldn't repeat itself. Ordulls would try to eliminate Mystiers— again.

I'd have to check security measurements around our library, the beating heart of our city, but first, get this man as far away from Wes as possible. I rubbed my beard, trying to calm my racing nerves, but that didn't work. I released the energy I had captured from the steam earlier and let it stream through my veins.

"Dad!" Wes ran out the back door, through the swarm of tiny mosquitoes, and straight into my arms. "Mom said we can go parasailing next weekend, and she said you can come too. You'll come, right?"

Crap.

I crouched down to his level and glanced around his slender body at the mystery man still standing against the tree, waiting. "No, bud. I just got an important work … conference … and need to stay at the library for a while."

His smile disappeared. "But we can start …" he leaned in and cupped his hand to his mouth, whispering, "… start training my Magik, right?"

"Soon." I kissed his forehead and tied it to hide my shaking hands. "But keep it our secret."

He mimed, zipping his mouth shut, gave me a thumbs-up, and ran inside. While he ran, his body flickered in and out of view, disappearing completely then reappearing.

Shit! I can't leave him. But, if I don't, he might not have a future. Or any of us.

A breeze fluttered over my face, giving me strength. I stepped toward Jadox.

I know what I need to do.

CASSIE SWINDON'S NEXT PROJECT:

The Linked Trilogy

a fantasy- romance/dystopian series
full of action and suspense

Prequels/short stories:

Isaac's Curse
Jadox's Spell
Kyra's Ruin

Potential Novel Titles

Scorched
Severed
Shattered

HERE IS A SNEAK PEEK AT THE PRELIMINARY BLURB OF THE FIRST NOVEL IN THE LINKED TRILOGY, POTENTIALLY NAMED

"Scorched"

Once upon a time, fury-driven, Kyra Kozelski wishes that all men would disappear, combust, disintegrate, or melt away—any of those would be fine. Little does Kyra know that she holds Magik that has the potential to turn her thoughts into reality. A fiery connection with an alluring stranger changes the course of humanity in an instant.

All males vanish.

In a world without a clear path forward, society becomes chaotic as new leadership battles the best plan for the future. Secrets of Mystiers are exposed. On the verge of being used as a sacrificial example, Kyra is determined to master her intense powers and find a way to recover her lost nephew from this mass disappearance. On her journey, she runs straight into the last person she expected,

The only surviving male.

Wild at heart and full of bitterness, Jadox Griffin has spent years in isolation because Ordulls are dangerous, wicked, and can't be trusted. Jadox's inner turmoil calms whenever he's around Kyra, a woman with a dynamic spirit who grounds him completely. Their connection is that of ancient legends, though, he must hide the truth about Magik from Kyra and trick her into completing his side agenda—one she would never agree to willingly. His plan is the only option for protecting his tribe, his family.

Lying and secrets are the only way.

The two don't see eye-to-eye, yet neither can deny the intense connection surging between them, a force out of their control. If they don't get on the same page, the revengeful force hunting them could destroy them both.

Cassie Swindon

Jadox's Spell

Cassie Swindon

Kyra's Ruin